THE BONE GUARD 1

THE MONGOL'S COFFIN

E. CHRIS AMBROSE

Rocinante

Rocinante

Nashua, NH

CONTENTS

CHAPTER ONE

Grant Casey dove behind the nearest statue, a huge sandstone lion with wings and curly hair surrounding a wise human face—at least, until the shots blasted its face into gravel. Bullets and bits of stone pinged off the display cases and the concrete walls, leaving gouges and sending ricochets that stung his exposed hands and cheeks. Grant scowled into his goggles. He'd seen someone come this way, someone who should have been to-hell-and-gone before the shooting started, but now he didn't dare to call out.

Along the corridor, ahead, he glimpsed a tall soldier—Nick—herding a small group of civilians out of the museum—a woman in full burka, with children, a pair of older men, looking flustered. At the sound of gunfire, Nick placed himself between the civilians and the shots and hustled them all out of sight. Good.

The latest barrage ended with a settling of dust, and shattered glass from museum cases glittered on the floor. He held back a sneeze. The statue's head wore a mask of pock-marks . A few other, smaller figures lay dismembered and rocking on the ground. If they had stronger fire-power, even the stone lion couldn't protect him.

"Chief, do you copy?" D. A.'s voice buzzed in his ear. Grant dare not answer

"He took off west," Nick replied. "Shots fired in that direction."

"Don't tell me the Indian's gone cowboy on us." Commander Wilson, the putative leader of this supposedly joint operation.

"It's not his first rodeo, sir. He's got a reason," D. A. answered. "Chief, the building's clear—team's clear, do you copy?"

"Y'all are intel, not ops—Casey, you get your people out of here," Wilson barked. "You are in defiance of orders, Lieutenant Casey, and—"

"Saving twenty-eight lives and counting, sir." D. A. cut in, begging to be charged with insubordination. "Chief called in the threat, you didn't respond. Did you expect us to sit tight while the place went up in smoke?"

"I expected you to follow orders—"

Grant snapped off his set, the argument dropping into silence. Cautiously, he adjusted his position, settling his back to the solid stone, breathing carefully, listening. This room sat only a corridor and a lattice-trimmed courtyard short of the entrance, where the rest of the team would be wondering, despite orders to the contrary, if they should come and get him now that they'd cleared the place of civilians. Only, they hadn't.

He caught a flicker of movement and a flash of a red heat signature in his left-hand lens, furtive, somebody slipping from the bulk of that leafy-looking column to the base of a nearby display of jewelry and tablets. Grant tracked the movement with his rifle.

"Allahu Akbar!" shouted a gruff voice to his right. The shooter, seeking his compatriots. No answer. So the third party wasn't his, and wasn't Grant's. Civilian.

Grant jumped back to the tail of the lion, caught the flash of red, the shooter's position. He fired three shots and ducked away again as the shooter returned fire.

Glancing over, Grant silently urged the civilian to get the hell out while the shooter was looking for him. Instead, the civ lunged along the display and stuck his hand over the top, snatching a jeweled diadem and pulling back, stuffing the piece into his dark tunic. A looter, in the middle of a firefight. Could be someone taking advantage, trying to fund a ticket out of the chaos that was Afghanistan, or maybe a museum staffer hoping to save something from the destruction.

Boots pounded up the hallway from the heart of the museum, accompanied by shouts of "Allahu Akbar!" and a hundred other things. Shit. His shooter called out in reply, then the air in the room sucked dry, something boomed, and the lion exploded. Grant dove away, toward the civ. He ran hard, gunfire spitting in pursuit. The civ dodged behind a wooden doorway that wouldn't stand up to automatics, never mind the rocket they just fired. He scooped up the civ with one arm and launched them both into the courtyard, rolling so he landed on top behind some kind of tomb. Ironic, if he bought it right then.

"Stay down!" he barked, first in English, then in Dari, the local dialect.

"Get the fuck off," the civ growled back in accented English, shoving at him. A woman? Yeah, he could tell now, despite her genderless tunic and trousers. The wrap slipped back from her face, revealing sharp green eyes, dusky skin, parted lips.

Women had every reason to need the cash to fund a getaway. He couldn't blame her for taking advantage. "Get out of here, lady. I'll cover you."

For a moment, their eyes locked, and those lips gave a slight quirk, then she gave a nod, and he rolled aside, taking a knee behind the low tomb, weapon in hand. When he popped up, peppering the stone lattice with shots, she checked her stolen diadem, tossed it aside, and ran: straight back into the chamber.

Grant ducked down again, the shooters taking pot-shots at his head, while the crazy woman flanked them, making for the same case she'd robbed moments before.

Leaning left, aiming upward, Grant fired again and heard a

shriek as a bullet struck home, then he pulled back, yanking out the magazine and slamming in another. His last. On the other side of the lattice, the shooters snapped at each other, loud enough to hear, too soft to make out the words. Draw their fire, or make for home? One last civ, and she was nuts.

When the rocket roared, Grant plunged left, rolled, and pounded down the side hall to come up next to their hide-out, already shooting, turning them away from the civ. Three heat signatures, one of them meeting his eye as he fired into the man's chest. The next one brought up his automatic, then he fell forward, blood spilling from his lips.

The crazy woman pivoted out of her stance, the gun still in her hand. Okay, not the usual civilian, not at all.

Between them, the last shooter froze, glanced behind him, then shouted a stream of fury at a woman in pants and swung his weapon toward her.

Two shots, chest and head, one from each direction, and the shooter went down.

She shoved the gun into her waistband and swung around the corner of the lattice.

"Hey!" Grant held up his off-hand to stop her.

Too late. She slipped her hands and feet into the diamonds of the lattice surrounding the courtyard and scrambled up, climbing fast to the roof and disappearing, even the patter of her steps fading in a heartbeat.

"Chief! We should be out of here—what're you doing?" Nick led with his gun around the entrance at the far end of the hall.

"Finishing the job." Grant released his gun and stepped back, the tether keeping it handy. Four insurgents lay in the wreckage of the museum, bleeding onto the remnants of what should've been their heritage. Maybe the crazy lady had it right, taking something away, rescuing what she could from the chaos. "I spotted a civilian, but she took off across the rooftop." He gestured up.

"Up there? Fuck. You sure about that?" Nick came up beside him, half a head taller, maybe seventy pounds heavier, a running back compared with Grant's track-and-field physique. "Commander's raising Hell on the radio—you heard?" Behind his helmet and goggles, Nick's dark face looked grim. "Could be bad news back on base."

"Twenty-nine lives and this place still standing? I'll take it." Grant swept the room, listening, watching: no more sounds, no heat signatures he could see.

"They all down?" Nick leaned a little closer.

Grant scanned the insurgents. The first one to fall shifted a little, moaning, his breath hitching. A living insurgent meant a chance to get some intel and get back to doing their job. Would it appease the commander? Unlikely.

"Trauma kit," Grant ordered as he stepped over the bodies, pausing to roll a body from the wounded man's legs. "Lie still. We can help." The words rang a bit hollow, given he was the guy who'd shot him, but it wasn't personal. Nick held out the trauma kit, edging into the space on the other side. The wounded man moved again, muttering, his arm underneath him as if he were trying to sit up. Nick's eyes flared, then he shouted, "Chief!" and launched himself over the downed man, knocking Grant aside as the insurgent's hidden explosive went off in a shower of blood and bone. Grant flew backwards from the thrust of Nick's tackle. He tumbled past the bulk of that wise, ruined lion, the stone wings fluttering in a breeze of fire, shielding him from the worst of the blast, and the even worse anointing of Nick's blood.

CHAPTER TWO

Minister of Antiquities Jin Wang-lo mopped his brow lightly with a kerchief as he gazed down on the gates to a tomb fit for an emperor. It contained instead, a criminal—one of the greatest ever known, but Jin did not begrudge him this final resting place. Indeed, it was the culmination of Jin's archaeological career.

In the narrow valley below, his Assistant Minister, a pudgy academic by the name of Li labored up the slope as the tomb doors shut behind him. "Minister," he panted, "it is done. I have confirmed the inventory." He stumbled to Jin's side and nearly slipped back again, waving a hand as if he expected the Minister himself to offer aid. Jin helped those who helped themselves. He smiled thinly. Indeed, when the rewards for this project came to fruition, perhaps in a decade or more. It would be Jin who then helped himself and his family.

"Seventy-eight crowns?"

"Seventy-eight crowns, Minister," Li confirmed, then tried a smile, though he was still panting from his exertions. "They are magnificent. What shall I tell the workers?" He gestured back at the thousand or so men in workmen's garb who labored in the defile with shovels and picks.

"No need, Li. Sub-minister Yang will take care of them." He gave a flick of his hand. Yang stood stiff as a terra cotta warrior in the shade of a cluster of trees, sunglasses shielding his eyes, his square jaw suggesting foreign ancestry. Still, Yang could be trusted utterly. Without glancing toward the Minister, Yang nodded and stepped up to the edge of the ravine. A line of men in loose beige clothing joined him, and another, similar line of men matched them across the other side. The mountains around echoed with a growl of engines as the tanker trucks finally arrived.

Li flicked his eyes over the arriving trucks. "So much water? Is it even necessary to re-supply the camp now that our work here is complete?"

"I do not suggest you drink what those trucks contain." They carried the last ingredient he needed to complete his life's work.

"Now?" Yang asked.

Jin watched the trucks maneuver into place, their pipes ready to dispense their contents into the valley below. "Now." He turned on his heel. "Come, Li, the cars will bring us back to Beijing to deliver our final report."

"Ah, yes." Li's head bobbed, then his glasses slid from his sweat-streaked face and he turned back, bowing to search for the spectacles as Jin walked down the trail. His foot hesitated over the ancient stone pathway. The first twang and whisper of bowshot reached his ears, then the screaming began, echoing in the walls of stone.

"Minister!" Li bleated, staggering toward him, then back toward the edge of the ravine. "What are they doing? Stop! You must—Minister!" He waved his hands, but Yang and his men continued to fire, launching volleys of arrows down into the valley below until there were no more screams.

Li's slippery hands clung to Jin's arm. "Minister." His eyes looked too big and altogether too round, like his flapping mouth. "What have they done? Why?"

"Because none must ever know about this tomb." Jin stared down at him. "You knew that when the project began, that our work, if successful, must be eternally kept secret. Have you suddenly forgotten?"

"No, of course not, but this—" he gave a helpless gasp, his hands translating his tremors down Jin's arm, his sweat marking the Minister's suit.

"Is in keeping with the requirements of the Party." Jin gave a twist of his arm to free himself from the other man's grip. "You did sign the pledge, did you not?"

"Yes, of course, Minister." His head swiveled back to the line of men in beige, still holding their bows, more like the terra cotta warriors of the First Emperor than ever. The archers froze, listening and watching below, then Yang approached the Minister's position.

"It is done."

"Tell the trucks they may proceed."

"But they're already dead," Li said. "What good can it do to drown them?"

"They were enemies of the Han people, Li, just like the man in the tomb. Persons without worth or status."

Li's round gaze rose from his view of the ravine, but he looked pale as a dumpling, swimming in sweat, owl-eyed without his glasses. At Li's back, Yang lifted that chin, his shining black lenses reflecting the Minister's face, the high sun, the rough terrain, revealing nothing. Jin tipped his head, and Li's flapping mouth gaped open, then filled with blood as his knees buckled and he bent backward over Yang's knife. Yang stepped aside in a fluid motion, like the finest masters of wu shu, away from the path of the blood.

"I will strip him," Yang said, "and add him to the others."

Liquid flowed from the tankers, splashing down the walls into the ravine and the smell already drifted toward them. Jin pressed his kerchief over his nose once more. "The knife wound may be conspicuous."

Yang held up the blade, its old metal dull. "I took the precaution of arming myself appropriately, Minister."

Jin gave a short bow of acknowledgment. They should recruit sub-ministers from the army more often, if all of them could be as efficient as Sub-Minister Yang. "It appears that I am in need of a new assistant. I should be pleased to recommend your advancement."

Yang placed his hands formally over the hilt of his weapon and bowed more deeply. His blade dripped blood onto the stones. The ravine behind reeked of death, and it sizzled. Minister Jin strode carefully down the slope to his air-conditioned limousine. He had achieved greatness. Now all he need do was wait.

CHAPTER THREE

Liz Kirschner yanked the earbuds from her head and tried to catch her breath. Music, just music, like all the other files, discs and records she had listened to. Or not. But this wasn't the kind of thing the music department cared about, not even Ethnomusicology. Mongolian was pretty obscure anyway, the most obscure concentration in a major already mired in obscurity. Asian Studies, then. Had to be. The last file uploaded to her iPod, and Liz pulled the disc out of the archive's antiquated machine, leaning back, her mind still racing. The Asian Studies department head, Professor Chan, hadn't taken kindly to Liz being appointed to organize the upcoming conference on the Arts of the Steppes, or maybe he just resented the entire topic of the conference She figured she had a couple of years to bring him around on that, but this discovery—this was too important.

The sound still echoed inside of her head, a deep, full-throated voice with the layered buzz unique to khoomei throat singing. It sang of mountains and rivers, the kind of landscape where horses roamed beneath a broad blue sky. The music stirred her—she blamed all those summers in Colorado—but more than that, it could just be the capstone to the coolest master's project in the history of the department. Maybe even more.

She stuffed the iPod in her pocket, slid her laptop into its case, and returned the precious discs to their archival storage unit before signing herself out of the archive, sharing a nod with the senior at the gate. "Not taking anything out, are you?" he grinned up at her. "I really should search you, just to make sure."

"Yeah, Marko, nothing." She opened her laptop case to display the machine, keeping it between her and Marko's desk. Her pulse quickened as he took a peek inside, rifling her notes.

He plucked out the ratty paperback and eyed the cover. "*Secret History of the Mongols*? Seriously? Hey, if you're into horses, my mom keeps a polo string—"

"Sorry, I've got a boyfriend, not to mention a thesis to work on." She flashed a smile, and took back the book. "Did you know the Mongols play a variation of polo using a dead goat? That's probably where the game came from."

Marko winced. "You should come over to the modernists. Phillip Glass is where it's at."

"Didn't he once hold a concert that consisted of sitting still at a piano in Harvard Square for half an hour?"

"No, see, people always misunderstand—"

Big mistake, picking on his project. Liz backed away. "Seriously, thesis. Gotta go." She marched resolutely away from his downcast expression. Outside, the autumn chill blew between the tall brick buildings, tossing her hair as she hustled toward the Liberal Arts admin building. After five already—would anyone still be in their offices? Worth a try. She didn't think she could settle down until she shared her discovery with someone who might actually get it. Liz bounded up the steps inside, clinging to the rail for balance. Breathless, she arrived on the top floor and scanned the faculty directory. There—Professor Chan, head of the Asian Studies department, on the right of Archaeology. The mutter of voices emerged from Archaeology, then from Asian Studies as well, the broad wooden door framed by posters about winter session in China, a local dance troupe, and a lecture on the history of the Hong Kong conflict. That event was happening tonight: she wouldn't have much time.

Still, Liz hesitated to interrupt until she noticed the door was slightly open. "Professor Chan? It's Liz Kirschner." She tapped, and nudged the door a little further.

"I appreciate your enthusiasm for the conference, Ms. Kirschner, but it has only just been scheduled, surely you can send a memo to the committee if there is more to discuss before our next meeting." His voice had a twangy quality that put her off. The professor pushed off from the desk where he was perched on an edge, folding his arms. Behind the desk sat a man in a gray suit with the sheen of silk, a purple pocket square drawing her eye. The suit about matched the silver threading his black hair.

"I'm so sorry to bother you, but this isn't about the conference, Professor. I'd like to consult with you on something else, something related to my thesis."

Professor Chan gave a nod, and tipped his head expectantly.

Liz glanced at the other man, the one who had taken the professor's chair. "I hope I'm not interrupting."

"Clearly, circumstances dictated you not wait. I, on the other hand, can afford patience." The man in silver chuckled. "And a good many other things as well." Despite his Oriental features, he spoke with a trace of a British accent, and lovely enunciation in a soft tenor. He had taken elocution lessons at least, and she wondered if he had ever been a singer. "I am Huang Li-Wen, tonight's speaker, by the invitation of Professor Chan."

Professor Chan's throat worked, his lips thinning. "How can I help you, Ms. Kirschner?"

"I found something in the archives, some recordings of Mongolian throat-singing. According to the researcher's notes, the songs can be traced back at least to the sixteenth century. I think they're older than that. A lot older." Their eyes on her made her feel foolish, self-conscious, and she took a breath to steady herself.

"Go on," said the man in silver. "I have a great interest in antiquities."

Professor Chan bristled, squaring his shoulders. "Sixteenth century music seems a difficult thing to trace, Ms. Kirschner. Even for the Han culture, which has records inscribed on turtle shells, never mind for the Mongols who remained illiterate until they subjugated China. And yet you think these songs are older? How old?"

"I suspect they date from the thirteenth century." She swallowed. "From the time of Genghis Khan."

CHAPTER FOUR

"Look, Mr.—" The prof tore her stare from Grant's neck long enough to glance down at the card he'd given her. "—Casey. This interview simply confirms that you are not an ideal candidate for the position. Security for a conference like this is a delicate matter, one of balancing academic goals, the material display, including valuable artifacts on loan from a variety of institutions, not to mention working with distinguished professors and researchers. I am not sure that your... particular style, would be complimentary to those ends."

"I speak a variety of languages, and am familiar with cross-cultural relations," Grant replied, still a little hesitant to specify which languages and cultures.

"Yes, well, the armed forces do have a perspective on such things," she said drily. "Nonetheless, it is not a perspective widely admired among academics of standing. An unfinished degree in history hardly prepares you to work with such individuals. We anticipate that the Chinese Minister of Antiquities himself will be present, among many others. These are not the sort of people who..." She trailed off, her eyes rising again to his neck, then offering the card back to him. "I do appreciate your taking the time to apply, but we shall be looking elsewhere for our conference security coordinator."

Someone had used the contact link on his website to send him the job posting, saying it sounded perfect for him, but apparently he wasn't perfect for it. Just like the other twenty-six jobs he'd applied for since he got out of Walter Reed. Still, the idea that anyone had found his website seemed like a positive development. "Keep the card, ma'am. It may be that you'll need someone like me in the future. Free-lance, on site security, that kind of thing."

That drew a quirk of her dry lips that might have been a smile. "We at the University are not in the habit of hiring mercenaries for virtually any purpose whatsoever, much less to serve as, how can I put this delicately, muscle? while we are engaged in the pursuit of our academic goals."

Grant stared straight back at her, hands clasping his folio behind him. "When was the last time you went out on a dig? Or even on a research exchange with an overseas institution? It's a crazy world out there, ma'am, and it's getting crazier all the time. The destruction of the Bamiyan Buddhas and the Mosul museum—that stuff is happening all the time. People are getting hurt and history is getting destroyed, and someone's got to step up and stop it."

"Primarily because you people haven't been doing the job so far." She dropped the card onto the only patch on her desk not covered by papers, journals and bits of pottery. "I do applaud your entrepreneurial spirit, Mr. Casey, and I do, of course, support the concept of veterans finding useful employment, but having found you unsuitable for the position at hand, I do not see how we can make use of your services."

Grant swallowed his irritation. It wasn't the job of the Armed Forces to defend other people's culture—that was exactly why he thought his business idea would work. The trouble was, how to get paid for it. The U had money, plenty of it, they just preferred to spend it on wine receptions and big-name commencement speakers, and some suave retired county sheriff to glad-hand the big-wigs at their conference. "Thank you for your time, ma'am." He tipped his head toward her, restraining himself from offering a salute. His neck remained stiff, but it wasn't the kind of thing you let bother you.

She ran her thumb over the logo on his card, a skull over a crossed shovel and rifle. "In terms of your free-lance prospects, I do think you might reconsider the name, 'Bone Guard.' It sounds rather lurid."

"I'll take that under advisement." He turned on his heel and let himself out of the office. Grant paused by the faculty directory to see if he should drop off cards with any other departments while he was here. Asian Studies? Middle-eastern Studies? Could be a winner. Grant pivoted and stalked down the hall. The squirrely woman from Archaeology let herself out of her office, dodging his gaze as she locked the door. Maybe he should've covered his ink; tattoos seemed to disturb academic types. If he got another interview like this, he'd have to keep that in mind. Grant smiled and gave a nod. She swallowed hard and hurried away.

Scanning the doors, automatically counting them in the back of his mind, Grant went to the Middle-eastern Studies office and knocked. Waited. Voices across the hall in Asian Studies, two men and a woman, the woman over-eager, the men cautious, then the woman frustrated.

Grant knocked again. Still nothing.

Across the hall, the door popped open, and a Chinese man in a rumpled suit ushered a young woman out. "Thank you for stopping by, Ms. Kirschner. It is an interesting line of inquiry, but tenuous at best." He bowed slightly. "Please keep me informed if you are able to find any...evidence of these claims."

She tossed back her red-blonde hair and leaned in, maybe hoping her feminine charms would persuade where her claims had not. "Professor Chan, if you'd just—"

"We have heard the songs, and your interpretation of them, Ms. Kirschner. At the moment, I have a lecture to prepare for. Perhaps before you continue to pursue such claims, you should partake of a few more of our course offerings. Contemporary Inner Asian History, for example, or Professor Warren's Tribal Influences seminar." He glanced over, noticing Grant and dismissing him in the same moment. "If you are able to complete your thesis in time for the conference, I shall look forward to hearing your presentation."

The other guy, by contrast, stood four-square in the door in his snappy suit, a smartphone in his hand, and his dark gaze sweeping Grant from head to toe, as if he were another operator sizing him up.

Balancing her armload of papers and books, the woman glanced at the second guy and paused, as if she didn't know what to say, then simply shrugged and walked away, starting to stuff her things into her bag.

"If you'll excuse me just a moment, Mr. Huang, I have a call to make, then I shall escort you to the lecture hall," the professor said before he disappeared back inside.

For a moment, the rich guy and Grant met eyes, then the rich guy tapped on his phone and turned profile, taking advantage of the better light from the prof's office.

Grant headed back for the stairs. Asian Studies didn't seem up for a pitch. The woman flew back around the corner, looking up at the last minute. Grant side-stepped, but she stepped the same way and crashed into him. He braced, dropping the folio and reaching toward his hip for—nothing. He turned the gesture into a supportive hand on her arm as she stumbled.

"Sorry, sorry. Oh, crap, are those your papers?" The woman freed herself and took a few steps, circumscribing the contents of his folio, now spilled all over the floor: lists of services and proposed costs; photos of himself and some of his buddies in uniform, making the whole thing look professional; resume showing his background and special skills; a scatter of Bone Guard business cards. She was pretty, and under other circumstances, he might have...no, who was he kidding? He'd had more first dates than he'd had job interviews, and they were turning out just as well: half the women were eager to save him, turning his scars into some kind of pornography, the other half couldn't understand why he wasn't up on the latest reality shows. They lived in a whole different reality.

Grant dropped to a knee and started scooping up his things. She bobbed a little, as if about to join him in the effort, then glanced toward the office she'd left earlier. "Sorry," she said again, and hurried that direction. "Professor—Oh. Excuse me."

"I presume you returned for your device? I was just now attempting to reach you to return it." The rich guy held out a sleek phone in his palm. His teeth gleamed a little too white.

Grant tucked his papers back into his folio and departed, already calculating his next angle of approach.

CHAPTER FIVE

Clutching her phone, Liz took a moment to secure her shoulder bag before she headed out again. It gave her the time to recover her composure after realizing she'd left her phone, then running into the stranger. Her shoulder still ached a little from the impact—he didn't look that formidable, but he was clearly all muscle under that polo shirt. Definitely not a student, not here. He had an even, low voice, carefully controlled and intriguing, the kind of voice that made you want to listen. Attractive, in a dangerous way, with his dusky skin and chiseled features. She couldn't quite place his ethnicity, but his hair barely hid the tattoo on his neck and she wondered if he were an ex-con. Under a bench in the corridor where she'd run into him a business card remained, white against the scuffed hardwood. Liz paused to pick it up, examining it as Professor Chan and his guest breezed by her.

"Grant Casey, the Bone Guard. Archaeological and Cultural tactical services. Defender of History." Seriously? It included a phone number, a website, and a QR code for direct dial. Liz snapped a photo. She had to share this with her study group. She snickered at the idea of having a tattooed body guard stand at her shoulder in a research library, or maybe asking him to rattle an archivist to get her what she wanted.

Professor Chan didn't believe her, though his guest had been politely curious. Whatever. She was onto something, something worthy of a book, not just a thesis; the kind of discovery that launched a career. She would track this all the way to Mongolia. It was about time she paid a visit, and Byambaa would welcome her—not that he'd appreciate her eyeing the Bone Guard.

Liz trotted down the stairs and pushed outside into the chill evening. Sodium lights buzzed overhead, casting patches of yellow light, and carving leafy shadows beneath the hedges. A few windows in the surrounding buildings showed the faint glow of people working late, but only a handful of other souls hurried along the walkways now, faces lit, as her was about to be, by the familiar blue-white of their tiny screens. She scrolled through a few messages, nothing important: Sara suggested dinner—too late for that; Professor Joyeux wanted to know if she could administer his motets practicum on Thursday. Sure. She tapped a response about the class, then brought up the image of the Bone Guard card to send it to Sara. Did she want to activate the QR code, her app wanted to know. As if. She stumbled over a root protruding into the pathway.

A hot breeze flashed past her and cracked into the tree. Liz spun around. A small round hole marked the trunk, edged with splinters. She turned again, the roots tripping her up. Another soft whistle and a burning sensation as splinters stung her arm.

Someone was shooting at her. Shooting? Liz clutched her bag and broke into a run, glancing around wildly. There! A blue bulb on top of a post marked a campus security box, but did she dare stop? How long would it take for help to arrive? Another bullet pinged the casing of the call box, and Liz dodged away.

Did she want to activate the QR code? Oh, yeah.

"Bone Guard, this is Grant Casey." A masculine voice reverberating in the tiny speaker.

Someone tackled Liz from behind and she screamed.

CHAPTER SIX

The woman's scream echoed from his cell phone and Grant sprang back out of his car, tossing the folio on the passenger seat. "Where are you? What's happening?"

"Shut up—no sound," said another voice, then the connection went dead.

Grant stood at the open car door, listening. The scream hadn't just been in his phone, it had been out here, somewhere close. Leave the door open, don't risk the sound of closing it. Crouching low, Grant ran in the direction of the scream. Cell phone back in its holster, hand itching for the gun that should have a holster of its own, but not on campus.

There, at his one o'clock, the sounds of a scuffle, a man's grunt of pain. Another man whispering, "Let me nail her." A sexual command, or a termination order? Grant put on a burst of speed. A darkened intersection between hedge-lined pathways at the back of a brick building. The blue light of a call box shining on a man in profile, standing over two people struggling on the ground. The man held a gun extended. Termination, then. Grant scooped a half-brick from the rough pathway and hurled it sidearm, slamming the gunman in the back of the head. He staggered, cried out, and spun, getting off a round that whispered into the leaves.

Light at the gunman's back. Stupid mistake. Grant dodged across the path from where he had been, keeping his eye on the gunman, but the guy swiveled and shot out the light, killing Grant's advantage. He dropped low and barreled into the man's legs, toppling him. The gun came up, gleaming and Grant caught his hand, giving a twist. The gunman let out a squeal of pain, then his knee came up into Grant's stomach. They rolled together. Grant slapped for the sheath concealed in his sock. The gun shoved against Grant's throat too late: his knife was already sliding between the man's ribs.

The other guy shouted in something like Mandarin.

Grant pushed off, already on his feet, the knife in hand. Somewhere behind him, sirens wailed, growing louder.

The struggle paused, the man kneeling on the woman's chest, the strap of her shoulder bag in his hands. She grabbed a corner of the bag and gave it a swing, knocking him sideways. Instead of letting go, he yanked on the strap and pulled it free over her arm, then took off running.

"Are you hurt?" Grant demanded

The woman gasped, a hand pressed to her chest as she struggled for breath. The woman from the hall, her bright hair a mess of old leaves. She managed to shake her head, and Grant started after her assailant.

A bright light flared out of the darkness, pinning him. "Drop your weapon! Hands where we can see them!"

Shit. Grant let the knife fall and kept his hands up. "The mugger is running—he's at your ten thirty, heading toward the student center." He started to gesture in that direction, in case the cop didn't get it, but the unmistakable ratchet of a rifle round being loaded stopped him cold.

"Still have your cell?" he muttered.

"Huh?" the woman moved around behind him.

"Ms. Kirschner. Your cell phone."

"Uh." A sound of assent, breathy.

"Snap the dead guy, his face. We'll want it later."

Another light joined the big one, smaller, moving over his face then toward the ground behind him. "Whoever's with you! Tell them to stand up, get where we can see them!"

"One of the perps is down," Grant announced. "The victim may need medical attention."

Feet trooped closer, then one of the cops was in his face. "Who the hell're you? Some kind of vigilante?"

"Grant Casey" he answered, suppressing a smile. "The Bone Guard."

CHAPTER SEVEN

Sitting in the too-bright police station, dazed, Liz answered questions about her missing bag, about the assailants, one missing, one deceased, and about the man who had saved her. She kept her hands wrapped around the cup of coffee they'd given her, barely sipping it, clinging to its warmth. Someone shot at her then stole her laptop, her copy of The Secret History, all her notes for that essay on comparative musical scales she was supposed to finish. Someone shot at her.

"You were heading for the call box, why did you call Mr. Casey? Why not the police?"

Liz took a swallow from the dark brew. "As I told the other officer, I had snapped his QR code. All I had to do was tap the screen." The call box had looked so far away.

The detective questioning her nodded, poking his notepad with a pencil. "How long have you known Mr. Casey?"

She giggled, then forced herself to calm down. "I don't—I just met him. Well, I didn't even meet him, really."

The detective made a little sound of disbelief. He leaned back in his chair, pursing his lips. Along with the gravelly tone of a smoker, or perhaps a habitual shouter, he had full lips and a long nose, the kind of face that could go bad quickly if he gained much more weight, but his muscular shoulders strained at his cheap suit. He rubbed his neck, giving a long sigh, and she caught a glimpse of something at the edge of his collar, a dark mark of some kind. A tattoo?

Liz sat up and pushed away the coffee. "You know him, too."

With a snort, the detective said, "You think so? Maybe you should join the force." He dropped the pencil he'd been fiddling with. "So your story is, you're walking home from a campus meeting, in the dark, and someone takes a shot at you. You start to run toward the call box, but you have Mr. Casey's number on your screen, so you give it a tap, then the second guy jumps you and starts wrestling you for your bag. The shooter comes over, apparently eager for the shot, but the guy who's got you won't let him. Then Mr. Casey shows up and takes out the shooter. The other guy snatches your bag and takes off. Right so far?"

Another officer arrived, laying a sheaf of papers by the detective's elbow, and departed. The detective glanced over them, then back at her.

"That's right. Does this mean I can go now? I'd really like to go home."

With a half-smile, the detective said, "Yeah, I can believe that. Here, read this over and sign it, if it's an accurate representation of what happened. Then you can go."

She drew the papers toward her, reading through her transcribed words before she signed off on the report. "What about Mr. Casey?"

"The Bone Guard?" The detective sighed again, as if Casey were a repeat offender, but one he couldn't quite nab. "His story matches yours, his use of force seems justified. We're looking into whether charges are warranted. Probably best if neither of you leaves town."

She pushed the papers back to him. "I just really want to go home." In the morning, she'd need a new laptop, and hopefully her most recent data were in the cloud so she wouldn't be too far behind. The attack left her shaken, and Professor Chan's outright denial of her work dragged at her like an anchor. Maybe she was all wrong about this and it was just a bunch of old songs.

Both of them rose and the detective stuck out his hand. "Thank you for your time. We'll be in touch if we need anything else or if we need you to identify any of your stolen items."

He walked her out to the lobby where a tall familiar form waited, giving that military pivot, his brows notching up just a little. "Free to go?" Casey asked.

"Yes, I guess so. Thanks—I mean, thanks for coming."

"It's what I do." He flashed a grin that did nothing to dispel the air of danger. He'd killed a man for her last night, and he didn't even have to change his clothes as a result. She couldn't decide if that made him just the guy she wanted on her side—or just another thug out to exploit her. The timbre of his voice still drew her, a voice she wanted to trust. At the same time, she knew he'd been trained to that tone—it was just as finely educated as Chan's visitor's, but with a completely different purpose.

The detective met Casey's eyes, but he had to draw himself up a little to do it. "Don't leave home, Casey. And stay out of trouble."

"How likely is that, Gooney?"

The detective's eyes narrowed. "Don't call me that. I didn't like it then, I certainly don't like it now."

Casey's grin widened, and he flicked a little salute. "Let me drop you off, Ms. Kirschner. My car is conveniently parked in the impound lot next door."

CHAPTER EIGHT

Grant held the door for her, and pointed her the right direction. In the growing light of early morning, she looked wrung out, with a slight bruise on her left cheek. She reached up as if to adjust the bag she expected to find on her shoulder, and frowned when it wasn't there. At the car, she let herself in, shooting him another of those worried glances, blue darts of concern. Did he need a change of image? The prof yesterday seemed to think so. No way the ink was going, and a year out of the service hadn't done much to dissipate its influence in his manner. Sorry, stuck with it.

Once on the streets, he looked for the nearest bridge, waiting for a bike courier to glide by, then navigating with quick turns, glancing in the mirror. Green Toyota.

"You'll want to turn here—" She pointed, then aimed the blue darts again. "Where are you taking me?"

"Someplace safe." He turned again, down into the tunnel, then abruptly changing lanes and popping back out again. No Toyota.

"Look, I appreciate your help last night, but I need to go home."

She had slid to the far side of her seat, turning a little, so she could face him.

"Negative. You think two Chinese-speakers attack you out of the blue because you're going home in the dark? After a meeting in the Asian Studies department?"

"The—"she swallowed and turned a little pale—"the one who—"

"The dead guy," Grant supplied. He swung another turn, into a restaurant drive-thru. "You want anything?"

"He wasn't Asian."

"The other guy called out for him in Mandarin. Whether he was Asian or not, they had a clear expectation of mutual understanding. What's your research?" To the speaker outside his window, he said, "Four hash browns and a large vanilla chai. Did you want something? The coffee at the station tastes like wash water. Gooney should do something about that."

Mutely, she shook her head. He pulled up to the next window and picked up the order, handing it to her. She balanced the steaming cup in its cardboard tray on her lap and they re-entered traffic. A block ahead, green Toyota. Damn, the guy was pretty good. Grant made for the freeway, hoping the food wouldn't get cold before they lost this guy.

"Who's Gooney?"

"Corporal Tony Gonsalves. Gooney, to his friends." Or those who thought they could be. "We knew each other in the service."

"Which branch?"

"This green Toyota has been following us since we left the station. He's hard to shake. You seen anyone like that around your place?"

"What?" She swung about, staring out the back window.

"Figure of speech—he's actually ahead of us now." Grant put on his signal for the next exit, pulling over and slowing. Several cars ahead, the Toyota followed suit. When the concrete barriers loomed ahead, dividing the ramp from the highway, Grant stomped the accelerator and shot back into traffic, racking through the gears and flying between trucks. Not many drivers out at this hour. Good news, bad news. Good for him—bad for his tail. "I think that got him."

Her wide eyes drank in what was happening. "You're crazy."

"It works for me." He found the Somerville exit and slid down. "You want me to let you out? Toyota man's probably happy to pick you up."

She laughed a little. "He's really been following us? God." She sounded better now, more relaxed. "I can't imagine anyone would—steal my research." Then she pulled the tray a little closer to her and the frown returned.

"Yes, you can. You're imagining it right now. But don't tell me. The car was in the lot all night, chances are, it's not secure any more. Shit." He slapped his palm on the steering wheel and slammed on the brakes. "Get out. Don't forget the goodies." He grabbed the go-bag from his back seat, dumped it on the driver's seat to confirm all the stuff in there was his. Were these guys smart enough to tag his bag, not just his car? Chance he'd have to take—for now. It looked like an old gym bag, complete with smelly clothes on the top, and only the array of electronics and survival gear underneath said otherwise. He stuffed his things back in, along with a few other items from the glove box and side compartments.

Kirschner's eyes flicked with his movements, watching him bundle up a knife, a spare cell phone, an extra clip of rounds into the gym bag and zip it up. "The goodies?" He pointed to the tray she had set on the roof of the car.

"Are you sure this is safe?"

The neighborhood of boarded windows and narrow, heavily barred shops looked about perfect to him—if you wanted your car stolen. "It's good. You have a Charlie card?"

She shook her head. "In my bag."

"I'll add it to your bill." He led her down an alley and into a T-station, swiping a commuter pass through the entrance gate and ushering her in before he followed.

"My bill? I don't think I agreed, that is, I'm not sure—"

"You didn't plan on a hired gun." He found himself waiting for the train with his hands at his back, parade rest, and forced himself to shake it off. Facing the client, he told her, "If someone's willing to kill for this, there's money in it somewhere."

"But it's just—" the train arrived, and they stepped into an empty carriage, too early for the weekend shoppers, wrong day for commuters. The doors hissed shut again, and they were on their way. She caught a pole, and laughed again. "Okay, yes there is. Treasure, in fact." Her eyes alight, she said, "I've found the map to Genghis Khan's tomb."

CHAPTER NINE

Jin's phone buzzed softly as he stood in the courtyard, hands frozen in a posture of strength. He executed a swift change, one leg swinging up, the other balancing his weight as he kicked, then jabbed his hand after it, felling an imagined opponent. The last of the daylight fled over the ancient walls of his hutong house, leaving the statuary and carvings in shadow, standing in for his enemies.

His son, Mingbao, froze as well, but could not help glancing down toward the phone, his eyes the only thing moving. Distraction could prove fatal. Jin pivoted to face the boy, who snapped his gaze back again, lips compressing. He sank into his posture, but the buzzing sounded again, and Jin relented, stepping back with a tip of his head.

Mingbao scooped up the phone. "It's your assistant."

At such an hour? Yang knew better. Or he had cause. Jin accepted the phone and tapped it on. "Speak."

"The raven is taking flight."

The words registered as a blow, sending shocks through his chest. He had expected to wait at least two more years. His son's eyes flared in the dim light, watching him. "Now?" Jin recovered himself. "Are you certain?"

Yang answered with silence. If he felt any uncertainty, he would not have called, and Jin had allowed his surprise to overcome his discipline. It would not happen again. "What actions have been taken?"

"Operatives have pursued the information, the chain of evidence, and the one who discovered it. Shots have been fired, and one of the operatives was lost, but the discoverer escaped that rather inept approach."

"Who is the chosen one?"

"Elizabeth Kirschner, a graduate student in Boston."

Not even a professor? That was unexpected, as well. Jin stalked away from his son toward the lantern by the corner where a footed bronze vessel from the Shang dynasty caught the growing gloom. "Has she any credibility?"

"A sufficient amount, at least within the academic community. We have already moved against her primary source, and she has taken on a mercenary, a former soldier. It has been difficult to learn more about her ally. He is the one who eliminated our informant's hireling."

Was Jin imagining the edge of emotion he detected in Yang's voice? Yang never showed any emotion face-to-face, but the idea of this hired soldier worried or excited him. "I am sure you can deal with an unexpected adversary."

This, too, was met with silence. Yang waited for his signal.

Jin stared down into the pot. Similar ones stood outside of every temple in China, full of sand, with incense sticks thrust into them, smoldering in search of a poor man's fortune, or a woman's prayer for a son. This one stood empty. Jin preferred to make his own fortune, but this was sooner than he had anticipated. He expected his secret to rest for a few more years, at least. What would happen if his secret were revealed now? He had prepared for a siege, a lengthy tactical game, and was now facing an assault of a very different kind. He weighed the risk of inaction, the very real possibility that the plans he laid might be fulfilled by someone else. The Han people had not prospered for five thousand years by taking hasty action. But then, the world moved faster today than Sun Tzu might ever have imagined. His son required the best education, and his wife prayed daily for the indulgence of a second child. For a moment, he could feel the weight of an infant in his arms and see the eager young eyes returning his gaze. A sense of anticipation welled up in him, a focus like that he used to feel before a match. When he first began work on Project Raven, he knew the risks he would take, but his family deserved the rewards his audacity could reap.

Yang's silence hung upon the open line.

"Let the raven fly." Jin tapped the line closed, and turned back to his son. "Are you ready to spar?"

Mingbao grinned at him, readying his stance, bare feet braced. "Yes, Father. I will take you down."

"No," said Jin. "You will not." With quick strides and an almost casual spin, he swept his son's feet out from under him. The boy's head knocked hard against the tiled yard, the breath rushing from him. Jin stared down into his face, suppressing the urge to sympathy. "Never be surprised by an enemy."

"No," the boy mouthed, still winded, then he whispered, "Again."

Jin smiled.

CHAPTER TEN

Casey cocked his head. "Genghis Khan, scourge of the steppes? That guy?"

Liz gained her balance on the moving train, still carrying the tray from the drive-thru, though Casey made no move to eat or drink anything on it. "That's the one. The Mongols had the largest contiguous land empire in the history of the world. With Chinggis Khan's leadership, they conquered all of inner Asia, half the Middle East, Russia, Eastern Europe, and eventually China, under his successors. According to legend, when the Great Khan died, he was buried along with much of the plunder he took from those places, and all the men who built the tomb were killed so they couldn't reveal its location. He was afraid his enemies would come and desecrate his remains. Not to mention stealing his treasure. People have been looking for the tomb for almost eight hundred years."

"If everyone who knew the location was killed, then how could anyone make a map?" He stood easily, not hanging on to a strap or a pole, his knees slightly bent as if at a martial arts dojo, waiting for the next attack.

"Someone had to do the killing, didn't they? Someone Chinggis trusted had to have stayed alive to plan the whole thing and carry out the Great Khan's wishes. His son, Ogodei, oversaw the arrangements —when he wasn't busy conquering China."

"You keep calling him 'Chinggis.'"

"That's the Mongolian pronunciation. Are you going to tell me where we're going? If your car was bugged, don't they already know where you live?"

"We're not going to my place." The train slowed, and he pointed toward the door, a sharp, efficient gesture of command. "This is our stop."

He led the way out onto an open street lined with shops and restaurants, and starting to get busy with traffic. They followed a tree-lined street up past a little park and turned in at a brick apartment building, a little run-down, but no worse than the dorms back on campus. In the sheltered doorway, Casey leaned on a buzzer, counted to five, and buzzed again, short this time. Another moment passed, then the speaker crackled. "What's your delivery?"

"Stone lions." Casey gave a soft chuckle at Liz's questioning look.

"You've got company."

"A client."

"Have her check the mailbox."

The door buzzed, and he pushed inside.

"A password?" She felt as if she'd moved into a spy movie, but not an upscale classy film like James Bond, something earnest and low-rent. Graffiti marked the mailboxes at the entrance. Casey rapped one with his knuckles and it popped open.

"Don't tell me there's a secret door, too. Is this whole place a government installation?"

Casey's eyes sparkled, but he just pointed. "Like the man said, check the mail."

The spy stuff gave her something to focus on other than being attacked and watching a man get killed on her behalf. Liz leaned down and peered inside the box, a small hole pierced the back, but it was otherwise empty. "Nothing." She shrugged and tapped the mailbox shut.

The inner door buzzed, and Casey ushered her through, glancing quickly around before letting the door shut after them. They mounted the stairs that formed a squared-off spiral around a central elevator, and arrived on the fourth floor. With a rattle of chains, a door opened to reveal a black man in a wheel chair, one leg propped up on the footrest, the other a stump below the knee, a tablet computer strapped one of his armrests. Liz swallowed hard and gave him a nod as he wheeled back to give her space to enter. As he turned, she saw the scars that ran along the right side of his face, neck, and his arm below his sleeve. Three fingers remained on his right hand.

"Chief." The man spoke with a deep, resonant voice. "Police band says you had a busy night."

"What happened to your leg?" Casey asked.

Liz flinched. She'd assumed that they served together in whatever war had molded the Bone Guard, so Casey's blunt question felt intrusive, but the other man gave a shrug.

"Conduction issues. D. A.'s re-tooling the cup for a better fit."

"Hey, chief!" hollered a woman's voice from the back of the apartment, over the low whine of some sort of equipment. "With you in a minute!" A corridor led back past a wall with a cut-out into an adjoining kitchen. The combined living room and dining room held sparse furnishings, carefully spaced, including a large-screen TV with a freeze-frame of Liz's face, her blue eyes wide and ringed with lack of sleep.

"How—?" she started to ask, then realized the routine with the mailbox had exposed her to the eye of a camera in that tiny hole. Liz stopped moving, her glance flitting between the image, the men, the apartment door, which was already rolling shut at other man's tap of a pad.

"Need a drink? Coffee?" Casey moved around the partition into the kitchen beyond.

"How about an explanation?" She pointed to the screen.

Casey poured himself a steaming mug from the carafe on the counter. "Nick Norton." He tipped his mug toward the other man. "Paranoia's one of the side effects."

"Of what?" Liz demanded, then regretted it—she had no right to this man's personal problems.

"The job," Casey said. "Sure you don't want a coffee?"

"Really, I want to go home." She folded her arms. Her hands felt shaky.

"Thanks, Chief, now she thinks I'm a contractor. She's already had a rough night. You were the vic, right? The victim?" Nick addressed her, hands spread, face open despite his scars and rippling muscles. "Hey, thanks for the chai—are those hash browns?" He lit up like a child as he took the tray from her. "Anyhow, I heard there was an attack last night at the U, a mugging, and someone was killed. Was that your first time as a victim of violence?"

"I'm an ethnomusicologist—we don't get much violence." A nervous laugh bubbled up, and she let her knees go soft, sinking her onto the couch across from Nick's chair.

"An ethno-who?" He sniffed the drink, then took a long swallow, giving a satisfied sigh.

"I study the relationship of music to culture. I'm specializing in peoples of central Asia—Tuvans, Nepalese, Mongolians."

Nick shook his head. "That's a new one on me. What got you into that field?"

"We hosted a Mongolian exchange student when I was in high school. He practiced singing all the time, and I guess I got hooked." In more ways than one, but these people didn't need to know everything.

Casey emerged from the kitchen and held out a second mug. "Decaf. You'll need some rest."

"Chief—get lost. We're talking."

With a slight bow of his head, as if he had been bested in a duel, Casey departed, heading down the hall to the back, finally swinging the gym bag off his shoulder. Liz took a swallow of the warmth, and settled into the sympathy she saw in Nick's dark eyes as she told him all about it.

CHAPTER ELEVEN

Grant rapped on the last door in the hall, then pushed through, ducking the black curtain that blocked light—and signals. Six monitors glowed among the racks of equipment, one of them showing the front door, one the dark interior of the mailbox, one a view of Liz Kirschner settling back on the couch, sipping and chatting, stifling a yawn.

D. A. Silverberg pushed back from the desk and studied the monitor with Grant, her short curls bobbing. "Damn, he's good. Who would've thunk it? From sniper to counselor in one explosion. We're lucky he didn't go all Phineas Gage on us."

Lucky. Right. "You're re-fitting his prosthesis?"

She gestured toward the humming and whirring machine in the corner, an oversized frame with a printer head pivoting and moving through its space, the pinkish rubber cup already taking shape under the thin stream of material. "On-target. Should be ready in another hour. What've you got? You said a client?"

"Maybe. Not sure where the compensation will come from, though. She thinks she's found the map to the tomb of Genghis Khan. Someone else believes it enough to steal her laptop and notes, and wouldn't mind leaving her dead." He slipped Liz's phone from the pocket where he'd stowed it when he appropriated it earlier. "Check I.D. on the corpse. I also need some intel on a Professor Chan, head of the Asian Studies Department, and Mr. Huang Li-Wen, some kind of high-powered businessman."

D. A. tapped a few keys and brought up the image of the perp, then sent it off to her own device and handed back the phone. "I take it you didn't get that security job at the University."

Since they left the service D. A. had appointed herself their den mother, which sometimes Grant appreciate more than others. He shrugged. "Thanks for sending the listing over though."

She shook her head. "Wasn't me. But that's how you got mixed up with this, right?" She tipped her head toward the picture of Liz. "Worth doing?"

"If she's right, it's high profile, the kind of thing that could set us up. Genghis Khan's tomb—people have been hunting it for hundreds of years. If I can get in on finding it, that could make my career, and I can get you out that telecom job you love so much, maybe get Nick on logistics."

D. A. slid back to her desk. "I'll get on it, then." Keys tapped and fingers slid over the touch screen.

"How's he been?"

She glanced at the screen again, where Liz slumped on the couch and Nick gently relieved her of her cup, spreading a blanket over the sleeping woman. "Not bad. Not combat-ready." The computer gave a soft chime, and she brought her attention back to the screen. "Great—I love a quickie. Don't know what to call this guy, though, let's go with 'Jurgen'—he's used that one for at least two of his passports." A few more taps and she populated a second monitor with images of the dead man in life, in the background with a few now-dead Mexican kingpins.

Grant leaned over her shoulder, scanning the list of presumed aliases. The guy was a free agent, living in Boston the last few years, suspected of drug-related offenses, but not arrested—not yet. What was a cartel mercenary doing with a Mandarin mugger? Or was he an operative, taking out the competition on behalf of some other party? Interesting.

"He doesn't look like a Mongolian. I'll keep digging, Chief. Get a few hours' rest."

Grant drained the last of his coffee and stretched, taking another look at the woman on the screen, the one who might be their ride to their next great mission—or straight to the grave.

CHAPTER TWELVE

Over—what else? Chinese take-out—Liz played the music, the dramatic overtones of Khoomei singing filling the apartment. Nick closed his eyes with a cat-like smile, apparently enjoying the deep voices and the other-worldly buzzing, while D. A., the woman from the back room, screwed up her face and shuddered. "That's some weird shit. You say that's all one guy?"

"The finest Khoomei singers can produce as many as three or four distinct tones. But listen: this one's about the mountains. The next one is about a river—there's even birdsong worked into the primary line."

"So your map is a song." Casey put down his chopsticks, resting his elbows on his knees, that dark-eyed stare utterly intent upon her.

"Actually, it's a cycle of nine songs—I've got eight of them right here—describing a journey, to the place of deepest rest and greatest glory, where the heart of our ancestor resides forever, beneath the great Eternal Sky." She spread her hands, picturing the mountains reflected in pristine lakes. "Each of the songs begins with a reference to one of the other places, so they can be placed in order. That's how I know I'm missing one. Together, they form a whole landscape, pointing to a single place."

"What makes you think it's the Khan, not just some bit of metaphor?"

"The horsetails." She stopped the playback, scrolled to another song, and started again. "Listen, they mention horsetails nine times—only nine, exactly nine. That's based on the number of horsetails in the war banner of the khan. And this one—"she scrolled again—"the song is about the mountains, but the word 'crown' appears seventy-eight times. That's the number of kingdoms the Great Khan is said to have conquered. Among the treasures in the tomb are the seventy-eight crowns of those kings."

"Seventy-eight crowns? Must be a very long song," said D. A. She stuck a finger in her ear and jiggled it, as if to get rid of the sound.

Liz tapped the music off.

"How come nobody else has thought of this?" Casey asked. "If all the songs are about real places, you can't be the first person to know about it."

"The recordings came to the U as part of the estate of a long-time Chinatown resident, a woman who had fled the Cultural Revolution. She left us ten trunks that hadn't been opened since the fifties. Poetry manuscripts, scroll paintings, most of them damaged—pretty random, like an Asian yard sale. The labels on the chests indicated they were meant to be delivered to Joseph Needham, but only the first chest was ever sent. It looks like she found another way out with the rest of her documents. We get these kinds of legacies all the time, usually from alumni, and the ones with little apparent financial or research value get set aside until some grad student—me—has time to sort through them.

"My job in the archives has been to convert the old reel-to-reel tapes and records to digital before they get any further degraded. My thesis project centers on the tradition of landscape imagery in Mongolian music, so I've been looking out for more examples. I'm not sure anyone's even listened to these recordings since they were given to us. The first one opens with a sort of introduction, the missionary who recorded them wanted to find the oldest songs he could. He was looking for confirmation of the Biblical Flood in local legends, so he asked the elders, and one of them responded with this cycle of songs, but wouldn't tell him any more about them. He said they were the oldest songs in all Mongolia." Liz stared down at her device. "Then there was an argument about whether the singers were even Mongolian any more, since the Communists."

"Who else knows you found them?"

Liz tapped her fingertips together. "Professor Chan, and that collector who was visiting him. My Mongolian tutor, Toregene, who helped me check my translations; Byambaa, my fiancé, knows a little. My room-mate, Sara, knows I found something, but she doesn't really understand what. Professor Joyeux, my thesis advisor. Oh—and Marko at the archives. He checks people in and out, so he knows where I've been looking, but probably not what it means."

"And one of those people wants to kill you."

She jerked back against the couch cushions, but Casey's face hadn't changed, his expression as focused as ever. "No way. They're professors and students—they're not like you."

Casey went still, and all the air left the room for a long moment. "If you think you don't need me, you can leave. Right now. I happen to think you're wrong."

Spreading her hands, Liz told him, "Everything we do in my department is theoretical or archival. We listen, we describe, we compare—we don't get shot at, and when we do field work, it's with microphones and cameras, not weapons and bloodshed."

"You're talking to the guy who brought the knife to the gunfight. Like it or not, Ms. Kirschner, I didn't start this."

Her heart drummed, and she glanced away. D. A. and Nick had a whole conversation in tiny gestures, ending with the woman scooping the take-out containers back into their bag and standing up. "This has been fascinating, but I've gotta get to work, and Nick has an appointment at the VA. Chief, I'm standing down. Give me the high-sign if you need to. Nice to meet you, Liz." She flashed a brief smile, more a baring of the teeth, and stalked into the kitchen.

"There's really no reason to connect the muggers with my research—they grabbed my laptop because they can pawn it." The whole thing was just too bizarre. She came from the academic world, not the military one. Earlier, in the tension after everything that had happened to her, she thought it might be possible, but now, in the light of day, she'd come to her senses. Nobody killed over music, even if the songs could mean what she thought. Besides, she had a lot more research to do before she could come to any positive conclusions. Even her potential academic rivals wouldn't act on the little she knew. Liz pushed to her feet, still tired, but eager to put some distance between herself and a man who could kill that fast without losing his stride. "It's not that I don't appreciate what you did for me. I... you probably saved me from worse than a mugging, so I owe you for that, Mr. Casey." She put out her hand. "Good luck with the Bone Guard."

Casey rose in a fluid movement. His grip was solid and direct, and she recoiled a little, imagining that hand plunging a knife into her assailant. "Good luck with the khan." A brief smile. "You've got my number."

As she let herself out of the apartment, Liz hoped she'd never have to use it.

CHAPTER THIRTEEN

"Told you this idea was nuts." D. A. dumped the trash and came back to clear the plates. "Academics either don't have money, or they don't do anything interesting. She's probably headed back to the library to spend the next twenty-four hours immersed in whack-o music and books you can't even understand."

"She's going to her apartment." Grant gave a shake of his head, then grabbed his go-bag. "I'm tailing her."

"You're what?" D. A. stood with a stack of tableware in each hand, like that girl statue from the Garden of Good and Evil. "Chief, she said no. She's not a client, she's just a music major with an obsession. I've dated people like that, okay? Forget it. She's probably right about the mugging and the attempted rape and all of that."

"Fine, I'll waste another day."

"Maybe you need a distraction. Have you thought about Maria, down at the VA? She likes you."

"Thanks, Mom. I need to focus on my job, or what it could be." He side-stepped D. A., only to find Nick blocking the door.

"The Bone Guard's a cool notion, Chief. But it's meant to be details, not ops. You get to hang out at some digs or museums, defending the artifacts, maybe bring some friends along when you need help." Nick sighed. "You're treating this like an op because you miss the Unit. We know that, we get it. Maybe you're a little sensitive because you escalated when you didn't have to and somebody's dead."

"Don't pull the psycho-babble on me, buddy, I don't need that." Grant tipped his head toward the door. "You gonna let me out, or am I going out the window?"

Nick wheeled back with a graceful half-bow, gesturing toward the door. "Just remember," he said, when Grant was already halfway out, "paranoia's one of the symptoms."

Grant flashed him the finger and pulled the door shut. He took the stairs two at a time and hit the street. As he walked, he shifted the bag from one hand to the other, pulling off his shirt, replacing it with one from the bag, adding a beanie and a set of headphones that didn't connect to anything. At the T-stop, Liz stood tapping her fingers as she studied the route map. Grant adopted the slouch of a slacker, fists in pockets, shoving his jeans down too far. He slumped past her and got into the next car when she boarded. Green line trains had only two double-cars, each articulated at the middle, rattling and flexing around the bends in the surface tracks, occasionally sinking underground. Transfer to the Red-line, back toward Cambridge. Tall blond guy, on at the same stop, off at the same, checking his messages—or not. Long-haired Chinese girl, waiting for a train, changing her mind and pushing through the turnstiles just after Liz. She tapped her fingers all the time, did she know that? It was a tell, but for what? Details, the team said, not ops. Work details: like a cop standing around at a construction site, waving through the commuters and getting angry looks. Was it true? Yeah, okay, he hadn't felt this pumped since his discharge. So what? He wasn't the one who used a password for his apartment and facial recognition software in his mailbox.

Redline crowded, as usual, mostly students. That one had a lump under his jacket that might have been a gun. Grant bumped him by accident, ignored the guy's protest. Turned out to be a magazine, rolled up. Besides, his paranoia had kept him alive for fourteen years —had kept all of them alive, almost.

Blond guy hailed a cab. China girl kept walking, phone to her ear now, smiling and laughing, showing a lot of teeth. Liz walked from Porter Square, with its thousand restaurants and sidewalk sales, along increasingly narrow streets to come up to a brick triple-decker, where she patted down her pockets, and let out a little cry of dismay. Her keys must have been in her laptop case. Grant fumbled with his own keys at a doorway a few buildings down, on the opposite side, where he could watch her reflection in the broad window of an empty shop. Grey sedan, recent model, in the Permit Only zone, but no permit showing. Looked like an unmarked.

Liz jabbed a button by the door.

Movement at the other end of the block, and blond guy stood in the shadows, shifted his weight. Grant swung around, ready to take him, his muscles already twitching with the need. The door in front of Liz popped open and Gooney filled it with his cheap suit and big hands. "Elizabeth Kirschner. Detective Gonsalves."

She stumbled at his appearance, and he caught her with one of those hands, one side of his mouth smiling. "Watch it there, ma'am."

"Thanks." She gave herself a little shake all over, and looked up at him. "What can I do for you?" Then shook her head again, frowning, looking past him. "Wait a minute—were you in my apartment?"

"Yes, ma'am. All in the line of duty." He hadn't let go of her elbow yet and Grant's grip on his go-bag tightened. Gooney stared into Liz's face and a uniformed officer, a woman, appeared in the doorway behind him. "We're here to bring you in on suspicion of murder."

CHAPTER FOURTEEN

"I haven't killed anyone—it was your friend, Casey, who stabbed that guy." Liz let them turn her around, handcuff her. Her arms felt limp and shaky at the same time. "Self-defense, right? Isn't that what you said last night?"

"The mugging wasn't the only thing that happened last night. This is Officer Tran. She'll ride with you back to the station."

They escorted her down toward a dark car by the curb, her building once more shut against her. God, all she'd wanted was to go home, to be done with this insanity. Instead, it was just getting worse. Tears stung her eyes, the cuffs cold and hard against her skin. The handful of people on the street all stopped and stared—the woman who owned the fruit stand shaking her head, probably thinking how Liz always seemed like such a nice girl. As they helped her into the car, Officer Tran planting a hand on her head to make sure she didn't bang it on the door-frame, Liz noticed the guy across the street, slouched against a vacant shop, beanie pulled low and headphones dangling at his neck. He lifted a hand, poking back the beanie to reveal his dark gaze, and flicked her a little salute. Casey.

At the station, they brought her into another interview room, a little sparser, with a big dark glass on one side, and the round bulge of a camera in the corner opposite where they placed her. Tran took off the cuffs and brought her a cup of the same bad coffee.

"Our conversation's going to be recorded, Ms. Kirschner, audio and video, just so you know," Gonsalves began.

"Does that mean you're going to tell me what's going on, Detective, because I honestly have no idea. I was mugged last night, that's all I know. I already gave you a statement about that."

Gonsalves ignored her, laying out a few items from a folder he had carried in. "Does this look familiar?" He slid a plastic bag toward her, and Liz leaned forward, squinting at it.

The bag contained a twisted rectangle of plastic and fabric, partly melted and blackened, but with a familiar logo on the back, and a bit of an address still legible on the front. "That's the tag from my laptop case, I mean, it looks like mine, but what happened to it? Did you find my bag?"

"Is there any chance you didn't have your case with you last night? Maybe you left it somewhere, before the alleged mugging?"

Now the mugging was "alleged?" That didn't sound good. "No, I definitely brought it to my meeting with Professor Chan. I'm sure he can tell you."

"Mm-hm." Gonsalves made a few marks on a pad, then he took back the bag and opened it, holding it toward her, but not letting her touch. "Does that trigger any memories?"

Liz started to shake her head, then she paused. An odor drifted from the bag: melted plastic and soot. "They burned my bag? Oh, crap—what about all of my papers, my research?"

Gonsalves brought out a small rectangle from the folder, keeping his hand over it. "Hard to say. Do you recognize this man?" He slid his hand across the table, then turned a photo upright, one of those semi-formal shots the admissions office took for student ID's. Young guy, cute, but with an irritating smirk and a pretentious tie in Ivy League colors.

"That's Marko, uh, Marko Therrien, I think. He works at the archives in the music department."

More notes. "How well do you know Mr. Therrien?"

"Not very. We've had a few classes together. Mostly I see him at the archives when I'm doing my research, a few times a week, I guess." She clutched the cup of coffee, that shaky feeling returning to her limbs and core. "Why? What's this about?"

"Never seen him socially?"

She shook her head. "He tried to ask me out a couple of times, but I'm already in a relationship."

"No personal connection." Gonsalves tapped the photo, drawing her attention back to the face. "Then you wouldn't mind if you found out he's dead."

"He's what? What?" Liz put down the cup, picked it up again when her hands shook without it.

"Around the same time of your alleged mugging, maybe a little before that, maybe a little after, there was a fire in the archives. The fire department arrived promptly, and were able to prevent the blaze from spreading, but they weren't expecting to find a body, Ms. Kirschner. Marko Therrien. We ID'd him from dental records, Ms. Kirschner. Do you know what that means?"

That he'd been burned beyond all recognition. The smell of the luggage tag—melted plastic, soot—turned her stomach and Liz scrambled to her feet. "I need the bathroom," she gasped, then clamped a hand to her face. She pictured Marko, twisted and blackened just like that, and she never made it to the bathroom before she vomited.

CHAPTER FIFTEEN

Gooney pounded into his office and slammed the door, then pivoted on one heel, with a moment of shock that made Grant wish he'd been holding a camera: an expression that stunned could've gone viral.

"How the Hell did you get in my office?" Then he stabbed a finger at Grant. "And get out of my chair."

After an instant too long, Grant took his feet off the desk and rose, offering the chair as if it belonged to him. Gooney's hand balled into a fist. "How did you get in here?" Gooney looked around, peering suspiciously at the window as he stalked to his chair and dropped into it. He tossed a file folder on the table, spilling a young man's photo and a few other things Grant cataloged in an instant.

"I told the receptionist you and I served together, same unit. She buzzed me in." Grant remained standing, arms folded. "Police officers respond to the idea of comrades in arms." He scanned Gooney's blunt, furious face, and shrugged. "Most of them, anyway." He deliberately softened his stance, letting his eyes crinkle a bit. "You can't hold her for this, you know that. She was with me most of the time, when she wasn't here at the station."

"With you. Because you are such a great alibi. I could tell the court some things—"

"Not without exposing classified information." Grant hooked over a guest chair with his foot and sat down, steepling his hands on the edge of Gooney's desk. "You don't like me. I get that. Doesn't matter. You've got too much integrity to let that stand between you and your job."

"Liking has nothing to do with this." Gooney stuck a hand in a drawer and came out with a pack of cigarettes. He shoved one in his mouth, paused, then tossed it on the surface of the desk. "Goddamn regulations."

Grant laughed. "Never dreamed I'd hear you say those words."

For a moment, he thought Gooney might bend, even a little. Instead, the detective thrust his head forward. "You don't get to tell me how to do my job, or why, or what's important, got it? You're not the chief out here."

"Look, Gonsalves, Detective, you were in the Unit long enough to put this stuff together." Grant ticked off his fingers. "A woman gets mugged, guy takes shots at her with a silencer, that's hardly street-issue, guy speaks Mandarin—"

"Says you."

"Says me, fine. Same night, the archive where she does her research gets torched, and one of the few people who knows about the project gets killed. I'm guessing it wasn't from smoke inhalation."

Gooney's hazel eyes flicked right, then down to the photo, back to Grant's.

"Some evidence left at the scene points to her," Grant proposed.

Another flick right.

"Maybe even something from that same bag, something with her name on it." Bingo. "You know what sucks, my friend? You were already in her place, before she got home. That makes it hard to know if her apartment was searched before your boys showed up. If something's out of place, it could have been taken by a cop, not a robber."

Gooney snorted. "You're paranoid."

"That doesn't make me wrong. Connect the dots, Gonsalves. Not just a mugging, not just a fire. Liz Kirschner is in danger. Someone wants to scoop her research, or at least, stop her from finishing it. I wasn't the only person who followed her home today."

Gooney picked up the cigarette and rolled it around his fingers like a magic trick. "What's the research?"

"Can't tell you—that's up to Ms. Kirschner."

"What the Hell, Casey, you're not a priest or a lawyer, you're a goddamn mercenary. You don't get client confidentiality." He pointed the cigarette in Grant's direction.

"I'm not a mercenary, I'm a soldier, an operator. So are you, for all that we're on opposite sides of the desk. You're one of the smartest guys I know, Gooney, help us out here."

"With what? You won't tell me anything, and your girlfriend—sorry, your client—is in the ladies' room being sick."

Grant sat up straight. "She was fine before she got here—what happened?"

"Girl trouble." Gooney rolled his eyes. "Just the idea of what happened to that kid freaked her out."

"So you know she didn't do it."

"I can't believe you're bringing a graduate student into an op. She's not ready for any of your crap."

Technically, she had brought him in, whether she meant to or not. "So you admit it's an op. But the thing is, Gooney, it's not mine. Who's running it? Who's the target and what's the scam?"

Gooney sank his head into his hands. "It gives me a headache just talking to you again. No scam, no, it's not an op. I don't know what the Hell it is, not yet, but I'll figure it out. All I know is, people don't kill over a research paper."

With a grim smile, Grant tapped the photo. "Somebody did."

CHAPTER SIXTEEN

"Thanks for doing this, Detective." Liz still felt shaky, but being back at her own place, under police escort, helped with that. Professor Chan confirmed she had been at his office with her bag, and it had been only a few moments between that meeting and her call to Grant—cell phone records confirmed it. She just didn't have the time to set a fire, much less to—but she didn't want to think about Marko.

"Least I could do after hauling you off in handcuffs," Gonsalves answered, sounding a little contrite.

At the door, Sara stood wide-eyed, blinking at the detective and the two uniformed officers, then managing a smile for Casey, the last one in line. Seeing that smile, Liz took another look at Casey herself. Tall, rangy, clearly athletic, keen-eyed and dead-silent, he walked in like he owned the place. Sara suffered from a classic addiction to bad-boys, dark and dangerous. Pretty much the polar opposite of the artistic and erudite men Liz preferred. Casey didn't just look dangerous, though, he was deadly. Sure, some women would be turned on by that, maybe even by knowing how quickly he could kill a man—at the very least, he'd get a lot of attention at the local pub with his looks and that kind of backstory. Even if she hadn't known it was true.

When the parade of cops had passed, Sara wrapped her in a hug. "Oh, my gosh, Liz, are you okay? I heard about Marko and the archive, but I had no idea about the assault. When you didn't come home last night, I just figured, well, you know. Byambaa's awfully far away and a girl gets lonely." Sara's head cocked toward Casey.

"It wasn't like that—not at all."

"Guess not." Sara couldn't seem to take her eyes off him. "Who's that then? He doesn't look like a student. Or a cop."

"He's my bodyguard." Sara's eyes got a little wider, and Liz groaned. "Not like that. Good grief, do you ever stop?" She moved vaguely into the apartment, which seemed bright and cluttered compared with Nick's austere place. "Were you here last night? They're worried we might have had a break-in."

"Wow! No, nothing like that. I was at church this morning, and I stayed for Youth Ministry, that's why I missed the detectives earlier." She stood shoulder to shoulder with Liz, both of them scanning the apartment with new eyes.

Liz went to her desk, all the papers neatly stacked, folders in their slots. A hook marked the board above the desk, empty. "I'm missing a thumb drive, twenty gig." She tapped the hook.

"Might it have been in your laptop case?" Detective Gonsalves leaned in to examine the desk.

"No chance. That was my local back-up. It never left here."

"Encryption? Password?" Casey spoke from behind her, and Liz caught her lip between her teeth as she shook her head.

"Just what are you researching, Ms. Kirschner?" Gonsalves asked.

She glanced back at Casey, who stared at her levelly, as if awaiting her command. Sara and the other two officers hung around the living room. "I'd rather not say just now." This earned her an imperceptible nod from Casey, and a full-on glower from Gonsalves.

"Look, Ms. Kirschner, you're going to have to tell me, or tell the court, if it's at all relevant to the—events of last night. A man's dead, ma'am, you can't just clam up."

She opened her mouth, but Casey tapped her arm and shook his head, tapping his ear and giving a gesture that encircled the whole room. Last night, he'd been worried that his car was bugged, now he seemed to think the apartment was, too. And he'd spoken literally two words since they walked in. The empty hook stared back at her from the board, slender and ominous.

Casey suddenly lifted his head, slid a hand into his pocket and came out with a humming cell phone, glancing at the display. For a second, his lips parted, breath hissed out. Gonsalves started toward the bookshelf, but Casey shot out a hand and grabbed his arm, holding out the phone for him to see. "Shit. Nick?" Gonsalves said. "Why the Hell did you involve him?"

"He's my wingman." Casey turned to Liz. "Get your things. Whatever you need for a week and make it fast. Nick's place was compromised."

CHAPTER SEVENTEEN

Gooney snatched a portable light from under the dash and hit a switch, spreading a blue, flashing glow and a siren that broke traffic in front of the car. "You could at least be grateful, Casey."

"When we find Nick, I will be. Just drive."

"How did they find his place? Even I don't know where he lives, for God's sake." He slammed the car around a tight curve and they shot onto the highway.

"Backtracked from the station where they found her."

"She's right here, you know," Liz called from the back seat where she clutched her backpack. A small wheelie carry-on rode at her side. In the mirror, she looked younger and paler than before. Gooney was right about one thing: she wasn't ready for ops. Not combat ready. Like Nick.

"You're so sure they didn't follow you? Why aren't you driving—ditched another car, did you?"

Grant didn't answer that. What would be the point? "Head toward Somerville."

"Where the fuck are we going, the park?"

"D. A. checked the park, right after she heard from Nick. He's on the move, or he was as of 1300." He rubbed the back of his neck, feeling the smooth patch and the ridge of scars, imagining he could feel the ink. Nick's apartment had been compromised. Where would the big guy go? They had to assume Casey's place had already been tossed or bugged, or both. Not the VA or the park where he liked to hang out. The violation of his space would have flicked the switch back to sniper mode. "Turn here, then left."

"Why do I even listen to you," Gooney muttered, but he continued to follow directions until they pulled up a few blocks from Nick's place, behind a new high-rise hotel.

Grant stepped out of the car, looked around, then headed for the lobby.

"Oh, I get it. Nick's pissed, his PTSD has been activated, so he decided to check in for the weekend?"

Grant pointed toward the desk. "Get us roof access."

Gooney hesitated, then turned for the desk, already bringing out his badge.

"What's going on?" Liz, still hugging her backpack, approached Grant.

"Someone invaded Nick's turf. He's freaked out. We're here to pick him up and bring him home." How had the enemy infiltrated Nick's apartment? Grant scanned the lobby while they waited. Lots of brass and mirrors, oddly shaped benches and poorly-lit corners. Ops nightmare. Unless you were already in. Gooney gave him the signal, and they followed a slim woman in a dark suit into the staff elevator where she used a key to unlock the upper floors, glancing warily at him and Liz. They didn't speak at all, and, despite shifting her weight, her eyes, wetting her lips, the hotel woman didn't either.

"Wait here, ma'am. And thank you," Gooney said, with his more-like-a-grimace smile. If he meant it reassuringly, it backfired. Grant took the lead out the door, walking bold, making it clear he was under no threat.

"Why are we here?" Liz asked again, edging around the door.

"This is the highest building in the area. I assume this is Nick's neighborhood. Chief—Casey—thinks Nick's on surveillance. If we're lucky, he's not armed." Gooney shifted his own sidearm in the holster under his jacket.

Half a city block at its base, the building narrowed to a ballroom and a couple of fancy suites at the top, with AC units and a set of emergency stairs opposite the concrete pillbox where they had emerged. Overlooking Nick's building two blocks away. Grant walked to the middle of the roof, avoiding the skylights, held up his arms, crossed, at head level, then broke the gesture and waited.

A few heartbeats later, Nick's voice echoed from the concrete box around the emergency stairs. "You sure, Chief?"

"Positive."

A moment later, with a scrape and the sound of a soft landing, Nick appeared around the corner, shouldering his rifle, limping slightly on his re-fitted prosthesis. Grant gave him a salute. "Report?"

"Two men, one Chinese, one blonde. Entered through the window on the landing, via the rooftop. Gained roof access by posing as repairmen. Cameras got three angles on them." Nick approached to five feet and stopped, taking a stiff pose, keeping his eyes straight ahead. "Flash drives, any loose media taken. Calendars rifled, travel folders accessed. No high security breached, but scans are running to confirm."

"How does a one-legged man with an assault rifle get to the roof of a crowded hotel?" Gooney said.

Nick's eyes met Grant's, and Grant answered, "I guess you'd better talk to them about their security protocols. Maybe you can convince someone this was all a drill."

"You brought him, Chief?" Nick asked.

"He gave me a lift. This is the part where I thank him." Grant gave Gooney a salute. "Thank you, Detective Gonsalves. It's good to know a citizen can count on the police."

"Shut up." Gooney let his weapon slide back into the holster and stuck out his hand. "Nick. How are you?"

"Combat ready, sir."

"You think?" He pointed to the rifle. "You better stow that thing before the hotel woman goes batshit on us."

"It's okay, Nick. You can stand down," Grant echoed.

Nick flipped the gun and broke it down in a matter of seconds, the components sliding into pockets, both obvious and concealed, the barrel slipping into a socket at the back of his artificial leg. The leg of his pants slid down over his prosthetic. As he straightened, it was as if the tension drained from him and a rush of something better filled its place, as if that fierce hunter had never been, and a pre-school teacher took his place. Sometimes, Grant envied him the change.

Empty-handed, Nick turned a radiant smile on Liz. "Ms. Kirschner. I am so sorry to see your day's not improving. I hope these guys are at least treating you well?"

She laughed, a nervous sound that broke into genuine pleasure and surprise. "I guess they're doing their best, but I'd like to know why they'd rather be killing each other."

"Sorry, miss, but I am not at liberty to say."

Grant scanned the rooftop again. Clear, and the hotel woman was inside guarding the door—as much from them, as for them, he figured. "This is a secure environment, unless they have eyes in the sky, and a helluva microphone. Detective Gonsalves, would you mind giving us a few moments privacy?"

"Can't do it. I don't care who you used to be. This is my city, and I don't like what's going down." Gooney puffed himself up, straining his uniform. Unlike most of the force Grant had seen, Gooney still worked out. "You claim I can trust you—what the Hell good does it do if you won't trust me?"

"Ms. Kirschner, where do we go next to track down this project of yours?"

She took a half-step back. "I was just, I thought I'd continue my research here. There are some more sources I can examine, even with the archive destroyed—"

"We have to assume, because they got to Therrien, that they know what you were looking at. You have copies, they have the originals, and the archive was torched to cover it up. Someone cares about this, a whole lot. More than you, it seems."

At that, a little color came to her cheeks, and a fire to her eyes. "No, they don't. But it's still all theoretical. The evidence is spread out. I have the map, or most of it, but I don't have where it begins."

"And neither do they, right? But they're now a few steps ahead of us. What happens if they get there first?"

"They publish, they get the fame, the credit for my discovery." She scowled.

Grant took a step forward, entering her space. "You're still thinking like a graduate student. The enemy isn't some rival trying to do you out of an assistanceship, they're killing people." She caught her breath, lips pressed together, and he repeated the question, "What happens if they get there first?"

"I guess it depends on who they are. The Chinese? They hate Chinggis Khan, and everything he stands for. He's the only foreigner who conquered their country and claimed it for his own. The Chinese and the Mongolians have hated each other for eight hundred years. If they find the tomb, they'll dynamite it before they ever let anyone else find out."

Gooney cocked his head. "Shit, lady, it's that important to them that nobody finds out about this dead guy?"

Grant answered, "He's an international symbol of Chinese humiliation, Gooney, what do you think they'd do?"

"Now, gentlemen, let's try to stay civilized," Nick interjected.

"Cambridge," Liz blurted, drawing their eyes back to her. Nick pointed down the Charles River toward Cambridge, the haven of universities, but Liz shook her head. "Cambridge, England. Home of the Needham Research Institute, the world's largest collection of Chinese documents and research materials. That's where the first chest in our donor's collection was archived, along with the missing song. I applied for a travel grant to go, but I haven't heard back yet."

"England?" Grant echoed.

Gooney gave a hoot of laughter. "You should see your face. Can't go in there slinging guns and skulking in doorways."

"It's a long story," Liz said. "The recordings I have came from Inner Mongolia, that's part of China now, and the woman who left them to us intended them to go to Needham. I don't have all the information—odds are pretty good what we need is there, at the Needham Institute." Then her excitement froze, and she said, "Whoever torched the archive knows that, too."

"How am I supposed to convince a court that some kid in Boston gets flamed over the search for some famous dead guy?" Gooney said.

Liz ignored him, looking up at Grant, her expression caught between fear and excitement. "I've been saving up to go back to Mongolia. There should be enough for a couple of plane tickets as far as London. I can't afford to pay you, not yet, but—"Liz broke off, her fingers tapping together. "I can't do this without help. Without you."

And there it was, his, quite literal, ticket to a new life. "Then we better get flying."

CHAPTER EIGHTEEN

Once their flight took off across the Atlantic, Liz turned to Casey. "So, Joseph Needham was a British scholar around the second world war. He was actually a biochemist, but he fell in love with a Chinese graduate student, so he taught himself Chinese, and became obsessed, really, with everything Chinese."

"All for a girl."

"I've heard worse reasons," Detective Gonsalves said from the window seat. He shifted again, bumping her with his shoulder. "God, I hate flying coach."

"Not like we invited you," Casey pointed out. "But it's better than jump seats in a troop transport."

"Hey, my murder turned into an OD, and my arson into an accident—that's what the crime scene boys are saying anyhow. One big ol' coincidence, according to the Powers That Be." Gonsalves cast a dark look at Grant, as if he didn't believe that verdict for a moment. "If I stay in Boston, I'll never learn the truth. So. I've got nothing better to do but keep an eye on you. Not like I have this much vacation time anyway. I'll be pulling weekends for the rest of the year. At least tell me we get wine."

"I'll buy you the bottle if you'll shut up."

Liz couldn't quite believe it herself, but the reports showed Marko had been passed out or possibly hallucinating when the fire started, probably as a result of a spiked joint that smoldered while Marko crashed. She wouldn't have taken him for an addict, but the toxicology didn't lie. It was only Casey and Gonsalves's paranoia that associated her own mugging with Marko's tragedy. She shuddered and put that aside in search of distraction. "If I'm getting this right," Liz said, "You guys served in the same unit, along with Nick and even D. A.? They all call you 'Chief,' so were you the commanding officer?"

Casey stared at the seat in front of him, his well-modulated tone barely faltering. "I'm not the subject, Ms. Kirschner. I'm never the subject."

"I don't even know what that means."

"Ask him no questions, he'll tell you no lies," Gonsalves muttered, then held up his hands. "Quiet now, all done talking!" He turned away toward the window, pulling out a book, but Liz caught his smirk. Whatever had happened between them, the detective couldn't miss a chance to tweak his old comrade.

"Anyway, you should call me 'Liz,' especially when we get there. That'll make it easier for the administration to believe we're working together on the research." She chuckled at the idea of passing off Casey as a fellow graduate student. What would his major be—killing and mayhem? Military history? That might be believable. Then she remembered how easily he had fooled even her with a few simple changes in his clothes and his demeanor. Maybe it wouldn't be so hard after for him to fit in after all. "It would be even easier if you read Chinese."

A smile ghosted across Casey's lips. "At your service...Liz."

"Seriously?"

"I hate the guy—I don't think you should count on him," Gonsalves said to the window, as if he were still out of the conversation, "but he does have some skills. Hey, listen to this—after helping the Mongolians throw out the Chinese, the Soviets destroyed all the statues of Genghis Khan, except one, but it's super ugly. Then a few years later, the guy who commissioned it gets bludgeoned to death, and the artist gets fired."

"Where'd you read that?" Liz asked.

Gonsalves displayed the cover of a Mongolian guidebook. "Figured I should get some intel on the territory."

"Just like a detective, to find a murder in a guide book." Grant's smile solidified. "So how does a Brit obsessed with a Chinese girl get the biggest collection of Chinese documents outside China?"

"It may be the biggest anywhere. So much was destroyed during the Cultural Revolution—professors and researchers were killed and imprisoned, their research was confiscated, libraries burned, universities shut down—anything that might not support the Communist Party's agenda was destroyed. Needham and some of his British Sinophile friends caught wind of it before it began. Chinese academics were worried, so Needham proposed to write a book, the Science and Civilization of China. Cambridge University Press accepted the proposal, and he got to go to China to do the research. Given they have five thousand years of history, and thousands of square miles of territory, not to mention a variety of languages and cultural sub-groups, it was pretty clear the book would be one of many. I think the series is up to twenty volumes now, either published or in process."

"All based on this one guy's research?"

Liz shrugged. "Sort of. When the Chinese intelligentsia learned he was collecting material, they started sending him everything they could, trying to keep it safe from the Communists. Scrolls, chests, trunks, baskets—Needham got a surplus army truck and drove all over the countryside just collecting everything people wanted to give him, then shipping it back to England with the help of the British army, straight up until they all got thrown out of the country. Scholars are still sorting through all the information he collected.

That's the mandate of the Needham Research Institute and the scholars who go there. We need to find any other music related to our collection, and figure out where the map begins."

"Sounds like some heavy reading ahead of us." Grant leaned back his chair and shut his eyes. "Better get rested."

In moments, his breathing evened, his face relaxing from its habitual alert. Liz stared, incredulous. "How can anybody fall asleep that fast?"

"It's an occupational bonus," Gonsalves murmured. "I've seen him do it standing up—but only if he's got his back to the wall. You sleep when you have to, when you're safe. Which is practically never." His gruff voice softened as he spoke, his jaw working as he studied his old commander.

"So if he won't tell me anything, will you?"

"We served together in a special operations intelligence group, entering combat zones before the soldiers, gathering the information they needed to make their attacks. That's about all I'm at liberty to tell you. Half of what I know is classified, and I don't even know the half of it, if you see what I mean." He shrugged.

"Fair enough. Can you tell me why you guys don't get along?"

His eyes roved over her face, then he closed the guidebook, leaving a finger to mark his place. "There's a few reasons," he said at last. "Here's one: the team was clearing a building, a museum in the mountains of Afghanistan. They weren't even supposed to be inside, just giving the information they had to the local commander for him to act on. Let's just say, special ops aren't known for following orders, and Casey's unit even less so. He'd had enough successes by then, the brass gave him a little lee-way, so long as he delivered the goods. So this museum thing, Chief is first in, last out, but he was taking too long. Nick went back in for him—he wasn't supposed to, but—" another shrug. "One of the insurgents wasn't dead. He set off a body bomb. Nick got the chief behind some statue, out of the way and himself into it."

"But Nick still calls him 'Chief' and clearly respects him," Liz pointed out.

"And I don't. Yeah. Casey claims he was still in there because of a woman, a civilian who was looting the museum while the shooting was going on. Nick never saw anyone, neither did the rest of the team see her come out. We call her 'the Phantom'. Poof, vanished." He made drifting gesture with his hands. "Casey should've been out of there, instead, Nick went in after him and they both got hurt. Got the team booted out of action." Gonsalves shook his head. "He'd always been reckless. Still is, I guess."

Which didn't explain why Nick remained devoted to the man who almost got him killed. Or why Liz herself felt safer with Casey at her side. "Where were you at the time?"

"Stateside. On re-assignment, courtesy of Grant Casey." Gonsalves broke his gaze and poked the call button over his head. "I need a drink."

CHAPTER NINETEEN

Three hours of studying tiny old-fashioned catalog cards and searching for bits and pieces were about as much as Grant could stand. Sitting in the library, wearing the guise of a mild-mannered academic made him restless and twitchy. The Institute occupied a rectangular brick building, ordinary and institutional, though with some Asian flair to the roofline, at least from the outside. Inside, the structure of the place, with lots of windows, aisles of books and other resources and numerous desks occupied by a variety of scholars was a logistics nightmare. Plenty of places to hide, half the visitors were Asian, and he knew their adversaries were likely here ahead of them. Could be anyone. Could be anywhere. No stone lions to defend his client or himself. Liz, on the other hand, looked eager and at peace in a way she hadn't before. She pounced from one resource to another, able to discern at a glance what might be of use to them, and what was not. Now, she had access to the sound library, while he was tracking down references to Genghis Khan's tomb. He carried his note of titles to one of the reference desks.

"Excuse me. This volume isn't on the shelf where it should be. Is there another place to look?"

The woman peered at his note, peered at him, peered at her computer screen. She tapped and scrolled for a moment, then said, "No, sir, I don't see that it has been withdrawn or passed along for university use. It is simply possible that someone else in the Institute is examining that work at present. Wait a moment." She took the note over and conferred with a colleague, who returned in her stead.

"The gentleman over here recently asked for assistance in locating *The Galician–Volhynian Chronicle.* Let's just see if he's about done with it, shall we?"

"No, I can—"

Without listening to Grant's reply, the chubby librarian hustled over toward a tall stand where a middle-aged Chinese man leaned over a book.

Grant ducked down, letting a bookshelf interrupt line of sight between him and the man the librarian was now accosting. Short man, slim build, spectacles, slightly balding. He didn't look like an operator, but then, with the blazer he picked up at a charity shop and scuffed brown shoes to match, Grant didn't look like one either.

The librarian pointed back toward Grant, frowned looking around, then spotted him and brightened. Great. The man listened, nodded, and the librarian headed back toward Grant and the information desk. Behind him, the man turned away, moving his hands over the book. His shoulders hunched into a violent coughing fit which drew the irked attention of everyone else in the library. He slid a hand into his jacket and came out with a kerchief, smiling and bowing an apology as he coughed into the cloth. After a moment, when his coughing did not subside, he closed the book and followed the librarian.

"I will return to finish," he managed between coughs. "When I have recovered. Thank you." He handed the book over, then moved off toward the exit, followed by the relieved gazes of many other scholars.

"Oh, you are quite welcome. Sir?" The librarian scanned expectantly, then startled as Grant rose from his crouch.

"Thanks." He slipped the book from the librarian's hands and walked back toward the study carrels, choosing one where he could keep an eye on the door. The previous borrower exited through the security frame and could be seen outside the glass, still fussing with his kerchief. A quick glance at the book showed it had no index. Great. He flipped a few pages to see if he could get a sense for the structure—no sense reading the entire life of the Khan if he could just —toward the back, a few pages had been neatly sliced from the book. The shadow of the stranger had gone from in front of the building. Damn. If he went for Liz, it would be too late.

Grant snatched up the book and shoved it back into the hands of a startled librarian. "It's missing pages. I think that guy cut them."

"But—"

Grant was already leaving, moving efficiently through the door into the dull British day, scanning. Gooney pushed himself off from the low wall where he'd been sitting. "What's up?"

"Short guy, Asian, having a coughing fit."

"Left, toward the stream. You need backup?"

A brief hesitation, then, "Stay on Liz. You've got the pix from D. A., right?"

Gooney gave a nod, and Grant took off at a run. Students moved back and forth between the venerable buildings of the colleges at Cambridge, a collection of grey stone structures as crenelated and decorative as any cathedral. The stream disappeared under tarmac and buildings, then reappeared, providing a line toward the center of town. A grassy verge bordered the stream, with dense trees overhanging it. There, the tall man, walking fast, a phone already in his hand. He didn't look back. Grant put on a burst of speed, a few students dodging as he closed the distance between them. His target turned to cross the stream, toward one of the long college buildings, Grant now only a hundred yards behind. As they came into the shadow of the looming structure, Grant made his move, coming in fast, as if in a hurry, and banged into the guy's right side.

"Sorry," he muttered as he grabbed the man's arm. To any

onlooker, he was providing support. In fact, he used his momentum to steer the man into an arched doorway.

"Excuse me!" the man nearly lost his phone, but he saved it, shoving it into a pocket.

"Those pages you stole. The Institute needs them back." He kept his grip on the man's arm, but his other hand slid into the man's jacket, searching, paper crinkling under his touch.

"How dare you suggest such a thing." The man tried to smack his hand away too late.

Grant pulled out the pages, and the man's lips pinched shut, then a small, round pressure thrust against Grant's neck. An unmistakable, utterly familiar, and, in England, totally illegal, handgun. The man in front of him relaxed as the one behind said, "You have grown soft since leaving the service. Rigor mortis could rectify that."

CHAPTER TWENTY

Liz removed her headphones, the sound of Khoomei still reverberating in her ears, while the flush of victory bubbled in her head. Using the information from the songs she had cataloged back home, she had found the missing recording. And, with a little help from a micro-device D. A. gave her before they left Boston, recorded it for later study. She hoped Grant had similar luck with the references to the grave site. Even with the last song, she couldn't be sure where the map began, and it seemed unlikely that the khan's heirs had left such an important site completely at the whim of musical memory.

What else did they have? It wasn't until Chinggis Khan ordered the creation of a script that the Mongols even had written language. They had other materials like felt and silk; livestock, mainly sheep, goats and horses; wood, but not much of that; stone—there were some stone markers in Mongolia that pre-dated the advent of their own written language, weren't there? That suggested a symbolic language of some kind. She wanted to get outside the library and call Byambaa to see if he had any ideas how information might have been stored and transmitted from that period to now. She hadn't had a chance to talk to him since the attack two nights ago. Just hearing his voice would help her feel better. Must be, what, five hours ahead?

Packing up her papers, Liz headed out of the listening library back into the main building, only to stop short, her pulse suddenly faster. A familiar figure stood in the corridor, speaking to someone behind him, turning, even as she entered. It took a moment to place him: Huang Li-wen, Professor Chan's visitor the night she'd been attacked. Liz hugged the papers to her chest, but Huang noticed her before she had a chance to retreat, and gave a slight bow, hands spread as if to show they were empty. "Ms. Kirschner. I should like to have a word with you, if you have a moment."

"Uh." She glanced around. Where was Grant? Did he know Huang was here? He had to—he was out in the reading room, and Detective Gonsalves was watching the entrance.

Huang kept smiling, his melodious voice soothing, his suit today a very subtle pinstripe of blue with hints of gold as he moved, gesturing toward a small study. "Here, you see? This lounge is not in use, and it has many windows. I assure you, you will be perfectly safe in my company."

She took a step forward, and another. What else was she supposed to do? Run? Hide in the listening library? Might as well at least hear what he had to say. Even if he was behind the attack on her, he wouldn't kill her in a library, would he?

Huang closed the door behind them and waited for her to take a seat before seating himself, with a little tug on his jacket so it wouldn't wrinkle. "Thank you for agreeing to see me."

"No problem."

He kept smiling, his eyes soft at the corners. "I was intrigued by what you said back in Professor Chan's office, about the music perhaps leading you to Genghis Khan's tomb. I believe that your idea has merit, and I would like to help you out."

Liz held back some inane reply and focused on him, the ring on his little finger, the perfect fit of his suit. "You mean, financially?"

"If I were a researcher, Ms. Kirschner, I would assist with the reading. Alas, I am not; I am a business man, and my ventures have been profitable lately. I have been seeking a worthwhile project in need of such assistance, and I would like it to be yours. Tell me, where are you staying?"

The name of the B & B was on the tip of her tongue, but she could almost feel the weight of Grant's gaze upon her. "I don't know. About the offer, I mean. I would have to talk with my associates."

"A policeman and a soldier. Unusual companions for an academic such as yourself." He set his fingertips together. "I am sure the policeman, at least, would be just as pleased to return to Boston, knowing you to be well provided for. Of course, the soldier may stay on, if you feel that his presence is an asset to your work. I expect that he may begin to lose interest if it remains in the academic sphere."

She found herself nodding at the truth of what he said, then asked, "How did you find me here?"

"I called at your apartment to make my offer, and your roommate expressed her envy of your European travel. She seems a most engaging young woman. A journey to Mongolia or even to China would have been expected, but this shows that you are a dedicated searcher, not merely chasing a legend." He gave a slight nod. "For a man like myself, overseas travel is an easy matter to arrange. I should be pleased to put my resources to use in your behalf."

And probably didn't require maxxing out anyone's credit cards to travel on such short notice. He offered her a researcher's dream—unlimited funds to bankroll a theoretical project with little practical application. "I'm sure that's true, but I still need to talk it over with them. What are you looking for in return?" A man like Huang would hardly put up his money without some expectation, and a co-authored paper probably wasn't what he had in mind.

Huang looked serious, and his voice took on a deeper resonance. "I should like to be the first to step inside." He leaned slightly forward. "I am in a position to purchase for myself almost any item or experience in the world. What you are seeking, this would be a singular experience indeed, one that no other person can claim. I realize that the privilege should belong to you, as the seeker, and, we may hope, the finder of the tomb. I would like you to sell that moment to me."

His words formed an image in her mind, a great stone entrance and herself at the door, about to step through into a place of wonders no one had seen for eight hundred years. She wasn't an archaeologist, certainly not some kind of tomb raider. Until that moment, until she heard the longing in his voice, Liz had not imagined actually being there, standing at the graveside of Genghis Khan himself. Her mouth went dry. "Is there a number where I can reach you?"

He slipped a gold case from an inside pocket and offered a creamy card imprinted with a phone number and nothing else. "I will be hoping to hear from you."

CHAPTER TWENTY-ONE

Grant dropped straight down, as if his knees buckled. The guy with the gun let off a round, very soft, very small. It might have taken out his partner if Grant hadn't still been holding the looter's arm, bringing him forward to slam into the shooter. Grant let go and pushed off from the building next to him, lunging to the outside, the pages still clutched in his hand. He ran hard across the green, toward the River Cam which wound through the town offering views to the punters. The river forced both foot and road traffic onto narrow stone bridges about as old as the rest of the place, meant to be easily defended, not easily passed. Hundreds of students strolled or biked around on the pathways, coming and going from the medieval buildings. Huge old trees shaded patches of the green and sheltered clusters of people enjoying the sunny day.

Did they want the papers, or did they want him? The gunman certainly had recognized him, by type, if not as an individual.

Grant dodged pedestrians, then swung about and ducked behind a huge rack of bicycles. Two men emerged around the corner he'd come from, breathless, glancing around, the shooter with his hand in his jacket, probably to conceal the gun. Sun glanced from the man's sunglasses, his square jaw hard. Grant pulled out his cell phone and jabbed it on. Purchased from an airport kiosk, it contained only a handful of numbers. He tapped the first one.

The men split up, heading opposite directions into the riverside park, the shooter making his way swiftly toward Grant's position.

"Detective Gonsalves," answered a gruff voice.

"Trouble," said Grant. "Two, one armed. I'm grabbing a bike. Get Liz to the safe zone."

"Copy that, Chief."

Grant took a couple of pictures as the shooter, scanning the crowds around him, worked closer. A bike near the end had no lock. Half-rising from his crouch, Grant slid back the bike, then climbed aboard, launching himself as someone shouted—the shooter, or the owner? He punched up the gearing and pedaled hard toward the road, zipping past startled students and dodging tourists. The river flowed alongside; to the other side, more buildings, and highways beyond. Grant chose the river, shooting across, his leg clipped by the mirror of one of the cars that cluttered the span, a colorful curse pursuing him into the wind. The shooter spotted him, tracking his progress, then lifting a hand to his ear. Phoning it in. How many of them were there really? On the other side, Grant swung down a side street parallel to the river, a narrow course of leaning Medieval buildings and dangling wooden signs.

"Here, you!" someone called as he passed, then a whistle blew. Bobbies. Excellent. Grant turned again, down a street lined with college gates on one side and churches on the other. He spun into one of the forecourts and jumped down from the bike, slotting it into a rack with a whisper of thanks to the owner. Ditch the glasses, pull the corduroy jacket and drop that in a rubbish bin as he eased into the tourist traffic. He had little from which to craft a new guise, but he straightened up, pulled out his phone and held it in front of him, walking slow as if filming everything he saw. He carried only a messenger bag with the requisite notebook that was his ticket into the Needham institute. Every so often, he switched the camera from the back of the phone to the front, selfie-style, and scanned the street behind him.

From a street vendor, he bought a King's College pullover and tugged that on, tucking his bag underneath in the front, giving himself a slight paunch. Satisfied, he ducked into a bookshop, browsing near the front for several long minutes. Then the shooter walked by, at the back of a group of Japanese tourists, with his hand cupped and aimed at the gate opposite in unison with several of his fellow travelers—but he didn't hold a camera. Grant stood too close to another shopper, a young woman, reading over her shoulder as if they were together. The book showed black and white photos of a man climbing all over the local architecture. Looked like fun.

The woman shopper shot him a glance, then a half-smile, as if she liked what she saw.

"Good book," he commented.

"Quite. American?"

"Canadian."

Her smile broadened. "On holiday or studying?"

"Yes." He flashed a smile of his own, and slipped out of the shop, trailing his pursuer in loose clusters of the crowd. The guy scanned methodically while nodding at whatever the guide was saying as she pointed first to a college, then to a church. Grant's ambiguous skin-tone, an asset while trying to blend in in a variety of Asian, South American and Middle Eastern venues, was a little more conspicuous here—not quite an American-style tan, and a shade or several darker than the average Brit. Much as he wanted to know who these guys were, his best course was to rendezvous with the others and study the pages these guys'd been trying to steal. He took a turn away from the river down an alley and almost walked into the guy who'd stolen the pages to begin with. The man, scanning the street, nearly glanced by him, then his nostrils flared and Grant knew he'd been recognized. He bolted, the thief's hand briefly connecting, then shaken off.

A few more turns took him out of the crowds. Which could have been a mistake. But it also brought him to the back of an aging church, gaps showing between Norman-era stones. Grant took hold and climbed up, swift and steady, his fingers finding purchase, his shoes edging the stones until he reached the roof and lay down along the lead sheathing, peering into the alley below. How long should he wait? Even as he wondered, bells across the city began to toll, and the alley he'd taken started to fill with orderly lines of parishioners. Grant lay his head on his hand. His stomach rumbled, but he couldn't eat paper. Damn. He slipped out the phone. Gooney would be worried by now.

"Gonsalves. Where are you?"

"Closer to God, but not as close as I could have been. Are you at the safe zone?"

"Yeah, we're safe, Chief. Not to worry."

Grant's eyes narrowed. "Not what I asked, Gooney. What's your location?"

"In the back of a Mercedes limo enjoying a nice Bordeaux, with some very pleasant company. Say hello, Liz."

Liz's voice came on the line. "Hi, Grant. Mr. Huang has an offer he'd like us to consider."

Huang's limousine. One of the handful of people who could have been behind shootings, mugging and murder. Perfect. "Sounds like you've already accepted."

"Hey, I'm watching out for her," Gooney protested. "Besides Huang's got the goods, no doubt. When can you get here?"

The bell in the church's little steeple rolled a note that Grant felt from his skull to his toes and he clamped the phone against his ear. "God only knows."

CHAPTER TWENTY-TWO

"I appreciate your hospitality, Ministers, but I find nothing else to say to you." The Mongolian spoke careful English, though Jin felt certain he understood Mandarin perfectly well—he simply refused to employ it. His gaze kept sliding back toward Jin, who had been introduced but said little so far. Wu shu taught him patience as well as speed, and now it was the former skill he employed.

Only four people occupied the elegant study, two Mongols, two Chinese, around a low table with a delicate lacquered surface that was the product of a hundred hours of painstaking labor. No mere chemical could achieve such a depth of luster. Time must be an ingredient in anything of beauty. Perhaps a people who never settled but merely flowed here and there at the whim of goats could not truly grasp the treasure of civilization. Each man had a porcelain cup of tea available, but none of them were drinking, the scent of green tea curling out into the room, filling the stony silence.

Deng, the Minister of the Interior, pressed his fingertips lightly together as he regarded their foreign guests. "The Russians are not in a position to be as supportive to your nation as they have been in the past, Mr. Khunbish. Until such a time as they are able to do so, you would serve your nation well to cultivate other friendships."

"It is our intent to be friendly with the People's Republic, but that does not extend to ceding our resources to you." The Mongol shifted in his seat, an antique piece with a beautifully polished rosewood back. Though Khunbish wore Western-style clothing, Jin thought he could still detect a whiff of horses about the man. "As your emperor once famously told the British before the Opium Wars, you have nothing that we want." Before this insult could sink in, the Mongol went on, "At least, not badly enough that we would sacrifice our sovereignty. You must understand that this is not merely land to us, but sacred—the birthplace of our people, and the burial ground of our ancestors. The spirits of this land watch over us. They guide us and defend us."

"Are they guiding you now? If so, then you follow them at your peril. The world has not stopped, and Mongolia is being rapidly left behind. To guard so vast a portion of your potential wealth because of these superstitions is short-sighted. The spirits may thank you, but your children most certainly will not."

Jin gave a slight bow of his head, drawing their attention. "Minister, please do not unduly insult our guests' beliefs. There is no profit to be won in that conversation. Perhaps we should rather draw their attention to our own history of stewardship." He gestured toward the scroll paintings that decorated the walls. "Here, you see an oil well developed before the Han dynasty united the Middle Kingdom." In the image, workers in wrapped clothing served a framework of bamboo and rope surrounded by natural stones and flowers. "They even siphoned the natural gas and used it to light their homes and forges, in perfect union with their place in this landscape. It was the scholar Shen Kua over one thousand years ago who first predicted the widespread use of such fuels.

"We have mines for cinnabar and silver in this nation that have been in careful and continuous use since before many nations were founded, and it is only considerate stewardship that makes this possible." He gestured to another image, this one of workmen leaning on shovels and framed by mountains.

"I wondered why a historian attended a meeting about mineral rights." Khunbish barely glanced at the image. "One billion homes and forges demand more than bamboo pipelines and simple shovels to keep them fed and warm. You wish to speak to me of history? My grandparents recall when our cashmere production rivalled that of any nation on earth—until the Chinese undercut our own processing facilities by offering higher prices than we could afford to pay. When our domestic processing industry failed, the Chinese buyers cut their prices, and my people had no choice but to continue to do business with yours. A generation of herdsmen now lives in poverty thanks to your stewardship." He dropped a sheaf of papers onto the table. "You make us a handsome offer, but it will show its ugly face sooner or later."

Back to goats again. The Minister of the Interior grew very still. Mongols had no sense of how to speak to prevent the loss of face, and now the Minister decided how to redress it.

Jin carefully gathered the papers, clearing the surface of the table, and held them out to the Mongol. "The discussion of history displeases you, Mr. Khunbish. Then let us consider how best to move into the future together. Please convey our regards to your Prime Minister along with our offer."

For a long moment, Khunbish stared back at him, then snatched the papers from his hand and gave a nod to his assistant. They rose together, and the ministers followed suit, offering brief bows as the Mongols departed.

"They are as uncouth as they have ever been," Deng growled. He pushed aside the tea pot and reached into his desk for something stronger. Tea splashed onto his desk with his irritation. "Why are you here, Minister? The President's message conveyed only that you would attend, but provided no explanation."

"So that they would recognize my face, my name, and my role as their ally." He plucked a brush from the canister where they provided a nice contrast with the modernity of monitors and tablets. With a few strokes, he transformed the spilled tea into a few characters.

Minister Deng followed his brush, then said, "Raven? I have heard only rumors."

"Have you noticed the origin of this character?" Jin covered part of the symbol he had drawn, then the other part. Like the lacquer on the table, the very language contained layers, built up over centuries.

"Mongol's coffin," Deng read. Their eyes met.

"Project Raven will give us leverage over the Mongols, exactly the sort of superstitious cultural connection they value so highly."

"Fortune smiled upon the President when you entered his service."

"And it will smile again, sooner than we thought. This negotiation has been only a single move in a lengthy game. With patience and forethought, Minister, the People's Republic is bound to emerge victorious." Jin took the cloth from the tea tray and wiped away the word. "Please convey my regards to the cabinet when next you meet."

"Perhaps on another occasion, I will have the honor of welcoming you to join us there."

Jin bowed to his senior. "The honor will be all mine."

CHAPTER TWENTY-THREE

Liz peered into the gloom of the old oak interior. The cheer of the raucous crowd created a palpable barrier, a thick miasma of sound she longed to escape. Huang and his driver, a man named Zhen, clearly felt just as ill-at-ease, and she wondered if that's why Casey had named this pub as their meeting place. To be ejected from the posh limo into this rough room full of townies and footballers gave Liz a shock. Travelling from her own university's archive to the well-lit and exquisitely organized Needham Institute maintained a comfortable bubble of academia. Now, with the tang of spilled ale and the curses that accompanied every pulse of the crowd, England became a foreign country indeed.

Huang, seated across from her, looked stiff, his polished smiles and easy deference set aside in favor of vigilance. The exuberant crowd included a number of people of Indian or Pakistani descent, but he and Zhen still stood out, and his vaguely British accent in these surroundings sounded contrived. The driver stationed himself at the end of the table, constantly searching the crowd.

"It's not so bad—wish they'd raise the ceiling a little, though," Gonsalves muttered as he lowered himself into the crooked booth beside her, pint in hand. "How the Hell did the chief even know about this place?"

"Google?" Liz suggested.

"What was the search term, 'brawler pub'? 'Where to look for a fight?'" Gonsalves chuckled and brought out an imaginary cell phone. "'Siri, what's the worst place in Cambridge to bring a girl?'"

"That would be the rugby field at half-term." Casey set down a tray of fish and chips, and tipped back the cap he'd pulled down over his eyes. "You might want to hire a new lookout," he said to Huang, indicating the driver.

Gonsalves shook his head. "He made you when you went up to order."

"When did you?"

Gonsalves merely grinned. "You're not the only one with skills. What would you do without charity shops?"

Crazy, how a guy like Casey could go from a military hero to a scholar to a footballer in a matter of seconds, just by changing his hat, and, more importantly, his attitude. It wasn't just costume changes, but as if the costumes were inside, ready to slide into place, a chameleon changing its skin. Grant Casey could be anyone. What did he look like when he was being himself? Liz wondered if he could even do that anymore.

Casey hitched over a chair and set his bag on the table, removing a few pages and sliding them over to Liz. "I saw a guy slice these from one of the books about the Mongol conquest."

Crowded text in an antique font marched across the page. Latin. "Have you read it?"

"I don't do dead languages."

"Yeah, it's a shame when a language up and dies on you. Any other kind of death, Casey's good with, but languages—"Gonsalves sighed deeply—"he just goes to pieces."

"When I'm going to pieces, Gooney, you'll know it."

"Ooh, can I watch?"

Liz tuned out their antipathy and studied the pages at hand.

Most of her Latin related to music, and it took a moment to dredge up her first years of basic study. Even then, she tracked the words with her finger and mumbled to herself, transferring the visual to the auditory memory.

Gonsalves took a long swallow of his drink. "How come Americans can't make cider worth drinking?"

"Or figure out how to fry a fish." Casey dug into his meal.

"It is a curious thing to agree upon," Huang observed, "given that the superiority of British cuisine is by no means commonly accepted." A small glass of whiskey sat on the table in front of him, ringed by his fingers, otherwise ignored. "You are not drinking?"

"I don't." Casey polished off the fish and doused the chips with vinegar.

"Interesting."

"Boring," said Gonsalves, draining his glass and standing up. "Anyone else need another round?"

Casey pulled a water bottle from his bag and took a long swallow as Gonsalves walked away. Liz frowned over the pages and shook her head. The Chinese built a mausoleum for the Khan in the Ordos region, a tomb widely considered to be a fraud, despite the thousands of Mongolians who flocked there to worship their spiritual ancestor. If this chronicler could be believed, the relics contained in that mausoleum might hold the key to the true burial. "Chinggis Khan died in 1227 outside Yinchuan, China, but this—" Casey tapped the back of her hand and she looked up. "What?"

He pointed toward Huang. "You're taking it for granted that he's part of the team. I'm not."

"How else are we going to—"

"We got this far." Casey cut her a glance, hard and dangerous.

Huang pushed aside the glass and leaned forward. "What sort of credentials would it take to convince you, Mr. Casey? I am prepared to bankroll the expedition."

"Because you want the thrill of finding the target. It's not about the money; this isn't a luxury cruise. We have to move fast and far, and be ready for enemy operators. They've already found us twice." He stared at Huang, whose face softened.

"And you expect that I might be one of them. This is, of course, why you are the man for the job. Myself, I lack the...killer instinct. I believe that you and I, in partnership, could achieve greatness."

"Casey doesn't have partners—he has enemies and minions." Gonsalves slid back into the booth. "You gotta chose which one you'll be, and heaven help you if you pick the wrong side."

"In your estimation, Detective, which is the wrong side?" Huang spread his hands. "You wish to be an entrepreneur, Mr. Casey, and I admire that. By what criteria will you select your clients, and why should I not be one of them?"

Casey set down his French fry with deliberate care, as if he were disarming himself. "Tell me what happened in Guangzhou."

Huang's fingers closed together. "I inherited a difficult situation of which I was not fully aware."

"What are you talking about?" Liz interjected.

"An entire city block collapsed during construction on a subway tunnel," Casey continued. "Mr. Huang owns the construction company. No charges, no reprimands. How much money changed hands to make your name disappear from the press?"

"I acted to save the company, and the several thousand workers who depend upon it. Building codes in China are not determined by engineers, as they are in America, but by donations." A hint of acid seeped through his tone, unexpected and painful. "One cannot anticipate that the inspectors in China have actually completed an inspection, or that the officials who approve a project have, in fact, examined the documents."

"It's not his fault if the building wasn't safe," Liz pointed out.

Huang gave a gracious nod. "In fact, one might imagine that the inspectors and the officials knew precisely what would happen and were merely disappointed that the collapse entailed no loss of life. The administrative fees they require are much higher in the event of human losses." He reached for his glass, fingers stroking down the sides, then drew his hand back. "I am from Hong Kong. A foreigner, so far as many Chinese are concerned. A tree full of ripe plums they are only too happy to pluck."

"So you want to stick it to the Chinese by discovering the tomb of the great conqueror?" Gonsalves laughed. "I like it. What about you, Chief?"

Casey studied Huang. "I say where we go, when we go, how we get there, what I need, and who goes along. Liz doesn't reveal everything she knows, nor do we. You get first entry into the presence of the khan of khans."

"Minion it is then." Huang put out his hand, and, after a moment, Casey shook it.

"Now he's got one of each." Gonsalves raised his glass. "I'll drink to that."

CHAPTER TWENTY-FOUR

Nick strode off the gangway, a Desert Storm camo backpack slung over one shoulder. Grant stepped up to meet him, but Nick's eyes latched onto Gooney. For a moment, the old Nick showed through, casting off the refined gentleman his head wound had made him in favor of the steely warrior. Disconcerting. After counting on Nick for back-up for years, apparently Grant had adjusted to his new persona, a fact he registered with some surprise. But then, when they woke up in the hospital, the new Nick felt more like an old friend coming back, emerging through the patina, like the discovery that all the Elgin Marbles used to be technicolor. Nick, as Grant had first known him, was rock-solid and lacking in color. Since the museum, Grant wondered if that persona had, in fact, been his true camouflage.

Now Nick stood, a statue, ignoring Grant's hand in favor of staring at Gooney. "What are you still doing here?"

"Taking a vacation, and it's good to see you, too." The detective deflated, looking away.

"He's a good shot—we might need him," Grant supplied. "Good detective, too."

"Gee, thanks."

"I'm the only shot you'll ever need, Chief." Nick clasped Grant's hand at last, then leaned back toward the gate. "Hurry it up, D. A.!"

She emerged, weighed down by a backpack and a laptop case, her curls held back with a band of cloth, eyes bright. "Chief. You got the intel I sent on Huang? Good. I didn't get to tell you about the cell, Liz's cell, I mean." One of the bags swung forward, and she hitched it back, but Grant lifted it off her shoulder and added it to his own.

"What about her cell?"

"The app you asked me to activate? It already had been. I lost track of that after the incursion. Won't happen again." She dodged his glance. They'd been out of ops for too long. The team was getting rusty—aside from Nick, who could still break down a rifle in seconds, even on a hotel roof-top. Getting soft, like the shooter said in Cambridge, his gun barrel pressed to Grant's neck, his voice a breath in Grant's ear. Grant slid that memory aside like so many others and focused on what D. A. had told him.

So the locator app on Liz's phone was active already. Huang. Grant had wondered how the guy found them—assuming he hadn't been the one who burned the archive and stole the recordings. For someone who had access to that intel, the move to Cambridge would be logical. No matter, they'd be one step ahead now: they had the pages, and the enemy didn't.

"What's the call, Chief?"

"Liz and Huang are meeting the flight from Ulan Baatar, then we all head to Beijing. We have a private club room for the layover, so we can talk logistics."

"Beijing? Still not Mongolia?" D. A. took two steps for each of Nick's, or so it seemed.

"We'll hop a local flight to the Inner Mongolian Autonomous Region. A Chinese euphemism for an occupied territory." They came into another hallway, and found Liz and Huang standing by another gate. An airplane taxied in, marked with the stylized horse logo of Mongolian Airlines.

Nick wrinkled his nose. "We're going to have to ride, aren't we? Maybe not today, not tomorrow, but some time on this adventure, there will be horses."

"The Arabs have a saying. There's no air so sweet as that which blows between a horse's ears," Grant said, for a moment almost feeling that wind on his face, riding for miles.

"Cool. Now say it in Arabic."

"Not on your life." Security guards patrolled the Frankfurt airport in pairs, geared up in Kevlar vests, toting guns, and topped with cheerful white caps, like some sort of wardrobe throwback to Popeye the Sailorman. Grant could only imagine the excitement a sudden burst of Arabic would have on the locals in an area far removed from any Arabian flights.

Gooney said, "What, you don't think you could take 'em?"

Grant watched a pair of the armed men stroll by. He envisioned every move: hooking the first guy's knee. He goes down. A hand to either side of the man's head. Pop his neck. Take his gun, one shot through the other man's chin. "Wouldn't be a fair fight. They'd be too concerned about civilian casualties."

"And you wouldn't be?" said Liz, not taking her eyes from the gate.

For a moment, he pictured himself through her eyes. The first night they met, he killed a man. The next day, he talked a sniper down from a rooftop. It wasn't a bad rep to have, but every once in a while, he wanted a woman to look at him without that flicker of fear. "I've already got the initiative. I'm not armed, so, for a minute, they're less worried about me than about their own potential for damage. By the time they decide how to react, it's over. No collateral damage. The civilians don't even notice until it's over. As long as I make the first move, I control the game."

"But you didn't this time, did you?" Gooney said, softly. "They came after Liz, went for the archive, hit the Institute. Not saying you didn't recover well, but still."

"Seriously, Gooney, if you're along with the team, you gotta suck it up and be a team player." D. A. tossed her curls.

"It's fine, D. A. He's like my conscience," Grant said. "Only if I wanted to, I could kick him across the aisle."

"Hope you're wearing steel-toed boots, Chief." Nick thumbed his water-bottle open and closed, open and closed. "So what does this Mongolian singing expert look like? Will you know him when you see him?"

"Oh, I'll know," said Liz, her eyes fixed and eager, her body straining forward, until a stocky young Mongolian man in a vivid blue jacket emerged from the gate, glancing around. His eyes locked to hers and they came together in an embrace, their lips finding each other's.

Gooney burst into laughter, while Nick averted his gaze. "Yep, I guess so."

Grant found Huang watching him. "An interesting twist."

Yeah, interesting. The glow in her face, the anticipation in her form, like a horse waiting for a race, or a soldier waiting for the go-sign.

The embrace broke apart, Liz smiling to herself, ducking her head, acknowledging the truth she hadn't revealed until then, her hand still clasped in her boyfriend's.

"In the future, Ms. Kirschner, I'd appreciate full disclosure on your end." Grant forced his shoulders to relax, his hands to take an easy posture.

"Grant Casey? I owe you her life, which I treasure more than anything." The boyfriend put out his hand, calloused and unscholarly.

Grant accepted that firm grasp, modulating his own pressure in response. "And you are?"

"Byambaa Torje. Torje is my father's name. Byambaa is fine." The man grinned, a wide smile in his dark face. Unexpectedly deep voice.

Women liked that. More so than a man who could drop an

assailant between one heartbeat and the next. "Welcome aboard." Grant turned and flicked a gesture to Huang to lead on. "We've got a tomb to find."

CHAPTER TWENTY-FIVE

Jin sat in the Landrover watching his men wrestle with a boulder, a thick finger of stone with carved images on one side. They shouted at each other, pointing, directing, grabbing the stone again when it looked unstable. What would Jin's professors say if they could see him now? Would they imagine he had turned aside from the entire history of China, or that he had embraced its new pathway, using his knowledge of the past to guide their nation into the future?

A small military jeep drove into view, followed by a swirl of dust that eddied out into the dry landscape of soft hills and dull grass. The jeep pulled up alongside and stopped, but it took a long moment for anyone to emerge from the vehicle. The dust died back to earth, then the door opened and Yang stepped out, offering a bow, a thick folder in his hands. "This arrived at the hotel shortly after I did."

One of the workmen let out a howl as the stone bashed his foot and Jin frowned. They hadn't much time. This ancient stone was critical, and his hirelings seemed incapable of wrangling it. "Tell me about England."

"Our scholar had the book you requested, and removed the

pages." He described the chase, and how they had been shaken off in the alleys of Cambridge, concluding, "The American soldier is very capable."

"More so than yourself?"

Yang aimed his shades in Jin's direction. "If you care to hire him, you may wish to look this over first." He held out the folder.

Jin glanced at the dossier from the Department of Information Services, covered with seals and labels warning him about the severe consequences for the misuse of what it contained. All the accessible military records of one Casey, Grant, and a few of his associates. The information took up only a few pages, adding up to a very ordinary career in the army. Yet if Yang could be believed, Casey was anything but ordinary. "Is this all?"

Yang made no reply, swiveling his head toward the struggling workmen.

Jin read through the pages more carefully, looking for any insight, combing the words as he might sift through a pile of rubble in search of a shard of pottery or a bit of bone. Stationed in Afghanistan, Saudi Arabia, a short stint in Germany. Distinguished marksman. Medical discharge for injuries sustained in unspecified action at Mazar i-Sharif. Maps flashed through Jin's memory, maps of today, maps of history, the two overlaid, and the name coming back to him from much more recently. Mazar i-Sharif, Afghanistan, near the western border of Genghis Khan's conquests. He closed the folder. "Casey cannot be allowed to reach the tomb, under any circumstances. Do you understand?"

With a nod, Yang climbed back into his jeep, which roared to a start, popped into reverse, then swung about, heading for Hohhot.

Even granted that it would take a few days for the Americans to understand the pages they had taken, and to add this to the clues they already possessed, Jin's plan ran short on time. For a moment, he wondered if he should have allowed the Americans to get even as far as they had. The entire Raven project could well become a disaster, irrecoverable, but to rescind the decision now would require remediation, an effort just as likely to draw attention as to deflect it. Nevertheless, he must be more vigilant. And move faster. The loss of Casey might cause sufficient delay, or even derail the American effort completely with no other action required. But Jin would not take that risk.

"Minister!" called a voice, edged with fear.

He pushed the folder into his attaché case and turned to the workmen, just as they lost control of their ropes. The huge stone toppled onto the foreman with a crunch of flesh and bone. One of his hands remained visible, shuddering, then still, the fingers curled like a dead spider, blood seeping into the loess soil.

The other four men backed off in a rush, heads bowed, swinging worriedly from side to side—from their dead leader to their living overlord.

Jin eyed the corpse. That was unexpected, but perhaps not disadvantageous. Little created an air of foreboding like the finding of unexpected corpses. One of the men began to speak, but Jin waved him off, removing a sealed packet of bills and holding it out. "This is adequate. Please see that his share is given to his family."

"Yes, Minister, of course." The speaker edged forward and snatched the money, then scurried back to the others. Like a pack of feral dogs they scampered to their truck, taking the money and tools with them. Before the vehicle left earshot, they would have divided the foreman's share among them, the shuffling of the bills releasing the sarin they had been steeped in. Each worker would thus receive a twenty-five percent larger dosage, causing the poison to take effect faster. They would end either in a flaming wreck as the driver succumbed, or perhaps in a mysterious death miles away, their bodies wracked with their dying miseries.

The ancient Shang and Tang dynasties originated the use of Gu, a technique of concentrating the potency of venom by trapping several venomous creatures together in a jar until they had killed each other, then milking the venom from the survivor. This fearsome poison carried not only venom to slay, but also the sorcerous weight of its violent creation. Four men dead in a truck, carrying shovels like the tomb-raiders they had been. Omen and warning to the superstitious people of the region. He anticipated a reduction in archaeological looting in the coming months.

The last drone of the truck's engine faded into the distance, and Jin was alone with the reindeer stone and the corpse. Silent witnesses. His favorite kind.

CHAPTER TWENTY-SIX

As she finished off her schnitzel, Liz enjoyed the irony of eating German food with a party that included American servicemen, a Hong Kong billionaire, and a Mongolian singer. D. A. and Nick carried the burden of conversation while Casey ate as if it might be his last meal and Gonsalves savored every morsel, washing them down with German beer and smacking his lips in pleasure. Byambaa did his best to answer every question from how was the flight, to when he started singing. The timbre of his voice still stirred her deep down, resonating through her bones and vibrating through her flesh.

"Wait a minute, you were eight years old before you ever saw a car?" D. A. leaned forward. "Seriously? That's insane."

Byambaa shrugged. "Not if you live in a ger in the wilderness and you move every few months. About half of Mongolians live in the city now, but even there, the suburbs are all gers."

"A grrr?" she echoed helplessly.

"Ger. Round white tent made of felt." His hands sketched it out in the air.

"Oh—a yurt."

Byambaa's round face stilled. "No. A ger. 'Yurt' is a Turkish word. Completely different."

"Are you going to sing for us?" Nick asked. "Your lady played some of that Khoomei. I've never heard anything like it."

He glanced at the others. Huang dabbed his lips with his napkin and leaned back with a smile, ready to listen. Casey said, "That is what you're here for." His expressions and gestures hadn't changed, but Liz detected the slightest growl to his voice since they had left the airport.

"This is the first song from the tomb cycle." Byambaa pushed back from the table, giving himself space, and took a deep breath, swelling his chest, letting his eyes unfocus as if he could see back in time. He began with a word that soared into a high, buzzing sound like dragonflies, the syllables articulated between long, low tones, his mouth shaping the sounds into a rhythm beyond Western understanding. At times, his throat produced the low and high tones simultaneously, buzzing, droning, merging again and coming back to melody before he finally allowed them to blend into a sustained ululation at the end of the song. Through it all, D. A. winced, though she tried to shake the expression several times. Nick's head nodded slightly as he listened while Huang maintained an air of polite interest. Casey sat with head bowed, cocked to one side, listening intently, and Liz wondered what he heard. When Byambaa finished, the others clapped with varying levels of enthusiasm, D. A. glancing at Liz as if to ask what she got out of that.

"The song says there is a watering hole, a place where the birds sing and insects buzz—"

"I heard that!" Nick declared, rapping the table. "The birds and the insects, yes." Then he laughed self-consciously and waved Byambaa on.

"It is a place of good spirits, of life in the mountains, where horses can rest and put off their burden. Death is the burden."

"A stopping place while carrying the khan's body," said Liz.

"So that's one of the places we'll be looking for." D. A. pulled a tablet and a portable keyboard from her bag and propped it on the table, taking notes. "What else?"

Byambaa sang again, this time of wind that cut between ridges in a narrow place and called as if from the Eternal Blue Sky. D. A.'s fingers flew across the keyboard, and she murmured, "Sounds kinda creepy if you ask me."

"The Eternal Blue Sky is like heaven; it's the source of everything, and where everything returns. Chinggis believed he had the blessing of the sky to claim all the lands beneath it," Liz explained.

"The Mandate of Heaven." Casey lifted his head. "No wonder the Chinese were pissed—that's what they always claim to have. The excuse in China, if your dynasty fails or the emperor gets dethroned is you've lost the Mandate of Heaven."

"When Chinggis and his heirs came along, they lost the mandate —big time." Byambaa grinned. "One of the other songs is about a forest. The Oigurat tribe were to plant trees at the gravesite and tend them faithfully."

Another song described a deer, and another imitated the howl of wolves circling their den. When Byambaa had performed all the songs Liz had discovered, Huang asked, "Where do we begin, then? To what does this map correspond?"

"Well, that's where the chronicles come in." Liz spread the torn pages on the table in front of her, along with her own notes, her memory of Latin supplemented by D. A.'s computer expertise. "We know that Chinggis died outside of a town called Yinchuan, and was transported from there by a team of horses and soldiers, probably his personal body guard. They wore silver belts to denote their status—Marco Polo is said to have received a belt like that from Kublai Khan years later." She shuffled through the pages. "The key is this one, it's an account by a Franciscan who was sent on an embassy to the court of the Khan. Chinggis was already dead a few months by the time the monk arrived in Mongolia, and the khan's heir, Ogodei, came down to meet the funeral cortege. Father Bartolomeo was not allowed to follow it. They had already departed Badu, under Ogodei's direction, but it was only three days before Ogodei returned, and it was then Bartolomeo started to hear the rumors that everyone who rode with the khan's heir had been killed. So only Ogodei himself knew where he had buried his father. He must have ordered the tomb constructed before he got there, and just rode the last few miles."

"So the tomb lies within a day and a half of Badu, more or less—it would've taken them longer on the way out than it did for Ogodei to get back and meet with the monk," Casey observed.

"The name 'Badu' is associated with a town a few hundred kilometers north of Yinchuan."

Byambaa spread out a map thick with Mongolian and Chinese characters, with a bit of Cyrillic thrown in for the Russian speakers, and they bent over it together, but it was D. A., after tapping on her keyboard a little longer, who reached in a freckled arm and poked a spot just south of the border of Mongolia.

Byambaa made a face and shook his head. "In China. Generations of Mongols will hate that."

"They'll be glad it's found at last though, right?" D. A. asked.

He tipped one hand, then the other. "He is almost a god to us. The place where he was born is holy—many people believe he is buried there as well, and nobody is allowed to hunt or to build in that place. My people...they are content with the land, to know the land contains the spirits. This is a reason mining is so controversial in some aimags. They don't even like it when paleontologists come and sometimes won't say where dinosaur bones are found. To find this tomb, it would be one part celebration, and one part..." His hands moved, searching the right word.

"Desecration," Casey supplied softly, and the Mongolian nodded. "Should we stop searching? Call the whole thing off?"

"Not if the Chinese have our great ancestor in their soil." Byambaa's dark eyes flared, gleaming. "They have not forgiven his conquest, and his son's claiming their imperial crown. If they find his tomb first, they will destroy it or conceal it so that it may never be found. At least if we find it, even if it is on Chinese ground, they will bargain with us and my people can be restored their god."

"To the God of conquest, our patron spirit, Genghis Khan!" Gonsalves raised his glass and roared his approval.

CHAPTER TWENTY-SEVEN

Huang's driver, Zhen, entered the dining room after a soft knock and offered a handful of key cards. "If you are through, sir, the staff wish to clean," he murmured.

"I believe so," Huang answered. "Take a room," he told the others. "In the morning, my private jet can transport us to our next destination."

"Private Jet?" Gooney echoed. "I'm liking this trip."

"Sounds conspicuous," Grant said.

"Not at all." Huang's ready smile had ceased to have any impact. "It is how I am expected to travel, and it comes without some of the restrictions of commercial flights. Some of the equipment you requested is more easily obtained outside of China. I have let my office know that I am bringing some potential investors to view one of our production facilities."

"Gotta be faster, too, Chief."

"Will I have to take off my leg for security?" Nick wanted to know.

Grant sighed, sliding a key card from Zhen's grip. "Let's do it. 0700 for breakfast, then we've got places to go."

Liz took a key card and flicked a gaze at Byambaa. Did he turn a slightly redder shade? Grant still stung about the fact that she hadn't told them about her boyfriend. At least, that's what he told himself he was stinging over. D. A. and Nick were already talking about how to access satellite imagery for the area in question while Gooney expressed sloppy enthusiasm for everything Huang had already done for the team. Casey slipped out the door into the main dining room where the tang of sauerkraut and the live Tyrolean band roused a hundred happy tourists. A few were even gamely trying to polka under the direction of a woman in a colorful folk costume. Beyond this the lobby opened in a sweep of dark wood and tasteful paintings of hunting scenes: a Disneyland of German culture. A few clusters of people stood by the door, just arrived or waiting for rides to someplace else. Six staff at the counters, assisting a dozen or so guests. A pair of children slumped by a heap of luggage, watching Grant go by with the dull gaze of jetlag. He gave a slight wave, and the boy waved back half-heartedly. Dark nooks at the edge of the lobby sheltered velvet wing-chairs and heavy wooden tables. From one of the nooks blue light rimmed another door and dance music throbbed against the glass door. Something for everyone. Next time, Grant would choose the accommodations. Huang would go along—and Gooney would protest. That thought amused him.

A mirror alongside the door to the club gave a narrow view of the lobby, the tourists moving back and forth, a woman rising from one of those deep armchairs, cell phone in hand, her face lit pale blue as well. Chinese, with a long sweep of black hair, narrow hips and shoulders, arms long with lean muscle. Several of the tourist groups in the restaurant and lobby were Asian, and a number of different languages drifted through the air. Grant paused a beat, then headed into the club, letting the flashing lights and pulsing American rock music swallow him. Tables outlined the dance floor, half-occupied, with a bar to the left, and an elevated viewing area containing more tables on the right, a door to the street at the far end. That door let in a breath of night air as a pair of women entered, already giggling and clinging to each other. Grant swung right, choosing a table behind a group of Americans who shouted conversation and tapped their phones, leaning together first in this combination, then that as they clicked photos.

It took a few minutes before she entered, strolling into the dim light, sliding back her hair with one hand. Long-legged, carrying a handbag of red leather. She glanced around, getting the lay of the land, not scanning—at least, not obviously—and headed for the bar. Mirrors behind the bar, cluttered with bottles of liquor, but not so many that the reflections couldn't be seen.

Grant waited for the next song to start, then, in the flow of dancers on and off the floor, he moved through the crowd toward her side, putting on his best American gigolo as he walked. He slid up beside her, inserting himself past the elbow of the man leaning nearby. "Haven't I see you somewhere before?"

She giggled, hiding her mouth with her hand as she glanced back toward him, coy, her eyes giving the slightest flick. "To Americans, all Chinese look alike." She gave a provocative half-turn that displayed her figure without quite inviting him closer.

"Not to me. What brings you to Frankfurt?"

"I was studying abroad. Now I am going home, but I have not been to Germany before. It looked like fun." She lifted her face toward him, letting her hair drape down.

"You want to dance?"

That brought up her sharp eyebrows, carefully defined. "You think?"

"Why else did you come in?" He slid her a smile, then offered his hand. After a beat, she accepted, pushing her handbag strap up to her shoulder where the little bag dangled against her back. He led her out onto the floor, among the couples and groups already in motion. The song twined around them, just slow enough to encourage the dancers to draw together. Grant slid his other hand around her waist, close, but not intimate. She moved gracefully, turning with him, easily finding the rhythm, but her face remained still, as if something else entirely moved behind her eyes. How long had it been since he had danced? Fifteen, maybe twenty years? Not quite, but close, and back then it had been Western swing. She felt warm beneath his palm, her hand strong in his, the muscles of her arms well-defined, displayed by the sleeveless dress. Maybe she did tai chi, but Grant didn't think that was all.

After a chorus or two, she relaxed into his touch, letting her hips sway, her hair sweep across her back, a smile play over her lips. Grant smiled right back at her. When the song ended, he drew her tighter, then released her waist. "Let's get some air."

"Okay." She let her fingers tangle with his as he drew her outside into the street, the gleaming tower of the hotel at their backs and a mumbling rush of traffic before them. Other people moved from awning to window, some entering the club as they departed, or going to the other clubs and restaurants.

"Which way?"

She looked around, and chose right. He let her lead, letting their arms draw out between them, then in the dark place between businesses, he tugged her arm, swung her wide, just as if they were on the dance floor. With a sharp flick, he reeled her in, until her purse hitched loose and fell around his wrist and she was wrapped against his chest, between him and the wall. Grant spoke into her ear. "Were you studying in Boston, by any chance?"

"What are you doing? Let me go." She struggled and twisted, pushing at him with her other hand as she tried to reclaim her purse. Her hair tumbled wild around her shoulders, then over her face.

His arm hairs tingled. She popped the clasp, then he caught her wrist, squeezing until she gasped. She brought up her knee toward his crotch, but he was ready for that one, using her instability to drop her sideways as he swept her leg higher. She hit the ground hard and cried out. The scene, to anyone else, must look like a mugging: tall, strong man looming over this poor, frightened woman. The syringe she'd been groping for lay on the sidewalk between them.

"Honey, are you okay?" Grant asked loudly, turning aside the curious glances of a few passers-by. Then he leaned down, scooping up the syringe—helping her up with her arm twisted at her back, her shield of hair now shielding his action as well. Grant led her in an iron grip toward the doorway of a shuttered souvenir shop, backed her into the darkness so only the gleam of her eyes caught the light. "What's in this?"

"Insulin. I'm diabetic."

He laughed. "You're quick, I'll give you that." He brought the syringe up to her throat, their bodies pressed together, barely room to breathe. Her throat fluttered against the needle. "What is it?"

"Don't!" she said.

Grant drew the needle gently across her skin and she swallowed.

"Digitalis."

"Thanks, but I'm a little young for a heart attack. Who do you work for?"

She stared at him, her lips pressed together.

Grant slid the needle into her vein and she froze, her body rigid against him, but he didn't press down on the plunger. "Who do you work for? Do you even know?"

No answer. He steadied the needle, watching the pulse leap at her throat. Pity. For a moment, he'd really been enjoying the dance.

Grant tapped the barrel of the syringe with his finger and she flinched, tears glazing her eyes, then he plucked it free, squeezing most of the contents against the wall behind her and displaying the near-empty vessel. "I tried to give you just enough to make you real uncomfortable, but it's hard to estimate the dosage. I suggest you get to the hospital."

He stepped back, releasing her and she clamped a hand to the spot of blood at her neck. She reached for her purse, but he tucked it under his arm, backing away, shaking his head. "Get out of here before I change my mind."

Where was she supposed to go? Was it, in fact, any mercy to release a failed assassin? She ducked her head, her hair sweeping forward, as she hurried into the darkness. Grant discarded the needle in a nearby wastebasket, and was already disabling the location settings in her phone as he re-entered the hotel. They'd already known where the team was staying, the only question was how many operatives they'd sent. Grant braced for the disappointment of the team when he roused them from their comfortable rooms to get out of here. He pictured the mutual adoration of Liz and Byambaa and decided to leave their room for last, hoping the thrill of reunion would be wearing off by then. Better yet, send D. A. Assassins, he could face; adoration was something else entirely.

CHAPTER TWENTY-EIGHT

Captain Guo Peizhi of the People's Liberation Army kept his shoulders square and his gaze rigid despite the dozen or more Party members who moved around him like a garden in a breeze. His eyes tracked Jin's progress across the room, but Jin pretended he was unaware of the other man's regard. Guo was a snake. He imagined himself swift and frightening, but would have little defense against the eagle. Or the raven.

"Ah, Captain." Jin bowed slightly, gracefully, but only to the point of politeness and not deference. "I should not be surprised to find you here."

"The Central Committee understands the value of a strong and agile military. Not all branches of government have made their worth equally clear."

Jin maintained his polite expression. "The Central Committee also understands the value of patience." He gestured toward the inlaid floor where they stood, with the pattern of characters and images devoted to the idea of longevity.

"Do you imagine me guilty of impatience? I am not the one who filed repeatedly for a second child. You must have been thrilled when the restrictions were lifted. I am pleased if mildly surprised to find that the salary of a professor of archaeology can extend to pay for the schooling for two children."

Jin's fingers tightened on his glass of plum wine. A quick retort filled the back of his throat, but he swallowed it down, taking a breath to steady his pulse. Guo must have serpents of his own in the Family Planning Commission if he were aware of Jin's applications, still trying to make up to his wife for the poverty and heartbreak of twenty years ago. No one would have kept a child under those circumstances. Certainly not a girl. "I believe that my current projects will strongly contribute to the future of the People's Republic. Apparently, the Council shares this belief."

"And you wish to make an additional contribution to that future in the form of another child. Very noble of you. In the days of the empire, it need not even be with the same wife. Does your interest in history extend so far, Minister?" Guo took a sip from his crystal snifter, then raised it in salute as another man approached.

"Ah, Captain Guo. And you have met Minister Jin. Excellent." Tian Pengwen, Councilor of Public Security beamed, his round face lit like a paper lantern at festival. Like a jack-o-lantern, Jin's wife would have said. Jin bowed briefly, the surface of his glass shivering with the tension. "Have you visited the garden? It is quite stunning at this time of year." Tian swept ahead of them, Guo and Jin falling in behind him. It was not a pleasure-chat, not merely a random encounter at a Party function.

A series of terraces led down into the garden where hanging lanterns marked the graceful pathways and decorated tea houses and pavilions among the drooping willows and shimmering water ways. Green and fertile, the garden contrasted sharply with the deserts and dry valleys where he had lately been spending too much of his time. Chunhua loved places like this and imagined they would one day own such an estate, their children, then their grand-children scampering down the pathways and startling the fish. Raven would make it all possible. Secure in this knowledge, Jin walked straighter, not allowing Guo's military bearing to put his own demeanor to shame. Tian brought them to a three-sided square tea room looking out on a planting of pine trees meant to conjure the western mountains.

Tian lit a cigar and took a few puffs to get it started, then blew the smoke sidelong into the twilight garden and gestured toward his underlings with the glowing tip. "I am especially pleased the two of you are becoming acquainted, as you will be working more closely from this day forward. Jin, I am assigning Guo as your military attaché for the fruition of the Raven project."

Jin imagined sweeping forward into a lunge, sliding the cigar from Tian's fat fingers and twirling it to place the lit end into the Councilor's eye just as it flared open in surprise. Instead, he bowed more deeply. "To what do I owe such an honor, Councilor?"

"To your continuing record of failure."

Jin's throat went dry as that desert he had so recently abandoned. "Our informant's initial error has been corrected, and the project is proceeding well, given the variables."

"The variables. Is that the correct term? Two operatives have been lost, and the American eluded a second observer in Frankfurt. This does not look like success to me, nor to the other members of the Committee."

Two? His mind raced. One in Boston, due to the contact's over-eager beginning. A contact who was a good friend, but not highly trained in this work. Who was the other? Not Yang, who had been with him in the desert. Then why hadn't Yang reported to him—surely he should have heard before anyone else.

"You honor me with your trust, Councilor," said Guo. "From the start, those of us at the Central Military Commission who are aware of the project have maintained it required a strategist and not merely an archaeologist. This most recent failure reinforces our position." Guo brought out his own pack of cigarettes and slid one between his lips. "A woman is good for only one thing, Councilor. Espionage is not that thing."

A woman. Zhuwen—lost? Lost again, perhaps permanently. Jin's stomach clenched, but he forced himself to speak. "On the contrary, Captain, Councilor, this setback demonstrates that our adversary is more determined than the military intelligence would have us believe. I will be pleased to have the good captain supply better information on which we may take action. The American is no mere mercenary, nor are the team that he is assembling. Now that the Committee is convinced of the urgency of the project, perhaps we will be granted broader access to the information that you, no doubt, possess." He gave a nod to Guo who stretched his neck up as he blew out a puff of smoke. Arrogant to cover his ignorance. Guo might be keeping track of people in China, but of the American side, he knew nothing.

Tian's smile only broadened, if such were possible. "Then I will let the two of you negotiate a balance. As you say, the Central Committee is behind this project. If it fails, it will reflect badly on many of us, but the center of that reflection, Minister, will be yourself." To Guo, he said, "Our Minister Jin is not just an archaeologist, but the architect of the project, from the beginning. What was it, ten, twelve years ago that you conceived this notion and began to create it? Twelve, yes. In the same year you celebrated the arrival of your son. A most auspicious year for the family Jin. Let us hope that this year proves similarly auspicious... For you, and for your family."

Guo blew out another breath of smoke. "The two do seem to be linked, project Raven, and the Jin family. If the one should fail, the other may find itself faltering as well."

Tian nodded slowly, like a sage who has heard great wisdom, and must incorporate it into his thinking.

"I shall do all in my power to ensure the variables are accounted for, Councilor, and that Raven achieves its goals for China."

With another puff and blow, Tian said, "I shall be missed at the gathering. Good evening, gentlemen." He tipped his head to each of them in turn, then glided off through the garden back toward the manor.

The smoke of cigar and cigarette curled and eddied in his wake, stinging Jin's nostrils. Guo chuckled. "Well, it appears you are not quite the favorite you might have wished. Of course, I will be honored to add my considerable powers to yours to ensure success."

Or to enforce punishment for failure. Jin swept his foot forward, his hand turning in the air almost casually, the Captain's cigarette caught between his fingers as he drew back. "You pollute yourself, body and mind." He flicked the cigarette into a sand-filled urn as the Captain stiffened, his own hand still searching for what Jin had stolen. "Good evening, Captain." With a slight bow, Jin departed before Guo's expression could solidify from startlement to anger. He managed to speak confidently with several other Party members during the evening, and even to exchange a few pleasant remarks with the Family Planning Commissioner, who had rejected every one of the Jin family's petitions. Even laying eyes on the man brought Guo's threats to mind, and Jin excused himself from the gathering after an appropriate interval.

As his driver navigated the streets of Beijing toward the hutong, Jin snapped out his cell and got Yang on the line. "I am informed we have lost another operative."

"Minister. Zhuwen has not reported in. Her papers were found in a hotel trash can, but she herself was not seen leaving." A silence hung briefly on the line. "Her objective was not achieved. I will, of course, see to it personally."

Jin rang off and rode the rest of the way in silence, home to his small family.

Chunhua met him at the door, dismissing the servants, who bowed out of their presence. His wife wore a rippling gown of Western style but made of Chinese silk with a pattern of plum blossoms. Once the servants had discreetly vanished, she kissed him lightly, also in the Western style. At times her forwardness and expressiveness excited him, yet at other times, these same traits disturbed him as evidence of her foreign upbringing. Mingbao resembled his father in both looks and attitudes. Would another child favor its mother? If Jin lost Raven, lost his position—lost face in such a public way—would another child cripple them all? Worse yet, his family would suffer repercussions for his failure.

"A successful evening, for my brilliant husband?"

"An interesting one in any case," he answered. "But from your dress, I feel I have missed the true celebration."

Chunhua's smile and her eyes glowed, with none of the modesty of the true Chinese. "I have been to the doctor," she murmured, a hot breath against his cheek. "He says yes."

CHAPTER TWENTY-NINE

Liz and half the team stood on a concrete patio in front of a run-down hangar. Across a broad expanse of asphalt tufted with weeds, a sleek, small jet caught the first rays of sunlight while Grant, D. A., and the pilot examined the craft, looking for signs of tampering. Crystals of sleep still gummed up her eyes as Liz tried her best to wake up enough for the conversation that flowed around her. "You can hardly call her another phantom when we've seen her passport," Nick said.

"A US passport," Gonsalves muttered back, arms folded. "Everything D. A. comes up with says Susan Chin's just a student, just like her whole purse full of girly stuff would imply. Some girl comes on to him, and he takes it as a threat. Maybe the guy's got a problem with women."

"You're just pissed you had to bail from the big hotel to sleep in a hostel." Nick loomed over them.

A hostel where the men and women slept in separate dorms, leaving Liz rooming with D. A. And longing for Byambaa.

"He can't even produce the syringe he claims would've killed him.

I tell you, man, Casey is desperate for another op, another adventure. He wants the rush."

In a sharp pivot that made Liz jump back, Nick turned to face Gonsalves directly. "You do not accuse the chief of lying in my presence."

Gonsalves put up his hands, but he didn't back down. "Don't let your loyalty blind you."

"Why are you even here, thinking this way? Why would you pick yourself up from cozy old Boston and ship out if you don't believe in the mission?"

"Oh, I believe in the mission all right." He jabbed a thumb at Liz. "Something's going down, and this young lady don't know what she's got herself into. What I don't want is this Bone Guard crap to make whatever it is worse than it already was."

Nick's brow furrowed. "If you are just here to look after Liz, then I'd have to say you've been superseded now that Byambaa's here."

"The singing boyfriend is hardly likely to be much use if things get ugly."

"He's a three-time national archery champion," Liz put in.

"Archery? Like some Robin Hood shit?" Gonsalves mimed drawing a bow and letting an arrow fly.

"He's also a nationally ranked wrestler."

"In Mongolia." Gonsalves arched his eyebrows at her, and Nick looked amused.

"Mongolians take their sports very seriously," Liz told him. "People train all their lives in the three Manly Sports of horse-racing, wrestling and archery—although most of the races are ridden by children these days, four and five-year-olds."

"Thanks, Professor." Gonsalves flicked her a salute.

"Riding again," Nick groaned. "Never my strong suit—even when I had two legs." Then he cracked a grin. "Chief'd do pretty well at those games. Especially riding. He was recruited from the rodeo circuit: fancy shooting from horseback—could pick off a tin can with the gun behind his head and his horse at a canter."

Liz tried to imagine Grant Casey as a rodeo rider. "Did he wear sequins and fringe and all of that?"

Gonsalves let out a gale of laughter. "God, I'd love to see that."

Nick's eyes narrowed, but the smile didn't leave completely. He leaned down to Liz and whispered, "D. A. has pictures."

The double doors behind them swung open to admit Huang and Byambaa himself, who slipped his arm around Liz and drew her into his side. "We have secured visas for everyone, under the names provided," Huang announced, returning their passports. "Although one does hope that they will not require close scrutiny."

"That must've cost—you still glad you bought in with us?" Gonsalves asked as he accepted his passport back.

"So long as future accommodations are more suitable than last night's, thus far I have no regrets."

"You probably will have, before this is over."

"Time to go." Nick pointed to where Grant stood by the aircraft, giving the all-clear.

On board, Liz snuggled against Byambaa's side and let herself sleep for most of the flight. She woke intermittently to watch rough mountains passing beneath the wing, then mile after mile of stony ground, the stones arranged into circles in many places where native herdsmen kept their flocks.

"It is hard to imagine how we will find the watering hole where horses find rest," Byambaa murmured, his voice a low rumble through his chest. "Everything may have changed too much in eight hundred years."

"Your people have ridden the steppes for more than two thousand. Even if the water hole has dried up, there must be some evidence of it."

"It would have been a landmark for miles in a wasteland like this. The khan wouldn't just leave it—he probably used it as a way-station on the Yam route, a place for his messengers to get food and fresh mounts between the front and the steppes of home."

"A building nearby, then—and a corral?" Grant asked, swiveling his chair around to face them. "There would be some remnant."

"Probably. Grain storage. There might be coins or paizi tablets allowing safe passage by the Khan and showing the authenticity of the messages."

"I didn't find anything like that in the official archaeological record—what I can find of it," D. A. offered.

"Inner Mongolia's not really a popular research destination," Liz pointed out.

"Byambaa raises a good point, though. Maybe we can find the station, like he says, but the other clues are a lot more ambiguous, right? How will we recognize a forest of family? Or know we're at the right den circled by wolves? And how about this one—"she pointed to the list on her screen—"running deer that run no more? What's that even supposed to mean?"

Byambaa shrugged. "Those are the only words. Deer, running, not running."

"When we get boots on the ground, we can start sorting out what we know, and what's available."

Liz tapped her fingers together. "The locals would know where to find a way-station, right? Even if it's a ruin, most of these people are still herders and farmers—they'll know the land."

"So we're looking for looters," said Grant.

"I didn't say that." She scowled at him, bristling on behalf of pastoralists everywhere.

He ticked off points on the fingers of one hand. "Locals. Who would be familiar with ancient locations, and know how to identify the time-period of Mongolian artifacts, but wouldn't have reported them to any official channels. Looters." He opened his palm as if letting something go. "Everybody makes a living somehow."

CHAPTER THIRTY

The plane approached an arid landing strip outside an accumulation of square buildings like the abandoned rubble of a quarry when the masons have finished a great project somewhere far away. Aerial antennas and solar panels sprouted from many rooftops, among a clutter of wires that drooped from leaning utility poles. The place reminded him so much of Afghanistan at first that Grant's skin went cold, his core muscles already tense for action. Peaked tile roofs came into focus and animal pens.

Huang leaned closer from his facing seat and Grant controlled the impulse to reach for a weapon. At the moment he was naked—unarmed save for his bare hands. That would change the moment they exited the aircraft.

"Our flight plan states we land at Hohhot, which is the city further east. Just a few minutes ago, we changed our itinerary and say we don't have enough fuel for the complete journey, so we will land here instead. Subterfuge, as you requested. If anyone has set up an ambush at Hohhot, we will disappoint them."

"Good work. Where is 'here?'" He indicated the uninspiring landscape.

"Baotou." Huang spread his hands, ring glinting. "Very near to the acclaimed Mausoleum of Genghis Khan."

"A fake," Gooney offered from his place across the aisle. He waved his guidebook. "There used to be these gers, a travelling memorial, but the Chinese destroyed that and brought the relics here. Except that those relics were destroyed during the cultural revolution and replaced with replicas. It's like something out of P. T. Barnum—thousands of Mongols travel there every year. No offense, Byambaa."

The Mongolian replied, "We are aware of the fraud, but it gives a connection to the great ancestor that many of my people prize more than the pride they lose when they bend to the Chinese—at least on this point. That travelling memorial, the Naimaan Tsagaan, were tended by an elite group called the Darkhad. Even today, the Chinese allow a few of them to watch over the fake."

"Why would your people put up with that? It's your heritage."

"And it has been under attack for eight hundred years, since the khanate itself. The Naimaan Tsagaan for a time were at a monastery, but this was destroyed by the Soviets. For the last century, we are tugged between China and Russia, like a bone fought over by dogs." Byambaa linked his hands, pulling first one way, then the other. "Russia gives us defense against the Chinese, and destroys our relics, then China gives us trade privilege to save us from Russian influence, and claims to have those same relics."

"Leaving you to appease both sides," Grant observed.

"Just so."

"Maybe we should visit the mausoleum," Liz suggested. "Some of the original relics might still be there, and if the replicas are at all accurate, they could give us some clues."

"We don't have time to play tourist."

"Hey, Chief, don't forget you got a team," Nick said. "I'm not much good for tracking looters—I don't even speak Mandarin, never mind Mongolian, but I can sure play tourist."

"Sure," said D. A. "We'll ask dumb questions and take lots of pictures. Lots of them. Then meet up with you guys at Yinchuan. But we might need somebody who knows what we're looking at." She shared a glance between Byambaa and Liz.

"Do you want to go see it?" Liz set her hand on Byambaa's, sliding her fingers into his palm.

Byambaa shook his head. "We are working to discover the truth. I have no need to give the Chinese any more faith or funding."

"Right."

Gooney sat across the aisle, knees wide, sprawled in the comfortable upholstery. "What's the plan for us then?"

"Huang is a collector. Let's go find him some artifacts."

A rough jeep ride through grasslands and low hills brought Grant's smaller team across the Yellow River into Yinchuan, a bustling city with towers of overly stylized Chinese pagodas standing alongside the minarets and onion domes of a huge mosque. "For the Arab-China trade expo!" Gooney shouted over the noise of the engine, another guidebook clutched in his hand. "Yinchuan is the capital of this tiny region called Ningxua, something like that. Supposed to be for the Muslim Hui people, but it's mostly Chinese anyway!"

Grant pointed at the guidebook. "How many of those things do you have?"

"D. A.'s normally on intel, but she's busy. Instead, you got me!"

At Gooney's side in the back seat, Byambaa studiously looked out the window, but Grant caught the twitch of his smile. At least Grant also had a solid go-bag stocked with a variety of survival tools, not to mention a new knife tucked in one boot and a couple of others hidden in his tactical clothes. For this assignment, the mercenary Indiana Jones look would serve. While Huang invited local dignitaries to his new suite at the finest tourist hotel, Gooney, Byambaa and Grant acted as his agents, combing the markets and back-alley shops for items that might please a wealthy collector. Chinese locals and workers crowded the stalls, calling out for their business, competing with a handful of ethnic Mongolians wearing their traditional Del robes, and a double handful of Muslim minority citizens wearing head scarves or skull caps. The trio worked their way through the throng, examining artifacts and interrogating their vendors without finding anything genuinely from the Yuan dynasty. Gooney's grumbling grew louder, Byambaa looked tired, and Grant began to think of other ways to find the watering hole they were looking for.

In a cramped shop carved out of an alley itself, they turned up a handful of Mongol arrow heads, while at an open stall, an ancient felt bag disgorged a few coins and a slim bar of bronze marked with strange symbols. Byambaa examined it intently. "Where did you find this?" he asked in Mongolian.

The woman behind the table, her mouth collapsing on ruined teeth, answered in muddy Mandarin, "Four hundred."

Byambaa asked again, carefully.

"Three eighty, final offer," she said, bargaining with herself. Desperate for money? Or just for business?

"Do you have more like this?" Grant asked in Mandarin.

"No more." She toyed with the ends of a dark band worn around her sleeve.

"Other artifacts of the Yuan dynasty?"

"These, these are good." She gestured toward a pair of porcelain vases, clearly much later than the Yuan empire declared by the heirs of Chinggis Khan.

Grant shook his head and indicated the pouch Byambaa was studying. "We pay for Yuan items. Things like this. They don't have to be pretty."

"No more things. No more Yuan." She spat the word, glaring at Byambaa. "You want that, I will give you a price."

Grant brought out a few bills from his front pocket. "I am sorry for your loss." He indicated the arm band.

Tears welled in her eyes. "Three hundred eighty."

"Funerals are expensive." He handed over the roll of bills and she snatched it from his hand.

"There can be no funeral. The Yuan killed him. No funeral without a crane or a bulldozer. Even his no-good friends don't come around, they took off, and took whatever they were digging for. They are afraid of his ghost. I cannot bury him, and I cannot leave where he will haunt me. This is all I have." She waved her hands over the table of statues, coins and other historical tidbits.

"I don't understand, Grandmother. China has been Chinese for hundreds of years. How did the Yuan kill him?"

"The reindeer fall on his head. He is crushed by the Yuan. Eight hundred years, they still won't leave us alone." She aimed another murderous glare at Byambaa, who bristled, without understanding her words. Grant lay a hand on his shoulder and said, "Grandmother. For your generosity, I can assist you to rent a jeep with a winch, or a bulldozer."

Her eyes flashed up toward his, then she clasped his hand and nodded. "You want to take everything Yuan? I have his maps, his notes—everything, if you have a crane."

"We should go soon, so you can lay his ghost to rest."

When he told Huang what he wanted, the billionaire merely nodded and got on the phone. Even then, it took hours to arrange the truck, the winch and the crew to operate it, not to mention obtaining a coffin, and paying extra for men willing to work with the dead.

CHAPTER THIRTY-ONE

The fake mausoleum rose above green plains of grass and well-tended rows of trees, a trio of vast round buildings, meant to imitate the felt gers of the Mongols, but topped by golden domes and spires. Liz tried to reconcile these garish pavilions with the spare solidity of Mongolian architecture.

Nick leaned on the window of their taxi. "All I'm saying, I want the Chinese to build my tomb. This is some spread."

"I'm holding out for a Taj Mahal," D. A. said.

"But then you've got to get married and have, what, twenty-two children? Yeah, that woman earned her rest."

The taxi turned between the long promenade and the broad steps of the white pavilions. Hundreds of tourists, many of them Mongolian, streamed up and down the stairs, posing for pictures with the golden domes, or with the verdant pathway behind them.

"That's a lot of steps." Nick slung a camera about his neck, and a backpack over his shoulders. "Come on, ladies, the Khan awaits." He offered an arm for each of them and they mounted the stairs.

At a kiosk, they bought an English-language guide to the site—a good thing, because most of the signs were in Chinese. On the broad marble plaza before the domes stood a tall gilded censor, smoking softly, with a pair of cushions nearby where visitors kao-towed toward the supposed burial place of the khan.

D. A. muttered, "Do we have to dip a finger in holy water?"

Liz shook her head. "For Mongolia, it would be vodka, and you flick it toward the Eternal Sky, and the fertile ground and the door of the family that hosts you."

A herd of small horses grazed among manicured hedges, flicking their tails while tourists stopped to photograph them. Nick raised his camera as well, perhaps to cover his grimace. "Is it okay that I'm happy about the jeeps? The less I have to ride, the better."

"Hey, you can't say that here! It's practically sacrilege." D. A. tugged his arm. "Let's get on with it."

The main hall housed an enormous white marble statue of the Khan himself, frowning down over his mustache, surrounded by murals of the Mongol expansion and maps showing their conquests, or rather, Liz was amused to note, their "punitive expeditions." The place was the Disneyland equivalent of a reliquary, complete with lots of Mongolian-style hats (no Mouse ears) and dolls dressed in colorful clothing. The wall murals fairly glowed with color, especially where they depicted bloody slaughter, but half the women in the images wore clothing a few hundred years out of date for the Khan, and Liz, despite her amusement, felt her heart sink. What could they find here of use to their quest? Corridors connected to the smaller pavilions, which contained brilliant yellow gers, decorated with blue offering scarves, and containing coffins said to hold the remains of the Khan, a few of his wives, two brothers, and a son. Nick dutifully snapped photos wherever he looked, especially when they exited to a life-sized panorama depicting the soldiers of the khan, bronze, mounted on proud bronze horses, drawing the portable ger on wheels that held the khan to his final resting place. Probably hundreds of miles from here. And the ger was made of concrete, not felt.

"Isn't there anything for real about this place?" Liz grumbled.

"Story goes," said D. A., folding back a page of the guidebook,

"That the khan intended to be carried back to his homeland for secret burial, but then a wheel broke on that crazy caravan, and that was it—they buried him here."

Liz glanced around. From this side, despite the gleaming golden false-gers, the place looked a bit shabby: the grass dried out, the trees more spindly. Then she spotted an oovo, a mound of heaped up stones with a tall staff thrust in at the top and piles of offerings—mostly blue scarves—decorating the sides and slope. "That's more like it." She led the way toward the oovo. A group of Mongolian tourists circled around it, paying their respects, and she stopped a little short to give them their space. "Mongolia is covered with monuments like this, marking high points where the spirits live."

A Mongolian in a bright blue del embellished with bits of brocade at collar and cuffs strolled past, keeping an eye on the tourists. His fancy, brand-new hat suggested he worked at the mausoleum—dressed up for the benefit of foreigners. Liz walked up. "Excuse me," she said in Mongolian. "You work here? Are there any true relics of the Khan?"

Taken aback by her approach, the man tipped his head, then gave it a little shake. "Please. You speak Mongolian? This is very uncommon." He spoke with an unfamiliar accent, but she could make out most of the words.

"I'm Elizabeth Kirschner, of Boston. My fiancé is Mongolian, of the Buryat tribe."

"The forest people? You should have looked for a husband from the valleys." He looked her over with an appraising stare, as if she were a horse, but apparently, he found her acceptable. "I am Nergui, of the Darkhad. The ancestral guardians of the Great Khan." He tapped his chest, then indicated the gaudy pavilion with a twitch of his chin. "It is a job. It means I send money home to my family. You asked to see the relics. Here, this way." He waved her along with him, Nick and D. A. Following to a small museum, dimly lit and nearly empty of visitors. Nick prowled among the cases, shooting photos of swords, spears, saddles, antique scroll paintings that showed the progress of the khan's funeral cortege, and the Naimaan Tsagaan monument, each of its component gers flying a banner, save one.

"Even these are mostly reproductions. The Chinese claim they have the Great Khan's bones, but—"he leaned close to her, whispering, "Nobody knows where the Great Khan truly rests."

Her heart quickened, and she leaned as well. "Not even your people?"

His nostrils flared, his voice echoing with pride. "Your forest boy likely has not even a drop of the blood of the khans. My people have honored the Great Khan for centuries, passing this honor from father and mother to children ever since his death."

"You hold the tradition, unbroken, from all that time?" Liz let her voice fill with admiration, her eyes with wonder. "Do you know stories, or songs, of the death of the khan?"

"Only stories that old men tell. They're not for foreigners." Nergui arched away from her, and his voice went flat. "Here, these are the true relics, and inside, the bodies of the wives, brothers, son. Enjoy your visit." He gave a short bow, and strode out the door, his del swaying over his pointed felt boots.

"I thought that guy was gonna take you home—what did you say to turn him off?" Nick inquired.

Deflated, Liz said, "I asked him about songs, and he got all huffy. His tribe might know something, but they won't tell outsiders."

"If we came back here, would he talk to Byambaa?"

She shook her head. "He has a low opinion of anyone from Byambaa's clan. I think it's a bust."

"In that case," said D. A., "We should get going. Unless you want a closer look at any of this stuff? We've got a bunch of pictures—and the chief has a solid lead in Yinchuan."

Liz and the others arrived shortly before dinner, a sumptuous affair in a local restaurant featuring barbecued ribs and great heaps of slithery noodles.

The next morning, they rode in a slow caravan of jeeps with the heavy equipment trailer, under the direction of the looter's widow, to a place miles from anything. There, in the scrubland of the rising mountains, with the soft grit of their arrival still swirling in the air, they found the corpse: a rotting hand and leg still protruding from beneath the boulder that had killed him. A boulder engraved with a trio of running deer that ran no more.

CHAPTER THIRTY-TWO

"That poor woman," Liz murmured, hugging herself. Byambaa tucked her closer to his chest.

"Real question is, what did he think he was gonna do with that rock?" Gonsalves asked. "You can't just sell that in the marketplace. Maybe he had a museum buyer or something?"

"Maybe the Chinese just don't want us to find the tomb. They would take away the markers," Byambaa said, his voice deep with ancient hurt and anger. He had told her about the widow's suspicion, acting as if he were the representative of the great Khan's army.

"Do you really think so?" she pushed away a bit to see his face, but made sure not to glance toward the cluster of vehicles where the whine of an over-taxed motor told her they had attached the cable to move the stone.

Grant, on the other hand, stood facing the scene, watching keenly. "During the Middle Ages, people in England made a hobby of going out after church to try to topple the standing stones and bury them as pagan artifacts. In Avebury, a guy got crushed by one of them." A flash of a smile. "Pagan vengeance." The motor stopped and a different hum began. Grant immediately stalked past, toward the other group. "Gooney, come on—need you to play Nick in Mandarin."

Liz watched them go, curious. Gonsalves crossed to the widow, who had started keening her grief now that the stone shifted aside. He started to talk with her in a low voice, turning her away from the ruin of her husband's corpse—while Grant made a quick search of the looter's pockets. Liz's stomach roiled and she spun away again, looking out across the plateau to where the mountains rose. People were dying. Grant was doing what he had to do to make sure she wasn't one of them. Maybe she should quit right now and let the Chinese bury the past, instead of burying the living.

"Eight hundred years, and they still look at us as the enemy." Byambaa, too, stared toward the mountains: North, toward Mongolia. "The people here used to be us, Mongolian, but when the Chinese claimed this land, they sent away the Mongolian men to work in the south, and sent Chinese men to tend the herds and work the mines. And tend the women." He shot her a look, his voice hard, the overtones she so admired vanishing into a flat fury. "So the next generation would be Chinese. We cannot let them claim the Khan."

She slid her hand into his, feeling the callouses of riding and archery. Behind them, engines started. The motor whined again, lowering the stone back into the dirt, but a little apart from where the body had been. The workmen loaded the coffin into the back of an antique pick-up truck, and the widow handed Grant a packet of papers, then bowed to him, and he returned the bow, just as low, just as long. "It's weird how he can just get along with people like that, but I saw him kill someone. It's like he's two different people."

"Two hundred people. Mr. Casey is a spy, or something like one."

Half of their caravan broke off and started driving back toward town, the widow accompanying the trucks, but the sound of their engines vanished as a helicopter swooped in from the direction of Yinchuan and hovered not far off in the desert. A ladder dropped and a curly-haired figure slid down the rails, hurrying toward Grant and

Gonsalves. Liz and Byambaa walked over. The corpse was gone, but a dark stain marked the pit where he had been.

"There's a big jeep overturned in an arroyo a few miles east, near a high mound," D. A. was saying, pointing in that direction. "Should we check it out?"

"Negative—I'll take one of the jeeps and investigate once you're off the ground. We need you in the air, looking for the next clues." Grant tipped his head toward Liz. "Which are—?"

"Well, we don't need to find the watering hole or the wolves' den—those were the first two, and the deer are the third, so that should narrow things down."

D. A. continued, "From the satellite imagery, we identified a few candidates for the combination of the waterfall, forest and canyon. It seems pretty clear the mountains are that way. As for 'the cliffs join me in singing,' we'll need our expert for that."

"Better take him along. Assuming Nick's driving, that leaves you one seat in the bird. Huang?"

"Or Liz."

Liz gazed longingly at the helicopter. Given the tooth-rattling ride they had to get this far, she didn't like the idea of spending a few more hours in the jeep, but she said, "Give it to Mr. Huang. He's doing so much for us."

"If you don't mind following on the ground with his driver. That also gives us a better cover story—just giving the zillionaire an aerial tour of the region."

"Guess I'm going with you then, Casey." Gonsalves sighed, pulled off his hat to swipe sweat from his brow, and slapped it back on.

"Let's see what our friend's bequest has to show us." Grant raised the papers, leading the way to the back of one of the jeeps where he spread out the contents of the bundle, and added a couple of smaller items. D. A. pounced on the cell phone, an old-fashioned flip model.

"It still works! Smells a bit funky, though." She squinted at the small screen scrolling through. "Most of the calls have been to and from the same number lately."

"Tracking enabled?"

"On a phone this old? Not without some hardware." She pressed a button and held the phone out to Grant who leaned in to listen, then shrugged and shook his head and she punched it off.

"A man said hello, then nothing. Definitely Mandarin, probably Beijing. My accent would've given me away."

D. A. popped open a laptop and started typing, glancing from the phone to the screen and back.

Gonsalves traced a line on a hand-drawn map. "This looks like the highway, Yinchuan is here, deer stone, here. Somebody gave him directions to get here." Setting that one aside, he said, "Someone also paid him for delivery of a thousand shovels."

"A thousand? That's a lot of digging." Grant sifted through the other papers, Byambaa and Liz leaning over them as well.

The papers comprised receipts and invoices, certificates of authenticity in several languages, partially filled out, printouts of photos showing various artifacts, including the woolen pouch and the paizi they had bought from the widow, then a bunch of landscape photos some of them showing overgrown ruins or collapsed structures. "It's like he was surveying the area, not just looking for something," Liz observed. "Some of these are probably locations where he was digging, but the rest are just canyons and riverbeds with no sign of occupation."

"Making a nature book for his retirement." Gonsalves scanned a few more receipts. "What I don't get, if this isn't legal, why did the wife just hand it over to you? Isn't she more afraid of the government than she would be of her old man's ghost?"

"Unless she thought he had the government's okay." D. A. held up the phone. "That number goes to an office in the Communist Party complex."

CHAPTER THIRTY-THREE

Armed with the looter's maps, the helicopter took off, Liz's jeep tracking its progress to investigate on the ground while Grant and Gooney took a detour to the wreck. Based on D. A.'s description and compass bearings, they sped across the dry plain, dodging the occasional stand of trees ringed by smart sheep and goats taking advantage of the little shade. In the distance, they spotted a pair of riders, mounted herdsmen, who disappeared back over their ridgeline. They hit a rut and bounced out again, Gooney slamming forward and cursing. "What the fuck, Casey, you trying to get me killed again?"

"It's what I do best, isn't that right?" Grant kept his eye on the route before them. Half the villages on the local map had no roads connecting them to the world. "Didn't do such a great job last time, though—you're still here."

"Yeah, no thanks to you."

"Look, just because you hate me doesn't mean we can't be friends." He slammed the jeep into a lower gear to take the next slope. Ahead of them rose the mound D. A. had mentioned, a towering beehive of dirt with ridges almost like the disintegrating steps of an ancient pyramid. The arroyo began here, a shallow depression that rose quickly on the side they were driving.

Up ahead, the rise showed a series of ruts that carved along the edge, then abruptly cut through. Grant pulled up alongside the grooved earth, staying low, and killed the engine. He checked the gun at his waistband, and smiled to himself as he caught Gooney doing the same thing. Couple of operators, like old times. Grant took point, walking in a crouch to keep his head below the ridgeline until he came up to a patch of brush a little shy of where the tracks cut over. A breeze chattered through the dry leaves, carrying the odor of old sickness, and Grant straightened, waving Gooney up as he looked over the edge into a ten-foot drop, a dry riverbed. The other side sloped gently up to a stand of spindly trees white as bone. In between, the jeep lay on its roof, half-crushed at the front where it struck first, and one of the passengers protruding from the doorless side. Another body lay a few paces away, drag marks showing in the dirt where he'd apparently crawled before dying. A couple of birds lay there with him, and one further on, dark feathers fluttering as if waving goodbye. Gooney started down the ridge at his end where the slope was less steep.

"Hold it! Gooney! The birds." Grant put up his hand, then pointed.

"What birds?" Gooney looked exasperated, his cop instinct sending him to the victims without thinking first.

"The dead ones. Unless they were smuggling vultures, those birds didn't die in the rollover."

Gooney stared and frowned. "Who poisons corpses?" The two of them squatted down, studying the scene below. "These guys had to be experts to drive around here. Unless they took off in the middle of the night without headlights, they didn't just run off the road. Likely, they were poisoned first, then lost control while they were in the throes," Gooney muttered. "You can see vomit on the windscreen." He turned and walked back, following the tracks for as far as they could be seen. "Here's more of it—somebody barfing out the door."

Grant walked slowly ahead, along the jeep's trajectory, studying the ground and the valley below. "Lucky the jeep didn't blow on impact. Check out those gas cans." The cans must have been empty, though, when they tumbled from the vehicle. Three plastic jugs lay on the ground with a variety of tools splayed in a course from the tumbled wreck.

"The perp was probably counting on an explosion. The way the land around here is, an incapacitated driver is a dead driver." Gooney leaned, squinting. "More looters, I'll bet. Picks, shovels, ropes in the trunk."

It looked as if the no-good friends of the woman's husband had come to a bad end of their own. Interesting. But the thing with the stone didn't look like murder. So the guys dropped the rock they were moving, killing one of their number, then took off before they could be caught with the evidence—only to be killed themselves. By whomever had hired them to do the job? Seemed likely. They were three days dead now, buzzing with flies. As long as Gooney didn't turn cannibal and snack on the poisoned flesh, there was no reason not to get a closer look. "I'm going down."

"Better you than me." Then Gooney sighed. "I'm the investigator, I'm coming, too."

They slithered down the sandy rim ahead of the overturned vehicle, then angled back toward it, still keeping a wide berth at first. That Afghanistan feeling crept over him, palms damp, senses preternaturally acute, scanning the ground for tripwires, pins, anything indicating an IED. As if they were likely to blow up a carful of looters in the middle of the Chinese plains. Aside from the vomit, the bodies looked pretty normal, the dry heat of the desert slowing decomposition. Gooney headed for the one guy who'd escaped the wreck while Grant moved toward the driver's side, keeping an eye out for any loose papers or items that might point to the perpetrators. The desert hummed with insect life, beyond the circling flies and the whisper of dry grasses. The soft sound of hoof beats rose in the distance as the herdsmen moved in search of better grazing. Then a puff of wind and the driver jerked in his seat. Grant was already in motion, ducking low, dodging, when the second shot slammed into the tire, another into the front end, then a searing streak of pain across his back.

"Shots fired! Gooney, get down!" The impact sent him sprawling, scrambling up and around the hood of the car, getting it between him and the shooter. But Gooney had nothing, he was out there with a corpse and a gun and nothing else. His own gun, a Norinco clone of a Sig Sauer 9mm, felt cold and solid in his hand. He pressed his stinging back against the jeep. The brush on the ridge above shivered without a wind. Grant dove inside the upturned vehicle as a shot slammed into the side. The corpse passenger crunched beneath his passage and emitted a foul breath. Shooters on both side, and what did he have? A car load of shovels and dead men. If he could get to his own jeep, he could radio for the helicopter. Grant worked his way between the seats into the back and peered out to the north. Gooney lay on the ground near the dead looter and his entourage of vultures. Shit. Grant's mouth went dry. Gooney always said Grant was trying to kill him. Please God don't let it be true. No stone lions, just him and the jeep full of dead guys, this one with a fistful of money still clenched in his hand.

Stones rattled against the jeep on the other side. Gooney rolled, grabbing the dead guy and heaving himself up, corpse gripped by the back of its neck, a human shield as he whipped out his gun and started shooting.

Someone on the ridge above grunted, then returned fire, making the corpse jump. Another shot from behind, but a different angle. The other shooter was on the move, trying to line up Gooney for a shot. A shadow detached from the trees. Grant crouched in the doorway and fired.

Zombie dance partner or no, Gooney was in the open—soon, there'd be two bodies out there. Both shooters had good lines on Gooney and not much on Grant, so long as he stayed by the jeep. Body armor. Mental note to wear it. Grant reached out and grabbed the shovel nearest the door. Holding it across his body, he launched himself out the door. He ran uphill, shooting. A bullet pinged off his shovel, and another grazed his fist, then he was pushing forward, swinging the shovel and bringing up his gun toward the shadow. With a crack of metal on bone, the shooter tumbled to the ground. Two shots, chest and head. Grant swung about, taking aim toward the far bank.

In the gully between, Gooney ran for cover by the jeep, letting the corpse fall as a bullet puffed into the ground beside him. The other shooter popped up from behind Grant's jeep, fired, dropped down.

Grant picked up the dead guy's rifle and slid behind the skeletal trees, sinking low, catching movement under his own jeep on the far side. He fired.

Grant's jeep lurched into motion, rushing toward the ridge, then over it. In Grant's eye, it hung briefly in the air, suspended over its twin in the gully below before it crashed down with a roar of metal and the leaping, hungry wall of flames with Gooney on the wrong side.

CHAPTER THIRTY-FOUR

Zhen piloted the Chinese jeep, driving fast, leaving plumes of dust as they pursued the helicopter overhead. Liz pulled her kerchief over her nose and mouth like a bandit, the speed and the mad nature of their quest suddenly striking her—thousands of miles from a research library, in more ways than one. Her hair tossed around her, as if lashing her on to greater adventures. Hopefully, they were all done finding bodies. The sight of that dead hand thrusting from beneath the reindeer stone still lingered whenever she closed her eyes. The landscape changed around them, rising and growing greener as they passed streams and small pools. The music of the engine changed as they climbed, deeper and more growly. Flocks of sheep and goats scattered before them, the mounted herdsmen staring as the jeep blew through. Liz waved, drawing their eyes. The helicopter pulled far ahead, a speck in the distance, then the earpiece D. A. had given her crackled.

"Bird to Tracker, come in Tracker."

She squeezed the microphone button. "Is that me? This is Liz—am I Tracker?"

"Yeah, that's you. Possible lock on the waterfall that flows over small stones, about twenty miles from your present location, west north-west. We'll hover, copy?"

"Sure, copy." She frowned at the compass on the dashboard, then tapped the driver's arm and pointed. "West north-west," she shouted over the engine racket.

They plunged into a river valley, paralleling the stream for a time, then cutting through where the water stretched out over a plain of stones. Around a pinnacle of rock, then the helicopter sprang into view in a broad valley that looked as if a giant hand had pressed down on the land, sinking a green patch between a series of narrow rivulets. One larger tributary crashed down over a precipice and gurgled over a channel of small stones. The helicopter drew off as they approached, then set down—grass waving in all directions—in the meadow not far away. Byambaa and Huang stepped out, the Mongol with a vigorous stride toward Liz, the businessman with a pause to smooth his safari-suit. The engines powered down, the blades swishing slowly to a halt, then D. A. hopped down from the front, pausing and peering under the cabin until Nick swung down on the other side with a shake of his pant leg down over his prosthetic. They walked together, her short strides echoing his longer one, but Liz hadn't figured out yet if they were an item or just close army buddies: The towering black man, the little curly-haired woman, his voice deep and powerful, hers nasal and enthusiastic.

"—not a lot of places with waterfalls, mostly cascades—that's when the water lies flat on the rock over a series of shelves." D. A. used her hands to demonstrate what she meant.

They stood a moment staring up at the waterfall, then Byambaa drew a deep breath, letting it swell his belly, and let it out slow. He stepped away from the group, walking toward the water as he breathed. When he had chosen his spot, he began to sing, a vibrating tone that imitated the sound of the water fall and its following gurgle.

D. A. sidled closer to Liz. "That doesn't sound anything like the music you had," she whispered. "I mean, it sort of does, but not the song, you know?"

Liz stifled her irritation. "He's singing a tribute to the water, to the local spirits, then he'll sing the song."

"Oh. Right."

After a few minutes of Khoomei, Byambaa fell silent, listening to the water. Liz watched him listening, the utter stillness of his body like a meditation, a part of nature rather than a disruption of it. This moment was one of the things she fell in love with about him. Years before, when he had come to Colorado, to her family's ranch, as an exchange student, they rode out into the plains or up in the foothills, and he would pause to listen, absorbing the wilderness of another nation, then transforming it into music. For him that was a sideline to the civil engineering degree he eventually pursued, but for her, it was a moment out of time and place, linking her with worlds away, not only in space, but in time, with a sense of universal being. When he began singing again, performing the fifth song of the tomb, his voice filled her to overflowing, echoing through her with longing. She wished the rest of them would pile into the helicopter and fly away, leaving him and her, the echo of the water and the smell of sweet grass. A rush of desire welled up in her, all concerns of the world falling away, and she wanted to lose herself in him, in this place, and be utterly devoured. That hotel room in Frankfurt had been one of the few times they ever made love indoors.

Liz reluctantly set aside that memory and focused back on the scene, on Byambaa and the waterfall. The tumble and sweep of the fall sounded right, harmonious, if a bit more abrupt than the tones meant to imitate it. The gurgle over stones, too, sounded a bit fast, but it had been eight hundred years, rocks were bound to shift. The power of the water itself would round them down, smooth them out and rattle them into different groupings.

Byambaa's voice trailed away, and he met her eyes, his lips pressing closed. She hurried over to him as Nick clapped and Huang expressed his surprise and admiration. "What is it?"

He shook his head, glancing up at the water beside him. "It doesn't feel quite right."

"Some things are bound to have shifted in the last eight hundred years. All it would take is a new stone falling into the pool to shorten the tone of the fall itself, don't you think?" She clasped his hand in both of hers.

"Could be." He stared at the water, his profile still and stern.

"But you don't think it is. It's also possible the original singer on the recording had remembered the song a little differently, or rushed the intonation."

His head lowered, his dark hair sweeping forward, and he gave her hand a squeeze. "Which is possible for all of them. A few changes in each song and the entire map dissolves into nothing but music."

"You do believe in the map, don't you? You think I'm right?"

He swallowed and faced her. "We promised each other honesty. This... The idea of a map so old, a map of songs, a beautiful idea. But can it be true? Can it have lasted for so long?"

"Then what are you doing here if you don't believe me? If you don't believe in me?" She dropped his hand, but he caught her shoulders and drew her closer to the cliff where the sound of the water echoed all around them.

"I do believe in you. It is an idea worth chasing."

"Even if it ends on Chinese soil?"

Another silence. For a singer, a silence could mean everything.

"Or did you just come because Huang paid for your plane ticket?"

"That hurts me, Liz. I came to support you. To follow your dream, to see where it brings us."

"Even if you don't believe it, and you don't even want it to be true. Yeah, I get it. That hurts me." She spun on her heel, her eyes stinging with tears as she stalked away from him.

"So it's not right? What, we keep looking? Tell me what you want," D. A. said as Liz pounded by. "I'll check the satellites and see if I can find another candidate," she called.

"Hush," said Nick. "Just hush. Human resource tension isn't always mission-specific."

"It may be wise to seek alternative locations," Huang added.

Liz walked to the edge of the wider river, golden in the full light, swirling over stones. Long distance relationships were never easy, especially ones that crossed international and language boundaries. He had learned English, she learned Mongolian, but would she ever learn his soul? She thought she heard it when he sang—had she been wrong about that poetry?

"Pardon my intrusion, Miss Elizabeth." Huang stood at her elbow, a little ways apart, head also bowed, a small paper held in his hands.

"Sorry. I—"she wiped her eyes. "Just, sorry."

"I have been reviewing the photographs of the landscape, and here is one I think you should see." He proffered the item on his palm, like a fine chocolate. Taken with a low-quality digital camera and printed in black and white, the image showed an open area, a stream, and a waterfall. The same one that flowed behind them.

"Oh my God—he was here, that poor man." She took the picture and spun about to compare it with the real thing.

"If your soldier's surmise is correct, then the deceased worked for those in the Chinese government who have a vested interest in preventing this discovery."

It took Huang's meaning a moment to sink in, then Liz could hear the throbbing of her own heart. "He was trying to throw us off, to destroy the clues before we could get to them, but the stone got to him first. They've already gotten this far." Liz took off at a run. "Come on! We can't just hang out here, we need to finish this, to find the clues before they do." She waved the picture as the others gathered close, Nick and D. A. eager, Byambaa hanging back warily. "They have the songs, they must have someone who can sing them and understand them. This guy, the dead guy, was scouting the landscape for them, just like we're doing. If we're in luck, his death will have slowed them down. We need to get moving." She stepped up to face Byambaa and forced herself to speak more gently. "I know you have doubts, but these guys are already ahead of us. Think of what will happen if they get there first."

He gave a single nod. "Let's ride."

She grinned, and was turning to D. A., but the other woman held up a hand and said, "On it!" She held a satellite phone pressed to her ear, frowning. The excitement in the group hesitated, like a long note extended in a thrilling aria. Then D. A. drew the phone back, glared at it, and jabbed it again.

"Chief's not answering," Nick supplied, and she nodded without lowering the phone. "Do you have good signal? We could go up, but it's noisy." He pointed toward the helicopter, then started out in that direction, D. A. drifting after him.

Liz blinked at Byambaa, but Huang said, "I have had enough of flying for now. I think you should enjoy the view." He waved them on toward the copter, and in moments they were airborne, D. A. trying again for a connection while Nick gripped the yoke, focused on his task. They rose, watching Huang and his driver board the jeep down below, then Liz took in the view for the first time—the low, old mountains that rose before her from the dry plains, the threading of canyons and valleys, and the thick plume of dark smoke rising from the desert like a funeral pyre.

CHAPTER THIRTY-FIVE

Grant darted left and right as he ran, slammed into the slope below the shooter and dove for the burning mass of metal. Inside the jeep, three human candles burning, an arm waving through the windshield, animated by the heat. He squinted into the glow, and saw another form slumped against the earth berm, arms raised, his only shield against the blast. About four feet of ground lay between the flaming wrecks and the undercut bank. Bits of metal and flaming debris rocked in the gap. Gooney crouched there, his back to the earth, his feet working against the unstable ground to hold himself back from the blaze, shaking and seared, suffering God knew what other injuries. But his gun was still in his hand.

Grant flattened himself against the earth wall, dirt and stones grinding against his injured back, and thrust himself toward his man. Gooney's pants smoked at his ankles, then caught fire.

Grant snagged Gooney's arm. Gooney's left hand slammed into Grant's face, knocking him free, the right hand coming up to level his gun, shaking.

"Gooney, stand down—it's me," Grant shouted.

Blood and scorch marks obscured Gooney's face, but his damp eye blinked back over the muzzle of the gun. "Son of a bitch," he mumbled.

"That's me. Let's go."

"Owe me a drink."

"Owe you a barrel." Grant caught his man's arm again, pulling it over his shoulders, hauling him to his feet. The heat drenched him with sweat as they staggered together along the narrow gap toward the steepest part of the bank, anything to get a little cover: he hadn't forgotten the shooter.

A few feet past the fire, Grant let Gooney drape against the wall while he smothered the flames at his ankles, catching a glimpse of the angry, red flesh. Ahead, a patch of shade showed the mound they had passed earlier. It'd have to do. He grabbed Gooney, pulling him up onto his shoulders and ran the last few feet into the shelter of the mound. This side showed those same ridges and the grooves of old rain—and more, a deep wound carved into the side, revealing nothing more than tight-packed dirt. A few broken red tiles scattered the base and the heap of dirt dug out in the quest for artifacts. A tomb or a temple.

"Wants you," Gooney muttered. "Not me."

Grant hadn't been involved with the quest long enough to piss someone off that badly, had he? "Stay here," he instructed, lowering Gooney into the opening at the side of the mound.

Footfalls approached, soft in the muffling sand. Grant leapt the smaller heap of displaced earth and started climbing, notching his hands and feet into gaps in the ancient earthwork. He reached the rounded top flattening himself out so his shadow wouldn't show, as the shooter slowed and approached the curve where Gooney waited. Dressed all in desert beige, with a Muslim's skullcap, the shooter crept forward, glancing around, never up. Grant unslung the rifle and took aim. The minute he jacked a round, the guy would make him.

Instead, a shot spat out of the hollow and the shooter jumped back. Grant jacked it, fired—nothing happened. Dirt and flecks of blood marked the chamber of the rifle from where it had dragged as he carried Gooney. The thing was jammed. He pulled his pistol.

A series of shots pecked the dirt below him, sending spurts of dust into his eyes, and he pushed backward, scrubbing his face to clear the dust.

Another shot from below, then the click of an empty magazine, and Gooney's half-sobbed, "Shit."

Grant smeared his arm across his face, blinking desperately, but he was out of time—or Gooney was. Leaping up, Grant sprang down the other side, slithering on the rough surface in a spray of gravel, the shooter, already leaning into his stance in front of the hollow, swung up to aim at Grant instead.

Too late. Grant slammed into him, and they both tumbled into the arroyo. Grant's cut hand let go, his gun bouncing away. He wrapped his left fist in the guy's tunic and reached for a knife. They grappled, tumbling over and over in the dirt.

The shooter's gun shoved up between them. Grant caught his wrist, sending the shot between their heads. This close, the man had a square jaw, Chinese features, black, determined eyes. Both hands to the other man's wrist, up to the gun, twisting it free.

The shooter jack-knifed his body, kicking Grant hard in the gut.

His heart pounded and his ears roared, dust swirling around them as the shooter broke free, slapping his hand backward, swiveling about with Grant's gun. The roar grew louder, and the shooter staggered, then ran, a dark shadow soaring toward him from the west.

The shooter was getting away—likely the crew of the copter hadn't planned on a fire fight, they wouldn't be ready on the draw. But they could chase him down, or they could get Gooney to the hospital.

Grant scrambled to his feet as the helicopter flew overhead. He caught a glimpse of Liz's hair tossing in the breeze. Waving wildly, he made the gesture for turn around, two, three times before they were out of sight, but he thought she turned. In a moment, the helicopter swung in a circle, returning. Unsteady, Grant walked the few steps to the mound and sank to his knees. "Tell me you're alive in there."

"No thanks to you. Again."

Grant let his head rest on the rough stone, breathing in great gasps that stretched the aggravated wound across his back. His teeth tasted like dirt, his eyes throbbed with it, the grit coating his senses. Distantly, he heard the helicopter's rotor hum and felt the harsh breeze of its landing.

After a minute, Gooney croaked, "Thought you'd left me."

Pushing off from the stone, Grant faced him in the gloom of the ruined mound. "That's how little you think of me? God Damn it, Gooney." The words scoured his throat. He found his feet and walked away, dropping to sit on the pile of earth, wounded by the present, shadowed by the past, still waiting for his benediction.

CHAPTER THIRTY-SIX

The smell of antiseptic wrinkled Jin's nose, but he set aside that irritation, checking to be sure his surgical cap stayed in place over the thick-framed glasses. Entering the hospital, taking on the guise of a doctor, brought his wife to mind. She glowed with her news, pouted at the fact that he did not share her joy. How could he, with Guo digging into his project, with the Councilor's stark warning that it was Jin who would be disgraced if this went wrong?

"Doctor," said one of the nurses as he passed, giving a nod. She wore the head scarf of a Muslim, and her features blended Chinese and Arab in dark skin and a fine nose.

"The Americans?"

She pointed. "In the private room. But one of them has been released, treated for minor injuries. I believe he is still here with his companions." She cocked her head. "Where is your badge, doctor?"

Jin patted his coat pocket where everyone else had a dangling identity badge. He smiled. "I seem to have left it in the changing room. I need to check in on this patient, nurse. Will you inform the orderlies to check the locker room?"

"Of course, Doctor—?" She raised her eyebrows.

"Ma," he said, giving himself a surname typical of the Islamic Hui people.

"Right away, Doctor Ma." Her smile brightened, and she bustled off, presumably to do his bidding.

He would not have much time. Carrying a clipboard, a stethoscope slung about his neck, Jin moved efficiently toward the private room she had indicated. Just beyond the corner, he caught a glimpse of those companions: two women, a tall black man, and the soldier, shirtless, revealing the heavy embellishment of tattoos down his right arm. A bandage crossed just below his armpits and another wrapped his right hand. Sweat streaked his skin where the nurses had not cleansed him, and dust caked his muscles. He twitched like a horse after a hard race. A tempting target, if Jin had the wherewithal to assassinate a man in a hospital, surrounded by his friends and a dozen strangers.

"I want security for Gooney—either we need to bring someone in, or one of us needs to stay here," he was saying, his voice hoarse with the desert air, but emphatic.

"Should be you, Chief," muttered the black man.

Security. That wouldn't leave Jin much time. He ducked through the door. Inside the private room, a large American filled the bed, his skin ruddy as if with sunburn, his legs bandaged, a plaster cast swathing his left arm, the right one outstretched to receive intravenous fluids. Jin reached for the medical chart at the patient's feet, and the man's eyes flickered open, his gaze sharpening in an instant, then relaxing.

"Here to spring me, Doc?" said the patient.

Jin furrowed his brow, studied the chart, then gave that too-wide smile that Americans expected and put on a rough accent. "Please to forgive. Not knowing all of English, yes? Two days in hospital, until healing." He held up two fingers. "Am to check, and to give shot."

"Another shot?" The patient rolled his eyes, then said, in careful Mandarin. "What is the shot for?"

The man spoke Mandarin. Interesting. Jin kept up his guise. "No worry. Can give to IV." Then the syringe was in the plastic, the liquid within already circulating.

The man's hand curled into a fist despite the reddened flesh. "Thank you. What is the medication?"

Jin nodded and smiled, then launched into rapid Mandarin. "This shot reduces local infections and in particular, it combats several antigens known to be present in the air, soil and water in this region, and which your body may not have the antibodies adequate for defense. You should feel a relaxing sensation, and the site of your needle may be cold. Do you feel cold?" He set his hand on the American's wrist, careful of the catheter site. The pulse began to slow.

"Yeah, cold," said the American. "Feels good."

Jin leaned closer, speaking in English. "You were a soldier were you not? Tell me about Mazar-i-Sharif."

"Can't. Wasn't there. The chief kicked me back to the states. Where is the chief? I wasn't very nice."

The drug was taking effect, making him talkative, if a bit maudlin. "But the chief was there?"

"That's where he saw her, the phantom. Look, can you get him for me? Seriously." The American started to move, sitting up as if to swing his feet over and get out of bed.

Jin pressed him gently back down. "I will let him know you'd like to see him, but he was injured as well, he—"

"Is he okay?" The American sat up, fumbling with his partially-imprisoned left hand to yank out the IV. Jin grabbed him, only to be flung away with a surge of strength. "Where is he? Where's the chief?" The American ripped free his cords and cables, and Jin stumbled back, finding a martial stance, then releasing it as the door slammed open.

"Gooney, get back to bed." The soldier shot Jin a glance, his muscles rippling under a collection of scars and drawings, as if he knew something more about the minister. "Sorry, Doctor." The soldier got his reaction under control. Disciplined, despite the circumstances.

"Sirs! Please to stay away from—"the nurse hurried in and Jin stopped her with an upraised palm.

"The patient became agitated. We'll need to run a fresh IV. He may have had a reaction to the morphine."

"Yes, Doctor, I see." Jin escorted her out of the room and she hurried to the supply closet, while he allowed the American's other companions to come between them, then faded into the hospital, one doctor among many, and, the moment he had left the building, stripping off his white jacket and cap, simply one more man in a suit, walking fast, thinking furiously.

Yang waited in the car, his jaw knotted with a bruise, his wrist shaking slightly when he wasn't occupied with cleaning his gun. His being simmered with anger, with the loss of face. Yang had lost his center during that fight. The fact was disturbing, but it might encourage him to act more decisively next time.

Jin shut the door and told the driver to go. Yang sat beside him, rigid and staring as if he held the Americans once more in his sights and was determined not to miss. "The number you were instructed never to call again. Call it. And send Casey's picture."

CHAPTER THIRTY-SEVEN

After the medical personnel had left, Grant stared at Gooney, and neither of them spoke. Gooney subsided onto the bed, breathing too hard, shaking his head vaguely as if to clear it. The nurse returned with an armload of supplies. "Doctor Ma, I—"she looked around the room, but the doctor wasn't there. To Gooney, she smiled and said, "Please lie down. Let us help you."

"He'll be okay," D. A. murmured, and the words echoed into the past, the same words she said when Grant woke up in the hospital, his neck and head swaddled in bandages.

"He should watch out for concussion, but I expect he'll make a good recovery," the military doctor had told her, fussing over some part of Grant's dressings, but Grant knew her words had been meant for his ears; the first thing he wanted to know when he woke up had nothing to do with his own recovery.

Grant pulled back, letting the Chinese nurse do her job. "Thank you," he said in Mandarin as he stepped aside. Gooney's eyes looked confused, blank, as if he hadn't recognized Grant, and whatever emotion had caused him to shout a moment ago had passed. Two other nurses and a doctor bustled in, and Nick called their party back into the hall.

"Zhen brought you a shirt," said D. A.

Liz and Byambaa stood close together, nearly in step, while Nick led the way. They circled around Grant warily as if he were a mustang on the way to breaking, and they couldn't tell which way he'd lunge next. Zhen, Huang's driver, held out a folded parcel and Grant accepted it.

"He doesn't get left alone." He stared at D. A. who nodded.

"I'll stay with him," she said. "I'll make sure he's taken care of."

"Zhen will remain here, on guard," Huang offered. "Please let us return to the hotel, and be comfortable, that is, if you are ready to depart, Mr. Casey."

"When he's recovered enough to travel, he goes home."

Nick tried a tentative smile. "His injuries aren't too severe, he should be up and around—"

"He goes home."

"If we're right about the—"D. A. glanced around then said, "escalation, then we might need back up."

"I can't work with someone who doesn't trust me." Shirt in hand, Grant stalked to the men's room. He filled a sink and scrubbed his face, swishing water around and spitting to clear the grit from his teeth. For a moment, his own face stared back at him, like a haunting from the days of Custer: high cheekbones, dark eyes, tanned skin that would hide some of the bruises. His hair stuck out in sweaty spikes and curled at his neck where he'd let it grow long. Instead of paper towels, the room held an old-fashioned cloth wrap-towel on a frame, the kind that you wiped your hands on, then advanced to a dry patch for the next person. The rest of the dirt would have to stay for now. Maybe a shower...except the shooter was still at large, and his team, whoever they were, had the same information to go on that Grant's did. The door swung open and Byambaa stepped through. Their eyes met in the mirror and Grant straightened, controlling his response to the spasm of pain that crossed his back. He pulled on the shirt and managed the buttons with special care, his right hand tingling.

"I do not think it's you," said the Mongolian.

"What?"

"Detective Gonsalves. His problem of trust. It's not you."

"What are you talking about?" Grant rested his hip against the sink while it drained, regarding the other man.

"I know what it is to be the object of mistrust." Byambaa spread his hands. "Chinese hate me, on instinct, it seems. You saw that old woman, her reaction. It is frustrating."

Grant nodded slightly. Frustrating was a feeble word for a hatred that spanned centuries.

"But it is not me. They hate, they fear, they worry over something else, someone else. They hate that they were weak, for a moment, for just long enough to be conquered. Gonsalves, he is the same way. You remind him of his fear."

Interesting. Grant rolled over what the man had said. "What fear?"

Byambaa shrugged. "This, I don't know."

"I still think it's a bad idea for him to be here."

The Mongolian spread his hands. "That is not my pasture. I came here for Liz, and for the Khan."

The door opened and a Chinese orderly started to enter but Grant fixed him with a stare, and the man bowed himself right back out again.

"So you're committed, even after this. Is she?"

"She hates that people are getting hurt for her songs. Especially Detective Gonsalves. And you."

Something in his voice caught Grant's attention and the corner of his mouth lifted. "I'm not the competition."

Byambaa gave the slightest smile of his own. "You do not mean to be. If you did, I do not think I could offer much of a fight." His gaze flicked over Grant's face, his figure from head to toe. "You saved her life, Mr. Casey. That gives a certain sentiment. But this...she is a student, a teacher, a musician. And now, she worries that she is no warrior."

"She doesn't have to be. That's why I'm here."

The Mongolian's chin rose. "And me."

"Does that mean we should get you a bow and a quiver?"

At that, he grinned, a sharp white pleasure across his face. "Mr. Huang already has."

"Then we have a tomb to find, and fast."

CHAPTER THIRTY-EIGHT

Byambaa emerged from the men's room looking mysteriously pleased, tempting Liz to make some sassy remark, but the tension of the group over all inhibited her. All she had to do was picture Gonsalves' scorched face or Grant's blood-stained shirt and that tension sped through her, making it hard to breathe.

Nick stood up straight, nearly at attention, at Grant's emergence. Dressed in a Chinese-style shirt of light silk, he looked like a Kung Fu master, coiled with strength, projecting danger despite the bandage across his fist—or maybe because of it. "We have places to go."

"Regrettably, we may have some difficulty in our departure," Huang said. He gestured toward the doors as they approached. Three men stood outside, one in a crisp, dark suit, the others in sharp uniforms with brimmed caps decked with red stars. Police.

Liz slipped her arm through Byambaa's, and he hummed softly, a soothing vibration she could feel through their contact.

"Good afternoon, gentlemen, and lady," said the man in the suit, in English. "I am Lieutenant Ma, of the Yinchuan City Security Services. We must request the opportunity to speak with you about the events of this afternoon." He gave a slight bow, but the two men at his back stiffened instead, negating the effect of his polite address. This was no request. Liz's wrists felt damp and achy as if she once again wore handcuffs. The Boston police station offered bad coffee and, when the matter was explained in accordance with the evidence, a quick release—even if neither Liz nor the lead detective believed the conclusion of overdose and accident really explained what happened at the archive.

"Of course you must learn what happened," Huang replied. "Will you please accompany us to our hotel? As you see, my bodyguard requires rest and refreshment." He gestured toward Grant, who took on a sudden, predatory alertness, but for Huang's benefit or for the police, Liz couldn't be sure. "We will be pleased to answer your questions."

"That is a very kind offer, sir, but our superiors have suggested that you come to the office." The man in the suit bowed slightly.

"Of course, we will be pleased to attend them at the office at an appropriate hour. Perhaps you would like to have your superiors contact me?" Huang held out a card between two fingers.

Lieutenant Ma hesitated, accepted the card and slid it into an inside pocket. "In the meantime, your hotel will provide a suitable venue. Would you be so kind as to allow your bodyguard to accompany us?"

"We will both join you." Huang smiled and glanced at Grant as if to acknowledge the transition from minion to master.

"Yes, sir," Grant answered. During the conversation, his posture shifted, his feet grounded, shoulders back, hands held lightly before him, the pose of military readiness. Another of his two hundred selves, this one the loyal soldier?

After Huang stepped into the long, dark vehicle by the curb and Grant ducked in with him, the others piled into their remaining jeep and Nick shoved it into gear, his face grown hard and eyes keen in a way Liz hadn't seen before.

"Why are we going to the hotel? Why not to the station?"

"The room's bugged—it's a tourist hotel, the best—that's why we had to wait a while for them to get the room ready," Nick called back to her. In a couple of maneuvers, he got the jeep on the police car's bumper and stayed close through the streets clogged with bicycles. "Also why the chief won't let us talk about business in there."

"They wanted us to go to the station to win honor by making the rich man and the tourists bow to them," Byambaa said.

"But Huang did bow."

"Barely—and he did it while he insists on his own way. He gives them a way to save face. Still, they will be angry."

"Damn straight," Nick muttered, then rocked the jeep into another turn and pulled behind the police car into the hotel's driveway. "Tourist jeep rental is probably bugged, too. Not the copter—Huang got it from one of his companies."

"How many does he own?"

Nick shrugged and turned off the engine. "One good conglomerate is all it takes. Everything here's supposed to be state-run, but mostly they farm out the work to the lowest bidder and just skim the profits."

"Which is why they have so many industrial accidents and building collapses," Byambaa said. He slid out and helped her down. "Easier to bribe the inspector than to do things well."

"I didn't know you were so cynical." She studied him, remembering his doubts at the waterfall.

"Only about the Chinese."

Upstairs in the suite Huang had rented, a pair of women added chairs and laid out a meal complete with two bottles of wine. Huang must have called ahead to say they had company, but the idea of lavishly hosting Chinese police in their hotel struck Liz as completely bizarre. It was like inviting the KGB up for snacks.

They settled into the comfortable sitting area, Huang helping himself to a variety of treats—little fried dumplings and slices of fruit. Watching him, Liz's stomach rumbled, but she wasn't sure she'd be able to keep anything down, not with the police guarding the door, their officer sitting straight on a wooden chair. He brought out a notebook.

"Mr. Grant Casey?"

"Yes, sir." Grant remained standing, his height and bearing intimidating even to Liz.

"You are employed as a bodyguard for Mr. Huang? For how long?"

"New hire, sir. This is our first assignment."

"Tell me what occurred in the desert today."

"Mr. Huang wanted a tour of the area. We could not secure enough helicopters for the team so we drove jeeps. One of the vendors we encountered requested assistance with the preparation of her husband's body for funeral, and we provided assistance in that regard."

Lieutenant Ma stopped him with a lifting of his chin, and turned his notebook back a page. "With a truck, a winch, and a company of coffin bearers. Is this accurate?"

"Yes, sir."

"Why did she require such assistance, and why did you deliver it?"

"Her husband had been crushed by a rock, sir. Mr. Huang is a collector of antiquities, with an interest in petroglyphs. Our interest was in the rock, sir." Grant's eyes twinkled, though his expression didn't change.

"And did you transport the rock?"

Huang leaned forward from his place on the couch. "We would do no such thing without the proper authority and permissions, of course. We merely offered timely aid to one who required it, as a gesture of goodwill to the local community."

The officer stared at him, the Chinese equivalent of Grant's deadpan stare. "And the jeep?"

"While my pilot—"Huang indicated Nick with a graceful turn of his hand—"was en route with the helicopter, he spotted a vehicle that apparently had been in an accident. Of course we could not leave such a thing uninvestigated."

"This is the job of the state, Mr. Huang, as you well know."

"Naturally. But I did not like to think that people lay injured while we returned to Yinchuan for such assistance. Certainly, we would have done so once the situation became more clear."

The officer stared a moment longer, then made a note. "Certainly. How did your jeep come to lie on top of the accident scene, Mr. Casey?"

"When my associate and I went down to the accident, we were attacked by two men. I assume, sir, that they were interested in stealing our vehicle, but instead, they crashed it."

"Nearly costing your associate his life, is that correct?"

His jaw clenched, and Liz became aware of Byambaa's quiet hum beginning again. Grant said, "Yes, sir. Fortunately, our job requires us to be armed, and we were able to return fire. It is the first time I've used a Chinese firearm, sir. I found it to be more than adequate."

If the officer took this as a compliment to Chinese engineering, he gave no sign. "Inflicting fatal injuries on one of these apparent bandits. And the other one?"

"Took off when the helicopter returned, sir. They came on horseback, I assume he left the same way."

"Describe him for me."

"About 170 centimeters tall, square jaw, nick in one ear lobe, sunglasses, short hair, right-handed, wearing sand-colored, loose-fitting clothes. Damaged knuckles, probably a brawler."

When his pen stopped moving, the officer blinked at Grant with an expression Liz interpreted as professional respect. The officer turned back a page again, then raised his eyes to Huang. "If you are concerned for your safety, Mr. Huang, why would you allow both of your security personnel to go on this investigation?"

"They do not comprise my entire team." Huang settled back again, popping a crisp morsel into his mouth.

The officer glanced at Nick and Byambaa. "I am struck by the fact, Mr. Huang, that you choose to surround yourself with foreigners."

"I am courting foreign investment, Officer. It serves me well to display my cosmopolitan interests. Please do sample the food—there is an excellent restaurant here."

A rapid beeping echoed suddenly, and the officer frowned, then slipped a hand into his pocket and found a cell phone. "Pardon me for a moment, Mr. Huang." He rose and left the room, the other two standing to either side of the door.

Grant and Nick shared a glance. Nick offered a shrug, then scooted forward to help himself to a few items from the buffet. "They're pretty hung up on foreigners around here."

"Because I am one," Huang answered. "We have placed them in a difficult position. The lieutenant especially. He must make a thorough investigation, but he does not wish to offend us or to turn aside possible investments which might be of benefit to his domain."

"Communist."

Huang laughed, a rich and musical sound that released the knot in Liz's belly. "Just so, Mr. Norton. Communist. They must always be aware what will have the most benefit. As, I am sure, the lieutenant will demonstrate when he returns. Our investment so far has been minimal—"Huang indicated the buffet—"but he may be encouraged to anticipate additional... investment."

Nick poured himself a small cup of wine that smelled of peaches, and raised it. "To the common good."

And that, finally, brought the smile back to Grant Casey's lips.

CHAPTER THIRTY-NINE

After the police officers apologized profusely for the inconvenience of questioning, and accepted a few snacks, they departed, closing the door behind them. Grant relaxed his stance, and said, "Bodyguard?"

"An effective rouse. Do we depart immediately, or do you, as suggested, require refreshment."

"Give yourself a break, Chief. At least for an hour. D. A. took some pix of the crash site as we flew over, if that helps." Nick grabbed another fried thing from the table. "These things are delicious—almost as good as hash browns."

The smells of grease, pork and onion drifted in the room, but Grant's scalp itched with dirt or crusted blood. "Save me some." He stalked toward his adjoining room and the welcome of its shower, then turned back at the threshold.

"Mr. Huang." The businessman raised his eyebrows. "Thank you." It felt inadequate—he felt inadequate—but the other man gave a slight bow, and Grant slipped into his own room.

He stripped off his clothes as he started the shower. It pounded against his head like his old sergeant's voice, like his grandfather's harangues. Grant leaned against the wall, careful of his bandages, as brown water flecked with blood rushed away, circling the drain. Now that he was still and alone, a hundred scrapes and bruises stung. Tiny lashes, prodding him to do better. Gooney, in the hospital. One of them should have stayed high, near the jeep, taken watch. The others accused him of paranoia, then he let his guard slip, and this happened. Never mind that Gooney was here on his own reconnaissance—theoretically not Grant's problem. He was Grant's man, whether either of them wanted that or not. In a military operation, some collateral damage was to be expected in order to achieve the objective—how much and what kind depended on the op, the objective, and the higher ups. And that was almost always sorted out later, in the recriminations, or, God forbid, in the press. Setting expectations for the next time based on the last time. Always fighting the last war.

But he wasn't fighting any war now. He was providing security and intel for a private venture, maybe a public good, discovering the location of a historic landmark of legendary significance, and doing so before it could be destroyed by the petty forces of the present. All over the world, agents of chaos sought to scrub away the signs of someone else's culture, to claim their lands, their rights as if that people had no value, as if history itself could be erased and rewritten not merely in books, but on the very ground where men had lived and died. His grandparents' history had been wiped out like that. Would he let the same thing happen to Byambaa's? If he did, if he retreated from this fight, what, then repaid Gooney's scorched flesh, or that of the young man who died in the archives?

History. People acted like it was just this story people told to each other, a test to take in high school and forget all about when they entered the real world. But history made that world. Eight hundred years later, the Chinese still hated the Mongols. Thousands of years and the Arabs still hated the Jews. First Nations still fighting in American courts for the land their ancestors roamed forever. How many battles had been fought for Jerusalem, for Rome, for Constantinople, not for today, but for yesterday? Why else had the Bone Guard been born? Grant ran his hand over the tattoo on his neck, his scars defining the wings and claws of that lion, jaws spread, ready to fight back.

And Grant had wasted enough time already. He shut off the water and scrubbed himself dry, his scraped skin leaving streaks of blood on the towel. Hopefully Huang was a good tipper to make up for the mess. In the bedroom, Grant pulled on fresh clothes and surveyed his remaining gear. His gun had been left at the fight, along with those he borrowed from their assailant. His go-bag blew sky-high with the jeeps. He pulled together a new bag as best he could: basic first aid kit, maps, extra ammo. He added some extra clothes. Zhen's jeep carried much of their equipment, the shovels, picks and cameras of the archaeologist or the tomb raider.

In the sitting area that joined their rooms, the team relaxed into their casual meal, sipping wine, talking vaguely about where else they should visit, how long their friend would be in the hospital. They quickened at Grant's entrance, then seemed to sink a little deeper into sofa and chairs when he sat down and filled a plate. "I think we should proceed with Mr. Huang's tour as soon as possible."

Nick glanced at his watch. "Suppose there's any place in town to get a good chai?"

"Chai? That would be Indian tea?" Byambaa smiled. "You must try milk-tea. It is a special thing of the steppes, Tibetans, Mongolians—we all drink this. It is made with green tea, milk or sometimes butter, and salt for the altitude."

Nick wrinkled his face up, reminding Grant of D. A. "Butter and salt? You making tea, or making an omelet?"

"No eggs. In the steppes, not so many chickens. For the khan's army, no chickens at all. If they must ride a long way, they survive on the blood of their horses."

"Y'all are nuts."

Half an hour later, their diminished convoy set out, acquiring replacements for some of their lost gear on the way. Grant and

Byambaa took the jeep while the others flew on ahead, transmitting GPS coordinates to the waterfall they had identified. "*Grasslands thick as winter wool*," Byambaa muttered, flipping through the looter's photographs. He squinted at three of them in turn, images like the prairie back home, maybe like the steppes of Byambaa's home as well. "We should have horses."

"Agreed. But for now, the jeep's faster."

"Only until we get there." Byambaa pointed at the mountains growing ahead. "*The mountains that call my spirit to rest.* You ride?"

"When I can. I grew up around horses." He dodged a tumble of stones that crossed the dirt track, then set out across the dry land. "But the cortege included carts, right? So there must have been a track to get close to the site." They ascended along a series of switch-backs and narrow paths between thrusting stones until they reached the top of the waterfall, and the broad, flat valley through which the river flowed. A herd of goats scattered, bleating, a pair of lean dogs holding their ground, stiff-legged, watching the jeep like wolves.

Overhead, the copter soared out in a broad arc over the surrounding cliffs, disappearing in one direction, then another. A pagoda rose from one of the crags, clinging with wooden struts, its red roofs crumbling, the whole structure subsiding into the grip of time. The radio crackled and Byambaa clicked it on.

"Go ahead."

"Bird here, no sight of the grass, but come east, uh, about ten degrees. Do you see the pagoda? There's a pass beyond it. Go that way." Liz clicked out, then came back and said, "Over and out."

Grant suppressed his laughter. They were amateurs, doing their best.

"You heard that?" Byambaa asked.

The jeep bounced across old ruts and swerved around a handful of trees. The streams spread fingers out among the valleys. The wind shifted, and Grant clenched the steering wheel. The wind smelled of ashes. He saw Gooney running, saw the jeep explode into flames. But that was miles away. They came around the crag with its lonely monument and through a crumbling gap in the yellow stone. A high valley opened here, more gently sloped and decked with the spikes of burnt trees. Grant slowed. If they'd been Stateside, he would have blamed the fire on a lit cigarette, a scorched area spreading from the road up the slope until it ran out of fuel. On the other side, on a rise by a trickling stream, a few large, round circles marked the ground, stones piled around their edges. The open circles, ringed by scorched earth, stood out like scars. Another heap of stones stood to one side, topped with a staff and a singed blue cloth that dangled limp in the breeze.

"Mongols," Byambaa said as he jumped down, heading for the circles.

The radio crackled and Grant scooped it up. This time, he didn't follow right away, but surveyed the area from his position by the jeep, a replacement Norinco pistol tucked in a new thigh holster. "Go ahead, Bird."

"What do you have down there?" The helicopter moved over the valley, then came back and hovered.

"Hard to say. Looks like a wildfire. A ger camp moved out not too long ago."

"After living here a long time," Byambaa said. He held up a stone with an image of a wolf. "The guide spirit of the clan of Chinggis Khan."

"The seventh clue, *a forest tended by family*?" Liz's voice shone by with excitement.

Grant swept the scene with his gaze one more time. "Maybe it was—until somebody burned it down."

Byambaa wiped the stone clean, his brow furrowed. "It is the Oigurat clan who were to tend the trees at the khan's burial site, not his own clan."

"So you don't think this is it?" Grant's hand dangled, the radio still in his grip.

Byambaa tipped his hand one way and the other, a gesture like a shrug. "We should look around."

"Hang on," Grant said into the radio. He set out paralleling Byambaa's course. The Mongolian paced slow and careful, then froze on the rise and his head shook. He stumbled a few steps, shouting in his own language, then plunging down the other side of the settlement.

Grant's gun was already in hand as he ran, taking the high ground Byambaa had abandoned, keeping the stone heap between him and any possible threat. His injured hand throbbed with the strength of his grip. Byambaa's voice echoed from the cliffs, a torrent of words that could only be curses. The Mongolian language sounded more like Russian than Chinese, gruff and melodious. Down below, a rough dam of loose stones backed up the river into a small pool. Between his position and the pond lay three blackened mounds with outthrust legs, ribs showing beneath cracked hide, necks stretched toward a post, but the ropes that tethered them had burned. Horses. Grant's jaw ached from clenching, and let the Mongol howl enough fury for both of them. The radio crackled. Grant ignored it.

At last, Byambaa turned from the sight, viciously wiping tears from his face. "They are barbarians. Nobody lets horses burn. Nobody."

Except maybe a gang of Chinese looters with a trunk full of empty gas cans. Grant holstered the gun. "Looks like the smoke took them down before the fire got this far."

"I should sing for them."

Grant squeezed the Mongolian's shoulder. "Later. For now, we should avenge them."

CHAPTER FORTY

The director of the Western Xia Tombs Archaeological Preserve kept his hands behind him, perhaps politely, but Jin thought otherwise. The man was restraining himself from wringing them. "It is quite an honor to have a visit from the Minister of Antiquities," the man squeaked. "I regret that the lack of warning has prevented me from offering a proper welcome."

Jin inclined his head magnanimously. "I understand, of course, Director. Truly, do not be troubled by my visit. I was merely in the area, and wished to view the collections." He gestured toward the museum. "Do not feel that you need to accompany me."

"If you are certain, Minister." He bowed again.

"I am anticipating a guest—perhaps you can direct him to the courtyard?"

"Of course, Minister." He hovered still, shifting from one foot to the other, his eyes scanning the museum's glass cases and antiquated displays. All of the signage was in Chinese, the cabinets dusty on their edges, the lights flickering—once the Director had located the switches. In the central case, where the finest of the Xia imperial grave goods should have been displayed, a prime location in the case held only a notice to the effect that an item had been removed for conservation, but the yellowed edges of the message suggested the item had been gone for a long time. Jin moved closer, reading the notice. It pricked at his mind, like an approaching assailant in the sparring arena. "The five-sided crown—which conservator is working on it?"

Arrested by the sound of his voice, the director scuttled forward, peering with him. "I will check on that, Minister." He swallowed a few times, blinked, turned away, then turned back, brightening. "I believe that your assistant, Li, provided the name of the conservation firm, he may recall—"

"Li has not been with the ministry for nearly eighteen months, Director." That sense of approaching danger tensed his muscles. "Assuming you promptly followed up on his advice, that implies that this valuable artifact has been off display for quite some time. Please find the information. I will expect to hear from your shortly."

The man bobbed his head, then gave a jump when a pair of people entered, the woman who handled ticket sales, and a man in the dark, crisp suit of the People's Security Service, a cap tucked under his arm, and his lips set in a grim line.

"A man to see you, Minister Jin," said the woman, then promptly bowed herself out again, setting a fine example for the director whose cheeks sucked in at the sight of the officer before he hurried away.

"Lieutenant Ma at your service." A click of the heels and the slightest bow. "My office has given me to understand that you interfered with a provincial investigation, Minister."

Blunt. The officer contained his anger, though not as well as he might believe. "There is information that your office requires to handle this investigation properly." Jin strolled through the doors into the courtyard beyond, the officer catching up in a few sharp strides. "The Ministry of Antiquities is always interested in the movements of a collector like Mr. Huang."

They emerged into bright sun, then passed again into a pavilion of dioramas that showed the stages of the Xi Xia empire's demise.

One impressive display showed heaps of dead soldiers with a few men still standing, fighting a desperate action against the Mongols, the unstoppable horde. Vivid artificial blood spattered the armor of the life-sized figures and the vast painting behind them, depicting the battlefield as an endless array of corpses.

"Mr. Huang's record is quite clear, Minister, and I was given to understand that he might be in search of local investment opportunities. Do you believe his acquisitions to be in doubt?"

"So far as we are aware, his collection contains only items of very clear provenance." Jin met eyes with the figure of Genghis Khan. "However, that sort of collector often brings out vendors of suspect items, hoping to achieve a capitalist dream."

"Thanks to our rich heritage, Minister, Yinchuan has its share of such persons. As fortune would have it, several of the most notorious were recently killed in separate accidents." A vertical line of consternation pinched between his eyes, and Jin interrupted his train of thought.

"Huang's new American associates are known to have frequented sites of looting in the Middle East during their tenure in the armed forces."

"Soldiers," the officer said, with a thrill of recognition. "Mercenaries?"

"Apparently. Or looters of a more advanced nature. Now that you've told me about these coincidental accidents, I wonder if they are not accidents at all." He spread his hands. "Lieutenant. I apologize for disrupting your investigation, of course. I merely wished to express the same concerns you, yourself possess—there is no need to unduly concern a person of Mr. Huang's stature. I have to imagine that, if his new associates are not of the best reputation, he is unaware of that." He glanced meaningfully at the heaps of painted plaster corpses.

"Minister, no need to apologize. I am grateful for any information which might advance my investigation, especially if it aids me in uncovering greater wrongs." He gave a sigh. "I was not able to separate the American from Mr. Huang's party, and, at the time, I had little reason to suspect his story."

"These men were not mere infantry, Lieutenant—they have numerous skills, and I am sure that deception is very high among them." Jin folded his arms. "One of my assistants is in the local desert in the area where Mr. Huang has shown interest. He may be able to give you the opportunity to question the soldier on his own."

"I would be most grateful, Minister."

"May I give him your direct line?"

"Please."

Jin's cellphone vibrated in his pocket and he slipped a hand around it. "In that case, Lieutenant, I wish you all success in your investigation."

They parted with a slight bow, the officer pressing his cap to his head and marching off to do his duty.

He slipped out the phone and looked at the display. Above the army photo of Grant Casey a single word appeared, "Yes." The operative had identified Casey, just as Jin had feared. It was a good thing he had already taken action. He slid the message away. Between the two of them, Lieutenant Ma and Yang should be able to solve this problem. The Chinese system of justice was robust—it had devoured men like that before. And some of those who emerged were never the same.

CHAPTER FORTY-ONE

Liz pressed her face to the curved window at her side, peering down at Grant and Byambaa. They stood close together now, Grant reaching out to touch him, a startlingly human gesture, but he still hadn't answered her buzz on the radio. Below them in the dell lay a group of mounds she couldn't identify, but Byambaa's reaction had been all too clear, his fury soaring full-throat. She buzzed again. This time, Grant gave a thumbs up, turning from Byambaa and leading the way back to the jeep. Sitting down, he finally spoke, "Three dead horses down here, killed in the fire. I suspect those looters might have been involved—they had a few empty gas cans."

"Oh, jeez." Liz stared down at her fiancé. "Those burnt shapes, those are horses."

"Horses? Shit, the chief must be spitting mad." Nick took them up a little higher, now that the concerns were laid to rest.

"I didn't realize he was such a horseman. No wonder they're getting on so well."

Nick grinned. "Good. What's not so good is that." He pointed toward a brilliant sunset glow on the western horizon over the rugged peaks. "Can't fly in the dark, not in an unfamiliar range. Radio the chief—tell him we need to call it a night."

"Right." Liz squeezed her microphone. "Bird to Tracker. Nick says we need to head back before nightfall."

"Affirmative," Grant replied, but his voice betrayed frustration. "Hate the fact that we're losing ground."

"I know what you mean," she said.

"I am not aware there is any alternative," Huang murmured from the cramped back seat.

Down below, the jeep started up, sounding rough, and the headlights came on in the gathering dusk. "What's my direction? Can we get out ahead?" Grant inquired

Nick pushed the yoke and took the copter out of the valley, following the narrow track below. The cliffs opened up into a broad, high plain, with a cluster of white gers about a mile away, glowing in the ruddy light of the setting sun. Dogs barked up at them and sheep huddled together in that protection.

"It is as if we look back in time," Huang said. "Imagine the camp of the great khan spreading in just such tents." His hands described it, setting imaginary gers all across the horizon.

"The way looks good. There's a ger camp ahead, and a road leading east west, back toward Yinchuan," Liz reported.

"Thanks, Bird. On it."

The lights of the jeep bobbed below, up and down over the rough ground, making Liz grateful for her comfortable perch in the air.

"You're getting pretty good on the mic—telling him what he needs to know. Nice work, for a grad student," Nick remarked as he guided the copter back toward the lights of the city. "Someday, maybe you'll be looking for D. A.'s job."

"Thanks. What is her job, exactly?"

"Sig-int. Signals Intelligence. Listening, tracking, researching, like that."

"Who are you guys?"

His grin looked too bright in the twilight interior. "Now? We're the Bone Guard."

The mic crackled and Liz answered it. "Tracker, this is Bird, what's up?"

"Out of gas," Grant sighed. "Thought we checked the auxiliary can, but it's dry—sprung a leak."

"You want us to come back for you?"

"Negative, you've only got one seat. By the time Nick drops you guys and comes back, it'll be dark. Byambaa's going to talk with the folks in the ger. Worst-case, we spend the night with the jeep. I've got a solid go-bag."

Nick and Liz shared a glance. "If you think so. Can I say good night to Byambaa?"

After a moment, Byambaa came on the line. "These nomads may know about the fire—they may be the same family. I hope they speak the same dialect."

"I'm sure you'll be fine. If all else fails, sing for them."

Byambaa chuckled, then he switched to Mongolian. "I miss you more than the steppes miss the sun."

Warmth spread through her, and she whispered back, "I miss you more than the flute misses the breath. Goodnight." She clicked off, and settled back in her seat.

"What'd he say?" Nick inquired.

"Things that only lovers should know," answered Huang, and she could hear his smile as they left the sunset, and her love, behind.

CHAPTER FORTY-TWO

Shouldering his bag, Grant followed Byambaa toward the ger camp, barely visible in the fading day. How could he have not noticed the leak? Blame it on the morning, on Gooney's injuries, on the appearance of Chinese police at the hospital. Too many damn distractions, and now Grant was screwing up his job. Byambaa practically bounded forward, eager to talk with the locals; it was a good chance for some human intelligence on the ground. This whole operation had been rushed, without proper intel from the start. Slow was smooth, and smooth was fast: his CO had pounded that one into him in Ranger School. Better to move carefully, deliberately toward the goal than to move too fast and have the whole thing go south. Thank God Huang had been able to defuse the situation with the police.

Tall grass swished against his legs, then he emerged onto the dirt track. Byambaa waited for him there. "If they invite us in, don't step on the threshold—that's bad luck. They'll direct us where to sit. If they offer a snuff bottle, accept it, even if you don't sniff."

"Good to know, thanks." An etiquette briefing, just like the kind they used to get—and sometimes give—before any trans-national operation. The two gers rose a little way off, glowing faintly through the wheel-like opening at their tops. Smoke curled up out of one of them, scented with roasting meat, and a faint strain of Asian pop music drifted toward them.

Dogs barked, then four of them sprang out of the darkness, tall rangy animals more like jackals than sheepdogs. Byambaa kept walking, and the dogs circled, backing up before them, forming a perimeter of bright eyes and sharp teeth.

Solar panels on stakes glinted, explaining the aerial antennas on top of the classic round tents. The door of the first ger popped open and someone leaned out, giving a whistle. The dogs waved their tails and grinned, drawing back, clearly pleased with themselves. The woman stood in her doorway, her face invisible against the glow of the interior.

Byambaa raised a hand in greeting and started talking, his voice both rich and soothing. Yeah, the guy was a singer—he knew how to use his gifts. He gestured back toward Grant, beckoning him up closer. The woman listened, her lips turned down, glancing over Grant, then back to Byambaa, finally, she bobbed her head and stood back.

Bowing slightly, hands together, Byambaa entered, stepping carefully over the threshold. Grant followed, ducking slightly beneath the brightly painted doorway, red with a pattern of white and blue. "Thank you," he said to her, first in English, then Mandarin.

Her face darkened, craggy as the moon with heavy-lidded eyes, and she said something.

Byambaa answered, hands spread in a shrug, and the woman laughed, waving them inward, offering them seats on a low wooden bed, a match to one on the opposite side. A small stove stood there as well, a couple of stools, and battered steamer trunks topped by tilting wooden shelves of supplies and household items. The two central poles and the wheel at the top of the ger bore similar designs to the doorway, bright and cheerful in contrast to the plain gray walls behind the lattice that surrounded the home. A few photos hung from the framework along with hooks carrying pots and pans, aprons, and various tools. It reminded him of the hogans of his grandfather's people, the memory stinging his injured hand. He forced himself to relax. He was thousands of miles from there, in another world, however similar it might appear.

"That's the women's side," Byambaa explained as he sat.

"What did you tell her?"

The Mongolian looked away, his fingers tapping, and Grant wondered if he had picked up the habit from Liz. "She asks if you are a spy, to speak in Chinese, and I told her no, you were a child—you just haven't learned to talk properly."

Cocking his head, Grant said, "I guess I should just be glad you guys understand each other."

That slow smile began at one side of Byambaa's lips. "She speaks a dialect, but yes, we understand. Her husband and sons went north to do some shopping at a settlement."

The woman stood over the stove where a large pot steamed. She repeatedly scooped and poured the beige liquid inside, then, apparently satisfied with it, set down the ladle, and displayed a small bowl with silver fittings, offering a sad face to the men as she spoke.

"She apologizes for not offering vodka—her husband is to purchase more and bring it back." Then he leaned a little closer. "I would say her family has gone to test the local vodkas before they make their selection. Nomads have little entertainment out here."

A small television, the source of the faint music, flickered from the top of one of the wooden shelves, showing a happy Chinese family sitting down to dinner at a modern table, helping themselves with chopsticks, the future intruding in to this woman's traditional home.

Outside, the dogs started barking again, but with a different tenor, and the woman again dropped her ladle, wiping her hands on her apron and springing to the door with surprising lightness. Voices greeted her, and, after a moment, three men entered, craggy and bow-legged, greeting Byambaa like a long-lost cousin, and pulling out snuff-bottles of glass painted with horses. Byambaa and Grant stood up, enveloped in the smell of motorcycle grease and livestock as the men eagerly tossed questions about. The oldest man, the husband, Grant assumed, wore a traditional deep-blue del covered by a leather coat, while the two younger men had adopted a Chinese version of Western clothes. Byambaa struggled to keep up with their questions, one after another, and the woman thrust back into their midst, triumphantly offering the silver-edged bowl. The men handed off the parcels they carried and she accepted them with exclamations of delight, while the oldest of the newcomers produced a bottle from his pocket. He poured a draught into the bowl and gestured the others back, silencing them with a wave of the bottle.

Carefully, he passed the bowl to Byambaa, who dipped one fingertip and flicked a drop toward the sky, and one toward the floor before sipping from the bowl, and offering it to Grant. "Do as I have done," he urged.

Grant accepted the bowl just as reverently, and repeated the ritual. When he took his swallow, the liquor burned down his throat and filled his nostrils while the men cheered, then he passed it to one of the brothers, until everyone had had a swallow. The father topped it off again, and drank, then handed it back to Byambaa, who took another swallow, without the flicking this time. Byambaa held it out to Grant, who murmured, "I don't drink."

The Mongolian held the bowl, and said a few words to their host who roared something with obvious disbelief, but Byambaa kept shaking his head, pointing to Grant.

The sons were in on it now, and the wife leaned in with a few words of his own. Their expressions ranged from amusement to a scowling suspicion.

"They say what kind of America doesn't drink. Now they are sure you are a spy. They want to know why I'm helping you, who you work for."

Grant took the bowl and took a big swallow, to a roar of approval. Vodka scoured his throat and coiled like a snake in his near-empty stomach, hot and dangerous. This was the snake that had ruined so many of his grandfather's people, killed his own parents, and almost been the death of him. It felt familiar, and that frightened him . "Why are they so worried about spies?"

One of the younger men pointed at Grant as well, asking a question.

"They want to know what happened to your hand."

"Tell them I was punching out spies." Grant made a fist and put on a furious expression.

Byambaa laughed, conveying his message, and the Mongol family grinned back at him. "They are worried about things going on in the area. Some people have disappeared around here. Some Chinese have been asking questions, wanting to know about the land." He turned to the family again, and they spoke of something that wiped the joy from their faces, Byambaa's mirth evaporating. "Their neighbors' valley burned, but the neighbors fled. These people helped them return for their gers. Most of their things survived, but the fire moved too quickly—they could not get to the horses, but had to ride out on their motorcycles."

"Maybe here would be a good place to sing for the horses."

Byambaa squared his shoulders, and drew in a breath. He addressed them quietly, but the woman reached out and caught his arm, shaking him urgently, shaking her head just as fiercely. The conversation ranged back and forth, Byambaa looking increasingly puzzled, then his mouth set, and he said, "The first to disappear was their best singer, the best voice in Inner Mongolia, she says. He never came back."

"The Chinese would have needed a singer to interpret the songs."

"They're afraid for me."

Grant held up his injured fist. "Tell them I will punch out any spy who tries to take my friends."

A round of back-slapping ensued after this, and the gathering finally sat, crammed onto the beds, to eat a stew of mutton and drink the salty tea the woman had been stirring. When the vodka bottle had been passed around—doing away with the ceremony of the bowl, and giving Grant the chance to fake a swallow—they finally allowed Byambaa to sing.

The first time he'd heard the Mongolian, in the private room at a German restaurant, the songs sounded strange, otherworldly, as if the earth itself were speaking, but the effect jarred with their surroundings. Out here, before the appreciative audience of his kin, Byambaa's voice took on an expansive quality, his gaze unfocused, his hands still as his being focused on this. Like Nick when he was shooting, the act of singing absorbed Byambaa in a perfection of form.

After the song, more vodka, louder voices, a few more answers to Grant's questions, mixed in with rumors: they didn't know who had taken the singer; there had been some big project in the hills last year, but they didn't know what for—they'd had to move to poor pastures; they were told someone's dog had come home with a human leg, but they hadn't seen it; Chinese spies were to blame for everything from sheep that threw their lambs early to the theft of the bones of the earth.

"Dinosaur bones," Byambaa explained. "We believe they are born of the earth and meant to stay there. Scientists come and take them."

"Not Chinese spies?" Grant felt comfortably warm and full, the sinister weight of the vodka dragging down his limbs and making him stifle a yawn.

"Hard to say what to know, or to believe." Byambaa's eyes looked glossy, and he smothered a yawn of his own. "The brothers say we can sleep in their ger tonight, and they will stay here."

"Thank you," Grant said, smiling.

The gathering broke up at last, and Byambaa and Grant moved to the next ger, accompanied by a lantern to find their way. The bed was short, but comfortable enough. Grant curled himself into it, and let himself sink into sleep, into dreams of story-tellers and elders, a hogan filled with friends and with enemies, with some he couldn't tell.

The dogs began barking, and Grant's eyes snapped open to darkness. Vehicles? Voices? The door crashed open, a harsh light flooding the ger, and a voice shouted in Mandarin, "Grant Casey, on the ground! Hands on your head!"

Jolted out of bed, Grant staggered, blinded by the light.

"Down, get down!"

His head buzzed, the muzzle of a gun glinting, a rifle barrel pressed to his neck, shoving him onto his face, keeping him down. "Grant Casey, you are under arrest for the capital crime of murder. Do not move."

CHAPTER FORTY-THREE

"What's going on?" Byambaa shouted from across the room.

"I'm being arrested—stay here," Grant answered in English, his face scraping the rough carpet.

A foot slammed into his side and the gun pressed harder. "Quiet! Stay still."

Clamping his teeth against the pain, Grant kept his hands on his head. Someone seized his wrists, twisting them down, slapping on cuffs. The gun withdrew and he was dragged from the glare of the light into the darkness. Dogs howled and barked.

"Shut them up or I shoot!" A different voice.

They dragged him up and shoved him forward, stumbling. His shins struck metal and he fell against the side of a vehicle. Grant let it support him, breathing carefully. Two officers stood by the door of the brothers' ger, training powerful lights inside, one of them shouting at Byambaa, but Grant couldn't hear any reply. To the right, their Mongolian host stood in a pale robe, each hand grasping a dog by the ruff. His wife and younger son squinted out from the doorway, the elder son a bit further from them, his hands raised and a rifle at his feet. Four more officers covered the family with rifles of their own.

"Don't hurt them," Grant said in Mandarin. "They don't know anything. They only gave me hospitality." He pushed himself up, unsteadily, to his feet, but kept the posture of the prisoner: slumped shoulders, head tucked, signaling his lack of threat. At least until he figured out what the Hell was going on.

"Of course they are ignorant, they're Mongols," said one of the officers, drawing a snort of laughter from his partner.

"That is enough," said a new voice—new, and yet familiar. "There is no need for violence, not here."

Later then. Somewhere else. The leader had spoken from behind him, near the first of the two vehicles. The same lieutenant who had spoken to them at the hotel. So much for Huang's intimations of corruption—unless the guy was about to ask for money to release him.

"Get the prisoner in the car. Let's go."

The pair nearest Grant moved toward him, one gesturing with his gun, the other reaching out, but Grant slipped his grasp, ducking inside of his own accord. Cooperation made no difference. The one behind him shoved him down, hitting his head against the metal floor, then pulling him back by his collar and yanking a black sack over his head. Doors slammed and the car—a big army-style four-wheeler—lurched into motion, rocking Grant between the seats and taking off at a bone-jarring pace. Someone turned on a radio, blaring Asian rock music. Bad to worse. His heart thundered. Murder? Capital crime. The vehicle turned apparently at random, rattling him at every pass. The vodka and the mutton started a riot in his stomach. Were they actually driving in circles? Trying to disorient him. It seemed to be working. Grant forced himself to slow his racing thoughts, to breathe, to relax every muscle that didn't need to stay tense. The jangling music made it hard to focus, to think of anything else. Grant cast himself back to his training days: simulated abduction and hostage situations. The enemy would try to get you to crack, to give up your friends, your mission, your HQ. Apparently, the Chinese had taken the same class, but from the other perspective. A warm sensation at his back told him that the bandage had failed: he was bleeding again.

After way too long, they stopped and the radio snapped off, letting in a blessed silence. The opposite door slammed open and hands grabbed his arms, hauling him out headfirst, dragging him. Gravel or broken stone, not grass, not the dirt of the desert. Someone shoved him against a wall, pinning him, while other hands groped down his arms, chest, legs, prodding and jabbing, finding and removing his knives. Orders were passed, curt and effective, who formed a perimeter, who stayed on guard. So they weren't at a station, certainly not back in Yinchuan, nor any settlement large enough to have a dog to bark or a car to drive by. The middle of nowhere. Not the place for a formal criminal investigation.

Pulled free of the wall, Grant passed from the chill of the night air into a stuffy chamber with a stone or concrete floor, a few cracks. They pushed him into a chair, then a second shackle linked his ankle, a rattle of chain, the other ankle. Locked to a bar of the chair. He shifted his feet a little, feeling the pull between, the slide of the chain against metal. He had about a foot, no more. His fingers traced the edge of the metal seat he sat on, a pillar up one side, flakes that gave way under his fingers. Rust. Interesting.

"Be still." A pistol cocked, the barrel nudging his temple.

Grant obeyed. The sack over his head felt like wool, scratchy and hot, so thick that light didn't penetrate. If he shifted his gaze straight down, he saw dim light that suddenly brightened. When a hand yanked off the sack, he was ready, eyes shut, the full-force of that bright light heating his face. He let his eyes blink open slowly, adjusting, squinting, but avoiding the temporary blindness they sought to induce.

A powerful light on a tripod stood nearby, aimed at Grant's face. Beyond it, the room was small, maybe ten feet square, windowless, but made of old brick, very old.

"Have you notified the embassy of my arrest, sir?"

The lieutenant, seated at a small desk in front of him, hands clasped on top of a file, blinked twice, his glance flicked to someone past Grant's left shoulder. "Are you even here legally, Mr. Casey? Is your embassy aware of your presence? Is your government?"

"Sir, I am an American citizen. If this is a legal action, the embassy must be notified."

"You are known to be a member of American Special Forces intelligence. The government will deny your very existence. Certainly they will not be eager to assist."

How could they possibly know that? Grant's record, like all intelligence records, was sealed. Not that he'd been very intelligent today. The gas tank had been full, the auxiliary tank undamaged. The vehicle had been sabotaged, and probably tagged with a tracer while it was parked the night before, effectively separating Grant from his team, and especially from the powerful Huang. He'd been set up—why? "What am I accused of?"

"The murders of four citizens of Yinchuan. Subsequently, you returned to the scene for unknown reasons, resulting in the loss of your own jeep and a fire which destroyed much of the evidence."

Grant made himself stay cool. "And resulted in the injury of my associate. What kind of an idiot do you think I am, sir?"

Lieutenant Ma's eyes flared just slightly, flickering back to the man behind Grant. A supervisor of some kind? Or worse, secret police?

"As we told you in the hotel, Mr. Huang's pilot spotted the crash and requested that we investigate on the ground. When we did so, we were attacked." Ambushed, just as he had been tonight. Why? Compared with Liz or even Byambaa, Grant didn't know shit—he couldn't lead them to the tomb.

"Why are you here, Mr. Casey? Why did Huang come to Yinchuan?"

"Looking for items to collect and investments to place, sir. As he told you."

"I recall something else we were told, that you had brought your equipment to the desert to aid a local citizen. I think this is a lie. I believe you intended to steal that monument, and the dead men, your confederates, failed you in an earlier attempt. In retaliation, and to silence them, you killed them."

"Sir, the widow will testify that we did not know the location or existence of the stone before we saw her table in the marketplace. By then, her husband and the other men were already dead."

Ma surged to his feet, his face painted with harsh light into a demon's mask, pointing into Grant's face. "How do you know? How do you know when they died if you were not involved with their deaths?"

"Condition of the bodies, sir. When we arrived, it was clear they had already been dead at least a couple of days. The airport will confirm when Huang's plane landed. We weren't even here yet."

"Then it is inconvenient that the crash of your own jeep destroyed the evidence. Unless the evidence would not confirm your story. I suggest you tell me the truth."

"I'm trying, sir." Then he remembered Nick's remark. "D. A. Silverberg, the American woman at the hospital, has photographs of the crash site taken from the helicopter before we got there."

That drew the officer's frown, and Grant pressed his advantage. "You must have questioned her about what she saw, sir. She would be happy to provide the images."

A whisper of wind, then something struck hard from behind, knocking over Grant's chair and throwing him to the floor. Pain shot through his left cheek and elbow and blood streamed into his mouth. "Do not imply that the People's Security Service are not capable of doing their job," said a voice behind him.

Grant coughed and spat blood. He tried to turn his head far enough to catch a glimpse of the other man. Here he'd thought good cop/bad cop was an American game. That voice sounded familiar too, but distantly. Not a supervisor, not like that, and he said "*their* job," not "*our* job." "Then let them do it. At the station, where we should be."

"Be quiet," the voice ordered, and a gun cocked.

Lieutenant Ma stood straighter. "Pick him up."

"He will not cooperate, Lieutenant," said the other man, switching to Mandarin. "He is here illegally, as you said, to steal our cultural heritage."

"And what if he is a spy? You think that killing him will not draw American attention?"

Apparently they didn't realize that Grant understood Chinese. Then the pain in his face receded as a new thought stung him. What if they did know, and this was just part of the game, trying to get Grant to give up his operational objectives? Three men in a remote location, in a windowless room, the only guards on the outside. Who'd know the difference if only two men came out? He'd been in firefights before; in infiltrations where, if someone found him out, he'd be shot on the spot; but every other time his life had been on the line, at least he had a chance, however slim, of fighting back. Tonight, he lay on foreign ground, bound and injured, at the feet of the men who would kill him, and he didn't even know why.

Grant scooted awkwardly onto his side, sucked in a breath, and managed a glimpse of the other guy. A glimpse was all he needed: square jaw, sunglasses, nicked ear, a gun aimed at Grant's head, just as it had been in Cambridge, and again near the overturned jeep. Third time was the charm, wasn't it.

CHAPTER FORTY-FOUR

Gooney had been moved to a private room at the far end of an upper floor, with its own row of benches. A square window showed murky light that could be midnight in a city of lights, or could be closer to dawn. Liz sat in the hospital corridor, head in her hands, while Nick paced, his prosthetic leg clicking softly as he moved. He stopped with sudden interest, and Liz looked up to find Huang moving toward them from the elevator, his normally smooth demeanor pierced by the news, his driver trailing after him.

"The police station says nothing. They pretend not to understand a Hong Kong accent, and will not give me access to Lieutenant Ma."

"No local embassy," Liz said, "and the Beijing one isn't picking up." She gripped her phone like a lifeline, as she'd been doing ever since Byambaa's call a few hours ago. At least they hadn't taken him, too. Immediately, guilt followed on this thought. Grant Casey wouldn't even be here if not for her. She called him. If not for him, she wouldn't even know her own danger. She would likely be dead.

"There's a good chance he's not at the station," Nick said softly. "They could've taken him in yesterday, nice and easy, if they wanted him at the station. They didn't. They came at night, heavily armed and set for capture. This isn't a misunderstanding. It's no accident they waited to get him alone, or nearly so. This fucking stinks." The shift in his tone made Liz jumpy.

"Like a rat," D. A. said. "Call Byambaa, is the sun up out there yet? We should get the bird in the air and go find him."

Liz poked the number and waited, but the call went straight to voicemail. She stared at the screen in despair. "He said his phone was low on batteries. I think it's dead." She flinched at her own word, and felt the intake of breath all around her.

Just along the hall, the driver, Zhen, made a soft sound. At his side, Gonsalves' room stood slightly open, a hand on the inside handle. D. A. hurried back, her curls bouncing, but the door opened all the way, and the detective stood there, his face red and glossy with ointment, his left forearm encased in a cast. He wore a hospital gown as if it were his uniform. "Where's Casey?"

"Arrested, or so they said. He was taken from a Mongolian ger camp in the middle of the night by a bunch of armed Chinese officers." D. A. folded her arms. "I don't think you should be out of bed."

"You think I could sleep through all this racket?" The detective's voice had a new rasp, from smoke inhalation or from pain, Liz couldn't be sure.

"I didn't mean sleep."

He waved that off and leaned against the wall. "Somebody snatched Casey. Not the police, or they would've made a show of legality—at least, not alone. Somebody wants him dead, off the scent. Somebody's trying to stop us getting there."

"Say something we don't know—or get the fuck back to bed." Nick's hands clenched and relaxed at his sides.

"We gotta get there, now, while they think we're distracted."

"And leave the chief behind." Nick's body tensed, his voice at a growl.

"Gentlemen, please, we must move with caution." Huang sidled closer as if to get between them, and Liz imagined blood spattering his clean safari khakis.

"What would he say, Nick? What do you think Casey wants us to do? Ride in to the rescue? Woo-hoo!" Gonsalves pushed off from the wall, meeting Nick's eye. "What's rule number one in the Unit, Norton—you know this, you know the answer."

D. A.'s shoulders sank, and she gazed at Nick with something like pity.

"I'm guessing it isn't no man left behind?" Liz ventured.

"We don't jeopardize the mission for one man," said Gonsalves. "Especially not the chief. Especially not if that's what the goddamn adversary wants us to do."

Nick exploded toward him, both women jumping at once, shouting his name. He wrapped a fist in Gonsalves' gown, the other fist balled up for a swing. "You don't give a damn if he dies! You'd throw a damn party."

Leveling his gaze, Gonsalves spread his hands. "He saved my hide out there—what's left of it—you think I don't know that? Yeah, okay, he pisses me off. That doesn't mean I want him dead. What are the odds he already is?"

"I surely hope you are mistaken," Huang offered.

"What are the odds?" Gonsalves let his right hand down, resting it on Nick's broad shoulder. "Nick. They expect us to go for him. Isn't that what they always do in the movies? They expect us to be blown to pieces by the fact we've lost him. From what I can see, you guys already are. He's the chief, I understand. He wouldn't be alive if not for your sacrifice, Nick, and you guys are both carrying that. Right now, you need to put it down. Go to pieces, go after him, we're dancing to their song. Finish this damn quest and crow about it—and, if he's still alive, they got no reason to kill him."

Nick shook off the hand and let go, withdrawing, but not standing down. Liz wasn't sure anyone but Grant could get him to do that.

D. A. spoke softly. "Look at it this way, we need to pick up Byambaa no matter what, and he's on the scene of the crime, right?

We head out there, we see what we can see. Maybe we learn more information and make a better decision."

"You're talking like the decision is made," said Nick. "It's not. Chief wants you sent home, Gooney. I don't know what you said to him, you son-of-a-bitch, but he wants you out. I'm the one who argued for you to stay. I thought we'd need you—but not to hand down orders that we leave the chief behind enemy lines."

"D. A.'s right. We can go to Byambaa. If Grant's not in the city, that's where we need to start anyway, right?" Liz said.

Gonsalves tried a smile that apparently hurt his scorched cheeks. "I'll get my shirt."

"You shouldn't—" D. A. started, but Nick cut her off.

"Oh, yeah, he's coming. So I can ditch him in the desert a thousand miles from home with a gun that only has one bullet. Fucker." Turning on his heel, Nick stalked down the hall.

CHAPTER FORTY-FIVE

"That's him, Lieutenant, the man who tried to kill us at the jeep," Grant said, as if it mattered, now that he could see they were working together.

"Your description was quite accurate," the officer answered casually. In Chinese, he said, "Please, pick him up. We have an interrogation to continue."

The other man held his gun outstretched, aimed at Grant's head. Abruptly, he swung it upward toward the officer. Grant lashed out as he pulled the trigger, the chained chair swinging around and catching the shooter's legs, staggering him.

The bullet cracked into stone—through and through, or a total miss, Grant couldn't tell. Lieutenant Ma dropped with a cry. The shooter took a step forward, shooting again and Grant flailed the chair at him, then dragged it back. He caught the back with his chained hands, braced his bare feet on the bar underneath and shoved hard with his legs. A bullet shattered the stone near his head. Another kick, and the chair broke apart, the chain sliding free.

"Come, come!" shouted the lieutenant. The shooter darted forward, then drew back, holding a gun in each hand now.

With a flex of his core, Grant curled into himself and pulled his joined hands around his legs to the front. He leapt up and rocked the tripod lamp into the shooter, knocking him off balance. Another bullet, two, three, but his left hand gun rattled away.

Snatching the weapon, Grant dropped behind the desk. The lieutenant lay there, clutching a hand to his bleeding side, slumping over, his eyes barely flickering open. Blood streamed from a gash in his scalp as well.

The door flew wide and four more men stood there.

"He has the lieutenant! He shot him," the shooter announced.

Grant went for it. He wrapped his grip around the officer's upper arm and dragged him to his feet, the gun held at the back of his head. In Mandarin, he said, "Step back, drop your guns, or he dies!"

The shooter stepped carefully, keeping his back to the wall as Grant moved himself and his hostage around the desk.

"Do as he says," the lieutenant managed.

The officers at the door split, a few guns thumping to the ground, then Grant was between them, hurrying as best he could, half-supporting the wounded man before he thrust him behind the wheel of the four-wheeler. He did a quick assessment, guessed the guy was in no condition to drive, and shoved him over into the passenger seat. With two shots he took out the side tires on the other car. "Keys!"

In the rearview, dimly lit by a pair of outside lights, he saw the officers re-assembling, snatching their guns from the ground.

The prisoner fumbled toward a pocket, and Grant snatched the ring of keys, jammed one into the ignition and stomped on the pedal, sending the vehicle rushing backward toward the re-forming line of police. They shouted, shots flying wild, one of them shattering the back window. Flinging it into gear, Grant steered the vehicle out, thumping over ruts and stones, getting out of there as fast as he could.

"Which way to the mountains?" He shouted over the noise of wind through the broken windows, then he glanced over. The lieutenant slumped in his seat, shaking. Going into shock. Shit.

The light of moon and stars illuminated a rolling plain ahead and left, and to the right, an uneven wall, too smooth in some places to be natural, too rough in others to be modern. The Great Wall of China, made to keep the barbarians out. Epic fail.

Grant swerved from its shadow and took off across the plains, the mountains dimly seen ahead of him, with rolling valleys and occasional outcrops in between. Behind one of these, he rocked to a stop and searched the keyring until he found the one for his cuffs, and another for the chain at his ankles, his bare feet throbbing from the effort of breaking the chair. Tossing his chains into the back seat, Grant eased down the policeman and stripped off his jacket. Through-and-through below the ribs, but not too far from his side. The guy might have dodged organ damage. He'd be better once the bleeding stopped. Grant tore the man's shirt and wrapped it tightly around the wound, applying pressure where it was needed. As Grant handled him, Ma woke with a gasp, staring into his eyes. Grant tucked the man's jacket around his chest, replacing a layer of warmth.

"Who was that man? Why did he try to kill you?" Grant demanded in Chinese as he prodded the scalp wound. No sign of fracture. Good.

"Yang, Assistant Minister of Antiquities. He shot me because he thinks I may believe you." The man blinked rapidly, his pulse pounding. "He is former army. Like you."

"I don't think that's a compliment." He performed a quick assessment. "Does it hurt anywhere else?"

"No, not a compliment." The man gulped for breath, then said, "No other injury."

"Good." Grant squeezed back behind the steering wheel, leaving the lights off, and set out southwest. "How far north did we come?"

Ma said, "You were to be disoriented."

"Didn't last. How far?"

"Eighty miles." The lieutenant protected his injury with his arm, watching Grant sidelong. "Why take me? Now they believe him, that you have shot me."

"If we stayed, he'd've shot us both, blaming me for yours, or claiming your death as an accident. Tell me I'm wrong."

The officer gave what might have been a laugh. "I think you are not wrong. Why do they want you dead? Not merely detained."

"Minister of Antiquities?" With a knowledge of the archaeological sites in the area, maybe even one they'd rather never be found.

"Assistant."

"Do you have other units in the area? Officers on call?"

"Eight men should be enough to hold you." Again, that ghost of laughter. "Thankfully, this, too, is wrong. I say again that now they will believe Yang."

"He knows the truth, and knows that we both know it, too. Now he's scared—"Grant didn't know the word for 'shitless' and guess it was probably better to leave that out—"because we're talking. Unless he thinks you're dead. You're going to be a problem for them."

"Minister Jin called off our conversation at the hotel. He told me that Yang would help me, and suggested you are the murderer."

Minister Jin, and his assistant, Yang. Two names he didn't have before. Grant played the informant game, and gave something back. "Those men in the jeep were poisoned. There were a few birds dead nearby, probably from trying to eat the bodies, or from exposure to whatever took them down. The jeep ran off the road when the driver died, not the other way around."

"This sounds strange."

Grant glanced at him, Ma's eyes now avoiding his. The cop still didn't quite trust him. "D. A. took pictures that will show the birds in place, before the fire. Can your office do—"he shrugged and filled in with the English word, "Toxicology. Testing for drugs and poisons in a body?"

"Yes, with suspicion of wrong-doing. Why poison them?"

"Those empty gas cans. There's a valley near where you found me, burned, including a few horses that died. My guess is the guys in the jeep burned it, on purpose."

"To what end?" The lieutenant took a few ragged breaths. "No use for arson in the wilderness."

"I need to get you help. You, alive, can clear me. At least get your people off my tail, right?" Grant saw an edge of light to the east. "Be careful—they'll be gunning for you."

"You distract me with my pain, my danger. You say poison, murder, arson. Tell me why you say this."

Apparently, the pain wasn't distraction enough. Grant slowed a little. Something moved in the grass outside, paralleling or maybe converging with their course, but still some distance away. "Did you have other vehicles there, besides the cars?"

"A motorcycle. Looters, with shovels. Why do you say arson?"

"I forgot about the shovels," Grant said, seeking a track through the darkness. "The man under the rock, his widow gave us his papers, everything he'd been working on in the last year or so. Apparently, he was doing business in shovels—he'd ordered over a thousand of them."

Ma coughed so hard that Grant stopped the vehicle and caught the other man's wrist, checking his pulse, staring at his face. Sweat sheened his features, but he bunched his hand into a fist, mastering his reaction. "A thousand shovels. You are certain?"

"Are you investigating a shovel-smuggling operation?" Grant released him. His pulse strong, investigator's mind clearly engaged.

"Why arson?"

"I can't tell you."

"Yet you are not on a mission. Not a spy."

"God's honest truth. Not a spy. Are you?"

A sharp breath, then, "No."

"But not just police."

"No."

"So neither of us is revealing everything." Grant smiled and punched the vehicle into motion. "Somebody's tracking us, to the east, between me and the sun. This car—it's got a tracer?"

Ma gave a slight shake of his head and shifted, wincing, using his right hand to pull out a cell phone. "This." He pushed himself up awkwardly and held it out.

"Are you Internal Affairs? Anti-corruption?"

Silence. The cell phone bobbed in his hand as they bounced across the plain. The guy needed to stop, to be still so he had a chance to recover. Grant could chuck the phone and keep driving—to where? But that phone was also Ma's lifeline, the most surefire way for him to get the help he needed and survive, for both of their sakes.

Grant pitched right and slewed down into a shallow draw near a series of stones or mounds barely visible in the dim light. He took the gun and the phone, leaving the door ajar, and slipped low through the grass to scramble up one of the mounds, watching to the east. The movement grew, shapes separating from the shadows, two of them, bulky and moving smoothly and quietly. As they approached, the one in the lead shifted shape again. A man on horseback, rising in his stirrups, something coming to his hand, then, as the sun edged above the horizon, the distinctive shape of a mounted archer, his bow drawn, an arrow aimed in Grant's direction.

CHAPTER FORTY-SIX

Jin's phone buzzed and he woke instantly, eyes staring at the ceiling. Yang must have finished the American. Excellent. It buzzed again, and Jin frowned. That was the wrong tone. He tapped the line open.

"How is my brilliant husband?" a voice purred.

"Trying to sleep. Have you been drinking?"

"There is little peace without you here." A clink and a swallow. "Mingbao brought home a perfect test today."

"Yesterday," Jin corrected with a glance at the clock. Nearly dawn.

"He is so like you. So smart. Was she like me?"

That stung, a probing blow from a beloved adversary. Jin deliberately misunderstood. "She will be. She will be beautiful, graceful and kind." Kind. Did Chunhua even know when she was being cruel? Did she mean to be? Jin schooled his voice to sweetness. "But drinking could hurt her, darling, you know that. Please don't do it again."

The decisive rap of a glass set sharply down. "This is the day that

I drink—the only day I drink. You know that. Someone should celebrate her birthday."

He did not ask whose, but closed his eyes, centering himself. Could she possibly know the truth? So many things would have to go wrong, to be revealed, for that to happen. Did he even know the truth himself? Since Guo's intrusion, he dared not ask. "Yes," he told his wife. "Someone should celebrate."

"Will you? Where ever it is that you are, doing your great work, will you honor our daughter?"

His great work. Today might indeed be the culmination of that work, and she asked him for this. His anger was fleeting. She asked for so little. She had been so patient, so charming with his colleagues, so self-sacrificing for their son, for his career. "I will find a way, Chunhua."

She sighed, sounding almost happy, and hung up. Jin clicked off the line. Curious, that an archaeologist should so focus on the future, while his wife gazed into the past. When the new baby came, she would join him in today, he was certain of it.

Jin rose and dressed in light clothing, then moved through a series of poses, taking them slowly, then falling into the rhythm, faster and faster: Kick, strike, slide forward, strike again, block, kick, kick harder. Honor her. Strike, kick, faster, until his movement was a blur, too fast for him to think and move, too smooth for him to remember and strike at the same time. Celebrate her birthday. The day that nearly killed his wife, and his marriage. Slide, block, dodge, slam that fist forward. From that day to this one, he fought to keep them, those things most dear to him. Chunhua sacrificed for him, for their future. And now, that future arrived. Kick, duck, lunge.

The door of his hotel room swung open. Lunge, thrust. His fist shot out, his arm like iron aimed at the throat of Captain Guo.

"I heard movement. I thought you were being attacked," the captain said. His hand gripped his sidearm, but had not yet drawn the weapon.

Jin could have disarmed him in an instant. He snapped back his fist and drew himself up into a line of darkness, threat and power. "Thank you for your concern. I did not expect you now."

"Councilor Xi received your progress reports. It seems that the time for action is imminent."

"It is not I who have been still until now." Jin bowed to the captain. "I have prepared for the day. Perhaps you should do likewise." He reached and shut the door, leaving the captain on the outside. Where he belonged.

CHAPTER FORTY-SEVEN

Liz wept silently into her hands. Byambaa—gone. Where? When? The Mongols weren't saying, or they didn't know—which was worse. Used to the friendly welcome of nomads, Liz felt the weight of the family's suspicion. She wished Nick were down here with her, ready to use that soothing voice. Instead, she had Gonsalves, moving stiffly, speaking little. He did clumsily set a hand on her shoulder as they climbed back into the jeep. Zhen sat behind the wheel, silent and efficient as ever.

"We're going on, kiddo. We got to. Or they win. He'll find us, you gotta believe that."

She flopped her head in assent, wiping her eyes, only to have the wind draw more tears as they set off into the mountains. *Wind cuts through a channel.* How the Hell were they supposed to find that? And without their singer, would they even recognize, *the cliffs join in the singing*? What if Byambaa were right, and the whole map idea was a crock? What if that's why he had left, not wanting to face her with his doubts? They had taken some of the supplies from the stopped jeep into their own, and now followed the shadow of the helicopter as it roved into the foothills and higher.

"What are we looking for?" Gonsalves shouted.

She sniffled, swallowed, and answered, "A narrow channel in the stone, someplace the wind cuts through."

"God, that could be anywhere." He held the radio in his hand, staring at it thoughtfully. "Well, no, not really. Which way's the wind blowing?"

Liz shrugged. "You mean, which way does the wind usually blow?"

He snapped on the radio. "D. A. Prevailing winds—are they always the same direction around here?" He listened for a while, then, "Yeah, so we're looking for something narrow, a slot canyon maybe, or a notch?" He glanced at Liz, an eyebrow twitching up, then crinkling with a wince of pain.

"She's right you know, you should be in the hospital," Liz told him.

"Hell with that. This one time, we had set up a cover story, man in need of surgery, one of us was a doctor, so we could infiltrate a hospital and abduct another patient, and they'd never figure it out." He took a swallow of water, and went on, a bit slow and gravelly still, "Our fake patient would do a switch-er-oo and take the place of the target's guard, all that bullshit. I'm supposed to be the doctor, right? because I speak the language best, so I push Casey in on a gurney, all moaning and groaning, playing the patient. And some local doc comes over to do an examination. I gave him my spiel." He took another swallow.

Li was in no mood to hear some rambling anecdote, but she could hear in his voice how much it was costing him to tell it, so she focused on his face, his words. "What did he say?"

"That was the thing, I didn't know. He was agreeing with, me, right? Then he throws in one or two words I didn't know—I could hardly download a whole medical dictionary in my brain, right? So I agree with whatever that guy's saying, and the next thing I know, this local is getting ready to give Casey a full alien probe-job, if you know what I mean. Shit, Casey starts screaming and chanting his prayers, and the doc backs off long enough for us to get through to the surgery." Gonsalves starts out with a grin, remembering, then it falls away. "Casey kept it together through the whole thing, dropped the guard and took over. Wasn't 'til we got back to base with the target that he slugged me. Looked like he wanted to ream me a new one, like that local doc was gonna do to him."

The detective blinked, his eyes a little glossy. He took another long swallow of water. "I deserved it that time."

"He sounds like a real professional."

"Sometimes." Gonsalves stared into the distance, grunting a little as they drove over ruts and stones.

"Wouldn't you have been more comfortable in the helicopter?"

"Not with Nick in there. That bird's not big enough for the both of us." The radio crackled, and he listened. "Now you got it. That's gotta narrow down the possibilities. Keep in mind the wagons had to get there, with all the treasure and shit."

The rough road for the next hour precluded much conversation, Gonsalves conferring with D. A. about this or that possibility. Then they suddenly rose to a high plateau. A steep drop-off formed a narrow trench along the far side, with a trickle of water at the bottom. "That it?" the detective pointed.

Zhen stopped and they piled out of the jeep, the helicopter landing nearby. Could it be? This would be the fourth possibility they had found worth stopping for. Dusty and tired, feeling Gonsalves' pain whenever he moved, Liz tried to put off her discouragement as she walked over, then dropped to her knees, listening. Nick killed the helicopter engine, and both vehicles ticked into stillness. She pulled out her mp3 player and brought up the eighth song, listening to that, longing for Byambaa's voice to interpret what she heard. She shut it off and listened to the narrow valley. Nothing. This channel lay too low in the ground, shadowed by other ridges and ravines—it didn't catch the wind. She slumped back on her heels and stared up at the mountains that grew around them. It could be anywhere. They guessed that the clues would be equidistant, but that was only a guess, after all. The sun rose full in the sky now, erasing shadows, dancing on the long grass and illuminating the pine trees on the opposite slope. Erasing most shadows, anyway. A thin edge of stone still shadowed the plateau, pierced at its center to let through a gleam of light.

Liz stood up and walked over. It wasn't the kind of thing that could be seen from above—you had to be on the ground to notice the gap. She scrambled up the slope and caught hold of the edge of the rock, feeling the wind as she rose beyond the sheltering cliffs. Cool and delicious. Liz climbed a little higher, until her own shadow covered the sun's gleam and she saw through a window of stone down and aside, back into the arid landscape of the lower slopes. The rugged landscape dazzled her eyes with sunlight and pale stone, a sweep of rubble led between the arms of a narrow gorge to the face of a steep cliff. She squinted against the light and distance, making out a level edge low down, just over the height of the fill, a lintel carved into the rock. Unless her eyes deceived her.

"What you got?" Gonsalves called up to her.

Liz descended slowly, pointing. "Maybe nothing, maybe a carving of some kind."

"More of those animals?"

She shook her head, and started walking, following the line of sight down the slope. The jeep trailed after her, loaded with the rest of the team. The plateau narrowed, emerging into full light, the grass ebbing until they stood more in desert than in the steppes. She started scrambling over the fallen stones.

"Hey, watch out there, lady," Nick called after her, loping along the top of the ridge. "Somebody wasn't so lucky." He pointed a little ahead of her. Weathered bones showed at the edge of the mound of stones and earth. Probably a goat or sheep caught by the rock fall. As she drew nearer, picking her way, Liz made out the two long bones, the jumble of smaller ones, the dull glint of metal. She reached down into the hollow of the stone and picked it up. An arrowhead.

Nick gave a low whistle.

"It looks genuine," she said, holding it up, but that wasn't what he was looking at.

Ahead of them, partially exposed in the end face of the narrow ravine rose a stone doorway, two posts and a lintel, carved with patterns like clouds or mountains, beneath them in the shadows, a bronze door.

"You found it, Liz. Holy Moly, Ms., Kirchner, there it is."

Liz found her eyes once more glazed with tears as Nick gave a whoop of excitement that echoed from the mountains around them. *And the cliffs join in the singing.*

CHAPTER FORTY-EIGHT

Liz, Huang and D. A. scrambled down the slope, stumbling and eager, to the door while Nick and Zhen watched from above, and Gonsalves resolutely scanned the horizon with binoculars. How he could ignore the discovery being made behind him, Liz couldn't fathom. She had promised Huang the first entrance —but first they had to figure out if they could even get inside, and if they could do so while maintaining the integrity of the site: it would need to have a thorough and proper archaeological study.

D. A. videotaped the approach and descent using a big, black camera that looked like a classic professional photographer's tool, but shot both video and stills. Her lens focused on Liz while she explained the songs and clues that had led them here, then she followed her down. An overhang to one side had deflected most of the rock fall, extending into a ridge for a while, then blending back into the mountainside. Tough-looking pine trees clung here and there, and formed clumps on the eastern side, where the more gradual slope would allow vehicle traffic, like the cart that had carried the khan. Had these very trees witnessed that moment? Pale old branches littered the slope around and under the stones—or so she thought until she drew closer. Bones, most of them clearly human. Arms reaching along the ground, skulls crushed by fallen rock, all of them weathered and yellow. Here and there, she caught glints of metal, the weapons, tools or personal belongings of the fallen.

"Wow. It's like a war zone. Seriously." D. A. focused on a skull not far from the edge of the rocks. "Gooney said the khan ordered everyone killed after his burial, the people who made the tomb, and the soldiers who killed them—to make sure no one would ever find it."

"And now here we are." The three of them stood at last on level ground, with drifts of rusty pine needles and old grass at the base of the broad, bronze door. A skeleton slumped against it, crumpled into itself, and Liz shuddered.

"No lake though," D. A. remarked. "Wasn't that one of the rumors, too? That they diverted a river to make a lake over the entrance to the tomb?"

"There are a lot of rumors." She stared at the skeleton, the empty, black stare of the skull over its missing teeth. "I guess some of them are true. Whatever earth covered the remains probably weathered away in the last few centuries, and that ridge means the only way to spot the door would be coming up from the direction we did. It was probably even less visible before the rockfall broke up the ridge."

"Chief should be here," D. A. sighed. "Byambaa, too."

Liz nodded, and Huang, at her side, bowed his head. "They will be located, I am sure. I have contacts working on this already. Please be assured that we shall do everything that may be done."

"We've got incoming! Looks like a motorcycle," Gonsalves called from above.

"A lot of nomads use them," Liz answered. "He's probably just trying to figure out why we left a helicopter up there on the plateau." But still...

The cast bronze face of a monster stared out with bulbous eyes from the center of the door. It wore a crown of human skulls, stylized, and apparently spiked through with spears. Its mouth gaped with sharp teeth and a thick ring under its mouth served as a handle.

Wisps of pale fabric clung to the ring, the remains of offering scarves left as a blessing to the dead. It was beautifully preserved, probably because of the sheltering doorway and cliffside, not to mention the dry climate. The door stood about seven feet tall, and three feet across, with a pattern of round, raised bosses surrounding the demon. Liz tried to ignore the skeleton slumped at the base of the door. She stood before the culmination of her research, not to mention these last few days of terror and excitement. "The monster is called a baht, it's supposed to chase away evil spirits."

"Right," said D. A. She shot a few stills. "So...who's knocking?"

"Or are we the very spirits they sought to dissuade?" Huang gazed at the door with something like awe. He reached out to touch the stone-carved pillars, then, very gently, set his fingers on the cheek of the monster. Liz drew back, her heart sinking, but they had an agreement, and he had certainly more than fulfilled his part with a private jet, sumptuous meals, fine hotels, cars, jeeps and a helicopter.

"Our biker's on the fly again, driving south. Coast is clear so far." Gonsalves sounded better now, as if the task gave him strength.

"Miss Kirschner." Liz and Huang shared a glance, then he motioned her forward. "Together?"

She grinned. "Together." She stepped up beside him, their hands on the great ring, then she threw her arms around him. "Thank you!" She gave him a quick hug and drew back again, as he chuckled, his cheeks warming.

Together, they lifted the ring and turned it. Inside the door, something groaned, squealed, and gave, the door easing inward, letting out a breath of musty air. The skeleton clattered to the side, sprawling into the door it had died to protect.

Gasping, she lurched back into Huang's steadying hand. He offered a reassuring pressure against her shoulder, the weight of life and dreams fulfilled. Liz fumbled a flashlight out of her pack and flicked it on, aiming at the narrow slice of darkness ahead, the disarticulated bones spreading before her, the skull still rocking slightly.

"Anything about booby-traps in those legends?" D. A. murmured.

Liz shook her head, but found she was holding her breath, and the flashlight jiggled a little. She took a deep breath and stepped forward, carefully stepping around the bones. "Try not to disturb anything else—just document it."

Something glittered there, a bit of metal or maybe even a gemstone. She reached forward, and D. A.'s camera flashed, capturing the moment, illuminating the chamber beyond. It winked with reflections from a thousand tiny sources. Wrapping both hands around the shaft of the flashlight, she stepped inside. Motes of dust, disturbed by the opening of the door, shimmered in the path of her light. The tomb seemed to be intact—a thrill for even an amateur archaeologist like her.

She startled, her light jumping, then steadied her heart and shone the light more deliberately. Pole arms, spears and swords decorated the walls, representing a dozen or more different styles and nations. Probably weapons captured from their enemies, including Chinese fireworks and long staves with more fireworks attached. A rank of soldiers stood before her, two dozen figures in armor, bows at their feet where the dead had released them. Unlike the skeletons outside, these were mummified, with dark, dry skin stretched over their ancient bones. In some places, damage or crumpled skin revealed hints of the bone beneath. They wore armor of leather and metal plates, helmets with dangling cheek-flaps and furred brims capped their tilted skulls. Tarnished silver belts winked at their waists, the mark of the khan's elite bodyguard. Wooden pillars propped them up inside the armor, and they stood in two groups, with an aisle between, leading to a dark opening at the back.

"Guards," she whispered. Still at their posts, after eight hundred years. She walked carefully, reverently, between them toward the arch at the back, where her flashlight gleamed off of gold.

Niches lined the circular chamber, every one of them filled with something golden or silver and glittering: crowns encrusted with jewels, some with fabric caps slumped or darkened by time. Looking at these, Liz felt a knot form in her stomach, hoping she hadn't damaged anything just by opening the door. Well, they wouldn't stay long—just long enough to capture some images, to document the contents and their discovery. They could split up, then, sending the copter back to Yinchuan to arrange for security and excavation. God, she hadn't even considered what should happen next. She hardly dared envision this moment, never mind the flurry of publicity and activity that was bound to follow such a major discovery.

A second flashlight beam joined hers, along with the flashes of the camera, then a steady glow as D. A. switched over to video again. In the strange light, Huang's eyes gleamed. He feasted on the sights around them, the dozens of crowns above, the ancient chests below, the heaps of golden coins and stacks of other relics.

"I expected the tomb might be more austere," Huang said, still speaking softly in the presence of the dead.

A third chamber opened off this one, both richly carved with images of deer, horses and wolves. Between the rows of carvings ran a strip of murals showing great battles between vast hordes of Mongols and armies of Persians with curved blades, Chinese with lances tipped by fire, and even European knights, their unfamiliar armor interpreted by an Oriental gaze.

"They're beautiful," said D. A., still following, tracking the murals down one side, then the other.

"Probably painted by Chinese captives. The nomadic Mongols didn't have much tradition of wall paintings like this."

"So the painter is probably out there in the rocks, with an arrow in his chest for all his hard work." D. A. snorted, then sneezed.

From behind them came the stumbling sound of hurried feet, then Gonsalves shouting, "Incoming—four jeeps, coming fast from the south." He caught his breath, then said, "Jay-sus. Will you look at this!"

"We are, Gooney," D. A. replied.

"Better hurry it up, we need some kind of show of force—or maybe some of you guys should get in the copter with the proof of discovery, in case these guys are here to shut us down."

"Good plan. Come on—quick tour."

Huang sighed lightly. "After eight hundred years, it seems the khan deserves more than a hurry, but we shall do our best."

They pushed on, down a passage, to a chamber even more grandly embellished, containing a yellow silk ger, practically identical to the ones at the false mausoleum. Liz frowned, remembering her encounter with Nergui, the Darkhad guardsman, and his reaction to her questions. His people knew something—maybe they even knew about this. Had they seen it? And might their descriptions have influenced the building of the fake?

Huang passed her, stepping up to the yellow ger and opening the curtain to one side, then shining his light inside. It fell upon a stone plinth, topped with a coffin of tarnished silver, richly embellished with images of the steppes.

She fought the urge to cross herself, a habit from childhood, and one so wildly inappropriate here that it made her smile. "May the Eternal Blue Sky shine forever upon you," she whispered in Mongolian.

From outside, Gonsalves shouted, "Now—come out now! It's the fucking Chinese Army!"

CHAPTER FORTY-NINE

Jin leaned forward in his seat, watching the distance. Four trucks of Guo's soldiers unloaded, spreading out along the ridge, some of them pursuing and shouting at the pair of people running north along the stone. Already, the helicopter's chop reached his ears: the pilot must have been ready for this. Whatever they had discovered, they likely now fled with the proof, ready to go in search of reinforcements. It was a good plan. Jin shouted at his driver to hurry. By the time they arrived, Guo and his men could well have destroyed everything.

Yang stayed on his motorcycle, circling a wide perimeter, watching out—and fortuitously avoiding Jin, who was seriously contemplating shooting his own assistant. No matter that the police may have collaborated in Casey's escape of the night before, he should never have been allowed to escape, even if Yang had to take down the entire Yinchuan police department. Yes, better that Yang kept his distance.

A few curious nomads trotted alongside the advance motorcade or watched from a distance, but the army markings on the vehicles encouraged them to stay back. Jin's official four-wheeler had tinted windows and air-conditioning, the only sort of vehicle that could keep him comfortable in his numerous expeditions to the distant provinces where most archaeological digs took place. He treasured the occasional salvage operation which allowed him to stay in a good hotel and use a proper state limousine instead.

Up ahead, the soldiers drew their weapons, and the helicopter launched in a flattening of grass, its shadow swooping over him, quickly out of range of small arms fire. Who had gone? Who had stayed? In the hot wind over the mountains, vultures soared, and a few ravens landed, croaking, in the pine trees as Jin stepped out of his vehicle.

Near the head of the ravine, the curly-haired woman stood next to a Chinese man Jin didn't recognize. Three ranks of soldiers stood on the slope ahead of him, the leaders hunkered down, rifles to their shoulders, a rank behind them, and another sheltering near their vehicles. Twenty-four men. Captain Guo occupied a position behind the door of his truck, near a familiar clump of trees. He gestured toward his men, and a small team started forward.

A gun cracked, and a voice shouted, "Keep your distance, all of you! I don't want to have to kill somebody." He said it again in respectable, if not fluent, Mandarin.

The big American should not be out of the hospital, but at least he would not be at his best. Jin couldn't see the man—he must have concealed himself among the rocks on the opposite ridgeline. The minister approached slowly, hands visible, but not elevated.

"What is the meaning of this?" Jin called back in English.

"Tell the soldiers to back off, or I start shooting." The voice echoed from beyond the ravine, making it hard to determine exactly where he was concealed. Assuming the man was a good shot, and had a supply of ammunition, he could readily mow down half of these men before they were able to take aim against him.

In Chinese, Jin said, "Captain, please. Have your men stay in place—tell those men to back up."

The captain rounded on him, glaring. "Don't be a fool, Minister.

These people are spies at best, foreign looters at worst—they are trying to conceal something. Look down there." He pointed toward the entrance, barely seen over the rubble of stones between. "Whatever it is, they've already been inside."

Ignoring the captain, Jin continued to walk slowly forward, hands visible and empty. "I am Jin Wang-lo, Minister of Antiquities. Anything you have found here belongs to the People's Republic of China. You can have no claims on our sovereign soil."

"We are not trying to claim anything," the woman said. "We just want to make sure this discovery gets properly excavated, and that the discoverer gets properly credited."

At her side, the Chinese man translated her words.

"Thieves," Guo muttered. "Foreign devils." He aimed his own sidearm at the woman's head. "Minister, we can take them all down, right now, and avoid any foreign entanglement." He sighted along the barrel as her curly hair tossed in the breeze.

From the trees overhead, a raven called for blood.

CHAPTER FIFTY

"Hang on! We're going in." Nick shouted over the noise, then swept the copter down close, the wind of its rotors tossing the grass and ruffling the uniforms of the soldiers. "You don't have to use it, Liz, just make it look good."

Liz nodded and leaned forward, the rifle huge in her hands as she aimed it out the door. On the other side, Huang did likewise.

Nick triggered something on his headset. "People's Army. Stand down now. Throw down your weapons, or we will fire."

The guy in the suit glanced up, then put his hands higher up, shouting at the others, translating, it sounded like.

D. A. and Zhen stood close together, covering each other. Liz bit her lip so hard she tasted blood. She could barely breathe, and put all her strength into holding the gun steady as Nick hovered, the soldiers, using their vehicles as cover, totally exposed from behind.

Again, the man in the suit shouted, and a few of the soldiers wavered, glancing up, their guns no longer pointing so rigidly. The army officer was shouting back, and Liz wished she could hear what he was saying. Did these men know where Byambaa was? Had they killed him? If so, she wished she could pull the trigger.

No, no she didn't. The idea of taking someone's life made her stomach roll and her mouth go sour.

Across the way, she caught a glimpse of Gonsalves, hiding behind a tumbled mound of stones. He dipped his gun, then the army officer flinched, his car door rocking. The star that marked the hood of his vehicle now had a hole perfectly centered and edged with bare metal.

She smiled to herself, then changed it into a fierce grimace, imagining herself a warrior—like them.

Another exchange of shouts between the guy in the suit and the army officer, then the officer took a step back, lowering his weapon. In a sweep across the ranks, the other soldiers lowered their weapons.

"Thank you, gentlemen," said Nick over the radio. "Now, we need all those soldiers to get out of here. They need to retreat at least five miles. Back to the river."

Another relay of orders, and most of the men started piling in the trucks, reversing and heading back the way they had come. Round one to the good guys.

"Praise the heavens," Huang sighed.

"Big time," said Nick. Then he tapped his headset. "Go ahead, D. A." He listened for a moment, then glanced at Liz. "Gotcha. You think that's smart?"

He turned the copter, following the four army trucks. The officer remained, along with two soldiers, and the guy in the suit. The copter lifted a little higher, tracking the progress of the retreat, then swung back around. "Liz? The guy in the suit. He's the Chinese Minister of Antiquities. He wants to go down and see what you found. He wants you to go with him."

"What? Wow." She looked down, then leaned back toward Huang. "Did the transmission go through?"

Huang replaced the gun he had been holding with an air of gratitude, and shifted the laptop belted in next to him. "Indeed. The complete archive has been uploaded to my account, and to the one designated by Miss D. A. Your documentation is secure. If my office does not receive continual updates from me every hour, they will post this information to the list provided."

Which included every major newspaper and television station around the globe they could think of. Liz drummed her fingers against the side of the rifle. "What does D. A. think?"

"She says he seems sincere, serious, but eager, you know? But she's not hum-int." He flashed a smile. "Human Intelligence."

"Right. If it means nobody else has to die, I think I should talk to him." She let down the rifle, and found that her hands trembled without it. As Nick lowered the copter, she pushed a ladder over the side, and climbed out to meet the minister.

CHAPTER FIFTY-ONE

"Does this mean you'll give me a nick name?" Byambaa asked, jogging comfortably along on his borrowed horse.

Riding alongside, Grant scanned the hills ahead of them. "No."

"I admit, it would have been a finer moment if I had gotten to shoot someone in your rescue." He patted the bow that hung in a special case from his saddle, ready to draw at a moment's notice.

Grant offered him a smile. "It was a great rescue. Best I've ever had." Byambaa had brought two horses, his go-bag, his boots, and a complete Mongolian outfit as cover. Yeah, hard to beat. Last time somebody tried to rescue him, the rescuer lost a leg and a couple of fingers, and Grant got a scar on his throat that looked like he'd been swiped by a tiger. Not a tough standard to exceed.

They'd left Lieutenant Ma with his cell phone, calling in for aid, and set out across the plains, putting some distance between them and their last known location. Then they spotted the helicopter, low and far off, racing for the hills. Now they picked their way across rough ground that rose steadily, in pursuit of the bird and the jeep that had to be following. When he realized the team wasn't heading north, the direction of his own abduction, Grant felt a queer blend of disappointment and pride. Apparently, Nick had finally absorbed the lessons of Mazar-i-Sharif: you don't jeopardize the mission for only one man, even for Grant himself. They were going after the objective, and Grant would rendezvous with them there.

"But no nick name?" The Mongolian sounded a little deflated.

"The nick names. They're not a compliment." A fox started up from a hollow and zipped away until its movement faded once more into the shifting grass.

"But you are called 'Chief,' this is a compliment."

Grant debated, guiding the horse with one hand, the other resting on his thigh. The sleeve of his robe turned back to reveal the scrapes around his wrist from the cuffs. Clothed, fed, sated by a bottle of salted tea. He glanced over at Byambaa who rode easily, born to the saddle. "I spent a few years on the rez—a reservation for Native Americans. You've heard of them?"

The Mongolian nodded. "Like the steppes, only..."He trailed off, frowning a little.

"Poor, drunk and dead-end. It's not all like that." But he didn't elaborate, not now, for this virtual stranger. "I got into riding, doing the rodeo circuit." Just to piss off his grandfather, but he didn't need to say that, either. "One of the routines was Cowboys and Indians. Guess which I was. Let's just say there's a big gulf between rodeo Indians and the real thing." He pulled the bottle of tea from a pouch on his saddle and took a long swallow. Tangy, milky and strange. "Gooney was the team leader when I first joined the Unit. He'd heard about the rodeo—he's the one who gave me that name."

Byambaa made a soft sound of understanding. "Not a compliment."

Grant stared into the distance, in time and space, smiling just a little. "I worked until I made it one."

"And you called him 'Gooney.' Which he dislikes."

"You got it. Tit for tat."

"And D. A.?"

"Don't Ask."

"Sorry." Byambaa looked disappointed, dropping his curious gaze as he stretched to pat his horse.

Grant laughed. "No, 'D. A.' stands for 'Don't Ask.'"

"Ah. Why doesn't Nick have another name?"

"That is his nick-name. When he joined up, he couldn't find his shaving kit one day. When the sarge asked him why he hadn't shaved, he reported the loss, and said that someone had 'nicked' his kit. After that, people swiped it whenever they could. His real name is Randolph."

Something cracked through his awareness. Grant raised his hand for silence, and both men halted. Gunshots? But no screaming. In the distance up ahead, the helicopter took off again, but circled back a moment later, the roar of the rotors covering most other sounds as the copter hovered.

Something was wrong. Grant nudged his horse into motion, cantering toward the foothills a couple of miles away. The grass thinned out, replaced by tufts and sparse brush, rocks growing more numerous as the ground rose. The bunch and stretch of the horse underneath him took him back through the years, fury beating at his chest as he stormed from the hogan, taking the reins and galloping across the plains, substituting speed for anger, for hurt, for the need to inflict that pain on others. Today was different: another man rode at his side, a worthy companion. And their friends needed their help.

Another crack of sound, much closer—the report of a rifle—and the horse's stride hitched, its breath suddenly strained. It pitched forward and collapsed underneath him in a rush of blood.

CHAPTER FIFTY-TWO

Jin stood in his clean, well-cut suit while Liz tried to straighten her grubby shirt. If he noticed her discomfiture or her clothing, he showed no sign, merely listening politely while she explained about following clues to arrive here, at the Inner Mongolian hills. She didn't reveal her sources or mention the songs, only that her research led her to believe she could find something exciting here.

"Myself, I was called in because of the looters. You have heard about them, yes?" Jin inquired, head cocked. With his silvering temples and keen gaze, not to mention the precision of his voice, he came across as an actor. Not like a Jet Li martial arts type, but an intellectual. "I see you have. In fact, I believe your companions aided the widow of one of the looters to retrieve his body for burial. You have done her a great kindness." He smiled genially. "I take it the reindeer stone is one of these clues you mentioned?"

"Yes?" She glanced at D. A., wishing Grant were beside her to give her a nudge if she said too much.

"Someone else is following the clues," D. A. put in. "Someone who's killing people."

"Ah! You do not believe the looter's death was an accident then? I have thought so myself. There are too many strange things happening in this little province, hence my own involvement. Have you learned anything about your rivals?"

"They're fast, ruthless, Chinese. Probably official." D. A.'s green eyes settled on the army captain who stood stiffly a little way off, with his two soldiers at his sides. The man glared back. "Well-armed, and capable of quick international travel."

Jin followed her gaze and tapped his chin. "I doubt any great quest or discovery could go on in my area of interest without my knowledge. My department must track the activities of looters and dealers in antiquities as much as possible. Sometimes, the items they bring to market lead us to important finds." His expression softened, like a disappointed professor. "But I am not aware of anything in this area." He waved a hand toward the ravine.

Liz leaned over and D. A. leaned in to meet her. "Maybe we should show him."

D. A. lifted her chin. Most of the time, she looked like a tech worker, or maybe a teacher, but every once in a while, Liz caught glimpses of the truth: whatever battles had formed Nick and Grant, D. A. had been there, too. "We believe that someone in your government is trying to stop us, Minister Jin. If your government understands what we've found, they'll bury it—pretend it never existed, maybe even destroy the whole thing."

Jin flinched. "You think that we would destroy archaeological monuments? We are not terrorists, madam. We are not jihadis like the Islamic State—"his voice rang with indignation, then he stopped himself, spreading his hands, giving a deep sigh. "I understand. In America, you hear about our Cultural Revolution and you protest the Three Gorges Dam project. You perceive us as barely able to tolerate difference. You believe that we will destroy the past in order to promote the future."

That was it, in a nutshell. Liz tapped her fingers, trying to work out a polite response. Could she agree with him, without insulting him, or bringing on the army? Was it possible they had misjudged the Chinese response? Eight hundred years of anger and prejudice—what if she had allowed Byambaa's own prejudice to sway her? Maybe it was better he wasn't here right now. She didn't think he could listen to the minister with any kind of objectivity.

Jin clasped his hands together. "Miss Kirschner. Although you have, until now, worked with your small team, if this find is, indeed, as great as you believe, it will not proceed without international cooperation. Without Chinese cooperation. It is, after all, on our sovereign soil." He glanced toward the army representatives, then stepped a little closer to Liz and lowered his voice. "If your allegations are true, it may well have been a certain conservative branch of the army which has attempted to prevent your discovery. Truly, I do not believe they would damage the past, but would they ensure that no foreigners saw it, much less discovered it? Yes, this I would believe."

"You think the captain is the one who was behind the attempts to stop us? In Boston, they killed someone and they burned a library."

He registered shock, then his face darkened. "Miss Kirschner. My position gives me a good deal of influence. If your find is genuine, I will bring the full strength of this ministry to support you, to ensure that the past is preserved."

"Thank you."

D. A. did not join their conclave, but remained where she was, and announced, "We've done a good deal of documentation already: video and still, with commentary. All ready to be transmitted to a dozen news agency to reveal the find. If we don't provide suitable passwords and updates, it all goes public."

"I see you have been very cautious. Justly so, given your concerns." Jin's clasped hands moved gently, pleading. "Miss Kirschner. Please. Will you show me what you have found?"

CHAPTER FIFTY-THREE

For a moment, Grant fell into history. Thunder, the best horse he'd ever ridden, the mustang he'd taken a part in breaking and made his own. Galloping hard, turning on a pivot, dropping the reins to take aim—an impossible shot for anyone but him, and Thunder made it possible. He still remembered how it felt, rising in the stirrups, Thunder just as eager as he, just as committed to the game. But the flower girls hadn't done a good job after the last race. A clump of roses thrown to the winner still lay, tousled and dusty, in the ring. Thunder's hoof landed straight and hard. And those roses brought him down.

The sound of bones breaking still echoed in Grant's memory, all these years later. Thunder screaming, struggling to rise. The smell of roses, dust stinging his eyes. The sight of his grandfather's stern face, the expression of the ring veterinarian confirming what Grant already knew. And he made the shot he never believed would be possible: he shot his own horse to stop him from suffering. Quick and relatively painless. For the horse.

This time, it was already done by the time he hit the ground. Grant jumped free as they fell, tumbling, coming to one knee with his gun already in hand, then diving to the other side of the downed horse. Its body twitched a few times as more bullets followed. The felt hat he'd been wearing rolled in the dirt then popped into the air and rocked away, a hole in its crown.

"Grant!" Byambaa shouted.

"Go long!" Grant shouted back, hoping the Mongolian knew what he meant. The horse was cover, the only cover he'd noticed aside from a few rocks as the ground rose toward where the helicopter had landed. For a moment, he closed his eyes and remembered the view, slope of tumbled rocks and scrub, at the top, an oovo, a Mongolian shrine of stones that marks a high point or a place of spirits. Vengeful spirits in this case.

The shooter had to be hiding there, it was his only choice. So had Byambaa heard and understood? Time to find out. Grant heard shouting—something like a battle cry—and peeked around the horse's jerking legs. Byambaa rode in a wide arc away from him, but still up the slope. If he kept going, he'd come abreast of the oovo. A few bullets pinged around or past the mad rider, then Byambaa dropped the reins and drew his bow. He aimed up the slope and pulled, nocked, aimed and pulled again.

Return fire from that direction. Grant got his feet under him, his right ankle throbbing, and ran. When he heard the next pop, he dropped low, diving by a rock barely large enough to block his torso.

Another ululating cry, and the whistle of an arrow. Grant jumped up and ran. The bushes ahead exploded in a puff of leaves. The shooter, trying to keep track of both Byambaa and Grant, was leading him a little too strong. Grant dodged right, into the line of the oovo, and back out.

Galloping hoofs off to that side and another swish, followed by a grunt this time. Then a flurry of shots and a horse's whinny.

Grant put on a burst of speed, slamming up the hill, rounding the oovo and dropping to a shooting stance. He got off two rounds. The shooter spun on him, an arrow thrusting from his leg. Grant fired again. The shooter jerked, his shirt tufting over his heart. Over his body armor.

Square jaw, sunglasses rocking on the ground nearby. Yang grinned, then his gun clicked. He tossed it at Grant, lunging forward at the same time.

Grant's shot caught his arm, then the guy was on him, punching, landing a kick that drew a wince from both of them. Grant gave way, circled to a more level patch, and knocked Yang sideways with a body blow. His right ankle burned, nearly giving out.

Dropping low, Grant caught the guy's leg as he kicked out. A jab landed hard on Grant's cheek. Both down now, grappling, Grant dragging Yang closer. Yang's next kick connected with Grant's throat. He gasped, tears rushing his eyes, but he didn't let go.

He pushed the gun forward, jabbed the vest and dragged the barrel low as Yang struggled. A fistful of dirt struck his face. Grant gagged, his lungs seared as he fought for breath. He dug in with the gun, feeling the softness of flesh, and fired.

The bullet tore upward, into Yang's gut, jerking him up as if he'd been shocked with an AED. Instead of starting his heart, this jolt stopped it, the bullet bursting out near his neck in a spurt of blood. Yang flopped back to the ground, still.

On his knees, Grant braced his hands, chest heaving, and finally got his breath back. His throat ached with the blow—lucky not to have a crushed larynx. He gingerly stroked over the injury. Shit, that hurt.

Quiet. A hum of engines receding somewhere behind him. Had they missed the party? Grant pushed to his feet, swaying, and limped past the oovo with its bloody offering, scanning the steppes. The horse stood on the next rise, ears perked back at him, saddle empty. In between, a patch of dark blue lay in the grass, a second tumbled form. Ignoring the pain of his ankle, Grant ran.

CHAPTER FIFTY-FOUR

At D. A.'s signal, Nick landed the helicopter on the plain below, and hiked up toward Liz and the others, his rifle slung over his shoulder, followed by Huang. From the rocky ridge beyond, a voice called, "Hey, can I come, too? Nick can provide cover."

"When do I get to see it? You at least got inside the door!" Nick hollered back, then sighed. "Fine, swap out."

He moved toward the narrow trail over the doorway that led to the other side, and disappeared among the rocks, the captain tracking his progress for as long as possible, then glowering. After a moment, Gonsalves emerged from the rocks, making his way not along the trail, but diagonally down into the small space before the door. "What are you waiting for?" he spread his arms in invitation.

After watching both men move across the uneven ground like dancers, Liz felt like an elephant herself, lumbering back down to the door.

Jin followed carefully, managing his balance by using his hands on the other rocks. He grimaced at the skeleton. "A looter or grave-robber, do you think? Except I believe I noticed others."

"Hundreds," said Gonsalves, using his rifle to indicate the heaped stones behind them. "All under there. You catch glimpses of bones everywhere you look. Lots to see from up there. Also, animals have been dragging them, scattering what they can reach." He smirked at the minister's dismay. "Thousands, maybe. Just like the legends say." He flared his eyes, an expression even more dramatic against his reddened skin.

"Legends?" Jin echoed.

Liz nodded. "This way, Minister."

She walked toward the door, but Jin paused, removing a pair of spectacles from his pocket and studying the bronze baht face. "Buddhist," he murmured, "but showing animistic influences. Workmanship is... Exquisite. I would say pre-Ming, certainly. Bronze must be dated primarily by style, and by the patina, of course, I—well, I am lecturing. Forgive me."

"No, it's fascinating. I'm not, uh, archaeology is not my specialty."

"You have not yet revealed what that is, Miss Kirschner."

"Inner Asia," she said vaguely, stepping through from bright sun and heat, into the darkness of the guard room.

"Mongolia." Jin stepped up beside her, both of them avoiding the tumbled bones of the skeleton who had fallen inside. "Wait—a thousand skeletons at the doorway, a Mongolian Buddhist entrance and now a room full of soldiers?" He caught her shoulder lightly. "Genghis Khan?" he breathed. "You found his tomb?"

And she could not conceal the smile that spread across her face. "There's more. Come on."

"The treasure—the sixty-eight crowns, are those legends also true?" They walked together, the others trailing, as she showed him what she had found. When they peered together into the silken ger, playing their lights upon the silver coffin, Jin said, "This is astonishing, Miss Kirschner. It will require further study of course, to be certain, but I cannot imagine what else this might be." He withdrew, pacing back into the treasure room, his borrowed flashlight tracing the crowns in their specially carved niches. The rest of the team clustered at the center, gazing around them in palpable awe. "How have you done this, when so many others have failed?"

"I followed the songs. I found a bunch of old recordings in our musical archive—that's my specialty, ethnomusicology?—and I translated and analyzed them. I had some help with the khoomei, of course, it wasn't all me."

Distantly, she heard voices outside, worry or excitement. Gonsalves detached himself and went to investigate, letting Liz concentrate on the minister.

"Still, you are to be congratulated." Jin took her hand in his, his warmth enveloping her palm. "It is the achievement of a lifetime. No, of a hundred lifetimes."

Grant Casey's unmistakable voice cut the darkness. "Let her go." Followed by the click of a gun being cocked.

He aimed a small flashlight at them with his left hand, propping his right hand where the darkness of the gun barrel matched the darkness of his eyes. The position of the light cast weird shadows on his face. No, not all shadows—some of the dark patches were bruises or blood.

"Stand down, Grant, this guy's cool. Liz is just showing him around." Gonsalves, his own gun slung over his shoulder, crowded Grant's elbow.

"That's right," D. A. chimed in. "He got the army to back off. He wants to work with us, to make sure the tomb gets conserved properly."

"Bullshit. He's behind the plot to bury this place. I just shot his fucking assistant."

Liz twitched at his language. Usually, he was so restrained—what had—"Byambaa! Where is he?" She took back her hand and stepped toward him, wanting to run, terrified of what she would hear next.

"Lost consciousness in a fall from his horse." Grant's eyes flicked toward her for the first time. "He's coming around by the copter, with Zhen. He'll be okay. The horse was used to hunting, didn't expect to become the hunted."

She knotted her fingers together, her knees feeling weak. Stay here, with the Minister and explain, or rush to Byambaa's side?

That black gaze returned to Jin's face. The barrel of the gun had never wavered. "Yang's dead, Minister Jin. You sent him for me, and he went down. What do you say, you wanna be next?"

CHAPTER FIFTY-FIVE

Jin spread his hands, staring the madman down. Between them, inadvertently blocking the shot with her nervous movements, stood the graduate student, Elizabeth Kirschner. "There is no need for rash action, Mr.—?"

Casey didn't rise to the question, and his compatriots, torn between loyalty to him and concern over his obvious derangement, said nothing.

"Let us adjourn to the sunlight. It is clear that Ms. Kirschner is worried over this... Byambaa, was it? Allow her to visit her friend, and let us clear the air as well." He smiled and shifted forward.

"Yeah, that's a good plan, Chief. Let's go out, get some fresh air," said the curly-haired woman.

"Look at this place, though, Chief! And she found it—she did it. You've gotta admit this is fan-tastic. Just the kind of thing you founded the Bone Guard for, right? Discovery? Protection?" The big American swung his flashlight from point to point. "A crown! And another crown!" He highlighted one after another.

Jin caught sight of one of the crowns—and fire rose at his core, his muscles tightening as if for a bout, but he concealed his anger and forced himself to watch Casey instead.

Casey's eyes flicked with the light, then back to his focus, as if he could bore two holes into Jin's brow with the strength of his gaze, his brows furrowing just slightly.

"Please, let us find a more comfortable place to discuss your concerns. Clearly, you have had some difficulty in recent hours." Jin finished his step forward, his motion releasing Liz to scurry past and hover in the corridor beyond, still uncertain. "Perhaps medical attention is in order?"

"Please, Grant," she said, holding the flashlight to her breast.

"Indeed, there will be time to view the artifacts and relics later, when we are all calmer," said Huang.

Casey was frowning, his gaze flicking back to the niches. Jin kept walking, side-stepping to get around him.

"This place is a fraud," Casey said, softly, distinctly, and Jin froze. Parting his hands, keeping the gun aimed at Jin, Casey pointed his flashlight toward a niche on the wall. "That crown. It hasn't been buried for a thousand years, not even a hundred. I was there when it was stolen."

CHAPTER FIFTY-SIX

Grant stared at the crown, tracing it with his eyes, the golden leaves, the cabochons. He had last seen it in a museum in Mazar-i-Sharif, in the hands of a looter, and now here it was.

"While these crowns are quite remarkable, they are not unique, as I am sure Mr. Huang will attest. Perhaps this one is similar to one you have seen before?" Jin waved toward the niches.

"Five leaves at the crown, red stone framed by blue ones, lapis lazuli," Grant murmured. Like he would forget it. Like it hadn't haunted his dreams for more than a year, in its glass display case before the shooting started, in her hand when she made her getaway, crowning the head of that woman, its image shattering into a thousand pieces with the blast that shattered Nick's leg. This was why they were trying to badly to stop him from getting here, not the whole team, just him. "It's a fake—this whole place is a fake."

"Nobody faked a thousand skeletons," Gooney pointed out.

"All you need is a thousand corpses nobody's going to miss." He swung about, and Jin retreated three steps, swift and precise despite the darkness, despite keeping his eyes on Grant. As if he'd been here before. "What the Hell? What do you people want?"

"Casey," Gooney started, "You sound—"

But D. A. put a hand on Gooney's arm before he could finish and say what Grant sounded like. "You're saying they faked all of this? Piles of treasure, mummies of warriors, a corpse in a coffin, not to mention a carpet of bones—how, Chief? Why?"

"Don't know. Yet."

Gooney brushed past her and leaned into Grant's ear. "Batshit. You're totally batshit crazy. What the fuck is wrong with you? We've been busting our butts to get here, to find this place, and you're what—trying to come up with a way to make it last? To turn the damn thing into an epic adventure? You look like hell, Chief, you can barely stand up straight: is this what makes you feel good? Getting the snot kicked out of you, and winning? Now you don't want it to end? Face it, it's over—it's a matter for Jin and Liz, and the Mongolian government. You did your part—stand down, salute, and fucking move on!"

Grant spun about and aimed his fist at Gooney's face, a mask of red, glaring at him in the gloom. He stopped short. "Get out. Get out of my sight, get out of my crew. Get. Out. Now."

Gooney didn't flinch from the fist that hovered at his cheek, he didn't even cut it a glance. Instead, he pivoted on his heel, rifle slung over his shoulder, and stalked from the tomb. A bone skittered away from his foot as he retreated. Liz wavered in his wake, as if she wanted to be swept along by his power. She glanced back at Grant, her face streaked with tears. This was her dream, the culmination of her work, and the beginning of a great career, a great life—with the fiancé that Grant had nearly gotten killed. Grant aimed his flashlight at the Phantom's crown, then ran it over the other pieces. What if he were wrong about this? How many lives would be ruined if he kept pushing, and for what? Because he thought he recognized a thing he had seen only once?

Huang cleared his throat, his flashlight held low, like a hymnal.

"As the Minister says, the artifacts are genuine. I have examined and purchased enough items from this era to know. He is a distinguished archaeologist and lecturer, an expert in the historical record of China—"

Grant turned his light to the billionaire, making him squint. "Just how well do you know him?"

The man blinked, several times. "As the owner of several contracting firms, I have had cause to know the minister, to ask for permits for salvage archaeology, and as a collector, I have found his assistance in establishing provenance to be invaluable."

"So are you on his payroll, or is he on yours?"

Near the tunnel, Jin fiddled with his glasses, a surprisingly awkward gesture.

"Chief..."D. A. used her warning tone.

She didn't get it yet, did she? But then, she hadn't been there when the whole thing started, when people started taking shots at Liz and Grant killed a man without even thinking. "D. A., somebody told. Someone told the enemy about the map Liz found, and there's only a handful of people who could have done that. A young man died for that, and the archive was burned. Her research was stolen, and we were pursued all the way—"he pointed back at Huang. "How did you find us at Cambridge? The cell-phone, wasn't it? It was you who turned on the tracking, before she came back to get the phone she left behind at Chen's office." He had been such a fool—but how could he show the others the truth? He had nothing but his own word and his memory of the Phantom, a looter no one but him had ever believed in.

"Why would they kill people over a fake tomb?" D. A. said, pleading. "Think it through, Chief. Someone wanted to stop us getting here, maybe that creep from the army, and they failed. Now Minister Jin is here to back us up, to back up Liz and her discovery. Much as I hate to say it, Gooney's right. It doesn't make any sense. Maybe the crown you saw was a replica of the one the Mongols took, have you thought about that?"

Jin stood, hands in his pockets, saying nothing. Grant had been in humint too long to think he was innocent, but what was he guilty of? Fake a tomb, then fake an adventure to carry it off? Why, so some foreigner could get credit for the discovery? Of course, because the rest of the world would instantly doubt the Chinese if they claimed this discovery. He flashed back to the interview he'd had at the University, when the archaeology dean mentioned that the Chinese Minister of Antiquities would be involved with the upcoming conference. Maybe scoping out the researchers, figuring out who to target with the clues that would bring them here. Or maybe Grant really was fucking insane.

Liz trembled, her shoulders sinking. He was saying everything she'd ever done was garbage.

"Look at the skeletons and the mummies—if you're right, then they should show signs: modern dental work, things like that. There should be other clues." D. A. sighed. "We should get Gooney back in here."

Grant held the gun rock-solid, but no longer knew where to point it. Just now, everything in the damn place was pointing at him. With a glance at Liz, hoping he conveyed some sort of apology, he stalked back up the corridor to the guard room.

"Very good. Let us move on," Jin was saying, "and begin the true discovery, Miss Kirschner."

"Somebody say my name?" Gooney stood at the threshold, but when Grant entered, he stiffened to attention, staring somewhere else. "I'm your back-up, sir, and there's no one to relieve me of duty, sir," he said pointedly.

But Grant wasn't leaving. He squatted down by the skull and picked it up. A few teeth were missing—knocked out in its fall? Lost in a life of hardship eight hundred years ago? Or wrenched out by someone who wanted to conceal the truth of modern dentistry? He stared at the bones. "Detective."

"Yes, sir." A snarl.

"How did he die?" Grant stared fixedly at the floor as Gooney stretched himself, blew out a breath, and finally stooped beside him, his cast pale in the sunlight through the door, another reminder.

Gooney studied the bones without touching for a long moment, then carefully rolled the rib cage, tracing the vertebrae. "There's a nick here, carved pretty deep actually, and another here. Stabbed, probably twice. Hard to say about the murder weapon. Trace analysis would give us the profile of the blade, and maybe the composition. We'd be able to tell if the blade were modern."

"Fascinating," Jin murmured, standing over them, but careful not to block the light.

Without looking at him, Gooney held out a hand to Grant to receive the skull, propping it for examination like Hamlet greeting Yorick. Then the detective went still, his jaw knotting, and he went on more slowly, his fingers tracing something only he could see. "Of course, that doesn't matter. Unless they were wearing glasses eight hundred years ago."

CHAPTER FIFTY-SEVEN

Jin raised an eyebrow at the men, watching the fortunes of his family rest upon the web the soldier was spinning. He had been inclined to doubt Yang's assessment of the danger, and now he saw that even Yang had underestimated. Could this still be salvaged?

"Wait a minute, this guy wasn't hit by the rock fall, right? He was by the door—maybe he was a looter or an archaeologist or something, someone else who found the tomb, but never made it inside," the curly-haired woman suggested, her voice sounding flat and distant in Jin's ears.

"Rock fall missed him because of the ledge over the door," the big American replied. "You can see that from the sniper's nest. I'll need to have a look at the other bones though." He rolled one of the long bones in his hand, displaying it in the streak of sunlight from the door. "The surface is a bit pitted, and darkened—from a distance, at least, the other ones looked the same. Likely all went down at the same time, under similar circumstances."

"So how could they be modern corpses? No hair, no clothing, no flesh—"the curly-haired woman glanced at Miss Kirschner as if concerned about offending her. The younger woman already looked pale and fragile, her research under attack as her Mongol companion already had been. Jin had placed himself on her side, but she seemed to be giving up already. Disappointingly weak. Indeed, he should have searched for right person rather than to fold her into his plan simply because of a few songs.

"This seems a reasonable point," Jin said. "Even should someone wish to do such a thing, to create such a complex undertaking, surely the manufacture of skeletal remains would be a step too far."

"For anyone looking for Genghis Khan's tomb, the stiffs would be the clincher." The big American stood up, his eyes rested briefly on Jin, then flickered away toward the door. "There's ways to de-flesh a corpse. We'd need a full chemical analysis of the soil to figure out what kind of agent was used."

At his side, Casey bore a half-smile. As if he had won. Jin fingered the device in his pocket. For a moment, he met Huang's gaze, the businessman watching him, impassive: the face he wore at auction when he did not wish anyone to know how high he would bid. His money had made the American expedition possible. Time to sow some doubt in these friendships of fortune. Jin tipped his head in Huang's direction. "Perhaps Mr. Huang can assist with your analysis, given his pharmaceutical connections."

Huang stiffened, a nearly imperceptible change. "I thought, Minister, that you had agreed not to exploit that history."

"Just how well do you two know each other?" The big American demanded, glaring at Jin.

"Perhaps better than you know your benefactor, if you are not aware that it is drugs, not buildings, that have been the foundation of his wealth."

Casey's already taut body twitched to readiness, as if Jin had shaken the ground beneath him, and forced a change in balance. Their attention shifted from Jin to the man they believed they could trust.

Jin drew out the device from his pocket and pressed the button.

CHAPTER FIFTY-EIGHT

An ear-shattering screech filled the cave, shooting through Grant's skull and dropping him back to his knees. Gooney clamped his hands over his ears, staggering against the wall, gasping. The sound reverberated and echoed all around them, causing streaks of agony. Across the way, Liz collapsed to the ground. D. A., too, was clasping her ears, mouth gaping and eyes popped wide. She swayed. Her ears, too, had been trained to a high sensitivity. Huang was somewhere behind him—had he known this was coming? Grant's head throbbed, his vision blurring, and he could hear nothing at all.

Jin calmly stood holding the palm-sized device, watching them through his glasses, the kind with attached hearing protection which, in the dim light, he had applied while apparently fiddling with the frames. His eyes met Grant's, then he tossed the device lightly, still screaming its attack, down the back corridor into the darkness. Giving a small bow, he exited the chamber, casually reaching a hand for the door.

Grant lunged forward, sprawling across the bones, grazing Gooney's legs as the detective crumpled under the auditory onslaught. The bones scattered without sound. Gooney turned with him, his mouth flapping silently. Grant hooked the rifle from his shoulder and slung it downward, jamming the butt into the narrowing gap of the door. The huge door moved ponderously and slammed against the metal gun, rocking its length without dislodging it, all without making a sound. Grant's vision still pulsed, as if the sensory overload from his ears had spread to his other senses. He didn't know how the hell he was still functioning, but was willing to bet on adrenaline alone.

Gooney was trying to talk to him, but moving his head around, as if he could shake out the sound, making lip-reading impossible. Tapping his shoulder, Grant flashed the time-out gesture, pointed to his eyes, to the door, circling his hand and flashing several hands of fingers, indicating that the enemy would have them surrounded.

Still shaking, Gooney swallowed hard and got himself under control. He faced Grant and spoke carefully, his training returning, including gestures, telling Grant to go after the device and stop it, while he got Liz out the door.

Grant flashed his gesture again. *Into enemy fire. No deal.*

Gooney mouthed a single word that required no training to read. *Shit.* He pressed a hand over one ear, wincing, then lifted his chin to Grant, asking, what have you got?

In answer, Grant forced himself up, glanced back to confirm the device was far away, and knocked over the nearest propped-up mummy. He pulled off the armor and helmet and wriggled into the chest armor, slapping the helmet on his head.

Circling a finger by his ear in the universal sign for insanity, Gooney crawled over and yanked down a warrior of his own. He had to slash open the leather on one side to squeeze into the armor, leaving his side vulnerable. Grant swiped a silver belt and slapped it around Gooney's waist, drawing the sides as tight as he could. Their eyes met, Gooney's face a mask of discomfort and uncertainty. He shook his head slightly, slapped his palm to his forehead, then pointed at Grant and gave a shrug. The closest he would ever come to an apology.

Huang straightened slowly, his hands clamped over his ears. He winced, tears flashing in his eyes. A drug kingpin and an ally of the Chinese, but he'd been left behind when Jin made his escape. Whatever else he might be, the guy was not an operator.

At a tap on his arm, Grant whirled, the gun in play again, but it was D. A. gesturing toward her ears, and holding out a handful of wool she'd pulled from one of the artifacts. What are they waiting for? She asked silently.

Grant stuffed his ears, grateful for even that slight reduction in the sound, and divided the rest of the wool between Gooney and Huang. The guy shrank in his high-end gear, like a little kid playing explorer. Grant jabbed a finger in Huang's direction, pointed at the man's flashlight, then emphatically gestured toward the back room. "Turn that damn thing off," he mouthed. Huang hesitated, sinking a little further, then stumbled in that direction, his light bobbing into the darkness.

To D. A., he replied with the sign for a kill, then gestured at the room around them. If the Chinese killed them in here, shot them, their pristine tomb would be a ruin, and all of their plans along with it. How worried were they? Could that work to Grant's advantage?

The light shifted and he grabbed D. A., yanking her out of the stripe of sun as someone got into position out there. What the hell were they doing?

By the door, Gooney pressed his back to the bronze, taking sharp breaths, fumbling through his pockets to come up with a small rectangle. The polearm from one of the fallen mummies lay at his feet and he picked it up carefully. Grant sighed to himself—if they couldn't hear shit, neither could those outside, and here was Gooney sneaking around like an infiltrator sure of his cover. Gooney wedged the rectangle in a notch in the ancient blade and lifted it, passing it carefully out the top of the door, and twisting the pole this way and that. Grant caught a flash and stared up. A signal mirror, reaching out the door, aiming down. Four soldiers were outside with a hose, two of them with guns aimed at the gap, one of them signaling to someone up the hill. Gas—could be just CO from the cars, a nice, non-destructive way to kill the occupants. They wouldn't have much time.

To do what? To blow their enemies' plans sky high. His eyes lit on the heap of fireworks.

CHAPTER FIFTY-NINE

"Project Raven is over. It is a disgrace, Minister. There is no reason not to simply shoot," Guo insisted. "They will not come out."

Jin held himself in a ready stance by the car, listening to Guo's harangue. "They will come out dead, like rabbits from a warren." At a sign from the soldier by the gate, he turned on the engine, letting the car run. If he ran out of gas, he would have it siphoned from one of the jeeps and still drive home in comfort.

Out here, the sonic grenade sounded distant, an alarm call, but one he need not answer. Down by the helicopter, the moans of dying men rose and fell. The Mongol and the Chinese driver were barricaded inside, with whatever weapons they had brought. Anyone who approached was shot, either by them, or by the sniper hiding in the rocks across the way. A small contingent of soldiers worked slowly across the upper slopes, trying to get behind him and take care of that problem.

"Have you not heard me, Minister? Raven is a ruin."

"No, it has merely had a setback. Surely in the campaigns you have run, Captain, you do sometimes face an obstacle unforeseen?"

"Unforeseen? It wasn't—it was Casey, the very man you swore your agents would take care of."

Jin focused on him. He imagined sliding back his foot, swinging it around, slamming the captain in the chest hard enough to stop his heart and letting him fall into the dust, perhaps hiring another chemical tanker to add his skeleton to the dead khan's guard. But no, it was the unplanned slaying of his former assistant that had provided enough evidence to back up Casey's otherwise mad claims. Who would fake a tomb, steal the artifacts, leave a thousand skeletons? A man committed to his task, who left no detail unplanned. And now a single, unplanned act had nearly caused the very ruin of which Guo now spoke.

"When we have overcome this difficulty, Captain, we will merely re-seal the tomb and wait. I did not expect Project Raven to reach fruition so soon, nor did the Councilor plan on it. The original timeline called for locating a suitable researcher to be guided here two years from now. I am a patient man."

"There will still be bodies to manage, and American connections to assuage. Not to mention the consequences of the death of a man like Huang."

Jin felt that blow, but he did not reveal it. "Indeed, there will be consequences, not least for you if you fail to assist as you have been ordered to do."

Guo gazed down into the valley. "It is gratifying to hear you admit that you require assistance, after all of your talk of controlling the situation. Very well. Sergeant! Get that door open and eliminate the intruders."

The leader of a group of soldiers, lying back from the edge, scrambled to his knees, keeping his helmet low, and gave a quick nod, then signaled to the two-dozen men behind him.

"No blood! Some of those artifacts are irreplaceable."

Swiveling his head, Guo stared now at the dead soldiers by the helicopter. "There has already been blood."

"Captain?" said the sergeant, hesitating, and Guo waved him in.

Two shots from the sniper across the way, and two soldiers went down, but the group of four on the slope above now had the man's position, and returned fire. Excellent.

Then the piercing scream of the sonic grenade went silent—only to be followed by a deafening roar.

CHAPTER SIXTY

Liz jolted awake when the floor rumbled beneath her. Someone held her in strong arms—Grant, she first imagined, then felt the brush of curly hair against her cheek. The awful screeching was gone, replaced by a rolling boom that echoed through the sudden silence in her skull.

D. A. grabbed her, pushing, pulling, until Liz stumbled to her feet, then the other woman pulled her forward. Something wobbled on Liz's head, and she steadied it, finding a leather helmet studded with metal outside, and lined with it as well. It weighed her down, along with a vest of similar structure. Ahead of them, two mad silhouettes stormed into the sunlight over the fallen door, Mongol warriors, but too tall, guns in one hand, pole-arms in the other.

Blood oozed under the huge bronze door near a twitching leg. Smoke billowed around the opening and the air reeked like the Fourth of July. She sneezed, staggered, and D. A. pulled her onward, over a scattering of bones, over a pool of blood and past the ruined face of a soldier. The woman didn't try to speak. Tufts of wool poked from her ears beneath a helmet of her own, and she, too, held a gun. The two warriors ran, stopped, shot, ran again, then split, one for the hillside, one for the rank of soldiers opposite, charging toward them. D. A. followed this one, scrambling up the slope, towing Liz.

D. A. pushed her ahead, gesturing toward the helicopter, and putting both hands out to steady her gun as she fired. Liz had never felt so useless, her ears buzzing and head rattling with so much sound and violence.

A hose snaked down the hill toward the blasted tomb and the dead soldiers. Another group of soldiers rushed up, using the parked car as cover. In moments, they'd be in place to take down D. A. or the warrior beyond.

Liz dropped low and grabbed the hose with both hands, yanking it up as the men ran close. Four of the six lost their footing, recovering quickly.

Jin, at the door of the car, turned to look at her, his face cold, all sense of shared excitement subsumed into a calculating stare. An arrow shattered the window behind him. Jin ducked into the car as the advancing soldiers regrouped, then the car lurched into reverse, smashing into the Chinese soldiers, bumping over their bodies and roaring away for a hundred yards before it swung about into a turn.

The army command car stood exposed by this departure, the officer's face round and furious, eyes darting from Liz to his fallen men, to the shiny sedan that had knocked them down like bowling pins.

She put on a burst of speed and reached the helicopter just as the door popped open to receive her. Byambaa's powerful hand helped her inside while Zhen, Huang's driver, slipped out, taking a shooter's stance beside the copter.

Across the way, Gooney shot at the remaining scouts, then clubbed one of them with his cast. Nick rose from nowhere, both of them covering Grant and D. A. who did a sudden pivot, moving like a pair of dancers in the competition of their lives. Together, they sprinted for the copter and dove in. Zhen turned to join them, but Grant shoved his gun into the man's face and Zhen backed off, not raising his hands, but not firing either.

D. A. scrambled into her accustomed seat, then braced her gun toward the soldiers. Grant dropped into the pilot's seat beside her, the medieval helmet framing his handsome face as he focused on the controls.

For a moment, Liz glanced back at the man beside her, dressed in a bloody del, his face bruised, but still grinning. Byambaa squeezed her shoulder, then reached across to slam her door. Grant flicked switches and the copter lurched into the air, its windows cracked, bullets pinging from the chassis. He swung about, diving down toward the remaining soldiers, scattering them. The captain lost his hat, his hair swirling with dust in the wind of the copter's blades.

On the far side, Gooney and Nick ran away from the tomb, and the copter gave them cover all the way back to the parked jeep.

The world throbbed around her with dangerous power: the violence of the men on both sides, the thrumming of the engine, the explosion of the bronze door that still reverberated inside of her, the desperate thunder of her own heart, then Byambaa lowered his weapon at last. His arms moved around her, drawing her close and humming so low it was more a vibration than a sound, and Liz was, however briefly, safe.

His humming reminded her of the music, of the past months listening to those songs over and over and the dawning realization of what they could mean. Only to now realize they meant nothing at all. Her dream was a fraud, shattered behind them and soaked with the blood not of Mongol laborers killed to keep the secret, but of soldiers and God knew who else, killed to conceal a terrible lie. Liz curled into Byambaa's chest and wept.

CHAPTER SIXTY-ONE

Grant paid for a few more hours of electricity and watched while the old man cranked up his generator, smiling so broadly that his eyes disappeared. Apparently, Byambaa's negotiations on their behalf had gone well, at least for the other guy. The blood-stained and battered appearance of his guests didn't seem to bother the proprietor, though Grant suspected it added a few thousand tugrik to the bill. "He can get us another jeep, Russian, and the gas to power it, in trade for the helicopter," Byambaa reported.

"Thanks," Grant replied, smiling and nodding to the old man. "Some point, we'll need to pay back that family for their horses."

"They were fine horses." Byambaa looked solemn in the long light of dusk. "Likely mine will return to her home. I will sing for yours."

Considering the horse had saved his life, with the bulk of its corpse if not with its speed and responsiveness, Grant said, "Make it the best song you've ever sung."

The Mongolian gave a nod. No doubt eager to rejoin Liz, he ducked between the old rugs that hung across the doorway of the squat structure, a white-washed building with cracking walls that fronted a beaten dirt road—the only one in town. Or what passed for a town in the Mongolian desert, a handful of similar buildings surrounded by a ragged spread of gers with motorcycles parked alongside horses. Rangy dogs paced the street, staring at Grant, while goats cropped the meager grasses that grew between the structures.

He ached from head to heel, but his self-assessment revealed no lasting damage. His ankle burned when he put weight on it, and his bruised throat ached when he swallowed or spoke. Dust and blood still itched on his scalp. It was not those things, the familiar aftermath of battle, that made him hesitate outside in the street. He knew what he'd see when he walked into that room: five expectant faces all turning to him, each one holding back the question. What now?

The silence of their flight had been almost a relief. Grant would've given anything for a hot shower and a firm bed, luxuries that might be available a few hundred miles away in Ulan Baatar, or in Beijing—the Forbidden City more than ever, now. Even here, he could scrounge up a tub and a pitcher of water, his hand twitching for a cigarette though he hadn't smoked since he came off active duty. The knowledge that he'd been right about Jin's treachery and the fake tomb only added to his discomforts.

Didn't matter. This was his squad, his people: Stuck in the middle of the goddamn desert, running from the Chinese army after abandoning their bankroller, after destroying the very thing they'd gone to seek. The Bone Guard. His fucking dream-come-true.

Wearily, he limped back inside, straightening as he entered the main room. Clusters of flickering oil lamps lent a warm glow to the low chamber, as if they sat in a temple.

"Byambaa says you got us a Russian jeep. How about a case of beer? Or two?" Gooney drained a bowl of vodka and winced. "Piva, isn't that what the Russians call it? Damn, shoulda kept up my language skills." He rested his cast on the edge of the only table, an assortment of chairs pulled up around it. Byambaa and Liz sat on the broad, Russian-style stove with its tiled extension making a warm sleeping platform. They curled together like a pair of parentheses.

"How far are we from the nearest airport?" Nick asked.

D. A. hunched over her laptop, scowling. "How should I know? I should be wiping the whole machine, at least doing a scan to make sure they didn't plant anything. You're lucky I navigated us here before we ran out of gas."

"We're seriously out of gas now." Gooney drained his bowl and reached for the bottle. "Forget the airport, how about a real hotel? Say what you want about Huang, I, for one, am gonna miss that guy." He lifted the re-filled bowl in salute.

Grant dropped into a chair at the table and ate a few dried cheese curds, the yak cheese tangy and unfamiliar, too dry in his throat. He washed it down with a long swallow of salted tea. "You missed the reunion, Gooney. He and Jin are old pals. Maybe he even helped Jin to cook up this whole plan about the fake tomb."

"What were they planning to steal from my people in return?" Byambaa said.

"Tell you what, though," Nick offered, his teeth glinting in the darkness, "those were some beautiful songs."

D. A. wrinkled her nose and gave a quick shake of her head, but she didn't deny it outright, maybe because Nick gave her a look. Liz had yet to speak about the deception, and how it had taken her in, but she had to be hurting.

"Whoever made those songs was a master. I can't believe they were written by Chinese sympathizer." Byambaa started to hum, then softly croon a section Grant recognized from the Running Deer song.

Grant listened, head cocked, frowning. Something about the music haunted him, but what? He took another swallow, longer, then set the bowl down deliberately. He pushed back his chair and turned. "I don't believe it either. Liz." Her head rose, her lovely eyes ringed by darkness. "How old was that chest where you found the music? World War II era, right?"

"Some of the letters inside dated to 1941."

"Seventy years ago? Jin wasn't even alive. I got the feeling he knew everything about that tomb, down to directing the thieves who stocked it. This tomb was a fake, but that doesn't mean the map was."

CHAPTER SIXTY-TWO

"Let it go, man," Gooney groaned, but Liz stirred and sat up out of Byambaa's protective embrace.

"You mean the songs might be real, the map might be true—but then, how could they lead us to the wrong place?"

D. A. rifled through her laptop case and held up a few pages of yellowed paper, her eyes bright. "Like this. Everyone knew you guys were going to the Needham Institute, and that Grant was with you—"

Grant snapped his fingers. "The library looter. He didn't have to cut the pages out, he could've taken the whole book, or just miss-shelved it, and we would've been stuck. He let me see him, let me chase him. Even Yang didn't take the pursuit too seriously."

Weariness dropping away, Liz pushed up and went to the table, taking the pages in her hand as if they were holy.

"All you needed was to find where the trail started, right? The location of the first song."

"But we found the third song, the Running Deer that run no more, with a dead man underneath it," she murmured, her eyes going round and liquid. "We thought they were trying to remove the stone or conceal it—what if they were planting it? By then, they had the songs—they knew what we would be looking for."

"I told you that waterfall sounded wrong!" Byambaa, too, crowded the table.

"But it sounded close enough, right?" Grant leaned in, looking as she felt, as if the weight of the failure had been swept away. "Jin wanted his fake to be found, so he waited for someone to think they were on the right track, then he planted just enough clues to re-direct the hunt and point toward his masterpiece."

"This doesn't help anything." Gooney slapped the table with his palm. "Even if the songs aren't bullshit like the rest of it, so what? You still don't know where to start. What're we gonna do, go back to Cambridge?"

"Go back to the intel. D. A., what else do we have?"

This punctured some of the rising enthusiasm, and Liz came around the table as D. A. tapped her keyboard, scrolling through lists, notes, images. "Hard to say, Chief. Lots of pictures of the other fake tomb, lots of pictures of this one. A few remarks from guidebooks and references, *Secret History of the Mongols*, that kind of thing." She shrugged and turned the laptop to face Liz.

"What's the oldest information we have?" Liz pulled up the copy of her own notes they'd accessed from the cloud, but most of what she had was musical, or translations of books written by Jesuit missionaries and other visitors to the Mongol empire. She closed that up, confronted with a window full of thumbnail shots from the mausoleum. A few of these showed her talking with the Darkhad guardsman, photos she hadn't known were being taken. After D. A.'s armed rescue during the tomb escape, Liz had finally reconciled the idea of this compact, frizzy-haired woman being a soldier and a spy just like the rest of them. Clandestine photography was probably the least of her skills. "Nergui knew something. He froze up when I mentioned songs and stories, then he told me the true relics were there, in the museum." She brought up the first of the images from the dim interior: weapons and armor, just like those in the fake tomb, stirrups and saddles, a painted scroll that showed the Naimaan Tsagaan gers, another painting of the same scene. She was about to click past when D. A. caught her hand.

"Why's the banner missing?" D. A. flipped from there to another image, the murals in the tomb showing the same gers, but painted recently. "Look, there's eight gers in the portable shrine, right? But only seven of them have banners in this picture—and eight of them here. Whoever painted the new version added a banner back in."

Nick's presence loomed over them. "Sign said that scroll painting hung in the chambers of Kublai Khan himself, the great Khan's grandson. Painted in the Chinese style, but made to remember his ancestor." His finger traced the outline of the banner, the one missing in the more recent image.

Across the table, Gooney started laughing so hard he got the hiccups, earning the dark stares of everyone around him. Liz appreciated all he'd done to help her and Grant, but seriously, she was starting to understand why they didn't get along. Now, he was apparently drunk, rocking back on his stool until he nearly fell over and crashed back to the ground. His face, still red from the fire, looked even more devilish until he flopped forward, his arms and shoulders taking up most of the table, still shaking as he giggled.

"Gooney—" Grant surged to his feet with a movement like an orchestra conductor about to bring down a crash of percussion the likes of which the audience might not survive. Liz caught her breath, but Nick put out his hand, stilling his commanding officer.

"Gooney. Seems like you need to explain yourself before you get tossed in a horse trough." Nick's voice, calm and deep, pierced through Gooney's mirth, and the detective pushed himself up with one hand.

"The banner," he said. "The missing banner, don't you get it? There was a banner stolen from the monastery where they stored the gers after they stopped travelling, the thing was supposed to be one of the clues to the khan's tomb. Red Army swiped it during the purges when they decided to wipe out the native religion." He hiccupped and grinned.

"Did you learn that from one of your guidebooks?" Grant demanded, but the surge of fury that had sucked the air from the room had dissipated.

"No—Wikipedia. Don't you guys do any research?"

CHAPTER SIXTY-THREE

Jin placed a steaming cup of green tea on the low table and sat carefully back on his own side. Across from him, Huang Li-Wen ran a finger around the cuff of his new shirt—tailored silk, rather than the safari-style clothes ruined by his earlier adventures. It took a second for him to notice the tea, and say, "Thank you, Minister. Most kind." By the time he lifted the cup, the slight tremor of his hand had gone.

"You are certain you do not require anything stronger?"

"This will be a fine beginning."

His hair still glistened from the shower, but he settled into himself more by the moment, enthroned in an elaborate suite in a tower hotel, once more surrounded by the fine things a man in his position must expect.

"Allow me to apologize again for any discomfort you or your man might have suffered," Jin began, but Huang merely tipped his head.

"You acted in defense of the People's Republic. I see that now. My presence must have placed you in a most difficult position."

"The Americans, much less a conspiracy of Americans and Mongols, cannot be allowed to infiltrate and damage the culture of the Han people—even a cultural period as dismaying as the Yuan dynasty. To put it quite simply, they have no right." Jin held Huang's gaze. "I am disappointed by your decision to be of use to such people, Mr. Huang."

Huang studied him in turn, with that keen gaze Jin knew so well. "Their expedition offered me an opportunity I could receive in no other way, Minister. You chose to keep me in the dark, as it were, then to suggest to the Americans that I have been involved from the start. Perhaps, had I been aware of your own plans in this area, I would have made a different investment." He drained his cup of tea and set it aside. "Perhaps it is time for something stronger."

"Plum wine?"

"I prefer whiskey." Huang settled back, waiting for Jin to wait on him. Jin controlled his expression and movement as he crossed to the cabinet and located the bottle, returning with that, and two glasses. He despised the piss-colored liquid; it had fire without depth, but this, too, he concealed.

"It does seem a satisfying adventure, this quest across continents and into an ancient tomb, which none had ever seen before. Very like an American film." Jin lifted his glass and took a swallow.

"Until we walked onto your set and the Americans discovered an uncomfortable truth."

"They seem to believe that history is inviolate, and yet deception has always been a part of the advancement of culture, like Zhuge Liang using straw soldiers to gather arrows from his enemy for the use of his own army."

"Indeed it was quite an adventure. A pity for both of us that it is over."

Jin offered a smile. "On the contrary. It may take some investment on my part to recover, but I do not believe that these events are irretrievable. We will simply need to find another adventurer. Or... To avail ourselves of an alternate narrative for this discovery. The military intercepted transmission of the footage shot by your Americans.

I see no reason that this footage could not be released to great advantage."

"Only if no one steps forward to dispute the tale." Huang's eyes narrowed just a little, his nostrils slightly flaring. He was, in some way, still invested in his own failed project, not so detached from the Americans as he pretended.

Jin let the whiskey fill his mouth, its vapors rising, its burn settling, then he swallowed and said, "You claimed to come to Ningxua in search of both artifacts and investments. I believe this offers a perfect chance to unite your interests. The Huang Li-Wen Institute for the Study of the Yuan Dynasty. It would be the first such center in China."

Huang laughed, his shoulders shaking. "That is clever. What should we say, then? That the discovery was made by one of my mining exploration teams? Something like that?"

"And we would work together to credential the scientists allowed to study and remark upon the artifacts. There is no reason yesterday's incident need be any setback at all. In fact, this approach will enable us to, how do you say it in the business world, to manage the roll-out?"

This only made Huang laugh louder, at least for a moment, then he calmed himself and leveled his gaze. "There is still the small matter of the Americans themselves. Or have you already settled that matter?"

"My colleagues in the military are in the process of doing so." Guo had been given that commission, and undertaken it eagerly. Now that there was no need for subterfuge, it should be within his skills, blunt instrument that he was.

"Then you need only make sure that no one can follow the music to the real tomb."

This time, Jin would see to it personally. When he discovered its whereabouts, that tomb would never see the light—nor would the Americans who thought they could find it: once they had been forced to do his bidding, they would become expendable.

CHAPTER SIXTY-FOUR

Byambaa checked the stirrups as Liz stood nearby, shivering slightly, flushed with anticipation. The householder who was putting them up needed extra time to get the new jeep, forcing a rest that Grant clearly chafed under, and just as clearly needed desperately. D. A. and Nick would comb through the images and data, seeking further clues, so they didn't mind the delay, and it gave Byambaa and Liz a chance to finally be alone, by the light of a spreading dawn.

"Hey, Robin Hood, you gonna want this?" Gooney stood by the door of the inn, holding up Byambaa's bow and quiver.

"Robin Hood?" Byambaa repeated, puzzled.

"Steals from the rich, gives to the poor, brilliant archer. Always riding off with Maid Marion." Gooney waggled the bow. "You want?"

Byambaa's shy smile edged out and he walked back toward Gooney. "Is this a nick name?"

"I guess so." He handed over the items. "You're not going far, right? Chief's taking a bath, and I don't know if I can manage a horse with this thing—besides, I'm starting to peel." He reached up to scrub at a bit of dead skin flaking from his scorched face.

"Not far—just to see the herds. I have some songs to perform for the horses." Byambaa gave a short bow and returned, strapping his quiver onto the saddle while his own mount stomped and tossed its head, as eager as Liz to get out of there.

She mounted and took up the reins, her horse, a small dun-colored mare, skipping a few steps until she took control, then rode up to Byambaa's side. With a last wave to Gooney, she kicked the horse and it burst forward, galloping down the dusty street. Byambaa whooped at being left behind, and caught up to her quickly, but she nudged her horse to another burst of speed and they soon left the little settlement behind, riding off into the grasslands. Like most towns in Mongolia, this one had no discernible road. The people looking for it came by jeep or Landrover with a compass as their guide. A sheltered location near a favored grazing area gave the place enough value to have buildings at all—half the Mongolian population were still nomads. Now, with the wind blowing through her hair and a strong horse beneath her, she could totally understand why. Byambaa rode one-handed, the other saluting her as he rode by, turning his mount for the lake that stood nearby.

They rode up over a hill and the water gleamed below. On the far side, a cluster of horses nipped up grass and nuzzled the water, flicking their tails. Their ears twitched up, a dozen faces suddenly focused on Byambaa and Liz, until they recognized members of their own herd and returned to their breakfast.

Liz and Byambaa dismounted, hobbling the horses so they could roam a bit, but not so far as to be out of reach. While Byambaa prepared himself to sing, Liz brought down the bundles from their horses: a thick wool blanket, a few parcels of food including a milky fudge made by the householder's wife. When he began, his voice rising from the earth and seeming to fill the sky, Liz went still, listening. She shut her eyes for a time, breathing in the earthy scents around her, the tall grass, the moisture of the lake, the slight sweat of their short ride. This was a song of mourning, honoring the horses who had been killed, most especially the mount who had given her life in the mad ride to reveal the truth about the false tomb. The song rose and fell, and finally drifted on the wind. Liz opened her eyes, expecting him to join her on the blanket. Instead, he turned to face her, and started a new song, one they had worked on together, melding the tunes expected in Western music, with the tones of the Mongolian tradition. Liz, too, stood up and sang with him.

She felt rusty at first, her voice scratchy and out of practice, but she soon found her melody line, bounding over his. It was a love song, of course, meant to be heartfelt, but this morning, he played the fool, spreading his hands, swinging his hips, wiggling his eyebrows until she could barely sing for laughing. When she broke down completely, smacking his chest, Byambaa enveloped her in his arms and brought her down to the blanket, smothering her laughter with kisses. Heat rose in her loins, a longing suppressed by the excitement and forced companionship of these last few days. She slid her hand to the back of his neck, feeling the silk of his hair. His tongue darted against her lips, then pressed them open, their breath mingled.

The sounds of the steppe shifted around them: the stamping of horses, the rising rush of the wind. They wrapped into each other, Byambaa lifting her, drawing her close with his hand at her thigh. She fumbled with the strange closure of his del, then let her hand slide lower, avoiding the buttons and loops entirely as she explored his powerful body.

His fingers crept between them, finding her belt and tugging it loose. Then a sound out of place—a ratchet and slide she had never thought to hear outside the movies. She pulled back despite Byambaa's moan of protest.

Rising above them, silhouetted against the day, stood a man with a rifle, backed by a half-dozen others. "Please continue," the man said in English thick with a Chinese accent. "It will give my men a reason to pause before shooting you."

CHAPTER SIXTY-FIVE

Grant's eyes snapped open to the dim light of the borrowed room. Sun filtered through gaps in the roof tiles, along with a chill Autumn breeze that ruffled his damp hair. At least he wasn't bloody any more. For now. Footsteps scrambling up the narrow stairs, then Gooney, breathless. By the time Gooney shoved past the rug at the door, Grant was on his feet, his hand resting on the gun.

"Chief. Shit. They rode out—not far, he had his arrows. They must have been taken by surprise."

"Back up and make sense."

Gooney caught his breath and straightened. "Byambaa and Liz took a ride at about o-nine-hundred, over to sing for the horses." This came out as a question, and Grant nodded—he already knew that much of the plan. "One of our host's daughters rode out that way to check on a foal, and found their blanket—empty, apparently abandoned. The two horses hobbled nearby. She found this on top." He held out a cell phone, black, sleek and unfamiliar.

Grant cradled it in his palm. "No blood? No sign of violence?"

Gooney shook his head. "No, sir. The bow and arrows remained on his saddle. Looks like they were surprised by a group, probably on horseback, given a lack of tire tracks."

"You investigated?"

"Not yet, Chief. Hearsay only."

"We should—"

The phone rang, and both men froze. In Afghanistan, the ring of an unfamiliar cell might just as well trigger a bomb as a conversation. It rang again, shivering in Grant's hand. He took a deep breath and popped it open, holding it to his ear.

"Have I the pleasure of addressing Mr. Grant Casey?"

A cultured Chinese voice, not the British style of Huang, nor sharp tones like the English Yang probably learned from watching movies. "Minister Jin, I presume."

A soft chuckle answered this. "You are a fine operative, Mr. Casey. The sort of man we would like to have on our side."

A pulse of anger shot through him, but before Grant could reply, Jin said, "Have no fear. This is not a recruiting call. I will not ask you to compromise your government. But I do believe you have the skills to do something that it will be difficult for my people to accomplish. I trust you speak Russian?"

"What's going on?" Gooney mouthed.

"Tell me what you want," Grant said evenly.

"The same thing that you do. The first marker on the map to the Khan's tomb. I presume you know about the banner. I should like you to bring it to me."

The Chinese probably had access to primary sources—they might have known about the banner all along, but it didn't matter until someone else knew how important it could be. "Why would I help you?"

"Because if you fail to do so, Ms. Kirschner and her barbarian shall dissolve in a vat of lye, never to be seen again. Feet first, I think. Together or separately, I have not yet decided. If you like, I can call when I place them inside. Perhaps you would like to put the call on speakerphone. Given their musical training, I am sure they will deliver quite harmonious screams."

CHAPTER SIXTY-SIX

Grant and Nick sat on an antique vinyl bench in the sparsely furnished office—a huge space in an over-sized concrete building. Nick clutched the case of camera equipment a little too tightly, while Grant studied every aspect of the room, for once enabled by his cover to do so openly. The Russian flag and another flag for the local administration flanked a large, framed portrait of Putin, wearing his most sardonic grin. Other than this, the room held only an accumulation of desks, apparently washed up from a century of former purposes, and three officers. Two of them rattled away on computers that probably still accepted floppy disks. The third woman, stocky and clad in a wool uniform not much different from that of the Chinese People's Security Service, peered at the credentials Grant had delivered. She stared at the papers, stared at Nick and Grant—a bit longer at Nick, then back to the papers.

She had already carried the documents into the office behind her, a corner of the huge room divided from the rest by windows of frosted glass. After a moment, she returned, still carrying their things, though he had no doubt they had been photographed or copied before her return. He took careful breaths, keeping himself calm. They couldn't afford to kill any Russians. That was a step too far, and they were already beyond the pale for most of his contacts to cover for him. He was so far out on a limb the best he could hope for if anything went wrong was enough rope to hang himself, and maybe leave Nick with some kind of deniability. They had the worst cover story he'd ever come up with, a handful of quickly forged documents, and half of D. A.'s beloved camera kit. And, of course, they had each other. No, if any Russians went down, he and Nick would be royally screwed by every government official between here and Siberia. For better or worse, it wasn't far.

"Has President Putin ever visited here?" Nick asked suddenly in Russian. He had to speak loudly to cover the distance between the bench and the broad school-teacher's desk where she sat.

The woman twitched at his voice. She swallowed, dark eyes round, then said, "We have not had such a visit."

"Yeah, the borders to the west concern him more, don't they?" Nick shrugged a little. "I wish we had the chance to cover him." He tapped the camera case. "He's where the excitement is."

She smiled faintly. "Excitement. Indeed. Putin tries to make the area strong again, to protect our citizens."

"So I hear." He bobbed his head. "Have you been in combat?"

"This is why I am surprised that you have been granted visas, even to visit here." She folded her hands on her desk top. "It is not a promising time to make a film of any kind."

"You got that right." Nick chuckled. "That's why we don't have much time." He gave a slight shrug.

She studied him again, then stood up. "I will consult with the Commandant." She turned and walked to the door with its inset glass, giving a soft knock, then entering.

In her absence, Grant flashed Nick a thumbs-up. Minister Jin's cell phone felt hot and heavy in his pocket, transmitting their location, and, mostly likely, serving as a microphone that broadcast whatever they said back to base. Since that call, half of Grant's conversations had been held across a keyboard or notepad. While they talked logistics out loud for Jin's benefit, they held a furious exchange of notes amounting to one conclusion: if Jin planned to get his project back on track, covering up any trail to the real tomb, all of them had to die. Jin would keep Liz and Byambaa alive just long enough to prove it when Grant turned over the banner. Then what? Not lye when good, old-fashioned bullets would do the trick. And with the cellphone as his spy, Jin could monitor their progress from afar. He sent photos of Liz or Byambaa every hour, making the phone jiggle in Grant's pocket, assuring him that, so far, they were still alive. The scant evidence Jin provided and D. A.'s research pointed them to the one-time commander of that border Red Army unit responsible for destroying the monastery, a Russian-Buryat with ties on both sides of the border. Would the guy even remember, after so long? They were lucky he was still alive. One way and another, the Bone Guard needed that banner just as much as Jin did, so they sat in the chilly office on the wrong side of another border, hoping their forged documents would pass the scrutiny of this backwater commission.

"The Commandant will see you now," the woman announced, standing aside to hold open the door as Grant and Nick rose and thanked her.

The old man leaned back behind a broad desk of his own, this one made of wood and topped with leather polished to a high sheen, displaying the fact that it was conspicuously empty. Thin and sharp-featured, he stared at them as they entered. Grant offered a hand, but the man gave a sniff. "My receptionist tells me you are interested in the period of the Mongol People's Republic and the Soviet Army's support of their operations. I cannot imagine why. Even I do not find that interesting."

"The American government calls it Nation Building, but it was the Soviets who pioneered it," Grant said.

"This is exactly what Putin claims." He folded his hands together. "But you are not speaking with Putin, or any of his people, you are speaking with me. Why?"

"We want the view from the ground, from people who were really there. Putin..." Grant gestured toward another image of the Russian president, this time mounted on a tall, bay horse, a rifle cracked open on his shoulder. The photo looked out of place among pictures of Mongolian buildings, steppes, horses, and group shots of soldiers, some of them in the classic mode of victory: grinning, holding up some trophy or another, near a building shot with bullets or broken by mortars. One photo showed the commandant, much younger, holding a bit of cloth along with another man, a Mongolian in a similar uniform. Both of them grinning. "Putin is a great man, but he is..."

The commandant's eyes shifted toward Putin and back, narrowing.

Grant focused on the photograph, yellowed with age, its image indistinct. Grant looked to Nick. "What's the Russian word for a dilettante?"

Behind his desk, the commandant gave something like a hiccup and his mustache bristled. Got him. The guy spoke English. "And you are, what? Film-makers. Artists? I have had enough of artists—I have never met one worth his vodka." He jabbed his finger toward one among the rank of pictures, showing a group of young officers, Russians on one side, Mongols on the other, shaking hands and grinning in front of a 60's-era relief sculpture, a blocky, stylized in the manner of the public art of the time, carved into a huge, jagged slab of white stone. "Do you see this? The ugliest statue ever made. The man who commissioned it was fired. The artist was fired. They deserved the misery they died in. We work so closely with the Mongolian Communist Party, we give gifts, we allow them honor, independence, and this is how they celebrate. With crap. Artists." He snorted.

Grant leveled his gaze and squared his shoulders. "No, sir. We are soldiers, like you. We want to reveal the military history of the region —we want to examine the influence of great military leaders, from Genghis Khan to Putin himself, but through the eyes of the men who served. Men like you." And they didn't have much time. Gooney favored a frontal assault, seizing the guy and putting a gun to his temple to get their answers fast. Maybe Gooney had a point.

"Soldiers." The commandant nodded slowly. "Then you are also drinking men." His mustache twitched upward, and he reached for his bottom drawer. "Or you are simply liars." He pulled out a huge pistol and leveled it with one hand while he tapped an intercom with the other. "Please send in two officers to handle our guests. They will be staying indefinitely."

CHAPTER SIXTY-SEVEN

Liz stalked from one end of her room to the other, then across, rubbing her arms as if she were cold. Her feet sank into the carpet, and she had to dodge the oversized bed. The whole place smelled of fresh carpets, new paint, and sawdust. She guessed they were in a brand-new hotel, not even open yet, maybe not even finished. Thick plastic covered the only window, from the outside, but that couldn't block the sounds of the street: quiet, compared with Boston. Few cars went by, lots of motorcycles and a number of horses. They had to be in Ulan Baatar, the only city in the region large enough to justify a lavish hotel like this one. Nearby, a periodic mechanical droning rose, accompanied by clatters and bangs on a more human scale, like someone using tools, along with occasional low conversations in Mongolian, and sometimes louder curses. The hissing and whining that sometimes joined in sounded familiar, but she couldn't place it, like a song she knew she'd heard before, but could not remember the words.

Someone knocked on the door and she startled, whirling around, but not answering. The knock repeated, and Liz stared at the door.

When Jin's man wanted to take her picture, he didn't knock, he just barged inside.

A third knock sounded, this time followed by a calm voice. "Ms. Kirschner. I would appreciate the chance to speak with you."

Huang. The traitor. "Get lost."

A long silence, then, "I can understand that you are not pleased to find me here." Another pause. "I trust the accommodations are at least adequate?"

"Best prison I've ever been in. Where's Byambaa?"

"He is nearby, also unharmed. Please, Ms. Kirschner. I have brought you American cola."

She nearly laughed. He brought her a Coke? And that was supposed to make her feel better? It was like something their advertising department dreamed up and discarded as too offensive to hostages. But the moment she thought it, she could taste the sweet and tangy flavor at the back of her throat and feel the bubbles popping on her tongue. After days of irregular and unfamiliar meals, the soda called her like a siren singing her to her doom.

Liz stalked over to the door, setting her hand on the knob. "What do you want?"

"The opportunity to make amends, perhaps to explain."

She yanked open the door, hoping he was leaning against it, but he stood in the hall holding a tray with a bottle of soda and a glass of ice on top. With his shirt-sleeves rolled up and no suit-coat, he might have been aiming to humble himself, but the effect was more like a politician's photo-op, when he wants to pretend he's hardworking. "Did you know about killing Marko? Were you in on that, too?"

"I have not been in on anything, Ms. Kirschner."

"Bullshit." She snatched the soda and crossed the room to plop into the room's only chair. She lifted the drink to her lips, breathing it in, then hesitated. What if it were drugged? Something to make her talk, or to make her sleep? *Paranoia is one of the symptoms.* Grant's voice echoed in her memory.

Huang advanced a few steps. "Would you not prefer it with ice?"

"You're not a butler—it doesn't suit you."

"No more does bitterness suit you." He set aside the tray on a nearby dresser.

She gave him a tight smile. "It was a present from a friend."

He tipped his head, his silvered hair as perfect as when she'd first met him, his clothes as impeccable, his demeanor...well, okay, he wasn't quite the polished businessman of those early days. She remembered his boyish excitement, the thrill that they shared when they opened that great door to the wonders inside. Before she knew the tomb was a fraud and, she now suspected, before he knew as well.

"Ms. Kirschner. The world often fails to provide what we seek. In these cases, I find it most helpful to enjoy what is found."

"A corrupt minister on his way to bilking the archaeological world and the Mongolian people? That is a treasure." She raised her bottle in salute and took a swallow. It effervesced in her mouth and poured syrup down her throat, filling up a place in her she hadn't known was empty.

"Friendship is a treasure," he replied. "And trust. A treasure once lost, hard to regain." He clasped his hands before him, lowered, like his face. Then his eyes rose to meet hers. "I hope that I will be given the chance to try."

"Is that what you want me to tell Grant when we get out of here? So he won't shoot you on sight?" Then her throat closed, the sweetness turning sour. She forced herself to swallow, to breathe. "Are we going to get out of here?" Jin couldn't afford it, to have any credible witnesses to his deception. Her chest felt too tight, and she looked back toward the darkened window with its mysterious rhythm of life going on, cars jacked up, a pneumatic lift, the curses of a mechanic familiar in any nation, in any language. It was a repair shop, of course. Score one for her exquisite hearing—thank God Jin's first assault hadn't ruined it forever. His second one would, however he chose to eliminate her. Would she at least get to see Byambaa first? Was Jin the kind of person who would force one of them to watch the slaying of the other? She shuddered.

Huang's soft voice brought her back. "The minister has made an agreement with Mr. Casey. I imagine that he will keep it." His eyes, more hazel than dark, looked damp and worried.

A man in an army uniform carrying a smart phone appeared at the door. Time for her close-up. He approached, raising the camera, not bothering to tell her what he was doing. With a trembling hand, Liz set down the bottle. She raised her fingers in something like an a-okay, and smiled, shifting her eyes, posing for maybe the last portrait of her life.

CHAPTER SIXTY-EIGHT

The cell phone buzzed in Grant's pocket, and the commandant frowned. "What is this sound?"

"Our buddies," Grant replied, "letting us know the bomb is armed."

The commandant jerked back, staring at the camera case, his weapon wavering. Feet pounded outside, and he shouted, "Stay back! Hold position!"

Nick surged to his feet with a roar. He threw himself against the desk, shoving it back into the startled officer, who tumbled then groaned as the huge desk pinned him against the back wall, hands flailing. With a swipe of the camera case, Nick slammed the guy's hand, the gun firing into a cabinet and flying free.

Grant spun the other direction, snatching up a visitor's chair and running for the door. Already, a hand was shoving it open. Grant slammed it closed again, the arm stuck inside, colorful Russian cursing outside. He opened the door a crack, slammed it again. Opened a third time and the arm jerked back, shaking and bloody. This time, he backed up the slam by shoving the back of the chair under the handle.

"You are—under arrest—for assaulting an—officer! Stand where you are!" the commandant shouted, gasping for breath between phrases.

Grant snatched the framed photo and completed his turn. His eyes met Nick's, the serious mask of the sniper flickering with something much more dangerous. Not combat ready. But doing a damn fine job. "Let's go."

Nick launched toward the outside wall, the arched window that looked onto a bleak and empty street. He held the hard-sided case before him, ducked his head, and ran straight for it. And people said Grant was crazy. The big guy flew through in a cascade of glass. The commandant twisted and ducked as best he could, glass shards scattering around him. Grant followed, clutching the photo, and grabbing the commandant's hat as he leapt onto the desk. He did a tuck and roll through the window, hitting hard, but safe, and was up again on the outside, still running. He paused to catch Nick's elbow and steady him. His prosthetic had been jolted by the fall, and he bared his teeth, staggering. Still, he gave a nod, and they rounded the building together.

The receptionist pounded down the steps toward their jeep, then dropped to one knee, bringing up her arms in a classic shooter's pose. Nick pushed out the camera case, and a bullet cracked into it, then he was in the back seat, Grant in the front, tearing out of there before the woman got off a fourth shot that burrowed into the cushion beside him. She was pretty good. She had scored another shot on the case that defended Nick's head and chest, and one that heated the air by Grant's ear.

"You good?" he shouted into the wind.

Nick's breathing sounded sharp. He groaned and shifted around, then Grant heard a plastic scrape and a mechanical click. Nick finally leaned against the front seat, bringing his head close to Grant's holding on as they pelted down the broad, pre-planned Communist streets. "I'm A and O and ready to go. The camera is a total loss. Anticipate pushback from sigint on the loss. Mission failure, sir."

Nick had gone mechanical on him, straight back to Unit protocols. Shit. "Stand down, Norton." Grant turned north, toward the mass of Russia, Siberia beyond—the age-old prison of Russia's enemies, and the hunting grounds of nomads not unlike the Mongolians.

"Negative, sir. Not out of the woods yet." His eyes darted, and his hands twitched in search of a trigger.

"I think what you mean to say is, you're fine, the camera's shot—literally—and D. A.'s gonna be pissed. Right?"

He peeled around corners, the few pedestrians leaping back, staring, taking notice of their speed and direction. Good. A few more turns like that, and he swung onto the highway, turning south now, driving calmly, the commandant's hat perched on his head. He projected the focus and frustration of an officer, catching a few curious looks and widened eyes, glances instantly straight ahead again as he passed other drivers. Somewhere behind and to the east, he could hear faint sirens. Not out of the woods yet. Maybe soon.

"Sir, the mission is incomplete. Are you calling off the operation?"

"It's complete as it's going to be. The Russian gave the banner to his Mongolian buddy."

"Phase two can't go forward without evidence, sir."

"We got that." Grant indicated the photo on the seat beside him. "Hey, look, the Commies have billboards."

Nick's face pinched, he flicked his gaze again, taking in the image of a woman in a fur cap with a bottle of vodka. He took a few deep breaths, and his expression eased, then he looked back. "What the Hell were you thinking, Chief, that's not even the right one—where's the banner?"

"Beats me. But those are the same two guys, along with a bunch of others."

"So now we're stealing trophy shots? Ugliest statue in the world." Still, Nick picked it up in one hand as they slid between other cars.

"Of—?" Grant prompted. The traffic thinned out, trucks still rumbling ahead, toward the border, Russian sedans taking exits toward the dense pine forests, headed for the local equivalent of vacation dachas or hunting retreats.

Nick studied the picture, then his brows rose. "Genghis Khan. Okay, but why do we care?"

"The man who commissioned it was beaten to death—they never found the killer."

"He deserved to be," Nick muttered. "No sense of proportion. Where'd you get that intel? Don't tell me: Wikipedia."

"Close. One of Gooney's guidebooks. Thing is this, all the other statues of the khan were destroyed, except that one. I'm betting, this Mongolian commissioner protected it with his life. He went down rather than admit what he knew." Grant looked ahead on the road. "Crossing ahead. Sit back and look official."

Nick leaned into the back seat, holding the black case beside him. Dodging the queue of trucks and motorcycles, Grant sped toward the smaller police gate. As they slowed, Grant glared at the young officer on duty and barked in Russian, "We have no time for this. Let us through!"

The kid jumped, glanced at his hat with the star, and gave a quick salute as he hurried to raise the gate. When the crossing vanished behind them, Grant pulled out Jin's cell phone. "Latest on Liz. Check it for me."

Nick squinted at the screen while Grant navigated the forest road into Northern Mongolia. "She's smiling, doing something weird with her hand, like she's a celebrity or something."

So far, every shot showed her fury—what had changed? "Take a picture on your phone send it to D. A." He didn't want anything else Jin might wish to send finding its way onto the rest of their devices. Hopefully, D. A. and Gooney had gotten close enough to civilization for a solid signal. Grant glanced at the picture beside him. Hopefully he wasn't risking all their lives for a snapshot of nothing and a stupid hunch.

CHAPTER SIXTY-NINE

Jin studied his computer screen, then made another notation on the map of Mongolia spread on the table beside him. Reindeer stones like the one in Ningxua were unusual, but not, unfortunately, unique. He had located at least a dozen, some marked out for tourists, others merely the location where one had been before being removed to a museum, and still others noted in travelers' descriptions, but not made public. For reasons of their own, the Mongols preferred to hoard their patrimony rather than to celebrate it. Except for the accursed Khan, of course. And he would soon take even that from them.

He trusted that the Americans would meet his deadline and deliver the banner. Americans were nothing if not personal in their definition of loyalty. While a Chinese might place the good of the nation above all, an American was just as likely to betray his country if he could save his friend. A curious priority.

His phone rang, and he answered, expecting it could be the American already. "Yes?"

"Minister Jin. This is Minister Deng. We have had another

communication from the Mongols regarding our offer." The Minister of the Interior sounded gruff, irritated, even for him.

"A refusal, I presume."

"When and how are you planning to deliver on your promises?"

Jin straightened away from the table, setting down his pen. "I am in Mongolia now, Minister, establishing additional groundwork. I have taken on a new partner, and we plan to be able to launch the public revelation of Project Raven within the next week. Does that suit you?"

"A week? This is more than I hoped for, much more. I am impressed, Jin. But you say you are already in Mongolia? Have you made contact with our people?"

"I have arranged a meeting in just a few hours. I will send you the samples for testing as soon as possible."

"I am very impressed with your efficiency, Minister. Your birth was an auspicious day for China."

Brushing his fingers over the map, Jin allowed himself a smile. He rang off, collecting his things into a case and calling for his driver. Within two hours, the Landrover parked in a copse of pines somewhere north of the only road, and less than a hundred kilometers south of the Russian border. A short walk up a grassy slope brought him to an overhanging slab of stone that protected a sandstone ruin. The rectangular structure supplemented by a few circular mounds of vanishing stone suggested a monastery, likely destroyed by the Russians during Mongolia's unfortunately brief span as a Communist republic. Clearly, the Soviet system proved untenable, while its Chinese counterpart remained strong.

As he approached the structure, sunlight warming his face and hands, making his suitcoat drag at his shoulders, Jin heard the walls humming. Thousands of tiny holes pierced the old stone, and shapes moved among them. Bees. Burrowing insects that had made the old monastery into their own hive. They chanted now, in their cells, as once the lamaist monks must have done.

Three men waited inside, lounging near a group of motorcycles.

The two Mongols were dressed in coveralls with dirt so ground-in he could not discern their original color. The third, a Chinese man, stepped forward, a hand beneath his jacket, bowing briefly to the Minister. He said something to his Mongol companions, and one of them dug into his motorcycle's storage to remove a packet, grumbling in his own language.

"Is there a problem?" Jin inquired.

"He says his family is suspicious. They want him to stop working, not to disturb the spirits."

Jin covered his disdain and smiled gravely, meeting the Mongol's defiant stare. "Tell him they will soon have a revelation that shows the truth, and they need worry no longer. The Great Khan himself approves his work."

The Chinese man spoke for a little while, but the Mongol seemed unconvinced, even when his friend joined in, waving his arms, and clearly enamored of the wealth their work could bring them. He pointed at their battered motorcycles and said something about the city. Apparently, the man had dreams he hoped that mining would fulfill. And so it could, but only if they had a solid supply, and a market, and that could only happen if the Mongols conceded their superstitions to the modern era. Jin reached into his case, drawing their attention, and withdrew a wrapped bundle which he offered to them. It gave a muffled clinking as the suspicious man took it from his hand. Jin continued to smile. The Mongols stood shoulder to shoulder as they opened it, the younger man looking eager, probably expecting money. The cloth wrapping parted to reveal, indeed, a glimpse of silver, then their faces stilled. The younger man lifted his hands as well, spreading the cloth, and what it contained, between them. A belt of silver plates embellished with wolves and horses, tarnished with age. Well, with certain chemicals that easily approximated that appearance. The silver cast dull reflections that lit up their faces, and they murmured of the khan.

The Chinese man glanced at Jin, and bowed a little deeper.

"I cannot leave this with them, but I wished them to see it, to understand what it means."

"The Great Khan is found," said the older Mongol in careful Mandarin.

"We believe that he might be," Jin answered. "You will be the first to hear."

The Mongol grinned back at him and bowed in turn, then lost his smile and handed over the packet he had brought, nodding and pointing. "Is good, is very pure."

Jin set down his case and opened the leather satchel to glimpse a group of canisters each containing a sample of mineral ore. "Thank you." The man barely heard him, returning to his examination of the belt, but his younger companion held it up to his waist and stood taller, no doubt imagining himself as a warrior, one of the khan's elite bodyguards. Hand-picked to defend him, hand-picked to die to seal the Great Khan's tomb. Jin slipped the satchel into his case and said, "Regretfully, I must return the belt for further study, to confirm what we have found."

The men's faces fell, but they reverently wrapped the belt in cloth and handed it back.

Jin's phone buzzed in his pocket. The Chinese man asked, "When will we hear from Minister Deng?"

"When he has had the chance to analyze the samples. If they are good, he will send payment, and inform you of the next steps."

"And of the discovery of the Great Khan's tomb, apparently." The man bowed with a congratulatory air, and herded the Mongols back onto their motorcycles. The sound of engines echoed in the ruined walls, then the trio had gone.

Jin composed himself when he saw the number on his screen. Guo. He tapped it on. "Yes?"

"The Americans failed and now the Russians are sending officers over the border in pursuit. It's time to follow through."

"Failed? Are you certain?"

"Your contact informs us they entered the office and departed again under fire within the hour." Guo cleared his throat. "You have failed."

Jin aimed his gaze at the hole-drilled wall before him, imagining it was Guo's head. "No, Captain. This was merely a loose end that can be tied off in another way. Shall I return to tend to those other...loose ends?"

"My men are already seeing to it, Minister. I trusted that you intended to be a man of your word."

"I am certain the Central Committee will appreciate your diligence, Captain." Jin tapped the phone off. No banner, the Russians chasing the American soldiers—sure to provoke an international incident, and a little too much interest in an area that Jin hoped to draw attention away from completely. Could the Russians be trusted to take care of those two? Jin lifted his phone and sent them some assistance. Guo and the army would dispose of Kirschner and her Mongol, the Russians could eliminate the two soldiers. That left two for Jin and his own people. In a matter of hours, they would contain the entire problem before it spread. Jin carried his case back toward the car, carrying the promise of Mongolia's past, and China's future. Bees hummed in the walls around him, working busily in secret on treasure only time would reveal. Very, very soon.

CHAPTER SEVENTY

For the first hour after the photo, Liz hoped for some response from the team. Where were they? Had they understood the signal she tried to send, and if so, was it enough? For the next photo, she tried the same thing, but the new soldier glared and ordered her to be still, hands down. After that, her hands simply would not be still. She tapped out the rhythms of every piece of flute music she had ever learned from Brahms to Navajo to Japanese fue melodies. Huang, apparently disappointed by his reception, had not stayed long, and now she missed him. She missed anyone who might even pretend to be friendly, and she stared at each wall, then the floor and ceiling in turn, imagining she had x-ray vision and could see Byambaa on the other side, in his own lush prison.

The door banged open again, and she startled, then wrapped her arms around herself. Two Chinese soldiers stood there, guns drawn. One of them gestured sharply toward the hall. When she didn't immediately react, he lunged into the room and grabbed her by the shoulder, hauling her before him. She cried out, and the other soldier stuffed a rag into her mouth, securing it with another. They brought her hands behind her, binding them tight. Liz shook her head. Surely the time wasn't up yet! They were being moved again, that was all. Another rough trip with a dark sack over her head, like the one that had brought them here.

Her heart thundered as they shoved her along down the hall. At a junction, they turned and she saw another group of soldiers clustered around Byambaa. He was on his knees, struggling to breathe around his gag, and one of the men was laughing, pulling his fist back for another blow.

With a wrench of her shoulders away from her guards, Liz sprang toward him. His head jerked up, eyes bleary with pain. Their eyes met, her terror mirrored in his face, their voices, the joy that had brought them together, stifled—maybe for good. Tears stung her eyes, but she shook them back.

An arm intervened, a hand with a gun that rose to press against her forehead, between her eyes, forcing her back.

"Up," barked a voice in English. The round-faced officer emerged from an elevator, a man behind him holding the doors open. "Get in."

Byambaa staggered to his feet, shaking off the torpor of the attack, and moved toward the elevator. Liz stumbled after, a little surprised when only one of the soldiers followed. Another man waited inside. As the doors closed, he caught Byambaa's arm and produced a syringe. The soldier's pistol dug into Liz's forehead, and Byambaa took a deeper breath, as if he would sing, but he stood still.

His last moment, his last breath, and he knew it. Liz screamed into her gag. She fought and struggled against the soldier. Dead, shot or injected, would it even matter? *Do not go quiet into that good night,* she thought. Poetry. Damnit, she didn't want poetry, she wanted music, she wanted to hear his voice. The second soldier grappled with her, wrapping an arm around her shoulders, but she slammed a kick into the man with the syringe and he struck the wall with a grunt. The officer's face darkened and he started to shout, drawing his own weapon, his back to the doors.

The elevator gave a ding and the doors slid open. The officer twitched, his head rearing back. A reflex of fury that saved his life as a bullet cracked the air and struck the back wall.

A second shot on a low diagonal furrowed the officer's leg, then he ducked low, taking a stance.

Liz's assailant swung his weapon away, and fell in a spatter of blood. She wrenched against the grip of the other man, ducking forward, dragging him with her.

"Here! To me!" the officer shouted in Mandarin.

Shouts echoed and the doors started to close, then Byambaa flung himself across the gap, half out of the elevator preventing it from moving. An alarm buzzer sounded.

Feet pounded on the nearby stairs, then, with another shot, the soldier's grip slid away, and hot blood seeped through her shirt, leaving her shaking.

The officer fired, straight ahead. A body fell and someone on the outside gave a cry. The officer swiveled in that direction, but Byambaa rolled into him, pressing him to the side.

A hand caught Liz's arm and pulled her. "With me, Ms. Kirschner. Please hurry. Byambaa, please!" a cultured voice, broken in fear. Huang. He pulled her in front of him, but tentatively, unsure how this was meant to work, unwilling to force her. "Go! Go. I will cover you."

He held a gun in his other hand, but his arm trembled. She wanted to laugh, to cry, to do as he told her. She stumbled a few steps down the hall.

Byambaa scrambled out of the elevator and the door slid shut as the officer readied his weapon. Zhen lay on the ground in a pool of blood, the gun still hooked in his hand. Even in death, he looked more effective than Huang, his arm straighter, his aim more sure.

The door to the stairs flew open and someone shouted, "Down, all down if you wish to live!" Two guns thrust into the opening, a rifle, a pistol, more shadows clustering, then they burst in, a squad of soldiers.

Byambaa got his feet under him and they fled around the corner, all three of them. "Here!" Huang called. "Here is the swimming pool."

The swimming pool. What good was that? Liz turned again, banging into a wall, her wrists tugging against her bonds as she instinctively tried to stop herself. Byambaa kicked open the door to the swimming pool and they ran inside. The pool stood empty in a surround of tiles still grayed with fresh mortar. Stacks of chairs waited their moment to be set around the narrow decking. Tall windows fronted one side, and a door onto a sundeck beyond. Byambaa tried to kick that, too, but it resisted.

"Please?" Huang said from behind them, then levelled the gun at the locked door, holding it with both hands. It still shivered. One shot shattered the glass, leaving a jagged opening they could never climb through, not with their hands bound.

Running footsteps outside.

Liz turned back, running toward the door. It slammed open just as she barreled into the heap of chairs. They teetered and fell, crashing into the soldiers as they burst inside, taking down the first pair, and leaving a tumbled heap of jutting enameled metal for the rest to navigate.

Another shot rang behind her. "Come!" Huang shouted. She obeyed, and they stumbled through the shattered door onto the sundeck. It didn't even have chairs. A tall fence surrounded the deck, clearly too tall to climb. Another gate stood there, topping an escape ladder that dropped the last story to the ground. The tall windows into the pool area showed flickering shadows as soldiers swarmed into the pool room.

Huang brought his gun to the locked gate and pulled the trigger. It clicked onto an empty chamber.

CHAPTER SEVENTY-ONE

"Bad news, Chief," Nick reported, leaning over the back seat, steadying himself. The narrow forest track they had taken to top the hill could barely be seen on the other side, so Grant paused to survey the wilderness.

"Company? The motorcycle?"

"Too big, still far off. I made the bike, too, but I don't see it now." He stood, shielding his eyes with his hand. "This one looks like army."

"Damn." Grant glanced around. They could take the track down the other side of the hill, but they'd be just as obvious, given the crunch of underbrush and the shaking of trees that marked the passage of the advancing enemy. How had the army even gotten here that fast? Grant's guess: motorcycle guy clued them in to the Americans' true destination. "Can you manage this terrain?"

Nick sank back to his seat and glanced around, one hand absently rubbing at the place where his stump met his prosthetic. He probably wasn't used to this level of activity since his injury, and Grant felt a twinge. Finally Nick answered, "Not for long, Chief. I'd slow you down."

"Don't talk like I'm about to leave you."

"Rule one, isn't it?"

"Fuck the rules." Grant slid out of the jeep and hit the ground. A taller cluster of trees sheltered their vehicle, making it harder to spot, but odds were the enemy knew this ground better than they did. Grant pointed up. "Can you handle that terrain?"

Nick gave a nod. "You got it."

"Don't fire 'til you see the whites of their eyes. We get lucky, we don't have to fire at all."

Nick flashed his grin. He slung their only rifle, a Russian-made hunting gun, over his shoulder, then entered the thicket of trees.

The sound of the engine growled as it drew closer. Grant snapped the stolen photo from its frame and slid it into his shirt. He pushed through the brush toward the south, then retreated more carefully, coming around to the track and choosing his position. When the truck roared up over the edge to the clearing at the top, it rocked to a halt, an extended cab army vehicle with a canvas back. The four men inside leaned, staring at the apparently abandoned jeep. They conferred briefly, then two of the men jumped out, Kalashnikovs at the ready, and stalked forward, one on each side. One of them, a guy with a trim mustache, dropped down, scanning underneath the jeep, then giving a nod as they approached

"They must be on foot," the man said, scanning the woods around them.

"Why leave the jeep?" called the driver.

He shrugged. "Too noisy. It's Russian."

"Louder than your wife," the driver replied, and the other men snorted their laughter.

"Shut up!" said the passenger, a thin, dark-haired man. He leaned out, listening, then murmured, "They can't be far ahead. Might've gone to ground." With a jerk of his hand, he loaded his rifle and stepped out. Cautious, letting the other men go first, looking for other signs. Instantly the most dangerous of the four. He reminded Grant of himself. Grant hoped he wouldn't have to shoot him.

"What's the point?" Mustache asked. "No harm done but to the old man's pride." He shrugged. "How long do we waste looking for these jokers?"

"It's a good point. I've got shashlik tonight—don't want to be late for that," said the driver.

"This is the job," said Thin Man. "We find the Americans. Period."

"We found their jeep," said the man on the far side of the vehicle. "I say we report in, and let the Mongolians find them." He shouldered his rifle and pulled out a cigarette as he sauntered back toward the truck.

"You think Putin's running a democracy? We don't vote on this," Thin Man replied. He made his own circuit of the jeep, resting his hand on the chassis and pulling it back. "You're wasting time. Let's go." He jerked his rifle, indicating the slope where Grant had broken through the brush. "Spread out. Let's go," he said again when the other two didn't follow right away. Mustache groaned and the other guy stuck the cigarette in his mouth, then they set out in rough formation, Thin Man taking point, quietly, while the other two stalked to either side, putting some distance between them, stomping through underbrush and cracking branches. Their noise receded down the slope. Still in the driver's seat, the last man slouched back, drumming his fingers on the frame of the open window.

Grant slipped from the brush where he'd been lying and moved in a crouch toward the truck. A voice in Russian, slightly muffled, called out, "Get off your ass and help us look!"

The driver sat up at that, sighed, and opened the door. Grant rose, clamping a hand over his mouth, wrapping his throat with his other arm. He squeezed carefully, lifting the guy away from the truck as he struggled, then slumped. Grant gagged and bound him, then stuck him back in the cab, pulling the keys and tossing them into the woods.

With a faint rustle of branches, Nick emerged likewise, coming close, mouthing, "What now?"

"Steer the jeep," Grant whispered. Nick climbed in behind the wheel, popping the brake, and Grant pushed it, started it rolling down the rough track to the west, Nick guiding the vehicle without turning on the engine yet. Grant took a moment to assess, glancing the way the Russians had gone. Behind him, canvas flapped, and he started to turn, a hand on his pistol. He turned into the blind eye of a gun aimed at his head.

CHAPTER SEVENTY-TWO

Liz caught her breath, looking away from Huang's anguished face, his silvered hair for once in disarray, his clothes disheveled, his suave demeanor utterly stripped away. Byambaa stood not far away, shoulders slumped. For a moment, a brief, glorious moment like the fanfare that announces the cavalry, escape had seemed possible, Huang's reversal a triumph that would carry them away. She drank in the sounds of motorcycles in the street below, the garage taking on another customer, the musical clanking of a rope against a metal edge, like a flag snapping on a flagpole. The last sounds she would hear before the gunshots that would end her life.

A zipping sound joined these, then glass shattered, but only a single pane, and smoke swirled inside the pool enclosure, the windows obscured by the billowing darkness, the soldiers thrown into chaos before the smoke swallowed them as well. Muffled thumps and groans followed from inside, then silence. A rope dangled over the glass wall, a man zipping down it, his feet braced lightly against the wall. Gooney turned from his task and grinned down at her. "Didja miss me?"

He rappelled down the rest of the way and dropped softly to the deck, unclipping from the line and moving toward them, quiet and efficient. "Huang. I wasn't expecting that. Next time, give us a call before you blow it, right?" He wore dark clothes, his left sleeve pushed back over his cast. A variety of pouches hung at his waist, and he plucked a knife from one of them. "Come on." With quick strokes of the blade, he freed their hands, then slid between them to the locked gate. Another tool, like a miniature crowbar, snapped the lock open with a brief application of force.

"Get moving." He pivoted back, taking a ready pose along the top of the ladder, a pistol held low in his hands.

Liz and Byambaa stripped off their gags, moving to a quick embrace, then he shook her off, pointing to the ladder. "Go."

She gripped the metal and swung herself onto the rungs, scrambling down. Her fingers felt numb, slipping instead of gripping, and she could hear her own pathetic whimper as she moved. The ladder vibrated with Byambaa's heavier tread, a sound that gave her a breath of relief. Suddenly, the ladder below her was gone and she tumbled the last several feet to the ground, rolling and pushing herself back up again, thoroughly disoriented.

A whistle caught her attention, and she found a three-wheeled truck waiting at the curb, a Mongolian woman waving to her. Byambaa clasped her hand as he landed on the ground beside her and they ran over together. "In, in," the woman said, unzipping the back of the tiny vehicle. She shifted a pile of felted hats and vests, and they crawled inside, then Huang came up, with Gooney right behind him.

"Sorry—didn't plan for three. You know how to ride a bike?"

"Bike?" Huang echoed, his voice raw.

"Get in," said Liz, pushing against the side to try to make room.

The Mongolian woman shook her head fiercely and spoke quickly. "The truck can't hold so many, so much."

"Get in," Liz said again and scrambled out. Byambaa reached after her, but she tossed the pile of hats at him. "They're looking for us together, a Mongolian and an American." She and the Mongolian woman pushed the vests into place, covering the two men, then zipping the cover over them. "Thank you," Liz told her, and the woman nodded as she hurried to the cab of the miniature truck.

"Come on." Gooney caught Liz's hand, tugging her with him. He led her down an alley and around a corner to a motorcycle. Once there, he gave her a quick inspection while he stripped off his dark shirt and tactical belt, stuffing them into a pack. From a shoulder bag, he pulled out a flowered scarf and a Chinese silk shirt, garishly colored. "Put them on. The scarf is for your hair. Okay, it was for D. A.'s but plans change. Here out, we're tourists." He smirked at her. "And we're in love, right?" He pulled on a fresh shirt of his own, slung the bag over his shoulder, and climbed onto the bike. "Hold on tight." He started the engine with a roar and peeled down the street. They turned, passing the open doors of a garage with a car up on a hydraulic lift.

Gooney pointed, partly turning. "Flat! I thought you meant the letter 'b' with that finger thing you did in the picture. It was D. A. who said flat! Like music! Like tires! Flipping brilliant."

Liz laughed, the breeze whipping tears from her eyes as she clung to his broad chest. Had she missed him? Oh, Hell, yes.

CHAPTER SEVENTY-THREE

Grant froze, his glance flashing from the barrel of the gun to the face beyond. When he met those eyes, sharp and green, he wasn't sure he could've moved if he tried. The Phantom. The woman he'd last seen stealing a crown in a museum in Afghanistan, a crown that turned up just days ago, in a false tomb in Inner Mongolia.

The Phantom stared coolly back at him, a brown scarf draping around her face. It should have softened or feminized her. Instead, it made her look all the more dangerous, obscure, as if she might vanish again at any moment. But the gun in her hands said otherwise.

"You are too easily distracted," she said, her voice slightly accented.

"I thought you were a thief, not a killer." He kept his hands low—she hadn't told him otherwise. Could he reach his weapon before she fired? Even odds.

"How would you know?"

Grant matched her gaze. Over the years, in the army, in ops, he had stared down a fair number of people who thought they were going to kill him. The ones who meant it never said a word. The

Phantom was capable of killing, he had seen that the first day they met; even capable of killing him. But it wasn't her first choice. Possibly not even her choice at all. "I'm a killer," he told her. "I know."

She blinked. She hadn't been expecting that. Her gaze narrowed, just a little. "Of course you are—your army bombs hospitals."

"Not on my watch, and not with my intel." Brush rustled off to the right, and both of them flicked a glance in that direction. The Russians would return at any moment, and he didn't like those odds. Grant shifted back, prelude to a step, and she steadied the weapon.

"Don't move, soldier."

He let his hands rise, still empty. "I'm no soldier—not for a while." Not since that day in the museum, or at least, since the aftermath. "What's Jin paying you? I don't think you signed on for murder."

She flinched. "This word depends upon your point of view. Is it murder to kill in warfare? Was it murder those men in the museum?"

Somewhere down the slope, Nick waited for him, another of those agonizing moments when you wonder, do you go back? Do you jeopardize the mission, for this one man? Grant knew the calculations there: last time, Nick hadn't left him. Nick's choice had crippled them both, and the last thing on Earth Grant wanted was to make him have to choose all over again. He had no doubt what Nick would choose. After all, he still had another leg.

"You looking me in the eye, doing Jin's dirty work when I can't fight back. Yes, that's murder."

"How many have you killed?"

"For my country, for my friends, for my life? Plenty." He stepped closer, letting the barrel of the gun brush his chest with each breath. "Like this? Not one."

This close, he could see the pulse moving at her neck, the way it sped up when he moved toward her, instead of away. "It is not murder," she said, nearly a whisper. "It is not personal."

Just for a moment, looking into those sea-green eyes, Grant kinda wished it were. What would it be like to have someone like her care that much about him, enough to kill him in passion rather than in cold blood. Not personal. "Tell me this before I die. What's my life worth?"

The scent of pine rose on the autumn breeze, fresh and clean, like a tidy kitchen, or a smooth pine box. His words hung between them, his voice dissipating into the trees, into the unseeing sky, and her eyes gleamed suddenly full of a fathomless pain.

The crashing of brush drew nearer. Grant rammed his hand upward, caught the barrel and turned it aside. Even as he moved, she squeezed, gentle and professional and the hot breeze of death whispered past his cheek. Their faces closed together, then he was twisting her aside, dropping her with a leg behind her. Or that's what he thought would happen.

Instead, she let her back arch, turning his move from aggression into support, flipping like a gymnast and snapping her feet into his head and shoulder. Grant staggered, the impact spinning him about. His right hand slid for the pistol, bringing it up, left hand on the slide, pivot, catch his weight, find her gun aimed directly at him, her compact figure crouched. Not murder, not any more.

"Hey! What's going on! Vanko? Where are you?" shouted the voices from below.

He had to get out of here, to catch up with Nick. Liz and Byambaa were depending on him. Too many goddamn people were depending on him. He had to shoot her. If he didn't, the Russians knew she failed. Jin knew she failed, and Jin had killed a thousand men just to fake that tomb. What would he do to her? She had to shoot him.

What was her life worth? What was his? "We can't both walk out of this." It came out on a breath, unintended.

He caught a glimpse of that well of grief. Then she fired.

CHAPTER SEVENTY-FOUR

Hours into the trackless steppes, Liz and Gooney crossed into a region of deeper valleys, shimmering blue lakes fringed with dense forest. The ground rose into a series of hills, with higher mountains in the distance, looking more like the Rockies of her home. Leaving the dirt road they'd been following, Gooney steered the bike into a cluster of small wooden cabins marked with a sign that read "Torists House, Welcome," and turned off the motor. Liz released him and he slid off the bike with a groan. Gooney stretched, cracking his back, then cradling his broken arm. "Shit—I'm getting too old for this stuff. Maybe I always was."

"Yep—definitely more mature than the rest of us," said D. A., emerging from the shadow of the nearest cabin, replacing her gun. Apparently, she'd been on look-out. She ran up and gave Liz a quick embrace. "You're alive! And you're brilliant! Wait'll the Chief hears about that signal. He's gonna want you on the team full-time." She grinned. "Come on, Byambaa's inside."

Grateful for that touch of warmth, Liz was even more grateful for the news. She hurried past them toward the door.

"So you've heard from them?" Gooney asked.

"Not since Nick sent the picture. When we made the plan, I texted him to meet up here. No idea if it got through."

"Shit," he said again, softly this time.

If they said any more, Liz didn't hear it. The small cabin contained a cramped assortment of furnishings like an American yard sale from a few decades ago: two beds that looked lumpy even from a distance, a Formica table and two metal chairs, an iron stove puffing away, a single wing-chair with ancient upholstery beside an ashtray stand, the whole place reeking of old cigarettes and coal fire. Was it better than the dung fires of the steppes? At the moment, Liz didn't care one bit. Byambaa rose from one of the beds and enveloped her in his embrace, both of them shaking.

The light shifted, Gooney's broad frame filling the door, then his voice, hard and tight with a barely-controlled fury. "Okay, Huang, tell us everything. How you know Jin, where the money's coming from. Everything—and make it good, or I can't promise I'll stop the chief from ripping your head off the minute he gets here."

Byambaa broke off his embrace, looking startled. "But it was Mr. Huang and his driver who freed us when they were about to shoot us both. It is not his fault the pool ladder was locked against us."

"You weren't there in the tomb, you didn't hear everything, but you must've wondered how he and Jin ended up so close." Gooney sat in the big chair, and Liz felt a momentary surprise that Huang hadn't already taken it. Gooney held a gun resting casually over his injured arm. The power had shifted with Huang on the receding side.

"He infiltrated the enemy—isn't that part of what you guys do?" Liz asked. Jin's insinuations at the tomb dimly surfaced in her memory, but compared with Huang's last-minute rescue, any friendship the two might have shared seemed hardly worth arguing about.

Huang, seated on a creaking metal chair, gazed into the bowl of tea in his hands as if he could read the future. Tugging Byambaa with her, Liz went over and sat on the bed nearest him. He glanced up at her with the briefest nod of acknowledgement.

"Opium, isn't it," D. A. added, squatting on a footstool beside Gooney.

"He's a fucking drug lord?" Gooney half-rose, his grip tightening on the gun, his cast sliding up to support it.

"Hey, simmer down—I didn't say that. Didn't have much of a chance to research before we got that photo and got the operation underway. By then, I'd broken a few encryptions, and made a few connections. Looks like it's the family business, but I don't know what role Huang Li-Wen plays." As she spoke, D. A. fished into a pouch, then held up a palm-full of pills of different kinds. "Besides, you look as if you could use a little oil of poppies yourself."

Gooney gave a snort of amusement and selected a few that looked like aspirin. He popped them back left-handed, and swallowed them dry, not giving up his gun. "Come on, Huang, I'm listening."

Huang bent forward and set down the bowl, then leaned back and finally raised his head. "As the young lady says, opium is my family trade." His voice sounded flat, distant in a way that made Liz want to reach out to him across that space, even as his words repelled her. "My great-grandfather on the British side settled in Hong Kong. It was he who amassed the original fortunes, encouraging his family to marry Chinese, to create advantageous connections. The British chaffed at the trade imbalance between these two great nations. The Chinese had banned the sale of opium, knowing the devastation of its effects, and the British went to war to force them to accept the opium trade. My great-grandsires' trade. They knew, those old men, where the money lay."

"They participated in the Opium Wars?" Liz asked, but Gooney growled at her, and she drew back from him. The anger of a cop facing a heroin epidemic wasn't something she was prepared to defuse.

"Get to it, Huang, Casey's the history buff, not me."

He pressed his fingertips together, a gold ring still winking on one finger. "Many members of my family continue in this tradition. I do not. But I have still benefited from the trade. My wealth, my home, my education, the investments that my uncles have made into my own business. My family's history is without honor and without pride. I invest in China to atone for it, but this debt has been accumulating interest for centuries.

"Jin did not exaggerate my past, nor are you wrong, Detective, to disdain me." Huang drew a deep breath. "All that I am, and all that I have, is borne upon the suffering of others."

CHAPTER SEVENTY-FIVE

Grant hesitated outside the cabin, hearing those words. He thought of the question he'd asked the Phantom, the question that seemed to jolt like lightning through them both. What was his life worth? What was Huang's? He rapped his knuckles on the doorframe and ducked inside.

"Jesus—you're alive." Gooney leaned back in the big chair where he was holding court. "Someday, maybe, I'll stop expecting to ID your corpse. What happened to you out there?"

With the slightest smile, Grant replied, "You wouldn't believe me. Trust me on that."

The gunshot rippled through his memory, the blood blossoming from her leg and the way she fell, her face a grimace of pain. The gun tumbled from her grasp in the moment he realized she'd shot herself, a flesh wound, but a nasty one. He twitched with the need to drop down beside her and tend the wound, to call for Nick with the trauma kit, but that would ruin everything she'd just bought for them both. Whoever she was, she could clearly take care of herself.

"You shot me," she hissed. *"Now get out."* She gripped her leg to control the bleeding.

"*Lucky for you I'm such a terrible shot*," he told her. He thought he heard her laughing when he took off down the hill.

What would he ever tell the team? What could he? That he'd met the Phantom for a second time, and for a second time, they had found each other worth saving? Some kind of crazy honor-among-thieves or just a wild attempt to prove to themselves they weren't killers. On that pine-thick hilltop, they balanced together on the edge of that terrible blade. For the first time in his life outside the Unit he'd met a woman who actually understood. Next time they met, he swore he would find out her name.

Liz was already on her feet, and he tipped his head in her direction. "Good to see you, Liz. And you." He took in the blood matting Byambaa's hair and the bruise on his face. "You okay?"

"I am alive, and we are together." He lifted their joined hands. "And we remain a few paces ahead of the enemy."

"Where's the jeep? Don't tell me we didn't hear it." Gooney demanded.

Grant shook his head. "Traded it for some horses. I threw in Jin's cellphone to sweeten the deal. Told 'em to call everyone they knew."

"Horses? Nick must've hated that." D. A., also on her feet, searched the door. "Where is he?"

"Not done cursing the horses and me along with them. He needed a little time off." Time with his prosthetic off, taking care of himself and getting his equipment back in order.

D. A. picked up one of the bags piled along the wall. "He'll need his kit, the joint oil and everything. Where'd he go?"

"Next door." He tipped his head in that direction and she set out, then hesitated, her dark eyes taking him in.

From the bag, she scooped him a handful of pills, dropping them into his palm. "Take a few—you look like you could use them."

"Thanks." Grant moved into the dimly lit space, and Gooney shifted, half-rising with a wince of pain, but Grant waved him back down. Deference from Gooney? Seriously? What had he missed? He jiggled the pills in his hand, then set them down on the tabletop in a little heap of nerve-dulling temptation. "Got any coffee?"

Huang stood up, his whole body leaning slightly away, like a dog waiting to be beaten. "Yes, Mr. Casey. We have coffee." He moved toward the stove, hesitating over the pot, used to having people to do that for him.

"The coffee is terrible," Byambaa offered, "but hot."

"As long as it's caffeinated." Grant dropped into a chair, his ankle giving a twinge as if to say it was past time. From his shirt, he pulled out the photo he'd taken from the Russian's office. "The Russians might still be coming for us. How about the Chinese army?"

"Yes, Mr. Casey, the Chinese as well." Huang offered the bowl, steaming and black and gorgeous. "They have lost a few, but Jin remains, and his Captain Guo."

"And I'll bet they're pissed. What went down?" He took a sip, searing the back of his throat, not giving a damn.

Liz stared at Huang, her eyes wide and damp. "Mr. Huang and Zhen fought for us. Zhen was killed in the shooting."

Gooney seized the lead. "That funky thing Liz did with her hand? I thought it was a 'b,' but D. A. said it was a flat, like that musical symbol?" He formed a circle with his thumb and forefinger, then pinched it in to change the shape.

"There was a garage across from the hotel where they were keeping us," Liz explained. "I could hear the equipment and some of their conversations. I couldn't think how else to signal that."

"Nice work." He took a more careful swallow of the coffee, bitter as anything, bitter as everything, really.

"So D. A. and I planned an op. She got some local support, a woman with a truck. I got to the roof from the other building, trying to work out which rooms they were in when I saw them come out by the swimming pool."

"Mr. Huang rescued us, or at least, he tried to."

Huang remained uncharacteristically silent, resuming his chair, stiff-backed, fingers pressing together, like a man expecting a sentence.

"That's affirmative," said Gooney. "He was out there with a gun that ran out of bullets, trying to manage the locked gate, and two people with their hands tied. Hard to say if he was on our side all along, or if he wanted to get back in good with us." Gooney shrugged expansively. "Makes sense he knew Jin, being into all that old shit, as for the drug connection, I guess you heard that part."

"Sounds like you're voting for leniency."

"I wouldn't go that far. Guy doesn't want innocents to die, that's a start, but what's to say he's not gonna waffle again?" Gooney sighed. "He's got no skin in this—no reputation, no honor. Jin's already shown he won't kill Huang if he can help it. Golden Goose and all that. All he's gotta do is step aside and let the rest of us go down: he's still got a life to return to."

"Acquittal," Liz blurted, letting go of Byambaa at last and leaning forward to confront Grant. "I vote for acquittal. When everything fell apart in China, we left them behind. You were suspicious, of course you were. But he stayed close to Jin, to help us out, right, Mr. Huang?"

"I have done my best," he said simply. "It has been very little. Jin did not trust me with the plan to abduct you, or I might have acted sooner, or behaved differently."

"It was enough," she reassured him, but Liz and her platitudes had no effect on the business man's demeanor.

"Even if he's not into the drug trade himself," said Gooney, "he's told us his relatives are. That's tainted money he's offering. I don't want any part of any poppy fields."

"He's trying to make amends, don't you see that?" Liz spread her hands. "He wants to break with his family, that's the whole point."

That wasn't the problem at all, Grant realized. Huang was haunted—by his past? By the death of his driver and body-guard? By the unaccustomed danger of the past few days?

Grant finished his coffee and set down the bowl beside his little mound of medications. Huang's fingers pressed together in his lap, his chin tucked down, staring at his hands, his shoulders too-square. He looked both smaller and stronger, as if he had found something within himself that he hadn't known was there, and maybe he wished he were still ignorant. Transmuted from gold into steel.

Grant reached across the table and lay his hand in front of Huang, the movement drawing the other man's attention, lips compressed. The expression looked familiar. It felt familiar. After the rush of battle had passed, when the recruit reached a moment of relative safety, a place where nobody was shooting at him, where he not need be prepared to shoot back, this expression arrived. Shell-shocked they used to call it. The eighty-yard stare. Nowadays shrinks and the press attributed the look to the terror of being under fire. Grant knew better. It wasn't the danger to his own hide that spooked a man so deep, it was the danger he suddenly found within himself.

"We've been there," Grant said softly. "The first time's hard for everyone. If it weren't hard on you, I wouldn't want you on my team."

Huang squeezed his eyes shut, with a quick shake of his head, then he stood, eyes glossy, and gave a deep bow.

CHAPTER SEVENTY-SIX

The next morning, Liz huddled in a woolen coat against the dawn's chill while the couple who ran the tourist lodge packed them food and offered lots of advice about where to go for their ride. "Not to the mountains," the woman warned her. "There are bad men up there, men who don't respect the earth." A small cluster of children watched the Americans, giggling and nudging each other.

"How would we recognize the bad men?" Liz held an armload of cheese, yoghurt and dried meat all bundled into a cloth wrapper. It weighed her down like her responsibility to these people. They needed to find the tomb, to preserve it for Mongolia—not just allow the Chinese to destroy it and exploit their own lies at the expense of the Mongolian people.

"They're not bad, just miners," the husband said. "My wife is very traditional. We can't live in the past, I say. If there is gold or other things in the hills, it should be us who benefits."

Shaking her head, the woman said, "These hills are sacred—let them dig somewhere else."

"Where?" he spread his arms. "Half of Mongolia is sacred, or it's protected for the wilderness."

"Look," she began, and Liz heard the tension of an old argument. Thankfully, she also heard hoof beats.

"Sorry, they're back—I need to go. Thank you again!"

Byambaa and D. A. had just returned, full of excitement, from their excursion into town, looking for any clues to the mystery of the banner and the statue.

"She'll meet us there," Byambaa was saying when Liz came out.

"The food? Great, let's load it on my mount and yours," Grant said, then, to Byambaa, softly, "Could you give Nick some tips? He's not the most comfortable on horseback."

Byambaa gave a nod and headed over to where Nick confronted a dun-colored horse, its ears already twisting from indifference to annoyance.

Grant turned back to the preparations. "I'll take the bike," he told Gooney. "Easier to steer a horse with one hand."

"I can still give you the finger with either one." Gooney continued stuffing things into the bike's storage.

"We may have to ditch it when we get to the hills in any case."

"I'm not ditching it." Gooney slammed the compartment closed, then straightened. "I'm ditching you." He glanced at Liz. "Sorry, Liz—nothing against you."

Grant said, "I thought we were square, at least for now."

Gooney swung about, and, for a moment, Liz thought he'd hit Grant. "I don't need to pal around with drug lords and hypocrites."

"He says—"

"And you believe him? Why? Never thought you were so desperate for a buck—maybe it takes a million to corrupt you? Good fucking grief, Casey, you're a reckless jerk, but I guess I didn't know your price."

Across the paddock, Nick straightened and turned, breaking off his chat with Byambaa, his face stormy.

"It's not about the money, Gooney. Not anymore. He needs us."

Gooney laughed, a harsh sound that made Liz wince. "The opium magnate needs us? What the fuck, Casey? How hard are you gonna justify this thing? If you want to prostitute yourself, just bend over and take it."

Grant's fist flew, catching Gooney low in the gut, then the cast came up, blocking another blow. Grant's foot slid in, Gooney stumbling and recovering himself, coming on fast, both fists swinging. Liz ran in. "Stop it! Both of you, please!"

"I say let 'em go," D. A. remarked. "They've been asking for it since the start of the mission."

"The team should not be broken for my sake," Huang said. "I—forgive me. I will go."

Byambaa started over, but his eyes met Liz's, and he turned aside, cutting across Huang's path.

Huang brushed past Nick as he came pounding up. "Lay off, sergeant!" Somehow, he slid between the combatants. Grant broke off in an instant, breathing hard, blood on his knuckles as the scabs cracked open.

Gooney stepped back, the bike at his side, his right hand still clenched, his left, protruding from the cast, quivering slightly. His breathing hitched with pain.

"You're pissed about the drugs. I get that," Grant said softly. He raised one hand before him, palm out, as if he could suck the anger from the other man. "When we get back to civilization, D. A.'s gonna dig on this for all she's worth. If he's dirty, she'll find it."

D. A. gave a nod, her curls bobbing. "Believe it."

Grant pointed toward Huang's receding back, Byambaa trailing him, talking softly. "He came looking for an adventure, right? Looking for an experience he couldn't get another way. He didn't sign on for the shooting."

"So you should charge more for your little adventure club. Value added," Gooney snarled.

Nick stood between them, a tall, dark wall, but Grant took a step to the side. "Do you remember your first, Gooney? Was it when you were a rookie, or when you joined up?" Grant took a stance, raised his hand as if it were a gun, aimed along his fingers, pointing straight at Gooney.

The detective stared back, eyes narrowed, breath coming in small gasps. His jaw worked as if he wanted to say more, to interrupt.

"Do you remember him looking back, you thinking, who's gonna win this time?" His thumb went down, the imagined gun going off, and Grant did a slow-motion recoil. "You win. The other guy dies. Then how come you're the one who feels it? It was Huang's first time yesterday. Did he win?" He was still holding the finger-gun, a gesture that should have looked childish, except he raised his hand, his finger tapping his temple. "Did he win, Gonsalves?"

The detective finally tore his eyes away. "Nice speech, Chief," he spat. "I don't remember you being such a sweet-talker."

"Maybe you're finally listening," Nick said.

"Oh, spare me." He folded his arms, scuffing his foot in the dirt.

"He needs us, not forever, maybe not for long. Because we know what it's like, and he didn't—not until yesterday." Grant relaxed his hand, but his fingers still shivered. Nick set his palm on his chief's shoulder, lightly, and D. A. let out a sigh.

Ever since that night on campus, Liz had been in fear for her life, but never for her soul, never for the kind of damage that these men, and women, were taking. Most of the time, they moved fast, fought hard, acted on years of instinct. And every once in a while, she caught glimpses of something else, a deep and primal heart within their actions. She pictured them in the helmets and breastplates they borrowed from the dead, their eyes gleaming, faces determined. Armed and armored and human. What must that be like for Huang, making the transition from a businessman above the world, to a warrior? Liz didn't know. She didn't think she ever wanted to find out.

CHAPTER SEVENTY-SEVEN

On the hilltop overhead rose the slab of white marble. Grant urged his horse forward, hoping Byambaa's contact would be there. So far, no sign of her. The backdrop of dense pines and growing mountains set off the white stone, its jagged edge meant to imitate the silhouette of the mountains where Chinggis Khan was born. A narrow road passed below, for the handful of tourists who ever came this far. Blue scarves flicked in the breeze from a staff atop the mound of stones nearby. The scent of pines filled the air, a smell he would forever link with the Phantom.

Movement by the trees had him reaching for his gun, but he drew back his hand as the old woman emerged, pushing a motorbike which she left on the ground. The others came up alongside, Gooney riding silent as death, pretending that gripping the handlebar wasn't killing him. His choice. He'd come this far, Grant wasn't pressing for more. Not yet.

Byambaa trotted up, guiding his horse expertly, then clucked it to a stop and jumped down. He greeted the woman who smiled uncertainly back at him. Her eyes kept shifting toward the monumental sculpture. Grant and Liz joined them on the ground, and she came close, whispering, "The woman says her husband ordered this—her husband was Tomor-Ochir." They followed slowly as the two Mongolians approached the sculpture, the towering outline of Chinggis Khan staring down at them, one hand lowering toward the earth, the other raised near the inscription describing his local and possibly miraculous birth.

"That's the guy who was beaten to death?" Gooney came up on Liz's other side, and Grant suspected that would be the way of it, Gooney keeping his distance. Whatever detente he'd hoped for was wiped away.

Byambaa pointed up, the woman pointed down, waving her hand as if digging, and he listened patiently. Guy would make a pretty good interrogator.

"She once offered to bury her husband here, but he said he was not worthy, not to be at the feet of the khan, she asked, and he got angry."

"Does she know about the banner?" Grant asked.

Liz waved him to silence, frowning. "She did it anyway. She thinks that's why Byambaa is here, asking questions, because he knows about her husband's ashes." Then she grabbed Grant's arm, her voice gone breathless. "Because something was already there!"

"Buried under the statue?"

"Where the khan is pointing, so she had to bury her husband at the other end, near the words."

Grant grinned. At last.

"You got something?" Nick called down from his horse. A guy that big on a horse that small looked a little absurd. His nervous mount danced and stomped, reacting to Nick's own nerves. Nervous sniper. Bad, bad.

"Don't suppose you've got a shovel in your kit?" Grant asked.

"Better," D. A. answered, "but let's wait until the widow heads for home. Hate to get caught disturbing the dead."

With many thanks and reassurances, Byambaa sent the woman

back to her motorbike and she rumbled off, spewing puffs of blue-grey smoke.

"She oughta get that engine looked at," Nick murmured.

D. A. dropped down, and pulled a long rod from her bundle, flipping a round paddle to the side. A metal detector.

"Be careful," Byambaa told her. "The widow says the whole monument is unstable." He pointed, and Grant could see the subsidence of the soil all along that side, maybe from people digging at it. In fact as he looked up, this close-to, he could see the slightest lean of the slab down toward them. Careful indeed. Dig too close or push too hard and the whole nationalist absurdity would come crashing down into the road.

"Gotcha," D. A. said. She approached the statue, careful not to touch it, and started methodically tracing arcs with the device, listening through earbuds.

"You asked for a shovel. I have the, what is it you called this?" Byambaa unstrapped something hung near his quiver and held it up. A trenching tool, its pick and shovel heads folded flat for easy transport.

D. A. really had thought of everything. "Huang, Nick, keep a look out, one of you at each end." Grant indicated with gestures where they should go, then took the trenching tool and followed D. A. The statue was certainly oversized and unappealing, but Grant still felt better knowing the thing was buried rather than hidden in some secret compartment. The Bone Guard was founded to protect history and culture, not to destroy it—no matter how ugly it might be.

"Chief!" D. A. waved her device back and forth right at the base of the sculpture. "Bingo."

He flipped out the shovel head and started digging.

CHAPTER SEVENTY-EIGHT

Jin scanned the horizon while Guo paced alongside the wooden house then said, again, "Are you certain this is the place? They have no streets, no addresses." He scowled at the antlers hanging by the door. "No culture."

"It is the place. There is a photograph in the records." Jin stood still, practicing his discipline. For once, they seemed on an even plain: Jin had lost the advantage in Inner Mongolia, and his operative had been shot instead of shooting the American, but Guo had lost both of their hostages, while under clear army control. In their competition for Party approval, neither man could claim the advantage. Huang's duplicity would be dealt with. Jin hoped to see to it personally. Once they could be located. In the meantime, they waited. Neither of them with patience, though Jin could counterfeit that at will.

At last, a buzzing sound echoed over the hills, then a figure on a small motorcycle emerged from the forest track, slowing as it approached. The driver stopped, turning off the engine and unsteadily dismounting.

"Are you the widow of the Communist Party official, Tomor-Ochir?" Jin asked as politely as he could.

"He said there'd be no police, no arrest."

This response made no sense. "I do not understand, grandmother. Tell me again."

"That nice boy with all the questions. He promised no police." She set her hands on her hips. "And you look like police." She squinted at them. "What tribe are you from? Not Buryat, certainly. Not Darkhad. I would know."

She thought Jin looked Mongolian. The idea irritated him, but he played along. "The young man told you the truth. We had some more questions."

Guo folded his arms, looking far too imposing for a man confronted by a single old woman. She shook her head. "This uniform—too many stars. It's like the Communists." She waved a hand. "Besides, I just left him—how did he even talk to you, to say you need more questions? Did his friends call you? Who are you?"

That nice boy she had just left. The Mongol singer, it had to be. Guo stared, understanding none of it. "Indeed, his friends called us. The Americans have some concerns about what you said."

She snorted. "The Americans. This is no business of theirs. This is Mongolian business." Again she studied Guo, getting close to him, her furred hat barely reaching his shoulder. "Not the business of ugly foreigners like you," she said to the captain. Again, he understood nothing. His expression did not change, and she fled for her bike.

"What—"Guo began to say, but Jin snared the gun from the captain's belt and fired. The woman jerked to the side with a scream and Jin fired again, into her chest, then replaced the weapon as Guo reached for him. The woman's body twitched and spasmed as blood streamed into the dirt.

"The Americans are already here. They've spoken to her. Let's go."

"Go where—you have just killed our source."

The soldiers, who had been waiting near their truck, came at a run, guns drawn, but Jin waved them back. "They are here, close by."

He was already in motion. "My operative said they took only a photo—"

"Of the dead woman's dead husband, yes."

"If all they wanted was to speak to her, they'd have done so here, at her home. Instead, she went to them." Jin climbed into the Landrover, waiting for Guo to get in the driver's seat.

The captain flung open the door. "Went where, Minister? I am losing patience."

"It wasn't a photo of a man, but of a moment. The dedication of a statue to Chinggis Khan. We assumed it was the man they cared about, of course it wasn't, it was the monument." He turned over the map and pointed. "This way, and east. We may still catch them." His fortunes, his future, his reputation and his position depended upon it. Not to mention the lives of his wife and child. Children.

Indeed, as they roared up the road, the white monument loomed in the distance, a small party of horsemen around it. One of them started waving. They'd been spotted. "Faster." The other two army trucks met up with them, conjured by radio from the junction where they had waited out of the old woman's knowledge.

In the vehicle ahead, a soldier stood up from the center, bracing himself and the large gun he mounted on the roof. He sprayed gunfire across the slope even as the vehicle bounced, chipping pieces from the fat face of Genghis Khan.

CHAPTER SEVENTY-NINE

"Mount up!" Grant was shouting. "Get behind the khan!" Another shovelful, another. He dug faster than any foxhole competition in basic training.

"Chief, get out of there."

"Come on, Grant!"

The shovel struck something hard, then bullets flew over his head, pocking a line across the Great Khan. Grant dropped down and dug in with his hands, pulling at the metal box. An ammunition container, marked with Russian stars. A perfect hiding place, assuming what they wanted was inside.

"Byambaa!" he shouted, and the Mongolian wheeled his horse, leaning down to take the box from Grant's hands. "Go, go!"

He still held the trenching tool, ready to wield it as weapon or shield. The trucks were still a ways off, gunning their engines to rush up the road. The huge slab shadowed him, leaning. So much for culture. He flipped the other side of the trenching tool, the pick, and used it to snag the edge of the marble overhead, pulling himself up like a mountaineer.

"The Hell are you doing, Casey?" Gooney shouted up at him, then his face cleared with recognition.

Grant balanced on the edge, dropped the tool and leaned into the surface, climbing higher along the monument's ridge. It groaned and shifted beneath him.

Another spray of gunfire cracked against the stone. Grant glanced back. Gooney struggled with the bike, swore, and ran, snatching for one of the horses. D. A. swung up behind Byambaa, and Huang herded the lot of them, riding like a sack of potatoes, but one determined to protect his team. Nick rose in his stirrups down below. "Chief!"

"He's taking it down!" Gooney spun his mount, steadied it, one-handed. "Come on, Nick! Ride!"

Grant reached the apex of the monument and it moved. He tugged and swayed, then he felt the shudder, and he scrambled away from the edge, toward the back of the monument as the slab of stone swung downward, crashing onto the oovo. The wooden staff at its peak shattered and the rocks tumbled and bounced away.

The lead truck swerved too hard and rolled over, bullets spiraling into the air. The second car slammed into it.

Grant dove off at the last moment before the monument hit the ground. He struck hard, the wind knocked out of him. The ground rumbled and jumped when the monument crashed down. Something cracked and stone screeched against metal. Someone screamed in Mandarin. Someone else just screamed. Scrambling up, dragging at the air with every breath, he ran. The left side of his body ached but who else was gonna do it? Nick? Gooney? He grabbed the trenching tool on his way and jumped onto the motorcycle, stuffing the tool into the saddlebag. The engine caught and Grant burst into motion, flying down the narrow track into the forest. Branches slapped at him, he ducked and dodged, finally catching up with the team as they splashed through a narrow brook. Liz had the last horse by the reins, easily managing her own mount and the spare. D. A., mounted double with Byambaa, gripped a handful of his coat with one hand while she carried the ammo box like a football under her arm. Nick stayed close beside them, still unsteady on his mount, but determined. Wingman through and through.

Byambaa led them at a gallop down the stream, Grant keeping pace on the narrow verge. Soon, he'd have to ditch the bike, no doubt. The rough track made his teeth ache—just like the rest of him.

They rode in silence save for the splashing of hooves, snapping of branches and the occasional grunt of pain from one of the guys. Grant could almost feel the heat of Gooney's glare, talked into staying to be a safety net for a man he couldn't respect, and now forced to give up the motorcycle, forced to show that Grant was right, even if he'd never admit it out loud.

WHEN THEY'D BEEN RIDING for an hour, the stream joined with a larger river in a broad, tree-fringed valley, and Grant called a halt. "But don't get off your horse unless you have to. Trucks can't come that way, but we don't know what else they've got."

Straightening away from Byambaa, D. A. scrubbed the rust from the ammo case, then snapped it open and unfurled something pale across her lap. For a moment, not a breath moved the team. The long strip of felt, gray-white on the back, unrolled down her leg to reveal designs like Celtic knot work and shells, a trident. D. A. held it out, turning it so everyone could see.

"It's Buddhist," Liz blurted, her confusion clear. "But Chinggis wasn't Buddhist. Maybe it's not the right one." Her eyes clouded with tears. The long adventure was grinding down her enthusiasm.

"The monastery was Buddhist, wasn't it? Maybe this is just some relic of theirs," Gooney said. He had dismounted and now paced around the small clearing, stretching his legs, cradling his arm.

"Then why bury it under Chinggis Khan?" Nick asked. "Maybe it means we're supposed to start at a monastery."

Huang nudged his horse closer and touched the banner lightly, tracing its patterns. "This is not Buddhist," said Huang softly. "This shell shaped like a horn. This is not a conch. And the fish—they are always two. This shows four."

"A funky shell and a pile of fish. Worth it now, Casey?" Gooney said.

"Where around here would you find shells and fish?" Grant asked aloud.

"A lake?" Liz suggested

Suddenly, Byambaa laughed, a great whoop of joy. "Not a lake—a mountain! They are fossils. A pile of fish, a shell like a horn. Things they would have seen and taken for sacred mysteries. Things someone else seeing the banner would take as barbarian mistakes."

Grant grinned right back at him. "We need someone who knows the local rocks."

"Miners," said Liz, and her horse pranced a little.

"So we stay with the water and head up the valleys. They'll need water."

"Affirmative," Nick replied.

Grant wheeled the bike over to a brushy patch near a rock fall to conceal it, Gooney's baleful stare following him.

"Grant!" Liz kneed her horse to catch up. "The woman at the hotel said the miners are bad men."

"They destroy the earth," said Byambaa. "It's a great controversy, especially here, in the hills sacred to Chinggis Khan."

"Then why do they do it?"

He spread his hand open. "All men need money. Here is no industry, no jobs, only tradition and stones and horses. So many move to the cities, or go to work in Russia. Those who stay love their land, but they exploit it in order to stay. They don't allow legends to stop them."

Grant took the reins of the spare horse. "What if we can prove the legends are true?"

"We can restore the pride of the khan, and remind my people what it was like to be great. There can be other jobs, but there can be no other land."

He swung up into the saddle and guided his horse toward the river. "Then let's ride."

CHAPTER EIGHTY

In a rough valley of tumbled stone and thick grass, Chinese soldiers mingled with a few dozen Mongols with grubby clothes and wary expressions. The soldiers' expressions looked little different, after the loss of two vehicles and the long, round-about ride to get here—and they knew their trucks could go no further. Above them loomed the start of the Mongols' sacred mountains, rough and golden in the growing light. Gold as the treasures they concealed.

"We should have a helicopter," Guo muttered as his soldiers passed out weapons and showed the Mongols how to hold them.

Jin stood in the shade, waiting. "Feel free to apply for the air space permission, Captain. Be sure to tell them you plan to fly over the sacred mountains. If the mere shadow of such a thing does not defile their wilderness, perhaps they will even grant the permission."

"Why not simply violate their airspace? Do you think the Mongol air force is so frightening? Do they even have one, or are they still using dragon-shaped kites and fire-crackers?"

The Chinese foreman, Ling, approached and gave a short bow, his manners dissolving during his long association with the Mongol miners. A Mongol trailed after him, a Chinese rifle slung over his shoulder. Jin recognized him as the older man who had been so suspicious when Jin came for the samples. "This man had some questions. He is a leader among the Mongols, Minister."

"What is it?"

The Mongol held up his rifle. "You said to them that we must stop the Americans. You ask us to kill them."

That wasn't a question. Jin kept his face clear, listening. Was the man a fool? What had he thought that Jin meant? "If the Americans are allowed to succeed, they will take all of this land from you. Your livelihood will be gone. How will your families survive?"

"But dead Americans are likely to be followed by living ones—soldiers and ambassadors. Many of our own people do not even know what we do here. Our livelihood is no less gone if we are imprisoned."

The other Mongol miners, initially excited by the weapons and the talk Jin had given, were watching them now, listening. Jin found a smile. "What you are doing for Mongolia will earn both the admiration of your countrymen, and the friendship of China. We are a very powerful friend. What can the Americans do? Have they stopped us building in the China Sea? No. Have they stopped us making friends in Africa? No. Make no mistake of this: we are the most powerful nation in the world. More powerful than Russia that knows only missiles. More powerful than America that knows only talk. The Americans have ruined so many nations with their intervention, while we have uplifted them. What China wants, China will achieve —with your help."

"China will defend us?" The miner shifted on his feet.

"Will we be paid extra?" called another man from the crowd.

"You will have the gratitude of the most powerful nation on earth. What do you suppose that is worth?"

The other man gave a whoop, joined by most of the rest. Most, not all. "Captain Guo, assign your men to two groups with these others. Make sure they are vigilant."

Guo flicked his fingers, counting them off, sending his underlings to organize the two parties. When the ground before them cleared, he said quietly to Jin, "You promise much, Minister. Do you have the assurances of the Central Committee? I do not think their mandate extended to organizing a foreign militia against the American government."

"If the Mongols take care of the Americans, we can take care of the Mongols—have no doubt of that." Jin checked the status of his own handgun. "In fact, you may give orders to that effect if you wish."

"Motorcycle!" called out a man stationed on the shoulder of stone above. He pointed, and Jin heard the engine's rumble a moment later. At last.

"Let it come," Jin ordered.

"The two reindeer stones are here and there," said the Chinese foreman, returning with a map. "They are at least two hours away by foot, and not all the men have motorcycles or mounts."

"Then they had best get moving."

Guo and the foreman took over, herding the two groups of men in divergent directions, emptying the makeshift camp with its wooden shelters and smothered fires, the minor tools of an inefficient operation. With proper equipment, the arms of the mountain could be levelled, and the mountaintop itself removed, carved down to more efficiently reach the rare earth ores at its heart.

The motorcycle edged past the last of the men and shuddered to a halt, then the rider rose stiffly, limping on one leg. A broad swath of bandages wrapped her thigh.

"You failed to kill the American," he said promptly in English, their common tongue.

"He fooled your Russians with a simple ruse, Minister. It was only I who remained alert to the possibility." She leaned slightly on her right leg, taking the pressure off of her injury. "I did not come here to justify myself."

"No? Perhaps you came to explain about the five-sided crown. How that particular piece came to be present." The gun felt hard beneath his jacket, although it would be more satisfying to snap her neck.

She shrugged, the movement rippling the scarf that shadowed her face. "It is no mystery. You ask me to find them, and this one I find at a conservator's workshop."

"None of them were to come from China, from Chinese museums. Your instructions were very explicit."

"And so it did not. Am I to blame if your little museums cannot control their inventory? There are no such crowns outside of China. It had to come from within."

His hand slipped beneath his jacket, resting on the grip of his gun.

She rubbed at her leg, and shifted subtly away. A natural movement to resettle the injury, or a response to his own slightest gesture. An interesting opponent, but he did not have time for sparring, not any more.

Jin took a step away, out of her easy reach, and pivoted, the gun rising in his hands.

She apparently didn't notice at all, her scarfed head bent to examine her leg as she spoke, "I did not come to explain myself, but to question you. I heard from Zhuwen."

Zhuwen, whom Guo described as lost in Germany. Jin hesitated, his breath sliding out in a long sigh, then replaced the gun. "Then she is not dead."

He thought he could hear her smile. "She will be gratified to know that you care, Minister. To know that you care about anything at all."

In that moment, he wanted to kill her more than ever, feeling the slide forward, the twist of his hand wrapping her chin, his other hand moving to her shoulders, as if to support her in a swoon, and the snap of bone. "You know nothing of my cares."

"Oh, Minister—"she finally faced him, her green eyes flaring, "we have more in common than you know."

CHAPTER EIGHTY-ONE

From horseback, Liz surveyed the refuse on the side of the stream where it emerged from the rock: a pick and shovel, a few food packets and basic living supplies, blanket rolled up under a lean-to.

"I hate to sound like a Scooby-doo character," said Gooney, "but it looks like someone left in a hurry."

"I thought I heard a motorcycle a little while ago, but it went the other way," Liz volunteered.

"Next time, say something," Grant said darkly, and she offered a meek apology.

"They're planning to come back, probably not even be out all night, not if they left their blankets," D. A. pointed out.

"We can't afford to wait. Let's keep moving," Grant ordered.

"This is the second abandoned site. What if we don't find anyone to ask?" Liz asked. Adrenaline could only take her so far, and even the prospect of finding the tomb began to pale with her exhaustion, both mental and physical.

"I wonder if there was a crackdown on mining," Nick suggested.

"The authorities came along and rousted these guys, or at least, spooked them into taking off for now."

Gooney swung down from his horse and walked through the narrow camp by the stream. "Probably gold-panning," he murmured, gesturing at the stream and the broad metal pans and sieves. He stepped carefully to lift aside the blankets, then opened the flap of a satchel that seemed to serve as a seat by the smothered fire. "Here we go." He reached in and lifted out a stone the size of two fists, a stone full of twisted shapes like unicorns' horns from a medieval tapestry. "How's that for you? Can't be far—can't imagine he'd want to lug this thing around."

"Exporting fossils is illegal—gold is easier," Byambaa observed.

"Maybe he wants it for his kids."

"Let's spread out and search. Stay within shouting distance," Grant suggested.

The territory here was more open, with sparse clumps of trees on the flank of the mountain. The low bushes glowed with crimson and orange leaves, standing out like fire against slopes of golden grass interrupted by dappled boulders. They spread out, Byambaa, Grant and Liz heading upward while the less stable riders, Gooney, Huang and Nick, guided their mounts to either side down below. D. A. now rode behind Nick, a second pair of eyes. They gradually receded from each other, and Liz followed a narrow trail up and North. A ridge of stone rose alongside her, herding her over into the next valley, a gorgeous vista of grass still green, with a herd of elk that paused and stared back at her, then casually loped away along the river.

"Marco!" called out Gooney's voice.

"Polo," Nick answered. "You know how ironic that is, right?"

Their voices echoed from the stones down below, but Liz didn't see anything promising up ahead. She turned her mount in the space by the ridge, then hesitated. A pale band of stone emerged within the gray and beige, a shape like the banner—a shape full of horns. She crowed her victory, exhaustion falling away as she brushed them with her fingers. "Here! I've got it!"

Hoof beats galloped behind her, then Byambaa was with her, his silky hair tossing as he slowed his mount, and together they looked down into the valley. "A watering hole," he murmured.

"Could it be?"

"Let us be sure."

The others clattered nearer from their disparate directions as Liz and Byambaa rode down into the broad green valley. A scatter of stones to one side could have been a shelter once, long ago, and the open mouth of the valley suggested where the khan's funeral cortege might have ridden through. Taller grasses and flowers past their prime rimmed the wider pool at the heart of the valley, and, this close to, she could make out the edge of stones that dammed the little stream. Below, it scattered into swampy clumps of low willow brush, buzzing with insects even now. These fell silent as they rode up, then started again after a moment.

Byambaa drew in a deep breath of the Eternal Blue Sky, then he sang the first song, his voice strong and stirring, the melody reverent, the overtones humming like insects. Once in a while, he added the trill of a bird.

By the time he had finished, the team gathered close, quiet.

"Yes," he said softly.

"Yes," Liz echoed. She reached out briefly and clasped his hand.

"Nice work, Robin Hood," said Gooney. "Now what?"

"It is beautiful," Huang said. "The song and the meadow." He smiled faintly, as if the Eternal Blue Sky touched him as well.

"Wolves circling their den," said Liz. She glanced back over her shoulder toward the ridge. "The fossil banner points here, the stream points onward." She followed it with her hand.

"It's a good guess," D. A. agreed.

"And an easy ride," said Nick under his breath as they jogged the horses in that direction. The valley rose there, the stream burbling down beside them, and they crested the ridge, taking a long view of the hills ahead. A dark smudge marked one of them, and they squinted into the distance.

"A cave." Grant gave his horse a nudge, then they were galloping, folded low over the horses' necks.

The mane of her mount tickled her face, and Liz couldn't stop smiling, once more riding with Byambaa at her side, this time flying over the Mongolian steppes, imagining herself as a bride of the Khan with silver in her hair and woolen boots decorated like the finest Persian rugs. Byambaa would sing for her, their voices rising in sweet harmony.

They topped the rise and slowed for the slope up to the cave.

"Mongolia is home to the deepest cave in Asia, some say," Byambaa murmured.

"But we don't have to go inside," said D. A. "Look at the boulders."

A tumble of large stones marked one side of the cave mouth. As they drew near, the cave opening high above, Liz made out shapes on the stone, faint markings chipped into the weathered patina. In some places, they had vanished completely, worn away by the intervening centuries, but in others, the pale marks showed plainly: jaws gaping, tails flaring out behind, a pack of wolves heading east. And beneath them, the clear imprint of a narrow tire. Someone else had been there first.

CHAPTER EIGHTY-TWO

Grant held up a hand for silence as he studied the track, then he circled his hand and waved them off toward the east as well. Gooney and Nick already had guns out, Huang stiffening in his saddle so that his horse gave a snort of annoyance. Byambaa loosened his bow in the case alongside his saddle. Robin Hood, Gooney had called him, and Grant smiled, recalling the singer's desire for a nick-name like the rest of them. D. A. slid down from behind Nick and hurried up the hill, keeping low, glancing to the side frequently, while Grant followed the path downward, past the cave entrance.

The track was only one, narrow like a motorcycle. Probably belonged to a herdsman or miner, and it did not continue beyond the cave. There, at the cave's entrance, lay a clump of pine needles. Out of place in a landscape of rolling grass and stone.

"All clear," D. A. called from above. "No sign of contact. I can see some big boulders in the distance, could be our next marker."

"That's the direction the wolves are heading," Liz observed. "*Running deer run no more.*"

The dark mouth of the cave opened before him. "Pit stop," Grant called back. "I'll catch up with you."

"I'll top out on the ridge," said Nick. Hoof beats receded, some pausing, some continuing on into the distance.

Grant slid down from his horse and tucked the long reins into the pinch between two boulders. He found a Maglite in his limited kit and held it at the ready, without turning it on. Keeping his back to the stone, Grant edged a few steps into the cave, moving soft and quiet, keeping his back to the stone. His eyes adjusted slowly to the gloom, a broadening hollow with a floor that dropped off steeply to one side. Across the way, movement, the waft of fabric on the breeze, like the shroud on a mummy in one of those old movies. A woman's scarf.

"What do you want?" he said, his voice echoing briefly.

"Shhh." She came toward him, limping, walking slow and careful, but, like him, without a light. The sun that slanted through the entrance lit her from one side, glowing on her profile, a gilt outline like a halo from a medieval painting. "I could have killed you," she breathed.

"I could kill you now."

"You are not a murderer."

Her voice sounded so certain—he wished he could be that sure. "Fine, so we're not killing each other. Get to the point, I don't have much time."

"If you win, save Jin's family."

Grant nearly laughed. "Excuse me?"

"Minister Jin has a wife who is pregnant, and a young son. If he loses, they will be imprisoned or killed. She will be forced to abort. If you win, save them."

The request struck him as so bizarre, that for a moment he couldn't answer. He hardly even knew where to begin. This woman could steal a crown from a war-zone and smuggle herself into Russia. She got the drop on him and chose not to use it. "Why don't you?"

"I am nothing. I have no standing, I have not even the Chinese language. I cannot do this."

"But you think I can."

"You ask me what your life is worth. What are theirs? They have done nothing. They are innocent, but they will suffer."

He couldn't make out her features in the darkness save the glint of that sunlight on her shoulder. "That's not my fight—I wouldn't even know how to start."

"Then find a way!" Her voice, suddenly sharp, bounced around them, and she stepped closer, but stumbled to the side, her back to the light. Grant turned, catching her arm, all hard muscle beneath his hand. She took a quick breath, getting her injured leg back under her. She had shot herself instead of him. People called him crazy, but that was only because they'd never met her. The Phantom eased back her arm, and he let her go, but she stayed in the darkness just before him, a form of shadows and heat. He sensed her there, as if he were wearing night vision, her shape so very clear, her slender waist, curving hips, firing the tension that rushed his body.

"What's your name?"

"Not your concern. Will you do it?"

He considered everything that would have to be done to bring Jin's family out of China, the diplomatic hurdles, the bureaucracy on both sides of the border. "It's too much. The Chinese won't talk to me, for sure. If word gets to the states about our little visit to Russia, I'm screwed. I can't do it."

"I did not think you were a man to say that you cannot when I brought you into this."

Grant stilled. "What do you mean, you brought me into this?" His mind scrolled back through the last few days, hung up on the curious coincidence of a man who could identify that crown being there in the tomb beside it.

For a moment, she simply breathed, sharp and worried, then said, "I follow you, online, since—the museum, I see this idea, the Bone Guard. Jin plans to use the American conference to find a dupe for his plan, to reveal the fake."

"You're the one who sent me that ad, to manage conference security."

"I think he is just fooling the scholars. I think, if you are there, you will see the truth and show his lie."

"So you don't support him lying about the khan, but you're willing to steal for him."

"I don't care about the khan or the lie. This is not for me, what I do. Now I know they kill his family. This I will not have—if you win, will you get them out?" Her voice became hard and urgent.

"I have to figure out how to win first. If I lose, Jin gets to live like an emperor, with his happy family beside him." And, like an emperor, he would build his fortune on the deaths of others, on the virtual enslavement of the whole Mongolian people. "I have to go—they're waiting for me."

"They cannot succeed without you."

"Hard to say," Grant replied, but he doubted it, not with Gooney's broken arm, and three members of the team barely tempered to gunfire.

She took another step, her palm flaming on his chest. "Pity." Her heel hooked his ankle and she jerked backward, shoving with her palm at the same time, toppling him into the black abyss.

CHAPTER EIGHTY-THREE

The drumming of hoof beats provided the soundtrack to Liz's growing excitement. She pushed her mount ahead, but Byambaa caught her. Somewhere behind, she heard D. A. call out for a lift, and Huang turn back to retrieve her. Gooney muttered a monologue about Holiday Inn, television and cold beer, but she ignored him. Complaining was his way, she'd come to understand, and she understood just as well—especially after his appearance at the hotel, just when they needed him most—that he was someone they could count on. She'd have to thank him for staying with them, despite his misgivings about Huang's past.

The valleys here rolled one into another, and the tumble of boulders D. A. had spotted proved to be further than she had believed. The next hill featured a densely forested brow, with shadows thick beneath them. In the span between, a single stone rose within a net of streams. "Could that be it?"

Byambaa turned in his saddle to holler to the others, "There's a standing stone ahead, a big one, in the next valley."

"Awesome!" called D. A., giving a thumbs up from behind Huang. "No sign of company?"

"Nothing."

"We should wait for Grant." Liz glanced to the figure of Nick on his horse at the top of the far ridge, already looking smaller.

"Fuck him. He said he'd catch up. Let's get 'er done." Gooney kicked his horse and started down the grassy slope toward the standing stone. As they reached the bottom, the horse's hooves stuck and squelched on the swampy ground.

The shadows under the trees shifted with a rustling sound. Byambaa rose in his stirrups, he and his horse both staring, then he shouted, "Gooney, no!" and fumbled for his bow. By the time he had it drawn, an arrow nocked, the first soldiers broke from the trees, shooting.

Gooney wheeled his mount, but the horse stumbled in the muck and slid down, landing with Gooney underneath. He floundered in the mud, the horse kicking and struggling to rise.

"Get back!" D. A. was shouting, but Liz met Byambaa's glance.

"Cover me, and I can get him."

He gave a single nod, and bent his bow, letting an arrow fly, then another. Some shrieked across the valley, then Byambaa kneed his horse, galloping in a broad arc, drawing their fire. Liz plunged her mount down after him, cutting back toward Gooney. His horse found its feet and struggled up, then staggered, jolted by a shot from the woods. The horse screamed. Gooney scrambled on his hands and knees toward the standing stone, the only cover available.

A few men broke from the trees, but they ran east, along the tree line away from the battle. Shouts and curses in Mandarin pursued them. "Cowards!" The remaining men maintained their line, keeping tight beneath the trees. Byambaa galloped hard across the valley, shooting arrows toward the Chinese position.

Liz splashed into the swampy ground and heard bullets flying past her. Her horse bucked and turned. She caught a glimpse of Nick, up on the hill turning as well, then, with a roar, drawing a weapon. Where was Grant? She turned the horse in a tight circle and urged it toward the stone, leaning down toward Gooney. "Come on!"

"Are you nuts? We got cover—you stay here!" He had his gun out, but mud obscured the slide. "Shit." He scrubbed it against his shirt, the only patch not already wet. Chips of stone flashed past and the horse reared, stomping. Gooney had a point. She slid down beside him and pulled off the scarf over her hair, handing it to him. The moment her weight left its back, her horse bolted for the hills.

Gooney used the kerchief to clear the slide and barrel as best he could. "God, I hope this works." He pushed himself up against the stone, glancing out and pulling back quickly. "Robin Hood's putting on quite a show out there. Makes it hard to get off a shot." Leaning on the stone, he met her stare and flashed a smile. "Thanks for coming, by the way, in case I don't get to say so later."

"Thanks for staying with us," Liz began, but his attention was already gone, squinting up the hill behind her.

"What the Hell are they doing up there? Having Trick-or-treat?"

Huang and D. A. seemed to be working together, digging into saddlebags. Gooney shook his head and got down to business, sticking his arm out, pause, shoot, and pull back. A few more bullets in their direction, the resounding noise merging with Byambaa's war-whoops and taunts like a battlefield rap song.

Into that melee, Huang rode his horse like a demon, barreling down, something flaming in his hand. Their assailants divided fire between Byambaa and Huang. The businessman still bounced on his mount, clearly a novice, but he wore an expression of grim determination as he splashed past the rock, then he flung his flaming grenade.

It exploded with a roar that briefly halted the firing, but the effect didn't last long. Gooney got off a few more rounds, rewarded with a scream from the forest fringe, then a horse shrieked and fell. Liz felt her breath stop in her throat. A man cried out. Gooney stuck his head out, down low this time. "Shit! Huang's down. Can you shoot?"

"I—"

He pressed the gun into her hands. "Just don't shoot me. I'm going after him." Then he was lunging from behind the rock and Liz stumbled up to his abandoned place, leaning too far. Byambaa dashed by again, but his quiver was empty, and for a moment, she wished he would lean down from the saddle, scoop her up and carry her away. Surely they could out-run the Chinese army.

In the space between them, Huang's dying horse thrashed, and he scrabbled in the muck trying to free himself. Gooney plunged forward and seized him by both arms, exploding with curses as he pulled, needing that left arm.

The Chinese, sensing blood, pressed forward. Liz managed a shot that went for the trees, then another, but they clearly didn't take her seriously. They edged forward, five men taking their aim, taking their time, four more behind them, still under cover. The leader's head erupted with blood and bone and he flew backward. The men retreated fast, but a second man fell as they did so. Then Gooney had Huang in his right arm and they ran together for the safety of the stone. Byambaa rode wide, clearing the way. Liz fired again and put the gun at her waist, reaching out to take Huang's hand and guide him beside her, Gooney hurrying after, pushing Huang's back. He breathed in great gulps, immediately clasping his cast to his chest as she took charge of the businessman. Her back to the stone, Liz stared in the direction of those excellent, terrible shots.

D. A. crept in the muck in the valley below, making her way toward the stone while attracting as little attention as possible.

On the ridge beyond, Nick stood with the rifle nestled to his cheek. He fired without worry, without moving anything but his trigger-finger, as far as Liz could tell, then the barrel of the gun swiveled with precision and he lined up another shot. Something in the mechanical focus and deadly accuracy chilled her to the heart, even as she knew he had saved their lives. The Chinese, scattered by his long-distance assault, argued on the other side of the stone, and the horse finally died. Somehow, miraculously, they were winning.

Then the waters of the spreading streams before her shivered with fresh ripples, and the cavalry arrived: galloping up behind Nick, at least fifty-men strong. The Chinese were cheering. They thought their Mongolian cohort had turned coward and run, when in fact, they were running for reinforcements. Nick pivoted and the lead rider clubbed him down as the horsemen streamed over the hill.

CHAPTER EIGHTY-FOUR

Grant opened his eyes on darkness. His head throbbed and he spat out blood. He hadn't fallen far, not as far as he had feared. Distant sounds of battle echoed in his skull, and he couldn't tell if they were real, or some lingering nightmare. He groped in the darkness, grabbing something with teeth in a cold frame of bone. He dropped it, then found his flashlight not far off, and flicked it on. The empty eye sockets of a sheep skull stared back at him. A few other bones winked white in the light's slender beam, organized into lines or shapes. For a moment, Grant thought he might have fallen into a prehistoric site of some kind bones arrayed in a ceremonial pattern, then he rose to his knees and played his light over the bones. They spelled a word that made him stifle a bitter laugh, the flash of green eyes shimmering in his memory: *sorry*.

He knelt on an earth floor with the cave roof high above and a slope at his back, steep and rough, looking as if it leveled off a good dozen feet over head. A drag-trail showed where he had tumbled down in the darkness, along with a few spots of darker earth where his blood-soaked in. No wonder he ached. A quick assessment found him battered, but not severely injured. His teeth had lacerated his cheek when he rolled, explaining the blood in his mouth. He collected the gun and a small knife that had been shaken loose when he fell.

"Nick!" He called, and his voice echoed back to him. The sounds he thought he'd been hearing receded, replaced by the drip of water far off. Grant rose carefully and examined the climb ahead of him. Didn't look good. He stalked to the right, shining his light up and forward, but the slope there grew steeper and merged into the roof above. Next time, agree to whatever the crazy woman wanted, negotiate later. Why had he felt the need to be honest with her? Because she'd shot herself instead of him. Crazy.

He stalked to the left and found that the centuries' accumulated dirt wore away here, with a damp channel drawing down the moisture of the surrounding stone, making it porous. Have to do. Gripping the light in his teeth, Grant caught the rough stone with his hands, dug in his feet and started up, every muscle protesting. His head swam, his stomach churning. Not good, but nothing he hadn't handled before. The bruises felt worst on his left and his shoulders, stinging the bullet wound left over from their earlier fire-fight. Details, not ops. Grant smiled to himself, aware of the smell of damp earth and stone, the plink of water, his hands and feet finding their way, his whole body working in trained perfection to drive him up the stone and back to the surface. He was alive—more alive than he had felt since he woke up in Walter Reed with his head being held on by sutures and bandages. The Hell with details.

At the top, he regulated his breathing and stretched out his hands. Full daylight still streamed through the open mouth of the cave but Grant moved carefully, taking to the edge so he could look out. The apology showed that she had scouted her location before manipulating him into position—she hadn't meant for him to die. She worked for Jin, but she wasn't in league with him, a minion, not an accomplice. And he still didn't know her name.

Outside, silence, but for a trickle of water and a few birds. Grant kept his gun ready, replacing the flashlight in his pocket as he stepped out into the day. His horse was no longer hitched where he had left it, but he spotted the dark bay not far off, grazing on a clump of darker green, another saddled horse beside it, its reins dragging and the saddle skewed to one side. That didn't look good.

Grant worked his way up the ridge, keeping low to be sure he'd see before being seen. Nothing moved down below, but the mud and narrow channels carving around the standing stone plainly showed the disturbance of people riding, falling—fighting. Five dead horses scattered the ground.

It took far too long to approach his newly skittish mount, speaking low, hands low, but he caught it at last, the other loose mare running further, then circling back toward them, following rather than be alone. Mounted despite his aches, Grant held the gun at his thigh and rode down into the valley. His mount shied and resisted, and it took all of Grant's coaxing to keep the horse moving, circling its dead kin. Bloodstains smeared the grass near the forested slope beyond the stone, and a scarf Liz had been wearing lay at the foot of the stone. In a couple of places, a lot of blood. Men had died here, but their companions had taken the bodies when they left. His jaw tightened, and he scanned the horizon. For maybe the first time, his team had done exactly as ordered—not returning for him. Still, they might at least have left him a sign to follow. Assuming they had won. Where had they gone?

Grant cantered to the high point and stared down at the grass. From above, the pattern of disturbed grass took on shape and direction. A large force of riders had come down from the east, over the slope where Nick had been waiting. They swept down upon the battlefield, and eventually rode off again to the northeast. A few shapes moved there, appearing to grow larger as he watched, a small contingent of riders, coming his way along the same course followed by the victors. Why return here? What remained—except the dead horses. They were Mongolian. Grant trotted across to the other side and waited, choosing his position, showing himself clearly. He tucked the gun into his belt, revealing his empty hand in a gesture of peace.

Seven people rode toward him, one of them a bizarre silhouette of swirling ribbons and flapping hides, a pair of antlers sprouting from its head. The one behind lightened Grant's heart: Byambaa, though he sat bare-headed, his quiver empty and his bow absent. Another man held Byambaa's reins, the singer's hands bound before him, allowing him to catch the high front of the saddle if his balance should fail him. Still, Byambaa's eyes lit when he saw Grant. The tall, lean man beside him held up a restraining hand when Byambaa started to speak.

"American. You are with these invaders." A bow hung at one side of his saddle, and a rifle at the other. He sat poised, with the ease of long practice.

The leader, the one with the antlers, shook its head in a wild flailing of metal tips and ribbons, then spoke gruffly. A woman? But older than her companions, probably a smoker as well.

"I came with my companions to honor the spirit of the Great Khan," Grant answered, catching Byambaa's slight nod.

"You would disturb his spirit," the other man snapped. "To defile his grave and defy his commands."

Again the ribboned one shook and grumbled, and the man fell silent, drawing back into himself, looking away. "We have a task."

"To sing for the horses." This earned him another nod from Byambaa.

The spokesman's eyes flicked back and he opened his mouth, then clamped it shut. He kicked his horse, passing the leader, and waving the rest down into the valley. Grant turned his mount and kept pace. The other man whipped him a glance. "You are not worthy to speak in this place."

"Let me prove my worth."

The man snorted, then shouted an order to the men. Immediately, two of them broke off, steering their mounts, and one pulled a long pole from a strap by his saddle. A loop dangled from the end and he held the pole out to one side as he kicked his horse into a run. Was the lasso for the horse or for Grant himself? He didn't wait to find out. Grant set his heels to his horse and they bolted as the loop slapped in the air next to him. The chase was on. He galloped back into the valley, then shifted course, staying clear of the sticking mud. At a nudge, his mount leapt one of the dead horses. The riders drew close behind, and Grant ducked low. The lasso swished again, this time catching a branch and drawing an oath from the rider who carried it. Grant galloped, the horse's mane lashing his face. The second rider pounded up alongside, and Grant swerved into him, forcing him back, crossing, splashing through the stream where it came together from its myriad courses. He left his stomach behind on the turn, his head beating in time with the horse's hooves.

The lasso man grinned, riding ahead, looking to cut him off. Grant slipped his foot from the stirrup on that side, then dropped his leg, letting himself slide to the side, riding sideways, his arm wrapped over the horse's neck. His mount tossed its head, his off-balance weight confusing it, but the horse's sudden turn made the lasso flick uselessly against its neck.

For an instant, Grant glanced up into the startled face of the second rider. As they broke between the pair of riders, Grant swung back up into his saddle, hooked his leg over and sat backward, letting the horse have its head for now. The lasso pole swung forward, reaching for him, and he caught it, twisting it aside and yanking the rider from his saddle. The man let go, caught in his stirrup. His horse, expertly trained, stopped abruptly.

Grant gave the lasso pole a turn, and shifted again, leaning his weight into the horse to jack himself back into the saddle. For a moment, he imagined he could hear the cheering of the crowds and feel a feathered headdress slapping against his back. God, this would hurt in the morning. Grant balanced the pole like a javelin and flung it hard. It slammed into the mud in front of the party of riders and he leaned back, halting the horse in its tracks, the animal still tossing its head, snorting at his unorthodox riding.

"How can I prove my worth?" Grant asked again, and his hand slid down of its own accord, patting and stroking the horse's neck, its ears settling, neck arching a little to encourage him to continue. He kept his focus close, his stomach threatening violence. Nothing would ruin the effect like vomiting.

When he looked up, the antlered one sat before him, dark eyes meeting his own. The rest of the strangers, except the lean man, concealed smiles, looking away, rubbing their chins or stroking their mustaches. Byambaa brought his bound hands to his forehead in a salute, and started humming, "Hail to the Chief."

CHAPTER EIGHTY-FIVE

Dusk came early in the narrow valley of their captors' encampment, leaving Liz shivering. The trees that sheltered this place towered in dense thickets with ancient trunks fallen beneath, forming the walls or roofs of makeshift houses. The four men set to guard them huddled around a fire, apparently not concerned about their escaping, and no wonder. They looked as ferocious as any men of the Great Khan's and rode with a fury to match. When they entered the valley, a wave of two dozen riders galloped hard down at the Chinese, drawing their weapons. The Chinese fired only a few more shots before scattering into the woods in the face of these superior numbers.

Nick had been taken there bound across a horse's back when he went down fighting—one of the men carried his prosthetic leg separately, and now kept it beside him like some kind of bizarre insurance policy against his escape. D. A. leaned next to Nick where he sat bound to a tree, but she kept silent since Gooney's outburst at the sight of Nick—and its violent result. Gooney's nose still oozed blood onto his leather gag, and one eye looked swollen nearly shut, but his expression remained determined. Liz imagined the running commentary in his head, railing against Grant for dragging them into this, then abandoning them in the middle of nowhere—no beer, no pillows, no way home.

When the riders had arrived, Huang, like Liz, surrendered quietly, hands up in the universal gesture. Liz tried to talk to them, until one of them brought out another leather strap, and she clamped her mouth shut. Byambaa, they had not touched at all. Seeing what was happening to the others, Byambaa rode back slowly, raising his hands, calling out for peace. Once they reached the encampment, Byambaa had been led away, and Liz hadn't seen him since. She had heard a group of riders set out a few hours ago. Since then, only the sounds of the men working around the camp had broken the peace of the wooded slopes. A thin river babbled through the center of the valley, giving the horses a place to water, and the men a place to wash off the blood of carrying the dead and beating the fight out of Gooney.

Were these the bad men, the miners their hosts had warned them about? Their leader, a tall man, wore a felt fedora and a kerchief that covered most of his face like an old western bandito. He took one look at the prisoners and marched away with Byambaa. Was her fiancé considered some kind of traitor? What would they do with him?

Her fingers pulsed lightly, her hands bound, but not brutally so. What could she do? Even if she wriggled free without getting noticed, the riders had watchmen posted around the camp. Huang's damp gaze met her own. More adventure than either of them had bargained for. Still, he held his head high, and she had heard his rush of thanks for Gooney's rescue. Honestly, she was proud of him, of them both. They came from such a different world than these men, even Byambaa had lived in the wilderness, hunting, trapping, knowing a harder life. Liz smiled at Huang, and he, wearily, smiled just a little, and gave her a short bow. She wet her lips. The scent of roasting meat and onions wafted through the camp, making her stomach growl. To distract herself, Liz began to hum, then to sing. *The mountains that call my spirit to rest.* The fourth song of the map that guided her. She could not do it justice without Byambaa's talent for Khoomei, but she knew the words, the rhythm. It hummed through her body, and she wondered if they would ever see the place that it described.

One of the men by the fire cocked his head, then frowned at her. "This is a Darkhad song. How can you sing this?"

He had an unfamiliar accent, but she could understand him. "You know the song?" she asked.

"All Darkhad know this song, but you are no Darkhad, neither was your forest boy. How do you learn it? No Darkhad would ever teach this. This song is for family."

She blinked back at him. Family? The forest around her seemed suddenly resonant with age and meaning. *A forest tended by family.* Where the Darkhad tribe remained to this day, watchful for the incursions of those who would break the khan's peaceful rest. "There was a recording, very old. A Darkhad singer—"

The man surged to his feet, a long knife in his hand, and he moved toward her. Liz scrambled backward, thumping into another tree. A commotion of sound to one side threatened to distract her, but she kept her eyes on the danger. D. A. sat up, then leapt to her feet, toppling into the assailant. He staggered and thrust her aside, intent on Liz. Gooney gave a shake of his head, keeping it tilted to focus his good eye, and growled as he, too, started to rise. Another long knife slid from its sheath by the fire and a Mongolian rider grabbed a handful of Gooney's hair, drawing back his chin, baring his throat to the blade.

"Yeah, I feel like doing that all the time," said Grant's voice. "But I don't think it's his day to die."

CHAPTER EIGHTY-SIX

The lean man, Nergui, said a few sharp words. The man holding Gooney released him right away, but the one stalking Liz protested, talking back, only to be silenced by the shaman who came at Nergui's side.

When the two men with knives drawn retreated, Grant let his hand relax off the grip of his pistol. He only had a few shots, not enough for the whole clan, but he'd make them count before he let anybody else slit Gooney's throat—never mind killing Liz. D. A. raised an eyebrow, and he gave her a nod, not surprised that her hands were already unbound as she sprang to Nick's assistance. Byambaa went to Liz's side, kissing her forehead before he worked on her bonds.

"I know you." Liz rubbed at her wrists, staring up at Nergui. "I spoke to you at the mausoleum in China."

"You have met me; you do not know me." To the group around him he said, "This does not mean you are not prisoners. You do well to listen to us, to cooperate, and to be quiet." Nergui aimed this last remark at Gooney.

Grant took a knee next to him, using a short knife to cut the leather gag and peel it away from Gooney's bloody face. "How come," Gooney whispered, "I'm getting the snot kicked out of me and you're treated like a fucking prince." His breathing hitched.

"Maybe 'cause I keep my mouth shut," Grant said. "Bend over." He tapped Gooney's shoulder, trying to reach his bound hands at his back.

Gooney gave a short laugh and shot him a look, then leaned forward and allowed Grant to cut free his hands. He eased back, his cast resting in his lap, his face gone pale under the blood with the agony of returning sensation. Still squatting beside him, Grant tipped Gooney's face toward him, scanning his jawline and nose. "Nothing broken. What hurts the most?"

For a moment, Gooney stared at him as if he didn't know where to begin. "Your pupils don't match, Casey. Might want to take it easy."

"Figures. I look like the walking dead, don't I?"

"Close to. What the Hell happened to you? Where were you when we needed you?" His voice rose dangerously, but Gooney held his fury in check.

That hurt, a sharp twist to his conscience, and Grant considered trying to convince him of the truth, but he could picture the explosion that would result. "I fell down a hole. Took a while getting back out." Grant put out his hand, rising, and offering to help Gooney to his feet as well, but Gooney spurned the gesture and muscled himself up. Liz and Byambaa fussed over Huang. Across the clearing, D. A. took custody of Nick's prosthetic, the composite muddy and scratched after such varied use.

"Check-in, Nick," Grant called. "What's your status?"

He half-expected to find Nick still embedded in sniper mode—he couldn't imagine what else would have caused the Darkhad to treat Nick as they had. Instead, the big guy took his leg, holding it before him as he sat on a log. He gazed at each of the Mongolians in turn before he finally replied, "Combat-ready, Chief. But these men have no respect for dignity."

Most of the men didn't understand his words, but Nergui stiffened, lips compressed. At his side, the shaman spoke in a low murmur. Byambaa straightened. "May I translate, with your permission, Nergui?"

The leader shook his head, and said, "I will translate. She apologizes on behalf of our people, saying that no man should be severed from himself."

Severed from himself. Grant rolled the phrase in his mind. That's what it had felt like, this last year of therapy and uselessness, rejected by women and employers both. Here and now, Grant was made whole.

"She invites you to join our supper, and then to leave our land without further injury," Nergui continued, waving them up and toward the larger communal fire beside the stream.

"We can't do that," Grant told him. "The Chinese are already here. With the exception of the banner, they have the same clues we did, and they're not going to be turned back by your desire to keep this place sacred. They've already built a false tomb for the Khan in Inner Mongolia—all they need to do is make sure the real one never gets found."

"I work there—no one believes that tomb," Nergui replied. "I returned home in case your questions meant you had learned the truth, or something like it."

"Not the mausoleum," Liz said, "another one, much more authentic. Minister Jin has been stealing artifacts and planning this for years. He's killed hundreds, maybe thousands of people to make it look like the real thing."

D. A. fished in her pocket and came out with a cell phone. "No," Nergui started immediately, and one of the men made a grab for it.

She retreated. "To show you the pictures, what Jin made." She tapped and slid, then held up the phone for Nergui's inspection. He squinted, frowning, his expression growing darker by the moment as he swiped through the images.

"For what does he do this? More tourist money?"

"Mongolia's money," said Huang. He stepped up beside them,

with a slight nod to Grant as if accepting the baton of leadership. "The People's Republic requires more resources than they have. Mongolia, this region you consider sacred, contains rare earth minerals they need for their aerospace and electronics industries." He continued, "Minister Jin operates for his own reasons, but this is China's reason, they want this land, and he serves China above all else. He will not be readily deterred. When the real tomb is found, it will be destroyed, along with anyone who knows how to find it. Very like the legends of the khan himself, slaying those who might reveal his resting place."

Nergui stalked before them toward the circle of stones, logs and camp chairs, head bowed. "Some of what you say, we already know. There are Mongolians here who work as miners, who know they defy us. They dig for gold, but lately have been digging for other things. When we find them, they are punished, but we are not here to fight other Mongolians." He spread his arms, turning a circle, the fire lighting his face from below. "This is our honor and duty. Our many-times great grandfathers are charged by the khan to defend his tomb, and so we have. When scientists come here, searching, we aid them with misdirection, with false reports and gear malfunctions. But they will not find it. Even we who defend the valleys don't know where to find the tomb itself."

"Someone's going to, and soon. You can't keep secrets from Google Earth," said D. A. "Not from ground-penetrating sonar, satellite surveys and metal detectors. Somebody's gonna come, sooner or later, with or without you. Do you plan to kill them all?"

"When we can, we kill no one." Nergui folded his arms, staring at her bitterly. "You have none of these things, how do you come here?"

"We have the songs," said Liz. "The map the khan's son left behind, so that his father would never be truly lost or forgotten."

"Jin has the songs as well, and is already following them, with the support of the Chinese army," Huang said.

"Maybe it's time for the khan to be found." Grant stood beside her. "Then it's up to you to decide what to do."

CHAPTER EIGHTY-SEVEN

Jin squatted next to the belly of a helicopter, inspecting the work as the painter finished his task. "Excellent." The painter bowed his head and started to clean up as Jin moved away.

Captain Guo stood nearby with a checklist in hand as a group of soldiers loaded cartons carefully onto a second helicopter.

"Do we have everything?" Jin inquired, more to be polite than from any concerns on his part.

"According to some members of the Committee, you have too much. And, at the very least, you have asked too much." Councilor Tian of the Central Committee took a cigar from his inner pocket and reached for a lighter, but Jin caught his cuff, swift, but light, to prevent him from striking a flame.

"Please, Councilor. Not around the explosives."

Tian shook him off, scowling, and rolled the cigar in his fingers. "These plans of yours grow too elaborate. There is already an investigation underway in the matter of the work crews assigned to Project Raven, and we have heard from several highly-placed members of Huang's organization, not to mention his partners who expected to hear from him. You last reported that Mr. Huang had agreed to cooperate with you in this, but the evidence now suggests otherwise."

"It is still possible that Huang will come around." If not, Jin vowed, there would be no evidence. If events developed to their most auspicious, Huang and his American friends would be there when the tomb was found, and would remain there when it was lost again, permanently. Word from the fight at the reindeer stone suggested that the victors were no more kindly disposed to the Americans than to the Chinese. It was entirely possible that part of the problem was already solved.

"Air support is ready, Minister." Guo bowed smartly. "The ground force is waiting."

"How much air support is required to defeat an army of a few dozen barbarians? If they even arrive in a timely fashion?" Tian demanded. "Likely they are celebrating their victory with fermented mare's milk and will sleep until noon."

"Then let us be gone and bring this project to a successful conclusion." As Jin moved toward the helicopter, the blades starting to churn the air, his phone buzzed in his pocket. He slipped it out and recognized his own phone number. His wife, calling on behalf of Mingbao to bid him goodnight. No time now. Soon, his son would wait for him no longer, but stand in a place of honor at his side. When the khan was buried beneath a mountaintop and his American friends along with him.

CHAPTER EIGHTY-EIGHT

D. A. insisted on at least a few hours' sleep for everyone, and they curled into borrowed blankets or piles of sheep and goat hides around the campfire. Liz lay down at Byambaa's side, feeling his heat even stronger than the fire. Across the way, ruddy light gleamed on Nick's eyes and dark skin as he cleaned his prosthetic. When he caught her look, he flashed a smile. "Go to sleep, Ms. Kirschner. Busy day comes too soon."

Beside him, Grant was already sleeping, and she worried briefly about his concussion. Wasn't he supposed to stay awake? He looked awful, even after cleaning up and having Nick stitch the gash on his temple. Somehow, he seemed stronger than ever, buzzing with a power that he barely constrained. At the communal fire, one of Nergui's riders told the tale of Grant's wild ride, much to the delight of the other Mongolians, but Grant didn't preen. Instead, he sat back, sipping his water, watching each of his companions in turn, as if to reassure himself of their well-being. He held up the bowl to her, and she smiled back, but wearily, warily, feeling like a gazelle camouflaged in a pride of lions. How did they even keep going? Back in the hospital, she had seen the winged lion tattooed at the back of his neck, accompanied by a swirl of other images that covered his arm to the elbow. At his throat, black letters formed words she couldn't read, embellishing a series of scars, like the score to the music of battle. Now, he slept peacefully, as far as she could tell, his breathing smooth and relaxed.

On the other side of the piled firewood, Gooney distanced himself from Grant, his breath catching and releasing as he tried to get comfortable, sounding muffled by his injured nose. His breathing took a long time to even out, but he, too, slept at last.

"Might I use your satellite phone?" Huang asked D. A. softly. "I wish to reassure some associates who will have expected to hear from me by now."

"Sure," she whispered back, fishing out the phone and handing it over. "Don't talk long—it's low on power." Thanking her, he receded into the gloom, his face lit by the bluish glow of civilization.

At a smaller fire beyond the first cabins, the shaman muttered to herself, and sometimes rattled bones or cast powders into the flames, making them flicker and smoke.

Liz closed her eyes, but that only magnified the sounds: the buzz of insects and the whisper of wind through the pine trees, the shaman's chanting, and Gooney's soft moans or grunts as he woke, shifted, and tried to sleep again. And inside of her eyelids, she saw the Chinese soldier, gun at the ready, about to blow them away when Nick's shot took off the top of his skull. Blood and bone, the screaming of men and horses, the mud sucking at her feet as she retreated behind the stone. Sucking at her feet like the hands of demons wanting to keep her down, to smother her there in the Mongolian earth, to punish her audacity in seeking the tomb and breaking the sacred perimeter.

Her eyes snapped open, focusing on the fire, on Nick's form, now prone and swaddled in blankets.

"You are not sleeping," Byambaa murmured from behind her, then slipped his arm around her and snuggled her close to his chest.

"I can't. I'm worried about tomorrow—all those men who died

today, what if that's us tomorrow? Jin's still out there somewhere, along with his army captain. How can we defeat them?"

"The chief seems certain. And so is Nergui. Determined to defend our heritage. He has sent riders to the other clans, to tell them he will seek the tomb."

"Are they okay with it? Would your clan be?"

"My father's family is very traditional—they would be angry the khan's wishes are not respected, but I think they would be pleased, too, when the Chinese are defeated in this. My mother's people run a ger camp for tourists. They would appreciate the discovery to bring more tourists." He laughed lightly, a resonant sensation she felt as much as heard. "Together, they are all of Mongolia: the khan is sacred, the khan is good business, either way, the khan belongs to us."

She settled into his embrace, holding his arm around her, wishing she could hold onto him, to that moment, and never have to face the morning.

"The shaman is still awake," Byambaa murmured, his lips close to her ear. "Let's get married."

Her eyes flared, then she giggled. "Yes!"

CHAPTER EIGHTY-NINE

For the second time that night, Grant's eyes snapped open at an out-of-place sound. The first time, it had been Liz and Byambaa's quiet footfalls, sneaking over toward the shaman's fire. Byambaa caught him awake, and gestured for him to follow. Grant rose and stepped among their companions, shedding the warmth of the blankets. His breath misted the air, but the chill felt good on his wounded scalp.

For a time, Byambaa and the shaman spoke softly together, and Liz leaned over. "We're going to get married—now, tonight." Her eyes glowed. "Will you stand with me?"

Standing for the bride at a wedding. Now there was a post he never thought he'd have, never mind at a Mongolian wedding. "What do I need to do?"

"We are supposed to walk three times around the family ger, then walk between two fires to our own place. I'm supposed to offer tea to the Eternal Blue Sky." She looked around and shrugged. "I don't really know—we're improvising. I should have a red veil, and my father should bring me to Byambaa's home, and give him an arrow to show that he's now the head of a household."

"Mission accepted." Grant melted into the night and took a few minutes to confer with D. A. who, like him, had awoken at the movement by the fire. He returned with a flowered head-scarf, but mostly red, and draped it over Liz's face, then brought her firmly to his side.

"Hey," Byambaa protested, then he stilled, standing by the shaman, his face lit by her small fire. She intoned a few words and lifted her hands, beckoning.

Grant brought Liz forward, and held out the other item he had found, one of Byambaa's arrows, retrieved from the battlefield. Byambaa accepted it, bowing his head, then took Liz's hand. Together, they walked around Grant three times, paused, then walked between the fires, off into the darkness, clinging to each other. Grant turned to find the shaman staring up at him, her antlered fur hat casting strange shadows on the trees all around. Her teeth flashed, along with the winking bits of silver and bone that embellished her robes. "You no girl?" she said, her voice raspy.

"No girl, not for me." He ruffled the hair at the back of his neck, his sutures tugging.

She shrugged in a jingle of charms. "Love like shadow. Sometimes see, sometimes gone."

Like a phantom.

The new sound that woke him had nothing to do with love. It was still so low that only the mountains of Afghanistan could have trained a man to hear it. He rose quickly, the night barely brighter than it had been hours before, and found Nick staring back at him. "Helicopters."

"Affirmative. Not too close, not too fast—unfamiliar with the territory." Nick pushed off his blankets, D. A. stirring and shaking back her curls. "We gotta go."

"I'll find the lovebirds," D. A. offered, and set out between the sleepers, while Grant sprinted to Nergui's wooden hut. A dog growled at him from the shadows, and the Mongolian opened the door before he could knock.

By then, the sound had grown from a breath to a whisper, and

Nergui struck a spark for his lantern. "The khan has waited eight hundred years—he waits no more."

Within half an hour, the camp was mounted, Liz and Byambaa looking tousled and better rested than the others, that dreamy look still haunting their faces. Excitement infused the Mongolians and Americans both: the dawn before a battle. Even Gooney wasn't grumbling as he accepted fresh ammunition. Most of the Mongolians carried only bows, but some had hunting rifles and a few had handguns, the product of their fathers' and grandfathers' military service. They took it in shifts to man the forest encampment for two months at a stretch, riding patrols, hunting for dinner, drinking vodka—like an extended vacation, though the home lives of most of the men weren't much different, he gathered. Yesterday had been their first blood battle ever, and the resentment over Nergui and the other captains' insistence on training like warriors had finally paid off.

Nergui and Grant led the party, with Liz and Byambaa at their side. They set out into a pre-dawn gray, riding up the valley, not too fast before the sun rose enough to show the narrow paths into the mountains. The Mongolians split into four smaller groups, riding out to rendezvous later rather than make such an obvious show of force. Let Jin and his soldiers be fooled by their numbers. The bulk of their own group waited in the tree cover as the leaders emerged onto the plateau above the encampment. "This is the forest we tend, as in the song," Nergui said. "I think there is no other."

"Then we're looking for a channel in stone where the wind cuts through," Liz said, and D. A. brought out a pair of binoculars, scanning the ridges above them. Byambaa drew a deep breath, and sang the eighth song, deep as the mountains, with a high, whistling tone that danced along it. The first time he heard khoomei, Grant found it bizarre, but now, especially out here in the land where it was made, it stirred him with the desire to ride, to hunt, to fight and not give in. From the expressions on the faces of the Mongolians, he suspected it had the same effect on them, even after hearing it all their lives.

"You guys have had the songs, but you haven't followed them?" Grant asked.

Nergui sat rigid. "Have you no taboos?" Then he softened. "These songs, they are sacred, a tradition. For us, they show the place where we live, the land we defend." He gave a heavy sigh. "Sometimes one of us thinks he will find the khan. He thinks he will do this so carefully, he is not missed, and his action is not known. He is always found. If the miners find him, he is dead."

"What if you find him?"

"He is left like the khan. As a boy, the Great Khan is captive, a board locked at his head and wrists. He escapes into the wilderness and is helped by wolves who become the symbol of his clan."

"So you put them in the stocks. Then what?"

Nergui eyed him sidelong. "We set him in the board. In the wilderness, like the khan. To be found by the wolves."

"Chief!" D. A. pointed high above, along the winding path up the mountain. A few crags rose from the talus slope and there, against the sky, a narrow slit marred the final ridge of stone.

"You're sure this is okay?" Grant asked. "I don't want to be left for the wolves." His horse danced a little, and Grant forced himself to stay calm, to project calm, even as he tried to suss out what worried him.

"You rode yesterday like a madman." Nergui squinted up at the stone, then shifted slightly in his saddle. "Do you also race?"

"We can't just—"Grant began, but the Mongolian was already gone, launching his horse with a shout of encouragement, and Grant's horse surged forward at his command. The trail switched back and forth, making the steep mountain's flank a little more reasonable, but still stones flew behind them as their hooves devoured the distance. For an inexperienced rider, the mountain was a deathtrap. And what did it hold for them? "Nergui! Stop!" He shouted, but his voice was lost in the wind.

Maybe it was the reminder of Afghanistan, the sound of helicopters at dawn and the knowledge that the birds were not their own, but Grant's neck felt stiff, his shoulders tight, and his skin tingled. They rode directly toward a narrow slot, exactly the kind of place where, if Grant had the first move, he'd lay his ambush. He kicked his horse harder, only to see Nergui's mount pivot and take the next stretch at a gallop, already high above him. Anyplace else, he'd've shot the horse out from under his ally to save the man's life, but here, horses were a man's life.

Abruptly, the trail levelled into the shadow of the stone, that narrow cut just ahead of them, the wind whistling through, sounding eerily similar to Byambaa's song. Nergui raised his fist and whooped his victory. Grant galloped up, breathless. Below, the others trotted or moved more slowly, the party strung out along the trail as they approached. Nobody fell. Nobody died. Paranoia was one of the symptoms, he'd told Liz a long time ago in another world. Maybe he was just feeling its effects. Then a speck of light flitted across the slope, like a firefly searching for a mate. Grant pulled his own gun and fired into the sky, watching his team scramble at the sound.

Some of them slid down from their horses, placing the animals between them and the direction of the shot. Gooney pointed, shouting, dragging his horse toward a crag that thrust up from the slope. The Mongolians looked confused, already riding hard up toward them. Byambaa and Liz, in the lead, kicked harder and the distance between them and their companions stretched out.

Nergui rounded on him. "What was that for? You alert them, if the Chinese are here."

"Somebody is here—didn't you see the reflection?" Grant pointed, trying to find the glint he had seen, but it had vanished.

"Then why aren't they firing?"

Nergui had a point. Surely the Chinese could pick them off with a decent sniper, out in the open as they were.

Grant shook his head, signaling for silence.

Both men paused, listening, watching. Nergui stroked his nervous mount with one hand as Byambaa and Liz rode up, breathless. "What's happening?" she demanded.

"Nothing." Nergui tipped his hand in a gesture of negation. "A soldier worries. It is always so."

The words, no doubt meant as comfort, grated instead. Then the flash came again, followed by the sucking roar of a rocket launcher somewhere above and to the right. The shot soared across the slope and exploded against stone. A section of the ridge above broke off, splintering and roaring. The landslide gathered speed with a rumble like thunder, sweeping down horses and riders, crushing them in a cloud of dust that rushed upward into the eternal blue sky.

CHAPTER NINETY

Jin felt the rumble of the landslide in the stone beneath his feet, and mused on the irony. Thousands of years ago, when a previous horde of barbarians descended upon China from the north, a brave and loyal Chinese heroine, Mu Lan, devastated that horde in the same way, by bringing down a mountain on top of them. Jin stood now in the shadow of those great heroes. Mongolia was the one nation that conquered China, and now, Jin would enable China to conquer them not by the rude means of invasion and bloodshed, but by seizing their own hero and placing his head firmly beneath the Chinese boot. This conquest would be economic and political—and complete. There was little they would not do in homage to the one Mongol who had ever amounted to anything.

His radio crackled, and he opened the channel.

"We have the singer, and the means to compel him."

"Bring him down." Jin clicked off and gazed up at the ridge where his men had captured what they needed of the Americans. He imagined the rest ground to pulp beneath tons of stone. An unfortunate accident in the mountains. Such a pity. He raised his binoculars. A dozen men now worked their way down the slope toward him, some of them armed, and some of them bound. Four prisoners. Well. It should be enough. He might need a few lessons before the singer understood what was expected of him.

Jin resumed scanning his surroundings, a high bowl valley, its rim cut by a series of ravines or rock falls, with cliffs between. A broad plain of rock provided the landing pad for their helicopters, and the jeeps stayed below, on the far side of the mountain he had identified using images provided, grudgingly, by Captain Guo. The clues all pointed here, and from the air, it had not been so difficult to locate. Water seeped from the face of one of those cliffs, filling a small lake at the heart of the valley, deep against the far wall and shallow at this end where the water barely trickled into another of those morasses, a swamp as impenetrable as the Mongolian mind. If they had only been reasonable about the resources the People's Republic required, so much effort would have been saved. But truly, Jin preferred it this way. Else he might have labored forever at the Ministry of Antiquity, cataloging the evidence of China's great history, and left out of its glorious future.

The landscape was quite striking, although it lacked balance and such trees as there were stood uniformly sharp and boring. What it lacked in trees, it made up for in cliffs. Which was the one that joined in the singing? Which one concealed the khan's tomb? He had had his men out on tracks barely fit for goats, examining the cliffs for tool marks or signs of excavation. So far, nothing.

"Minister." Captain Guo gave him a short bow that seemed almost sincere as he brought up the prisoners, two Mongolians, two Americans—one of them the singer's girlfriend. Perfect. Guo's men had gagged them all and bound their arms behind them. The soldier looked as though he'd already been through an avalanche, but his expression was cool, his eyes the rust-brown of an ancient weapon, settling on Jin, flicking away, taking in everything. If not for the hike into the valley, Jin should have had the man blind-folded as well, but he didn't want him dead. Not yet. The strange Mongol glared at Jin defiantly, chin raised, eyes wide in what was, perhaps, meant to pass for ferocity. The woman, on the other hand, looked terrified, and the singer seemed caught between these two poles, unable to master the icy resolve of the soldier, unwilling to give in to the frank terror of his partner. This, too, was perfect.

"One of these cliffs conceals the tomb of Genghis Khan, is that correct?" Jin asked.

The Mongol flinched, the singer glanced away while the woman trembled closer to him, ducking her head, trying not to give anything away. The soldier never moved. The time for drugs and seductions had passed.

Jin stepped forward and set his arm around the singer's shoulders, drawing him away from the others even as he dragged his feet and twisted in Jin's grasp. A strong jab at the right pressure point, and the man's resistance stuttered. He nearly fell, but Jin caught him and set him facing the others, then plucked free the singer's gag. "We will not help you," the singer said.

For a moment, Jin considered Grant Casey, the cocksure American he had been hounding all these days, who had twisted like a fox out of every trap. Casey stared back at him, face to face, unfazed. Jin would take him down like any cocky opponent. But he guessed the singer had grown attached to the American, and that attachment could prove useful, at least for a little while longer.

"The other Mongol," Jin directed, and one of the soldiers removed the man's gag.

"You think I would help you?" the prisoner spat. "I would—"

"You would sooner die?" From his waist, Jin plucked a handgun, dark and sleek. The Mongol squared his shoulders, ready to meet his doom, or at least, he imagined he was. "I do not need you to die, only to scream." Jin angled the gun and fired, shattering the man's knee. The Mongol dropped with a shriek that assaulted the ears, and the singer cringed away from the sound.

Jin turned his weapon toward the woman. "Perhaps you would like to re-consider your position?" He suggested with a smile.

CHAPTER NINETY-ONE

Byambaa's hands were freed, and Liz could see them trembling. He stared at her, resolutely ignoring Nergui's agony, though it showed in the pinching at the corners of his eyes. He took a deep breath, preparatory to singing, but it hitched and he broke into coughing instead.

"Bring him a drink, if you please," Jin directed, and one of the soldiers complied, offering a canteen. Byambaa accepted it and took a swallow.

Nergui's wail dropped low, to a series of ragged sobs.

Liz hummed softly, waiting for her husband—her husband!—to look at her again, then she nodded slowly, keeping time, letting her body move, just enough. After a long moment, he nodded as well, then his lips parted and he drew down the morning's chill, taking in the Eternal Blue Sky and exhaling on a tone. For a few minutes, he warmed up his voice, taking his time. It was, after all, the performance of a lifetime. For now, the enemy needed him, and so, the others would live. What if the cliffs didn't sing, what then?

"What are you doing? Stand up," Jin ordered, pointing his gun.

Liz saw Grant freeze, half-crouched at Nergui's side. He rose slowly, like a serpent uncoiling, or maybe just not making any sudden moves. Did he have a plan? How could he?

"Don't sing," Nergui panted. "Don't reveal."

One of the soldiers leaned down and tugged Nergui's gag back into place, stopping his voice.

Don't sing. The Mongolian nation could be left on its knees to the demands of its stronger neighbor if Jin succeeded. If they resisted, Jin would kill them all, no doubt. She pictured the blood spurting and the shattering of bone for each knee, each elbow—where would he shoot after that? Abdominal wounds were notoriously painful and deadly. He'd avoid head or chest wounds, he didn't want this to be too brief. Byambaa would be last to go, right after Liz herself, when Jin had no other threats to hold over him. Was it the more courageous choice to die and let the tomb remain hidden? But Jin wouldn't stop: he would take the entire valley apart, stone by stone and tree by tree, until nothing remained of the Darkhad's legacy but a pile of rubble. The other searchers, the adventurers and scientists, failed because they were careful, respectful, engaged on a less visceral level. Jin had none of those restraints. How long would it take the Mongolian government to become aware of their presence?

Grant, at her side, kept staring at the helicopters. Did he have a plan? Byambaa's singing could give him the time to enact it. But he was only one man against dozens of armed Chinese soldiers. Liz felt her heart drop. One man. Because the others were already dead, they must be: she envisioned D. A.'s curly head crushed in the rock fall, Nick's good leg battered, Gooney's sharp tongue forever silenced. The helicopters. They were painted with the Russian flag. If anyone had seen them fly over, they would be negotiating with their prickly neighbor to the north, not the real enemy. Her eyes burned and she forced back the tears. Byambaa needed her strong. He might as well sing—they had no hope of rescue save to drag out the time and pray.

The tones and overtones rose in the morning air, deep and resonant. *And the cliffs will join me in singing,* the final song in the map to the tomb of the khan. It made her want to weep.

Byambaa stood, chest swelling, nostrils flared, eyes closed. While the other songs created a tapestry of tones, unbroken and complex, woven with sounds like the river or the birds, this one held silences, long breaths between passages, as if the singer, indeed, waited for an answer. It did not come.

He broke off, wetting his lips, then taking another swallow from the canteen. "I think I must be closer to the cliffs."

"Very well. The trail is here." Jin gestured with his gun. With a slight bow, he transferred authority to Guo and escorted Byambaa toward the trail. "Captain?" he turned back, his handsome face bright with excitement, "Ready the explosives. We don't want this to take any longer than it must."

At a series of orders, one group of soldiers began unloading crates from the helicopters, then preparing the wires and boxes of trigger mechanisms. Nergui gave a grunt of protest, and Guo stepped closer, drawing a gun of his own. "There are still two hostages. Is it necessary to have three?" he mused aloud in Mandarin.

Across the valley, Liz heard the song begin again, Byambaa's lonely voice. She turned, tracking his progress. Six distinct cliff faces rose between the tumbled slopes, though one of them plunged straight down into the lake, forming its back wall. He wouldn't be able to sing there. Water seeped down the face to accumulate below, but the song contained no water, no trickling sounds, nor the noise of insects buzzing around the lake. Maybe they weren't even in the right place at all. Her chest felt tight. She stared into the lake, wishing it would swallow her tears and devour her pain. Then her breath stopped altogether, and she knew. No water. The song contained no water—because the water didn't belong. Liz whirled toward Grant.

"Be still," Guo ordered, swinging the gun to face her. She shook her head, motioning toward the water, flaring her eyes. Grant frowned, head cocked, one shoulder rising in a gesture of mute confusion.

"Be still, I told you!"

With a moan of exasperation, Liz stared at Grant a moment longer, hoping he'd understand. Hoping this time he would follow her lead, then she burst into motion, running for all she was worth across the grass and leaping into the lake.

CHAPTER NINETY-TWO

"After her! Someone get her!" Guo was shouting, waving his gun.

Grant let the wave of movement toward the lake carry him forward. What the Hell was she doing? Sacrificing herself so she couldn't be used against her husband? It didn't seem like her to give up—and why was she so keen for him to pay attention? Didn't matter—she was his responsibility, and he wasn't going to let her drown on his watch. Grant brushed against one of the soldiers, swiping the knife from the man's belt, twisting it in his grip and hacking at the rope, then he was running, tucking the blade at his back. He yanked free his gag with the other hand.

"Stop him, he has a weapon!" someone shouted. Byambaa's song broke off in a cry of panic.

"Let him go—let him find her!" Guo barked.

Grant drew a deep breath and dove into the water not far from the ripples where Liz had vanished.

Painful cold slapped his skin. Grant forced himself down, paddling, searching. With the sunlight shining down and the mountain clarity of the water, he followed the trail of her bubbles as she sank, her hair reaching out into the water around her as if it stretched for the surface and the air beyond.

He kicked hard, frog-kicks, propelling himself after her. Stone cliffs loomed ahead, then suddenly a face loomed out of the depths, a snarling demon with three eyes and an upraised sword. Grant nearly gasped, but held back his vital supply of oxygen. The bubbles drifted ahead, sunlight filtering down. Another face, this one stony and serene: Confucius. Had to be. A forest of statues surrounded him, sages and spirits of distant lands, stone and bronze and glittering with inlays of gemstones. Ahead, he caught a glimpse of the cliff's base, marked by a massive carved portal into darkness. Grant pushed off an inscribed pillar, searching, his lungs burning. There!

She fell against the statue of a woman, holding a veil, head tilted. Kwan Yin, the goddess of compassion. Liz struggled then, kicking, trying to dodge the stone arms. Drowned by the goddess of compassion. Ironic. Unworthy. Grant caught the end of the stone veil using it to push himself deeper, and got hold of Liz's arm. He dug in his fingers and tugged her sideways

Pushing off, he launched them both toward the surface, dragging her upward against his chest and finally shoving her above him, getting her face out of water. Kicking strongly, he broke the surface, gasped a breath and let himself submerge as he towed her toward the edge. Another breath, a glance toward land, then kicking again. Other hands grasped her, pulling her free of his grip up onto the shore, and Grant clung to the stone at the water's edge, breathing deeply, his wounds stinging.

Byambaa ran down, dropping beside Liz and ripping away the gag, slapping her back as she sputtered and gulped at the air. "Don't leave me," he said, over and over, English and Mongolian. "Don't leave me."

Cradled in his arms, she panted, and grinned.

"Stupid woman. Do you think your death—"Jin stopped, even as her expression fled, then he glanced up, stared at the lake, then back to them. "The tomb, it's underwater." He turned sharply. "Guo! The bombs, place them there." He gestured toward the far end of the lake where a gentler curved berm led into a swampy area of willows and wandering streams. Soldiers hurried to do his bidding.

From his vantage at the surface of the water, Grant could make out the shapes of the stones beneath the berm, stacked regularly into a dam. Legend again, this time, the rumor that a river had been diverted to conceal the tomb. Something Gooney read in his goddamn guidebooks. Grant scrubbed a hand over his face, wiping away that thought. Time for grief later—for now, he still had a team to serve, a team to save.

Byambaa had freed Liz's hands and she rubbed her wrists absently, his hand stroking her shoulders as they watched the Chinese soldiers stacking explosives on the ancient dam.

A dozen yards away, Nergui squirmed and Grant started to lift himself from the water, but Guo raised his gun, aimed and fired. Nergui's back arched and he spasmed in a rush of blood. Guo pivoted toward Jin. "Minister, now that we know the location—"

Grant didn't wait to hear him finish. "Hey, Robin Hood, can you swim?"

Byambaa blinked, then he grabbed Liz's arm, both stumbling to their feet for the two paces back to the lake. Together, the three plunged beneath the surface, stroking hard toward the great khan's tomb, and Grant prayed it would not become their own.

CHAPTER NINETY-THREE

Liz swam after Grant, his long body and powerful limbs sending him straight and hard. Byambaa kicked and struggled along with her. He could swim, sure, but he'd never been a big fan. Most Mongolians never had the chance to swim in any case.

They swam through the cluster of statues toward a looming darkness. A leap of faith. Could they even get through, or would the way be barred, another bronze door blocking them forever, just as they ran out of breath.

Grant got there first, clinging to something, waving them forward. He reached out and grabbed Byambaa's arm, pulling him into the vast rectangular shadow.

Then it was Liz's turn. Grant's strong hand caught hers, pulling her down, both ducking under the stone lintel into the darkness beyond. She could feel the waves of Byambaa's passage, but the sunlight did not penetrate. She pressed her lips together, desperate to take a breath, knowing she could not breathe water. Her chest squeezed more by the minute, Grant's hand still clasping hers, gripping her tighter as if telling her to hold on.

Her right hand, reaching into the water, dragging herself forward, brushed stone, then nothing, and she was bursting upward, gasping. Her kicking feet stubbed against something, a rising slope of stone and she let go of Grant, scrambling up the slope out of the water. She ran into something solid and gave a cry, but it caught her by the shoulders.

"We're alive," Byambaa said, his voice resonant in a narrow space.

"So far, so good," Grant muttered. He was shifting in the darkness nearby, shoes and cloth scuffing against stone, then a thin flashlight beam broke the darkness. She could make out little but the glint of his eyes and the brief flash of his smile.

"How did you know about the tunnel?" Liz asked.

"I could see the entrance when I dove down for you," he answered with a movement that might have been a shrug. "Had to be an upward slope, or the khan's burial would be soaked. I was betting there wasn't a door."

"Lucky bet," Byambaa replied.

The water roiled and the distant sound of an explosion penetrated the stone around them. The water surged upward, soaking her all over again, then sucked backward, gurgling down the tunnel.

"Better get moving. It'll be a little while before the water drains enough for Jin to avoid getting his feet wet. We want to be ready."

"But—it must be a dead end!" Liz blurted.

Grant shone the light ahead. "They both are, one way or another." He started walking, his light moving ahead, catching the edges of a series of niches in the wall. She caught glimpses of boots with pointed tips, and he raised the light, tracing a pair of legs in silk trousers up to an armor skirt of leather with metal strips, a breastplate, the gleam of a silver belt, broad shoulders, a helmet topping a leering skull.

She caught her breath and Byambaa squeezed her hand. "They're just like the ones at Jin's tomb," said Liz.

"Well, he was a scholar first," Grant observed.

"These are the warriors who accompanied the khan on his journey home." Byambaa gazed up at the vacant face, then asked,

"Who is to say he will not simply blow up the tunnel and leave us to rot with the khan?"

"He's a scholar. Even if he hates the Mongols, even if he can't wait to crush the khan and everything he stands for, and he stands to gain a lot of fame and fortune when he succeeds, I don't think he could resist being inside one of the great mysteries of the archaeological world." Grant shone his light along the wall, from one niche to the next, leaving the beam low, on the boots and not the hideous faces. There must be a hundred of them at least, the finest of the khan's men, willing to die for their leader.

"There's another thing," said Liz. He glanced back at her. "It's personal, you and him. I don't think he'll go until he knows—"she broke off, not wanting to finish the sentence.

Grant held the flashlight beneath his chin, casting his face in eerie shadows. "Until he knows I'm dead." He swung the light away to one of the skeletons, playing the beam over the empty eyes and the teeth like rows of tombstones. "I'm counting on it."

CHAPTER NINETY-FOUR

Lake water gushed through the broken dam, spilling into the channels and willows beyond. Where the curved dam had been now gaped open, stone and mud flung wide. Dozens of bones protruded from the mud, freshly revealed. The last resting place of the builders who had made the lake possible. Long bones thrust up and smaller ones speckled the edges of the fresh crater above the flowing water. Mud oozed from the jaws and eyes of a handful of skulls, witnessing the ruin of the work they had died for. He wondered if they had been shot with arrows, as his own workmen had, but this seemed hardly worth investigating, compared with the mysteries still concealed by the shimmering pool.

Jin watched the water level drop, ebbing down the sheer face of that tallest cliff. The barbarians must have excavated down to the level they chose, so that even the shape of the valley itself did not reveal its secret. Jin might not have reached the same conclusion the woman clearly had—unless her leap into the water had truly been an attempt to remove negate Jin's power over the singer. He did not think she had that sort of courage. Would he now see their bodies at the bottom of the lake? He did not think so. The soldier tried one last time to outwit him, but there would be no escape that way, not through a tomb meant to remain forever hidden.

There! At the lapping edge of the water, the top of a mighty lintel carved into the stone. The patterns resembled the cloud shapes the Mongols to this day used to decorate their gers. Jin felt a rising curiosity, as the waters receded, to find out how much he had gotten right in his own interpretation. At the very least, he would bring the khan himself back to China to be reinterred, then even genetic analysis would support Project Raven. Perhaps there were other artifacts worth removing before the site was obliterated. He had brought enough explosives to bring down the mountain, and had enough contacts among the local miners to pass this off as a mining accident.

Guo gave a soft whistle behind him, and Jin turned, following the captain's gesture. At the base of the slope from that gap in the rock, a soldier led a pair of horses, heavily burdened. Each horse carried one of the dead Americans, the black one, and the big one from the hospital, their hands and feet occasionally brushing the rough ground as the man approached. The other soldiers, waiting by the water, parted to allow him through.

The man bowed quite low, if somewhat stiffly. The discovery of the corpses must have taken some effort. The corpses themselves dripped with blood, their clothes torn and scuffed from the stones, but they appeared remarkably intact, save that the black man had lost a leg.

"What of the third, the woman, and the businessman who accompanied them?"

"I cannot say, Minister," the man answered gruffly, then smothered a cough. "Forgive me, Minister. I found these below a promontory. It appears they attempted to climb to safety."

"It appears that they failed," Jin observed.

"I made sure of it, Minister."

"Good work."

"Minister, the water," called one of the soldiers.

The pit below revealed a crowd of statues clustered around that tall, rectangular opening. He recognized Chinese sages and South Asian hybrid deities, the guardian spirits of a dozen dead empires, and the idols of a dozen more. A stone Madonna stood among them, the baby in her arms dripping Mongolian water beneath the Mongolian sun. Did they weep for their capture by the horsemen who had terrorized Eastern Europe? Or did they weep at this new salvation, revealed beneath the heavens for the first time in eight hundred years. A few puddles remained and water still slowly trickled out at the far end, but the drainage also revealed a smooth causeway down from the edge near where they stood, leading between the sculptures and into the dark passage beyond. That would be pathway traversed by the Mongol's coffin and its final companions. No sign of the three who had leapt into the water. Jin would have liked to be the first living man to walk this path in eight hundred years. Instead, he would be the first to walk it, and emerge alive. It held a certain reflective beauty that he, too, would keep this secret to the grave, a death far into a glorious future, marked by the honor of his family and of his nation. One day, he would share this victory with his son, or even with his daughter. Their father, through his wisdom and forethought, redeemed his nation from the memory of the barbarian conquest by despoiling the khan's tomb and carrying home his coffin as a trophy. Yes, it would be a tale worth telling.

"What shall I do with the bodies, Minister?" the gruff old soldier asked.

Jin gestured among the statues. "Dump them down there." They would be buried when the cliff came down, mere yards from the tomb they sought. An apt resting place.

Jin strode toward the conqueror's final path and claimed it for his own.

CHAPTER NINETY-FIVE

Liz and Byambaa walked up the slope, the beam of the light seemed smaller by the moment until it suddenly fell upon something pale, rising from the gloom. Liz flinched, but no ghost stood so broad or so round. A huge ger, woolen and unadorned rose before them, and she felt the briefest let-down, remembering the painted richness of the false tomb, with its mounds of weapons, niches full of crowns and yellow silk tent. But the Mongols had never been great painters, nor were they known for their architecture. They were nomads, roaming herdsmen turned warriors by the ascent of the Great Khan himself, who turned their skill with the bow away from their own clans, and outward to the world. She shone the beam over the surface of the wool, tracing its outline. To either side, pitching outward, sat rotting heaps of wood, their shapes no longer discernable. When she brought the light downward, she found bones, but these looked long and unfamiliar, until she reached the skulls. Nine horses, laid out in a row before the huge ger.

"The khan's wheeled ger," Byambaa murmured. "They must have taken it apart, collapsed the structure to bring it inside."

"And the horses who hauled it." Together, they moved forward, past the skeletal steeds who still bore the silver ornaments of their harness. A tall pillar rose at the front of the ger, topped with ancient bunches of horsehair. Liz raised the light up the length of it, then caught a shimmer, and lifted the light a little higher.

The ceiling far above winked and shone with stars. She recognized the Big Dipper, Cassiopeia, Orion. The beam of the flashlight barely reached. Between the gleaming constellations, the ceiling looked a rich, deep blue.

"Eternal Blue Sky," Byambaa breathed, simultaneously an oath and a recognition. "It must be lapis lazuli, that pigment. And the stars —silver? Or diamonds."

Liz became aware she was holding her breath and expelled it softly. "We should be looking for weapons, or at least a place to hide." She swished the light around, and found another rank of warriors.

Byambaa headed in that direction, and carefully removed a bow made of horn and sinew.

"No way the string will have lasted this long," Liz said.

Reaching into a pouch at his waist, Byambaa said, "I have a spare. And he is a Mongol. If he has oil, that will have lasted." Finding what he sought, Byambaa started rubbing grease from a wooden canister into the bow. Liz searched for a knife, but the damp had pitted the blades with rust. Better than nothing, she supposed. They moved on, back toward the huge ger, and she lifted a corner of the door flap, shining the light inside. The darkness glittered with gold, silver, gemstones. Her beam found the points of diadems and the fall of beaded veils, the bowls of golden chalices, the sheen of embroidered silken robes and the fierce glare of captive gods. The lost wealth of a conquering hero, found at last.

"Where is the khan?" Byambaa whispered.

Both of them spoke and moved with reverence, as if they visited a cathedral, or a throne room where they feared to raise the ire of the lord. She let the flap fall silently back, the smell of damp wool lingering in the air, and they moved on, behind the huge ger.

The flashlight found gold again, winking from a deeper darkness.

A thick carpet, richly patterned with flowers and vines covered the floor. The finger of light pointed to a crown, gold with leaves of emerald, then another, this one of enameled panels in the Byzantine style. The crowns sat on the ground, carefully arranged in a series of rings, playing audience, subservient to a broad throne of carved wood, low as a couch. An eye caught the beam, and Liz froze, then let her breath out and found another one. The eye was stone, a carved sphere set into the face of a wolf hide that spread across the wood, its fur thick and silvery. On the wolf pelt sat the khan.

Arrayed in battle armor of metal plates over a del of pure Mongolian blue, the conqueror waited, one booted foot tucked in front of him, the other resting lightly on the step as if he might rise at any moment. A sword lay upon his lap, a bow and quiver at his side, his withered hands still resting on his weapons. Edges of fur framed his fearsome face, his skin smooth and leathery, his eyes narrowed as if he gazed into the distance, as if he had seen them coming. A dark mustache draped his lips. As Byambaa knelt to his great ancestor, the founder of his nation, the khan's dry lips seemed almost to smile.

CHAPTER NINETY-SIX

Lights grew at the mouth of the tunnel, footfalls echoing, but nobody spoke. Even the Chinese felt the weight of this place, the mountain towering over them, the ranks of the dead staring down at them. Grant waited, still as stone. Powerful flashlights swept the floor, cut from the living rock and still moist from the retreating water.

"Spread out and be careful! They could be anywhere," barked the captain.

Quicker feet moving with trained precision quick-marched up the corridor. Five men, soldiers, hurried past, then another group, moving a little more slowly. Half the men carried lights, the other half had their guns at the ready. Hopefully, Byambaa and Liz were ready, too.

"Be careful with the artifacts as well. We may wish to retain some of them for study." Jin's voice, educated, confident.

"Minister, someone might have noticed the helicopters, we should—"

"Then they will be calling the Russians, very, very politely, given recent Russian aggressions in other areas. The Russians will, of course, deny everything, and the Mongols will be stuck. Even if someone saw us land, Captain, they will likely misjudge and assume we landed on the other side of the border." Jin's voice grew louder as they approached. Good—the wool boots made Grant's feet sweat and the corpse crowded him into a space as narrow as a grave.

Other footfalls echoed with those of the two principals. More soldiers in escort. Five more? The echoing corridor made it hard to judge.

"There are few people here, Minister, but there are people. What about the rest of that clan who shot up my men? They were not all taken by the rock fall, certainly."

"Do you practice wu shu, Captain?"

"We study hand to hand combat, of course." The officer snorted.

"Wu shu teaches centeredness, Captain. It seems to me that you might benefit from that." Jin paused, tracing one of the dead warriors with his flashlight, so close now that Grant could see the gleam of his eyes.

"You sound like one of those Qi Gong fanatics who wave their arms about in the square. Centeredness makes for easy targets."

"Hardly," Jin began, then broke off. The sound of gunshots echoed up the corridor—not from the tomb, but from outside. Jin spun on his heel. Grant dared to hope for more than Byambaa. The Darkhad had come to avenge their fallen leader.

Grant flung his dead companion out of the niche, aiming for Guo.

Cursing, the captain leapt back, the skeleton slamming against him bones rattling apart, silken clothes tearing and tangling. By the time the captain had his gun up and aimed in the right direction, Grant had Jin by the back of the throat, his knife held under the minister's chin. "Drop your weapon, captain," he ordered in Mandarin. "Tell your men to do likewise."

From the left, a shriek, a thud, gunfire and a shout, "We are—"cut off with a gurgle.

Grant gave a high-pitched whistle. After a moment, two sharp notes answered. Not ready yet. Damn. Well, Grant couldn't help them now—he had his hands full. "Let's walk out together. All of you get in front of me. I'll take the minister."

"Do as he says," Jin commanded, but his voice sounded complacent. As well he might be—he still had twenty or thirty men on the outside.

Grant pricked his chin. "Let's go."

Guo and the others let their weapons clatter to the ground, and the captain herded his men out ahead of them. He started to wave a hand, urging them to hurry, but Grant shouted, "Slow! Stay in sight."

The men hesitated.

"It is not as if you will kill him," Guo remarked casually.

"He doesn't need to die," Grant said, "Only to scream." Under his fingers, he felt the quickening of the other man's heart.

CHAPTER NINETY-SEVEN

Jin walked slowly, as requested. He considered how to break the grip, how to snap the American's arm, slam his hand into the American's jaw and snap his head back. But he could afford to take his time, in spite of the man's threats. Casey needed him in order to get out. The sounds of violence grew as they emerged, shooting, shouting. They emerged together into the sunlight. At the rim of the barren lake, the Chinese soldiers stood shoulder to shoulder facing outward, firing. Whatever threat confronted them, they met it with efficiency, under control. The sergeants Guo had left in charge called orders, the men replied with action though arrows and bullets flew in response.

The grove of statues rose around them, and there Jin saw the old soldier with the two horses, the two dead Americans at his feet. Jin gave a subtle pivot, guiding his captor's path, and his view, toward the bodies of his dead. He heard the sudden hiss of the man's breath and felt his grip tighten.

Jin swept his hands up even as he ducked his head forward. He caught Casey's blade, holding it off with one hand and jerked him off-balance. The flashlight he still carried swung backward, toward Casey's core, but he wasn't there.

Casey moved with Jin's fold, shoving his head downward and stepping to the side, maintaining his grip on Jin's neck, digging his fingers in as he pushed. His knee slammed into Jin's gut.

Jin stifled any reaction. He found his center, letting the flashlight fly and reaching for his gun. Left-handed, but still effective at such close range.

Casey didn't let go, but swung them both, like an ice-skater turning his partner. Jin's left hand cracked against the damp Madonna and the gun tumbled free. His fingers felt numb. Still half-bent, he must look the fool, bowing to this mad American. So be it. Jin shifted his grip on the American's knife-hand and flipped him up, hard.

That hand at his throat released as Casey flew overhead. Before Jin could finish the move and break the man's wrist Casey caught himself, somehow landing on both feet, turning already. For a moment they were face to face, both slightly breathless. Casey rocked his fist into Jin's solar plexus, counting on the resistance of their joined hands to keep Jin braced for the blow.

Jin let go, allowing Casey's blow to carry him backward, his feet sliding smoothly on the damp stone, his balance perfect.

Someone took a shot that pinged off a bronze. Jin leapt forward, swinging a kick that caught the American in the side. Casey caught his ankle and twisted. Again, Jin gave way, letting himself drop to the ground, forcing Casey off balance and snapping him to the ground. Casey struck the stone hard, but he hadn't let go. He slashed with his knife, plunging the blade into Jin's calf.

A bolt of pain slid up his leg. Jin wiped the pain away and jerked his leg back in spite of it, taking his enemy's knife with him. Casey was up already, lunging forward. Jin rolled, and found the gun. His shot furrowed blood across the American's side as he twisted to avoid the bullet. He landed with his back to a wild, winged demon, its tongue lolling and eyes bulging over the American's head. Blood streamed down his side. Jin slid his leg up, snatching the knife, and rose, a breath of fire from his nostrils as the pain struck again.

Casey caught the statue's arm and swung his body up. Jin's shot burst into the demon's bronze chest, just where Casey's head had been a moment before.

A thrum of helicopters rose overhead as he tracked the American's movement. He crouched on the demon's sword-arm, eyes drawn briefly upward, framed by the muscular bronze arm and the enormous, upraised sword, viciously curved and pointed. Guo and his five men, unarmed, thanks to the earlier command, rushed forward and gave the statue a hard shove. The bronze teetered, and the American swung, losing his balance. He tucked for the fall and caught himself well. Admirable, truly, but Jin held the knife in one hand, still dripping his blood, and his gun in the other.

As Casey unfurled himself, ready for the fight, Jin slid in low.

He shoved the knife under Casey's right arm and upward toward the shoulder, sticking him like a pig for the slaughter as he brought the gun down to his prisoner's ear.

CHAPTER NINETY-EIGHT

Grant gaped in agony. He couldn't move—the long blade paralyzed his arm and he froze in that half-crouch, blood streaming down his side. Overhead, three helicopters circled, and a cheer rose from the Chinese. Just for a moment, he believed they would get the better of this handful of men, the Darkhad warriors assaulting them from above while he dealt with their leader down below. Three helicopters. Chinese. Boldly, and openly.

Jin smiled at him, almost gently. He cocked the gun, aiming at Grant's eye.

A ragged shadow loomed up suddenly from behind, a strangely shaped club in its hand. "Nobody kills him but me," Gooney growled, and he slammed Nick's prosthetic leg into Jin's head.

The minister staggered and lost his grip on the knife. He raised the gun and fired. Gooney dodged and slipped, tumbling from the causeway under the arm of the fallen demon, its tongue mocking the sky, its first raised, sword bared in defiance of the sky itself, but lying now halfway across the path.

On the fringe of stone overhead, silhouettes of soldiers were turning their way, guns drawn. Even Jin, alive, would not save his team now. Grant staggered to his feet as Jin brought the gun around again. The man was fast, silent and deliberate. The world stilled, just then, the rattle of gunfire falling away, the scent of blood, sweat and mud vanishing as the moment reduced to this: Grant, sorely wounded, his adversary deadly serious, the black barrel of the gun between them.

Grant reached toward him as the gun levelled. He stepped straight in, catching Jin's elbow with his left hand, letting the butt of the gun ram his chest as he bent the elbow back. The bullet flared upward, singeing his cheek. Jin did as he always had; he gave ground, pretending to lose face to fool his opponent. Grant moved with him, a dance that could have only one end.

The gun twisted, lodged under his chin as he took the last step and finally pivoted aside as a bronze blade plunged upward through Jin's chest. Grant's falling weight shoved the minister more firmly onto the blade, the demon who bore it staring goggle-eyed as blood streamed down its arm.

Dropping to his knees, Grant pinned his right arm at the elbow, the knife trapped there, a stinging agony. Three helicopters.

Nick, on two legs now, snatched the gun as Jin's dead hand relaxed, and fired, cool and accurate, up toward the ring of soldiers. A few more targets down wouldn't matter at this point.

Gooney, spattered with mud, his cast almost unrecognizable, plunged from the thicket of statues, his fist clenched in the uniform of a Chinese soldier, an older man, his hat tumbling away. "You called them! You fucking bastard!" Gooney shouted into the man's face. Huang, in disguise.

"Let him go. What's the point?" Grant breathed, but they couldn't hear him.

"Yeah, he did," called another voice, a woman's, familiar. D. A., her curly hair bouncing in the breeze. Another face appeared beside her, a bullhorn raised.

"Army of the People's Republic, you will stand down on the

authority of Prime Minister Xi. Captain Guo, order your men to stand down." The voice echoed around them, way too loud.

"Who are you to give me commands?" the captain barked back from his position behind the stone Madonna.

"Lieutenant Ma of the Central Committee Anti-corruption Commission." The lieutenant lowered his megaphone, moving stiffly, bulky bandages outlined beneath his shirt. He watched over the army with a keen gaze. The Darkhad men clustered at the end of the causeway, their faces furious, their own weapons still firmly in hand.

Guo echoed the Lieutenant's commands, guns lowering all around them, the silhouettes transforming from spiked and dangerous back into men. Gooney stared up, then brought his eyes back to Huang, and lowered him gently to his feet, taking back his hand, standing there awkwardly. "Sorry."

"No need to mention it," said Huang, but his smile edged back to his lips.

Nick, stationed at Grant's side, lowered himself down, his prosthetic uncooperative. He wrapped a strong arm across Grant's chest. "Got you," he said, adding pressure to stop the bleeding. "But D. A.'s gonna have to print me a whole new leg when we get home."

Home. For a few terrible moments, Grant had been certain none of them would ever go home again.

From the entrance of the tomb, Byambaa emerged, a bow slung over his shoulder, Liz on his arm. The Darkhad let out a whooping cheer, as if the khan himself had emerged, once more victorious.

CHAPTER NINETY-NINE

Grant's shoulder still throbbed few weeks later, as he drove himself to Logan. He shouldn't, he knew—the doctors said he shouldn't do anything, really, and that he shouldn't expect to raise his arm over his head for the next year, if ever, and no gymnastics—certainly no swinging himself into the arms of pagan gods. Grant smiled to himself. He'd beaten worse than this.

Back in Mongolia, Byambaa and the Darkhad worked through a series of secret meetings, talking with the government about how to handle the re-discovered tomb. Would it remain a secret, be made into a tourist trap, or be held as a shrine for the Mongolian people? Grant couldn't say—that wasn't his choice: he had fulfilled his mission in defeating the Chinese plan to steal Mongolia's own hero, and protecting his client through it all. Liz placed her thesis project on hold until the determination could be made, and stayed with her husband. Huang returned to his home in Hong Kong, looking older, standing straighter. He told Grant he would be in touch about other opportunities for the Bone Guard before he bowed very low.

The rest of the team had come to visit when Grant was discharged from the hospital. Nick and D. A. returned to the apartment for some much-needed rest, swearing that, next time he called, they wouldn't answer—but she had winked as they climbed into their taxi and Nick gave him a quiet salute. Gooney hovered awkwardly nearby, his arm in a fresh cast, finally spruced up, but looking like he needed a real vacation. They faced each other for a long moment. Gooney opened his mouth, closed it. Took a long breath, and let it out slow.

Grant lifted his chin. "Gooney—"he gave a shake of his head. "Detective Gonsalves. Thanks for coming."

"Thank you for your service," Gooney muttered. "You're no civilian, Casey. You never will be." He sighed, then his mouth twitched into a smile. "But you're damn good at what you do. Most of the time."

Grant laughed. "Maybe, but I still need back up."

"That's what Nick's for, right? He lives for that."

"Gooney." Grant met his gaze. "You came through, no matter what. I won't forget that."

Gooney shook his head, waved him off, and stepped into the waiting squad car, already back on the job—no doubt facing a mountain of paperwork.

Was he a civilian now? He couldn't say. But the Bone Guard had delivered, and discovered a little more than he bargained for. Like today. The missing link between Jin and the states revealed at last. Grant made his way into the terminal, and saw her waiting, a willowy Chinese woman. She spotted him, ducked her head immediately, blushing. When he came close, she finally glanced up at him from that fall of hair. "I am sorry. I thought it was the best way, what my father wanted. My...fathers, I should say."

Susan Chan, the daughter of an Asian Studies professor, one of the few who knew about Liz and her songs. She was as beautiful as that night in Frankfurt when she tried to kill him. A new rush of passengers, many of them Chinese, streamed from the International Arrivals portal, and they turned to watch for a woman likely neither of them would recognize, but when they saw her, moving hesitantly, a teenage boy at her side, her dark eyes roving the crowd, Grant knew her right away. She was the image of the woman at his side, but older, more tired. She pushed a luggage cart, then stopped abruptly, lips parting, when she saw Susan.

"Zhuwen," the woman breathed, and the young man, a smaller version of Jin himself, took over the cart, his face shyly averted as his mother moved forward, reaching out a hand to touch the younger woman's face. "He tells me you are gone, never to be seen again. We were too young, too poor for a baby. I didn't think I would ever see you again."

Zhuwen/Susan smiled, blinked, tears streaming from her eyes. "He brought me here, to his old friend." She sniffled, then added, "Mother."

They came together at last, and Grant shared a glance with Jin's son, both looking away from the women's joyful tears. Grant had said he couldn't do this—he didn't know how, but Huang did. And, with a little help from Lieutenant Ma, they had done it. It felt strange to be here, to witness the arrival of his enemy's family, but they had, as the Phantom said, no part in Jin's schemes. Would they adjust to their new life in America? Who knew—but they had Jin's American daughter to help them find their way.

Grant's phone buzzed in his pocket, and he moved away, sliding it out, getting used to doing everything left-handed, at least for a while. A text message, from an unfamiliar number. A single word: *Akilah*. Not just a word, a name. Her name. Grant was smiling too, walking out into a brand new day.

THE END

ABOUT THE AUTHOR

E. Chris Ambrose also writes dark historical fantasy novels as E. C. Ambrose: the Dark Apostle series about medieval surgery, from DAW Books. Developing that series made the author into a bona fide research junkie. Interests include the history of technology and medicine, Mongolian history and culture, Medieval history, and reproductive biology of lizards. Research has taken her to Germany, England, France, India, Nepal, China and Mongolia as well as many United States destinations. In the process, E. C. learned how to hunt with a falcon, clear a building of possible assailants, pull traction on a broken limb, and fire an AR-15.

Published works have appeared in *Warrior Women*, Fireside magazine, YARN online, Clarkesworld, several volumes of New Hampshire Pulp Fiction, and *Uncle John's Bathroom Reader*. The author is both a graduate of and an instructor for the Odyssey Writing workshop, and a participant in the Codex on-line writers' workshop.

In addition to writing, E. C. works as an adventure guide, teaching rock climbing and leading hiking, kayaking, climbing and mountain biking camps. Past occupations include founding a wholesale sculpture business, selecting stamps for a philatelic company, selling equestrian gear, and portraying the Easter Bunny on weekends.

Made in the USA
Columbia, SC
12 July 2018